W9-BTO-524

epic!

ADVENTURE KINGDOM

Written By
STEVE FOXE
Illustrated By
PEDRO RODRIGUEZ
Colors By
SONIA MORUNO

Adventure Kingdom created by
Steve Foxe and Pedro Rodriguez

Adventure Kingdom text and illustrations copyright © 2021 by
Epic! Creations, Inc. All rights reserved. Printed in China.
No part of this book may be used or reproduced in any manner
whatsoever without written permission
except in the case of reprints in the context of reviews.

Andrews McMeel Publishing
a division of Andrews McMeel Universal
1130 Walnut Street, Kansas City, Missouri 64106

www.andrewsmcmeel.com

Epic! Creations, Inc.
702 Marshall Street, Suite 280
Redwood City, California 94063

www.getepic.com

21 22 23 24 25 SDB 10 9 8 7 6 5 4 3 2 1

Paperback ISBN: 978-1-5248-6982-3
Hardback ISBN: 978-1-5248-7078-2

Library of Congress Control Number: 2021934738

Design by Dan Nordskog

Made by:
King Yip (Dongguan) Printing & Packaging Factory Ltd.
Address and location of manufacturer:
Daning Administrative District, Humen Town
Dongguan Guangdong, China 523930
1st Printing — 6/28/21

ATTENTION: SCHOOLS AND BUSINESSES
Andrews McMeel books are available at quantity discounts with bulk
purchase for educational, business, or sales promotional use.
For information, please e-mail the Andrews McMeel Publishing
Special Sales Department: specialsales@amuniversal.com.

TO THE GREATEST JEROME I KNOW.
THANKS FOR ALL THE MAGIC, DAD.
S. F.

TO GEMMA AND MAYA.
P. R.

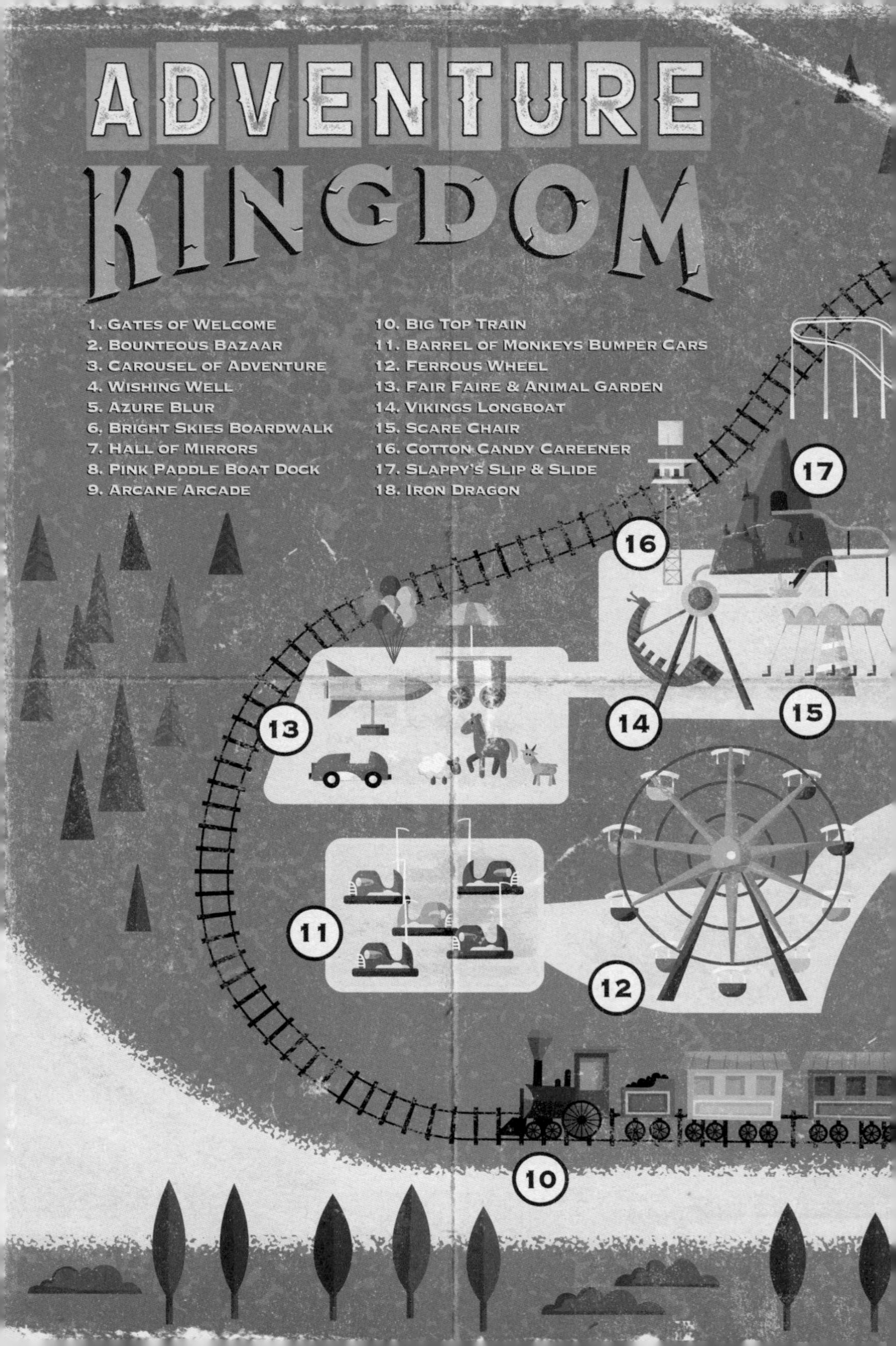
ADVENTURE KINGDOM
1. Gates of Welcome
2. Bounteous Bazaar
3. Carousel of Adventure
4. Wishing Well
5. Azure Blur
6. Bright Skies Boardwalk
7. Hall of Mirrors
8. Pink Paddle Boat Dock
9. Arcane Arcade
10. Big Top Train
11. Barrel of Monkeys Bumper Cars
12. Ferrous Wheel
13. Fair Faire & Animal Garden
14. Vikings Longboat
15. Scare Chair
16. Cotton Candy Careener
17. Slappy's Slip & Slide
18. Iron Dragon
17
16
13
14
15
11
12
10

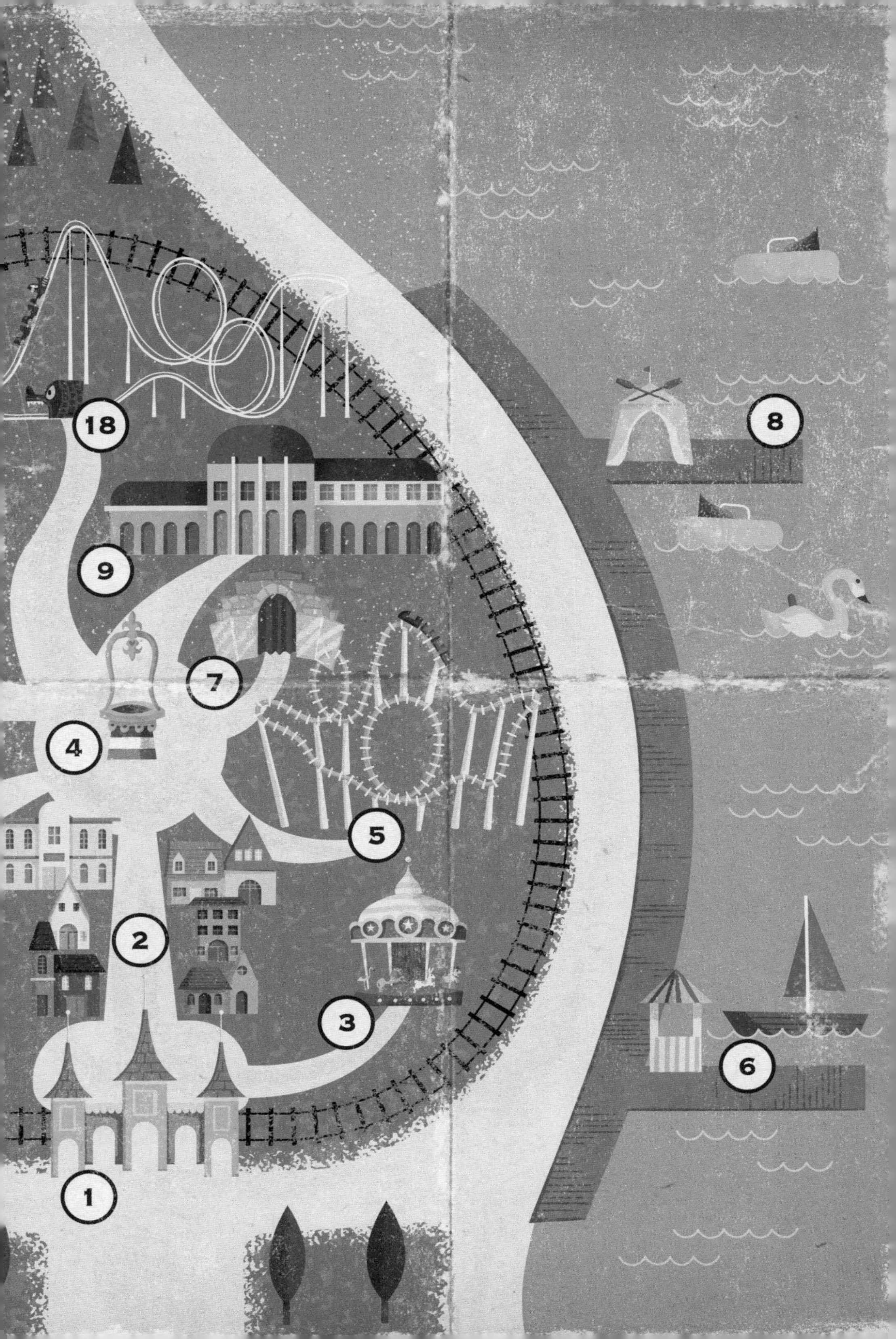
18
8
9
7
4
5
2
3
6
1

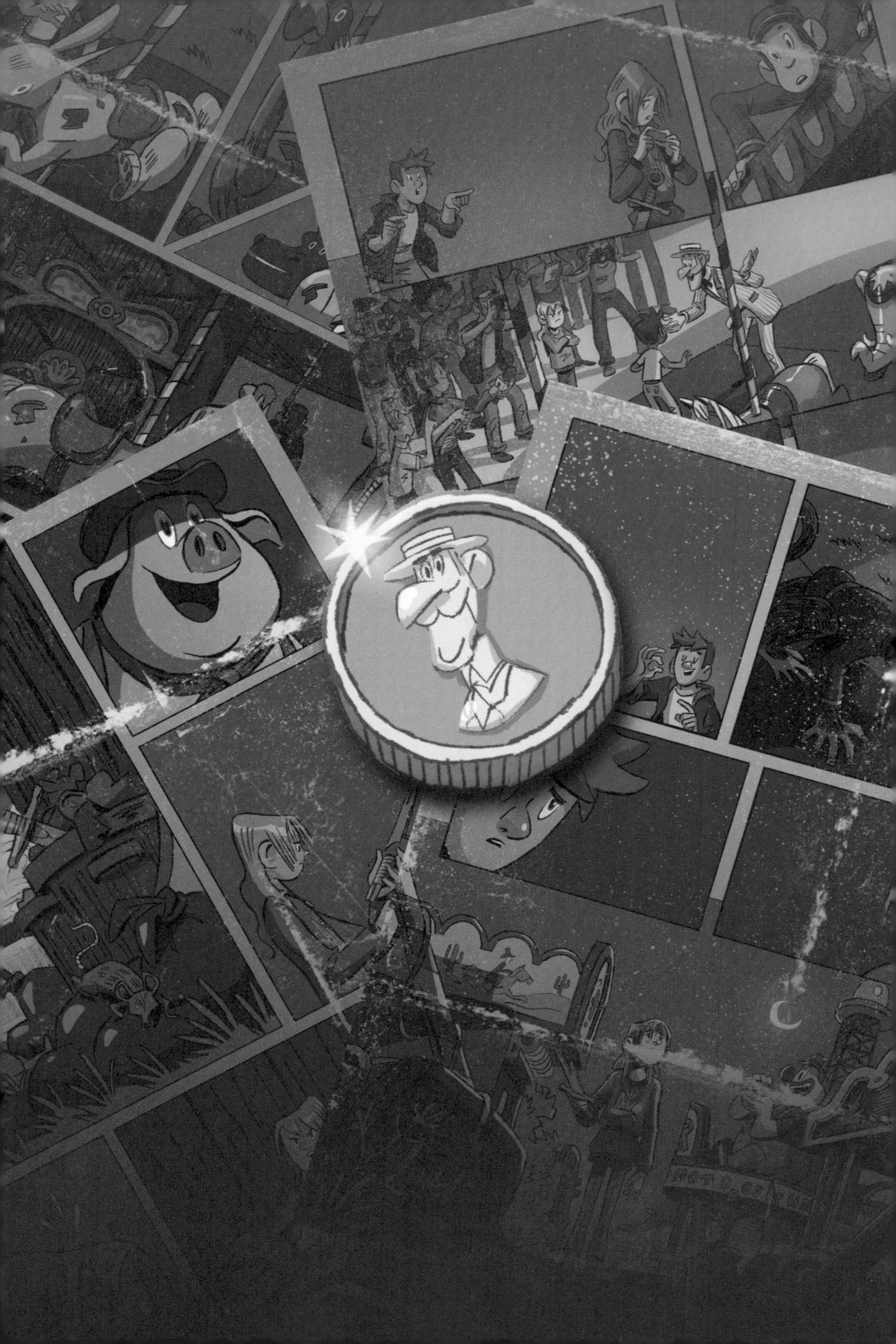

CHAPTER 1
KEY TO THE KINGDOM

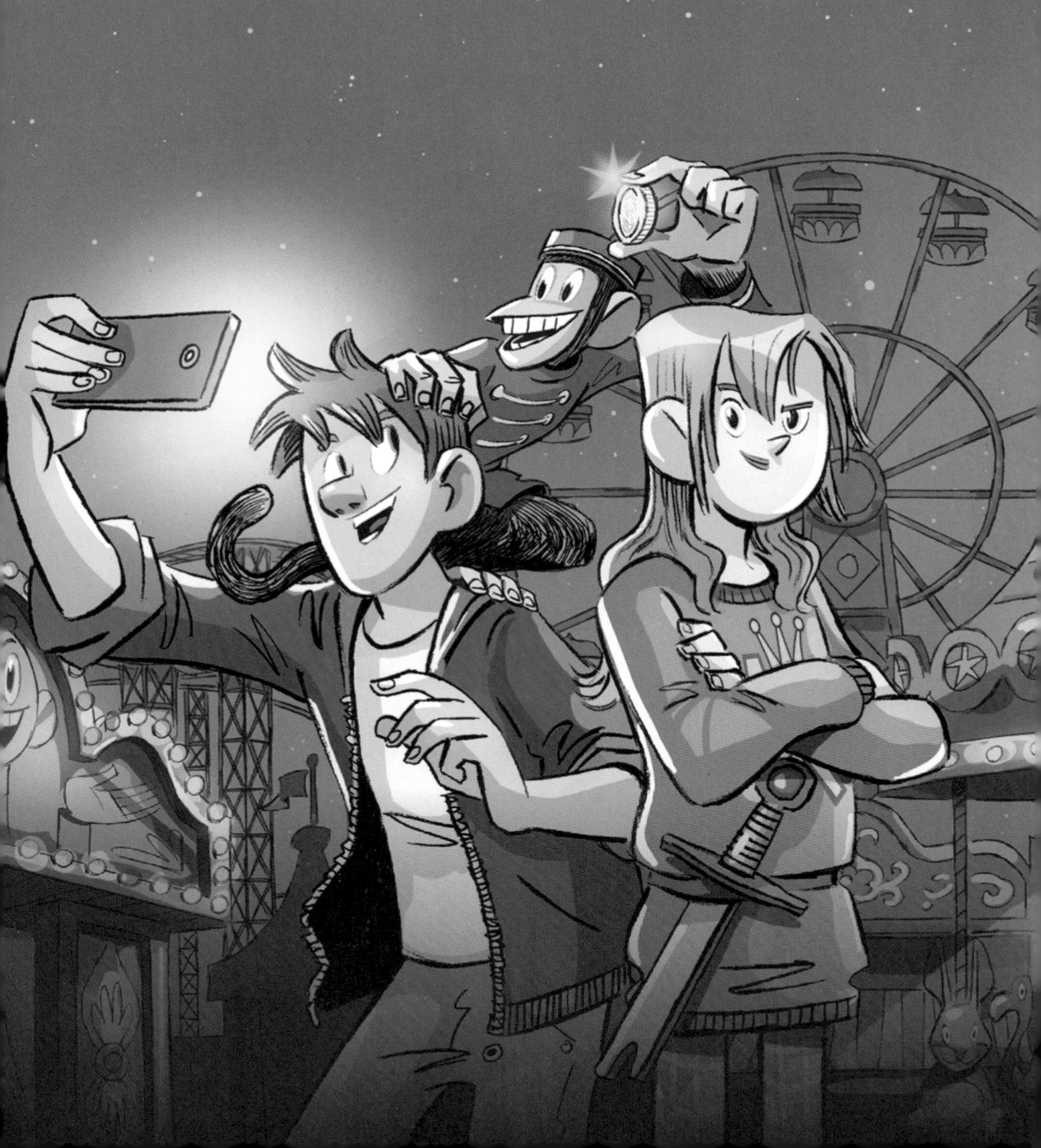

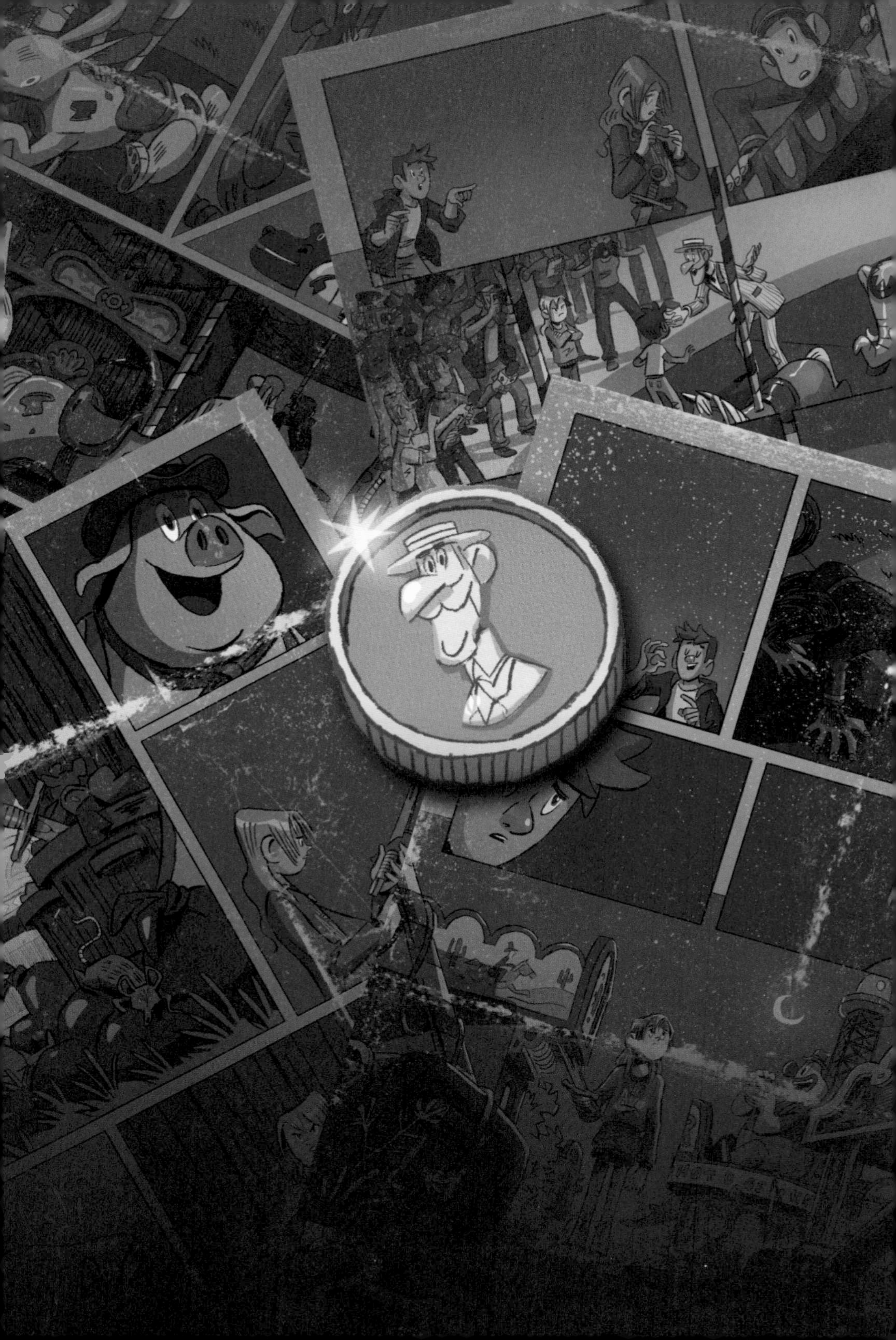

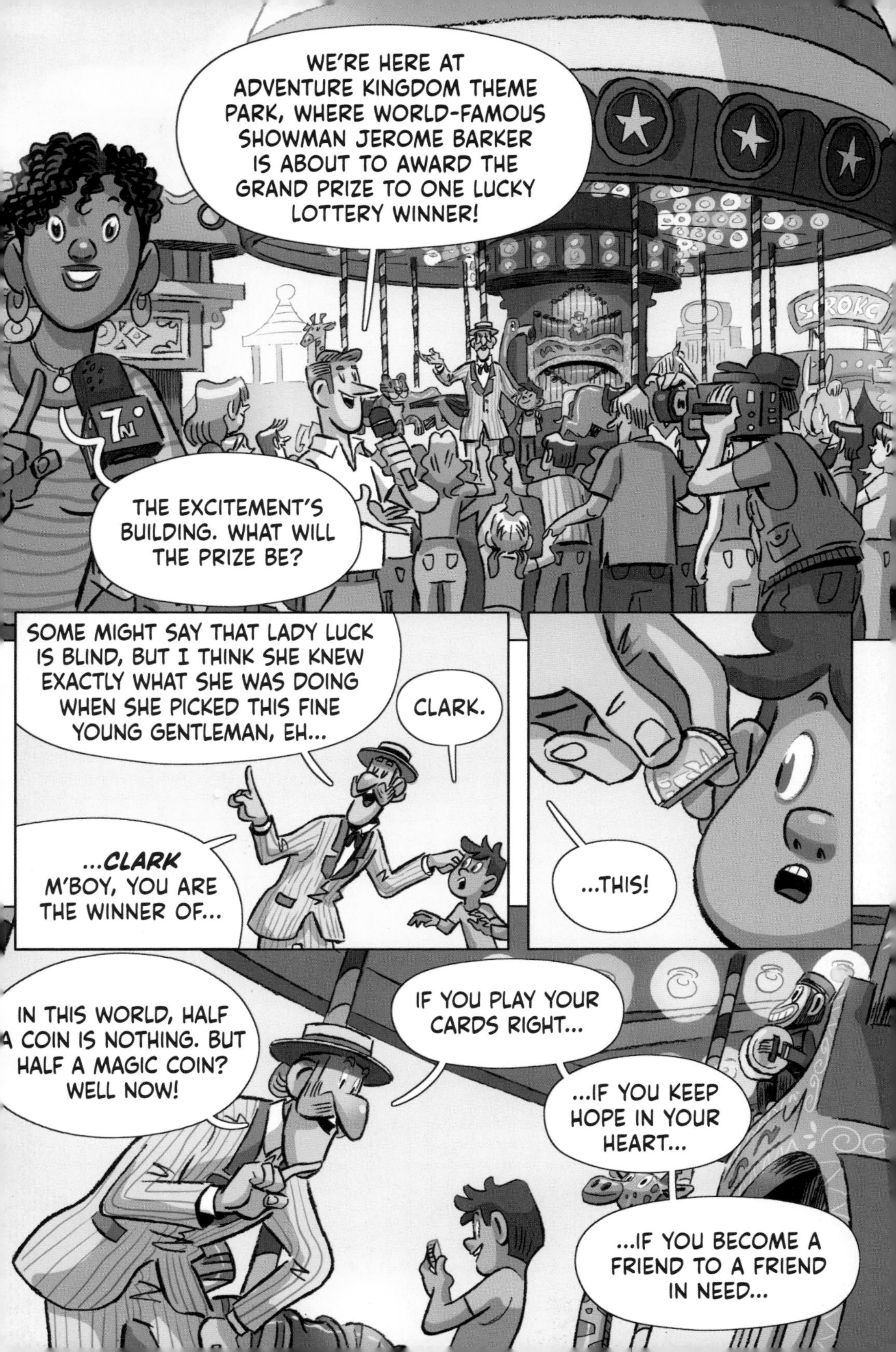
WE'RE HERE AT ADVENTURE KINGDOM THEME PARK, WHERE WORLD-FAMOUS SHOWMAN JEROME BARKER IS ABOUT TO AWARD THE GRAND PRIZE TO ONE LUCKY LOTTERY WINNER!
THE EXCITEMENT'S BUILDING. WHAT WILL THE PRIZE BE?
SOME MIGHT SAY THAT LADY LUCK IS BLIND, BUT I THINK SHE KNEW EXACTLY WHAT SHE WAS DOING WHEN SHE PICKED THIS FINE YOUNG GENTLEMAN, EH...
CLARK.
...*CLARK* M'BOY, YOU ARE THE WINNER OF...
...THIS!
IN THIS WORLD, HALF A COIN IS NOTHING. BUT HALF A MAGIC COIN? WELL NOW!
IF YOU PLAY YOUR CARDS RIGHT...
...IF YOU KEEP HOPE IN YOUR HEART...
...IF YOU BECOME A FRIEND TO A FRIEND IN NEED...

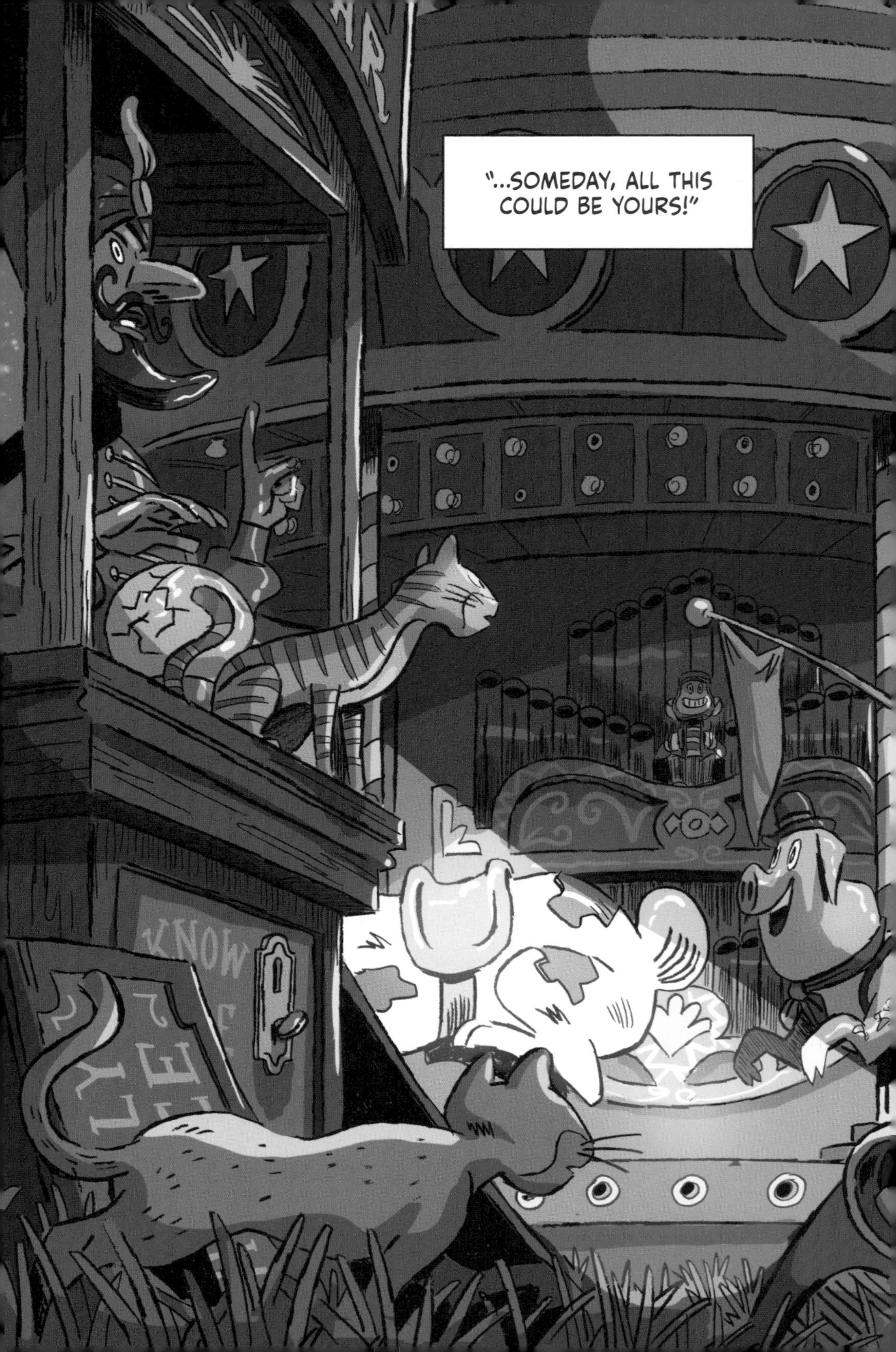
"...SOMEDAY, ALL THIS COULD BE YOURS!"
KNOW

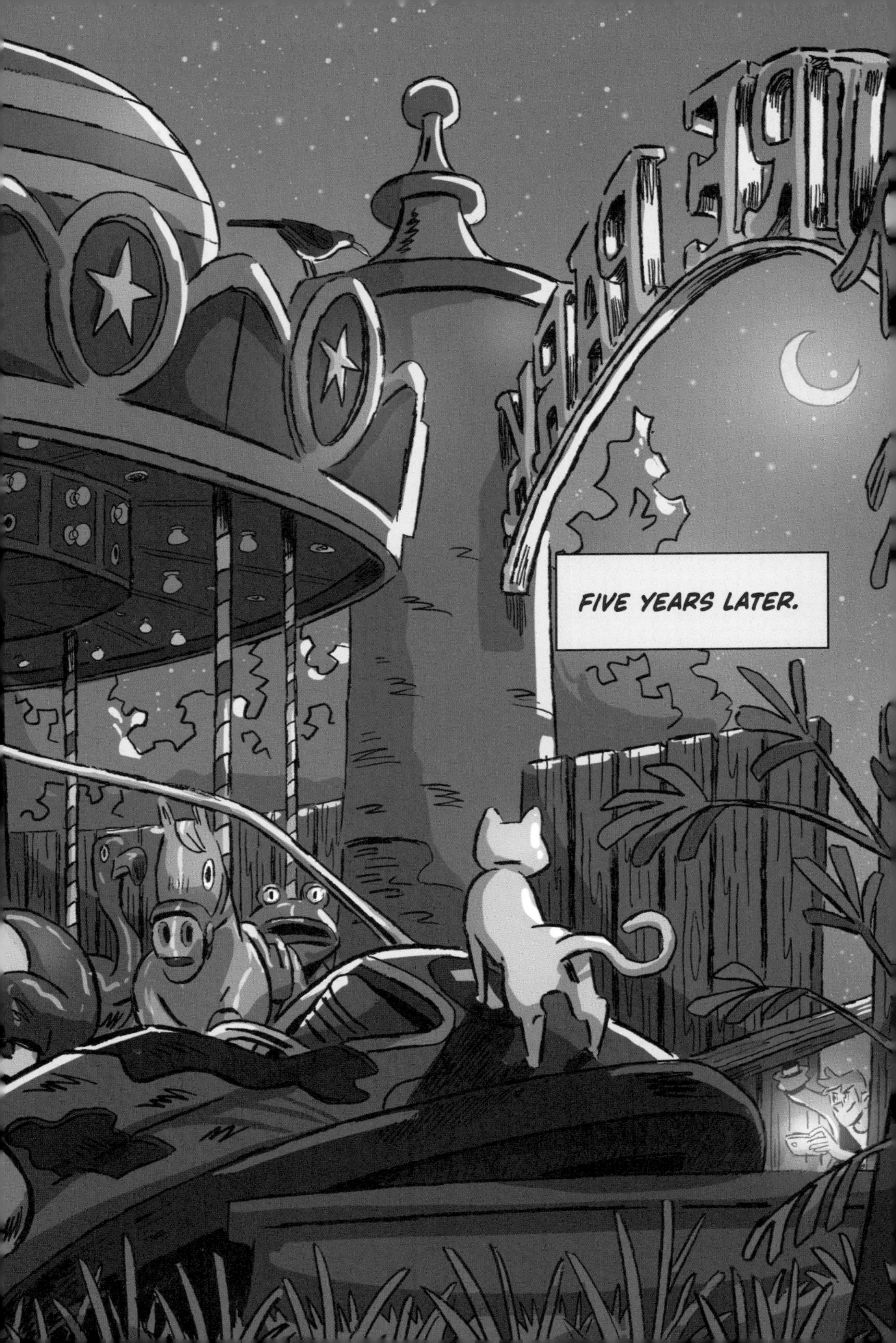
FIVE YEARS LATER.

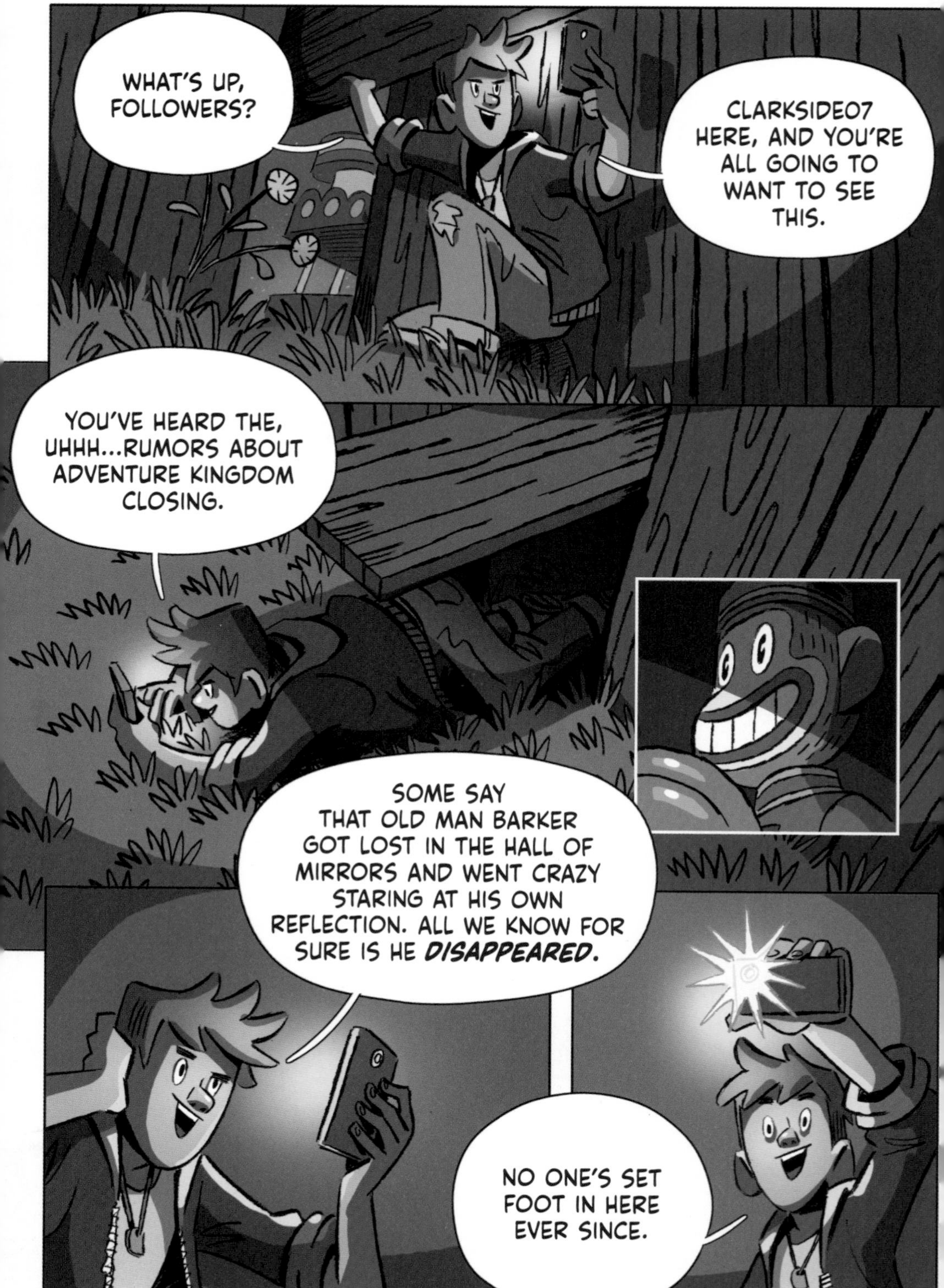

WHAT'S UP, FOLLOWERS?
CLARKSIDE07 HERE, AND YOU'RE ALL GOING TO WANT TO SEE THIS.
YOU'VE HEARD THE, UHHH...RUMORS ABOUT ADVENTURE KINGDOM CLOSING.
SOME SAY THAT OLD MAN BARKER GOT LOST IN THE HALL OF MIRRORS AND WENT CRAZY STARING AT HIS OWN REFLECTION. ALL WE KNOW FOR SURE IS HE *DISAPPEARED*.
NO ONE'S SET FOOT IN HERE EVER SINCE.

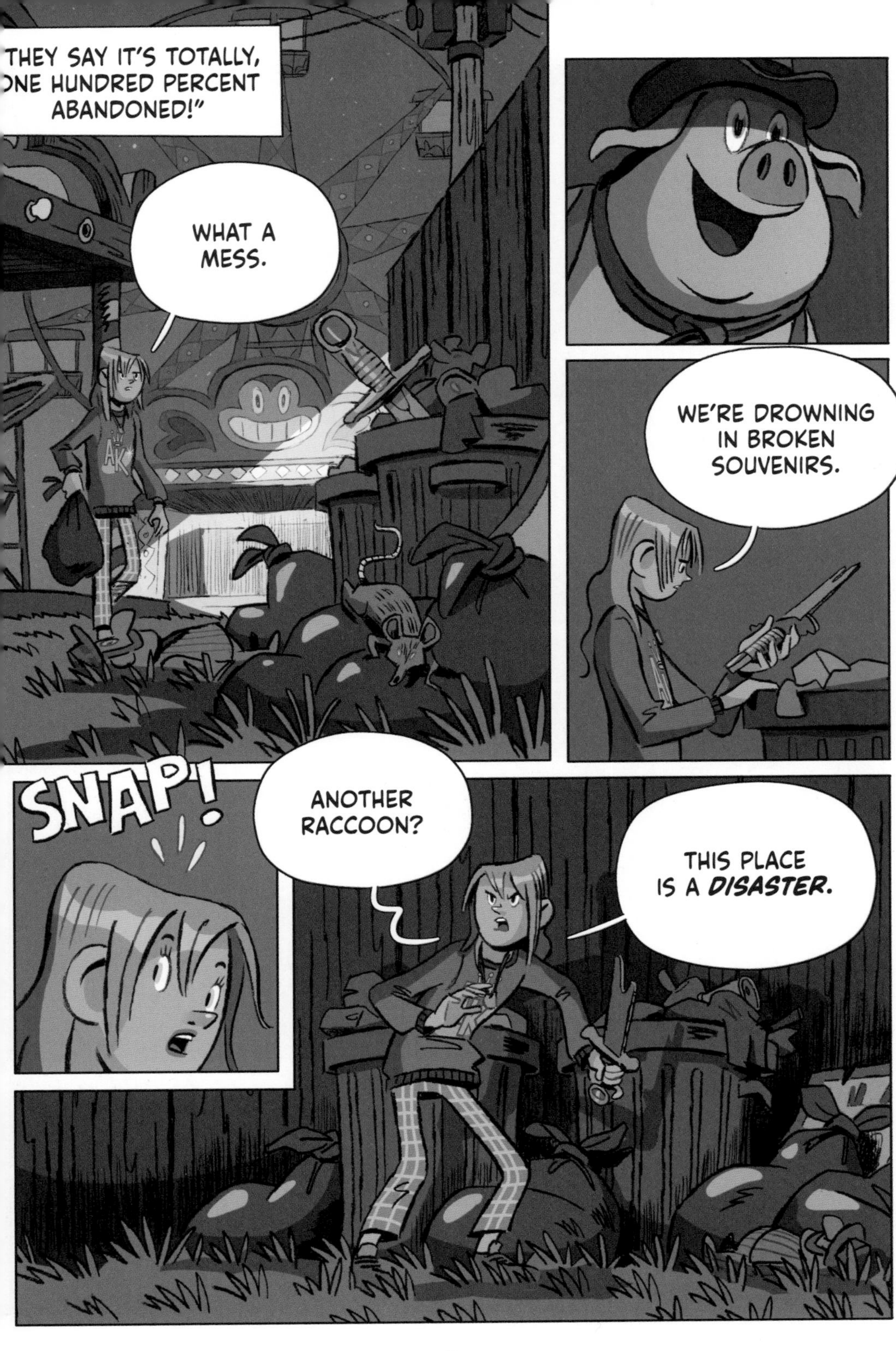
THEY SAY IT'S TOTALLY, ONE HUNDRED PERCENT ABANDONED!"
WHAT A MESS.
WE'RE DROWNING IN BROKEN SOUVENIRS.
SNAP!
ANOTHER RACCOON?
THIS PLACE IS A *DISASTER*.

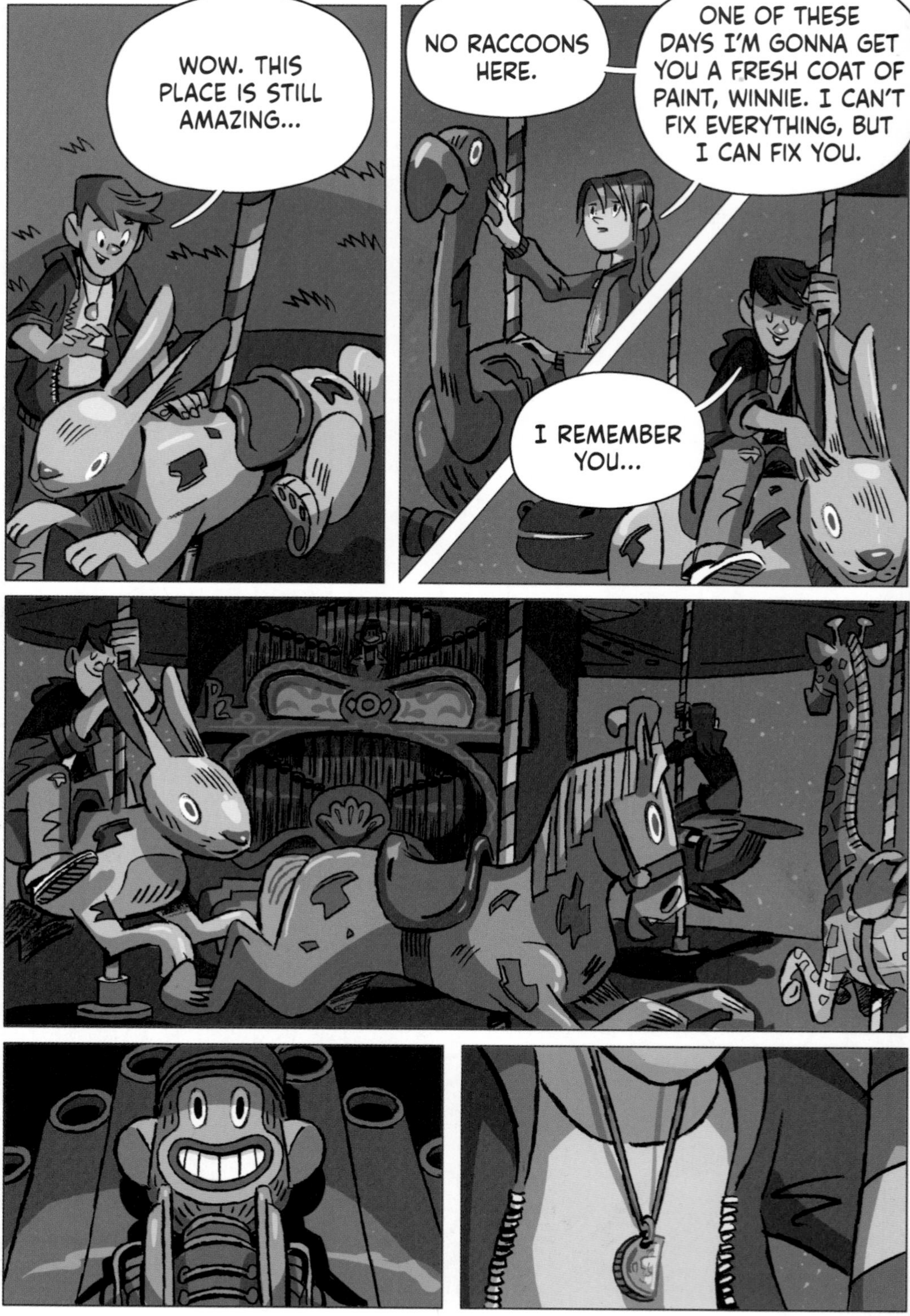
WOW. THIS PLACE IS STILL AMAZING...
NO RACCOONS HERE.
ONE OF THESE DAYS I'M GONNA GET YOU A FRESH COAT OF PAINT, WINNIE. I CAN'T FIX EVERYTHING, BUT I CAN FIX YOU.
I REMEMBER YOU...

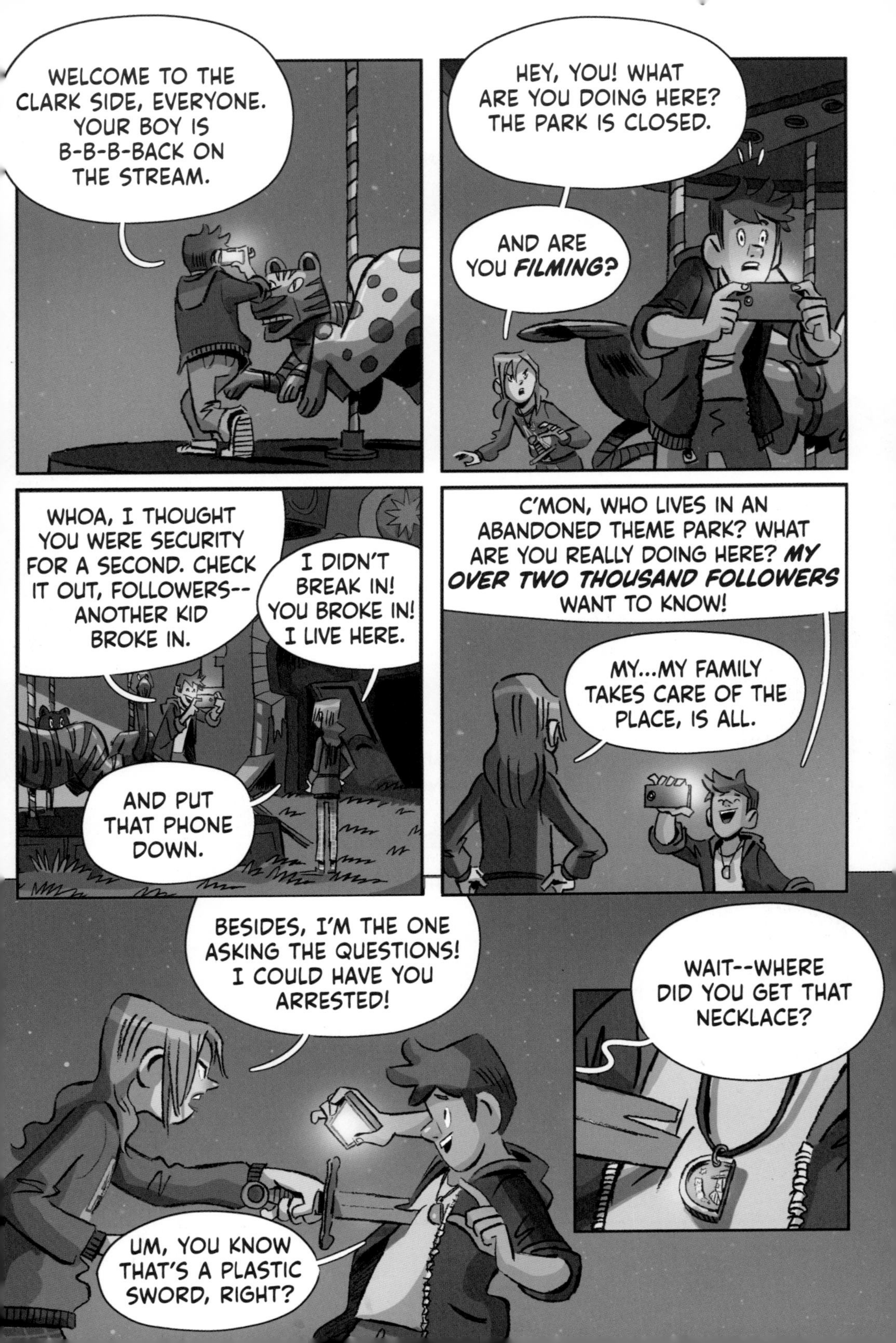
WELCOME TO THE CLARK SIDE, EVERYONE. YOUR BOY IS B-B-B-BACK ON THE STREAM.
HEY, YOU! WHAT ARE YOU DOING HERE? THE PARK IS CLOSED.
AND ARE YOU *FILMING?*
WHOA, I THOUGHT YOU WERE SECURITY FOR A SECOND. CHECK IT OUT, FOLLOWERS-- ANOTHER KID BROKE IN.
I DIDN'T BREAK IN! YOU BROKE IN! I LIVE HERE.
AND PUT THAT PHONE DOWN.
C'MON, WHO LIVES IN AN ABANDONED THEME PARK? WHAT ARE YOU REALLY DOING HERE? ***MY OVER TWO THOUSAND FOLLOWERS*** WANT TO KNOW!
MY...MY FAMILY TAKES CARE OF THE PLACE, IS ALL.
BESIDES, I'M THE ONE ASKING THE QUESTIONS! I COULD HAVE YOU ARRESTED!
UM, YOU KNOW THAT'S A PLASTIC SWORD, RIGHT?
WAIT--WHERE DID YOU GET THAT NECKLACE?

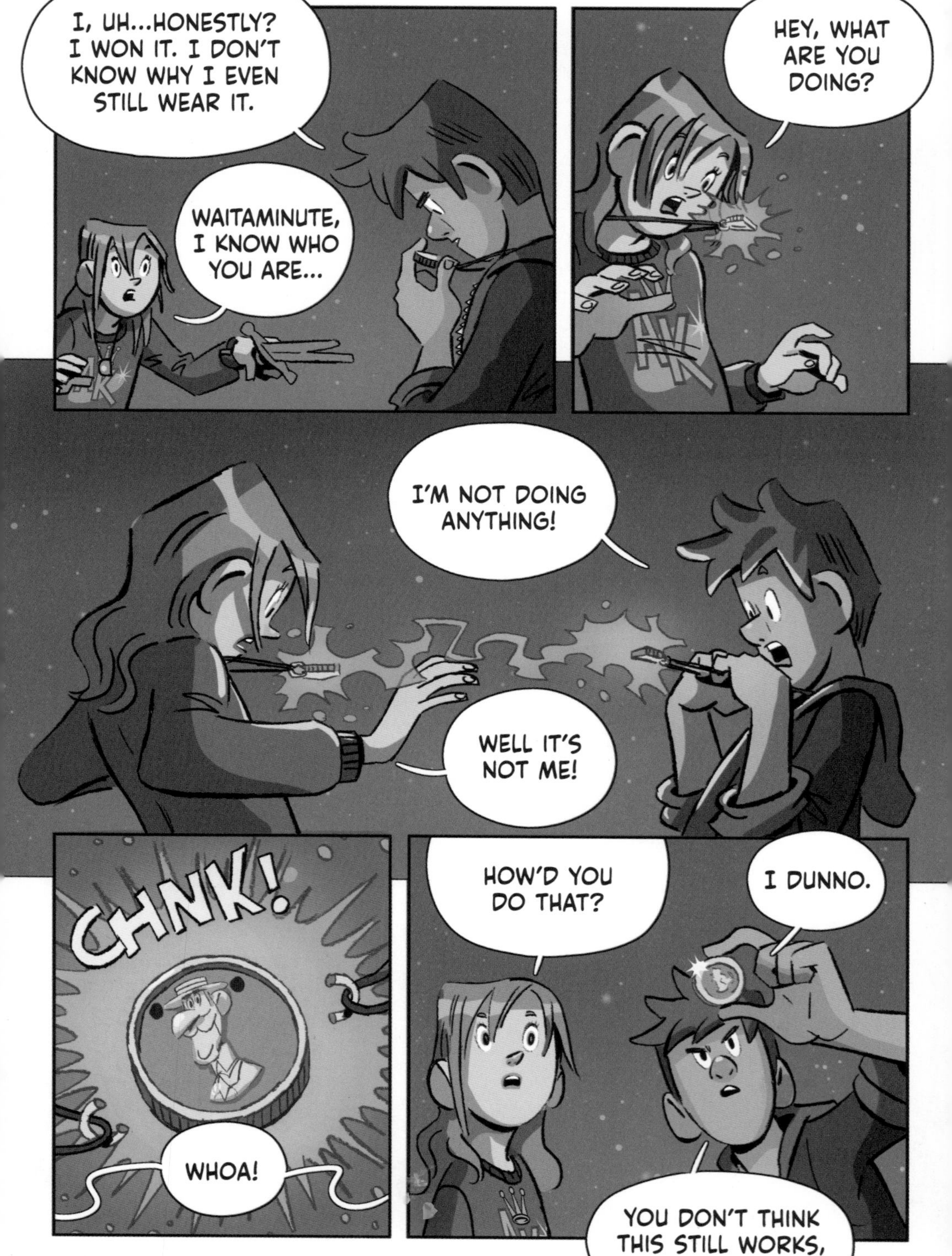
I, UH...HONESTLY? I WON IT. I DON'T KNOW WHY I EVEN STILL WEAR IT.
WAITAMINUTE, I KNOW WHO YOU ARE...
HEY, WHAT ARE YOU DOING?
I'M NOT DOING ANYTHING!
WELL IT'S NOT ME!
CHNK!
WHOA!
HOW'D YOU DO THAT?
I DUNNO.
YOU DON'T THINK THIS STILL WORKS, DO YOU?

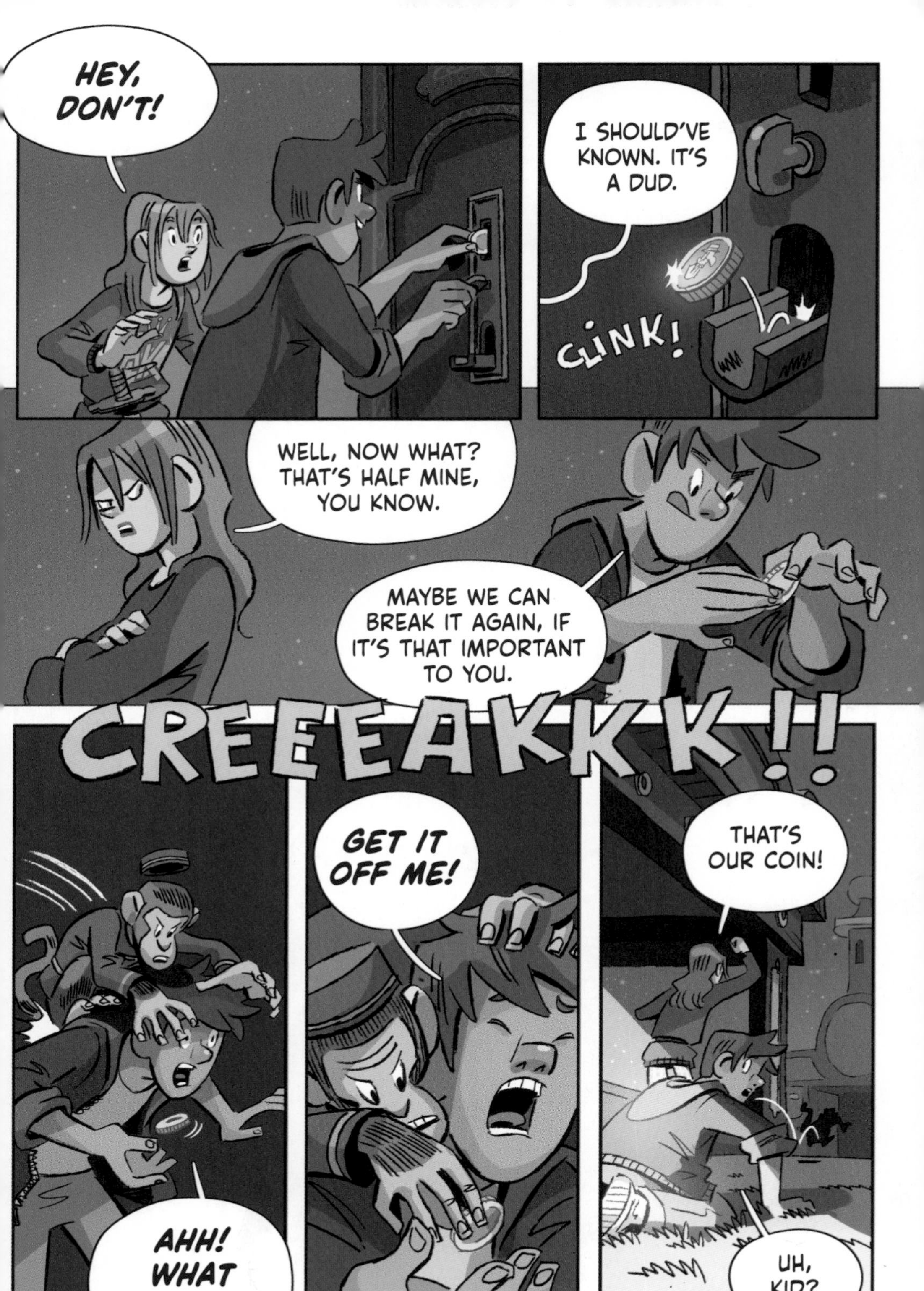
HEY, DON'T!
I SHOULD'VE KNOWN. IT'S A DUD.
CLINK!
WELL, NOW WHAT? THAT'S HALF MINE, YOU KNOW.
MAYBE WE CAN BREAK IT AGAIN, IF IT'S THAT IMPORTANT TO YOU.
CREEEAKKK!!
AHH! WHAT IS THAT?
GET IT OFF ME!
THAT'S OUR COIN!
UH, KID?

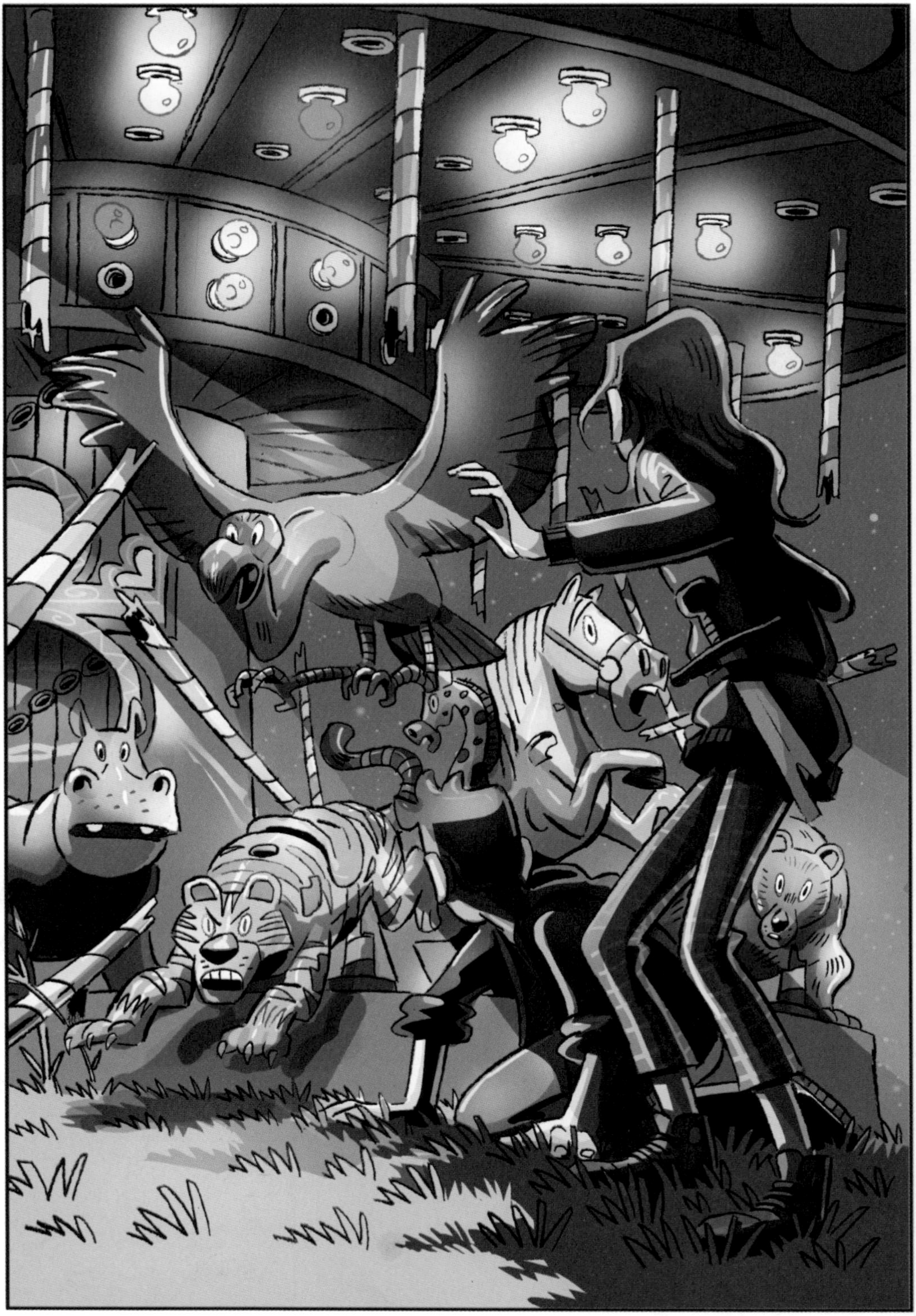

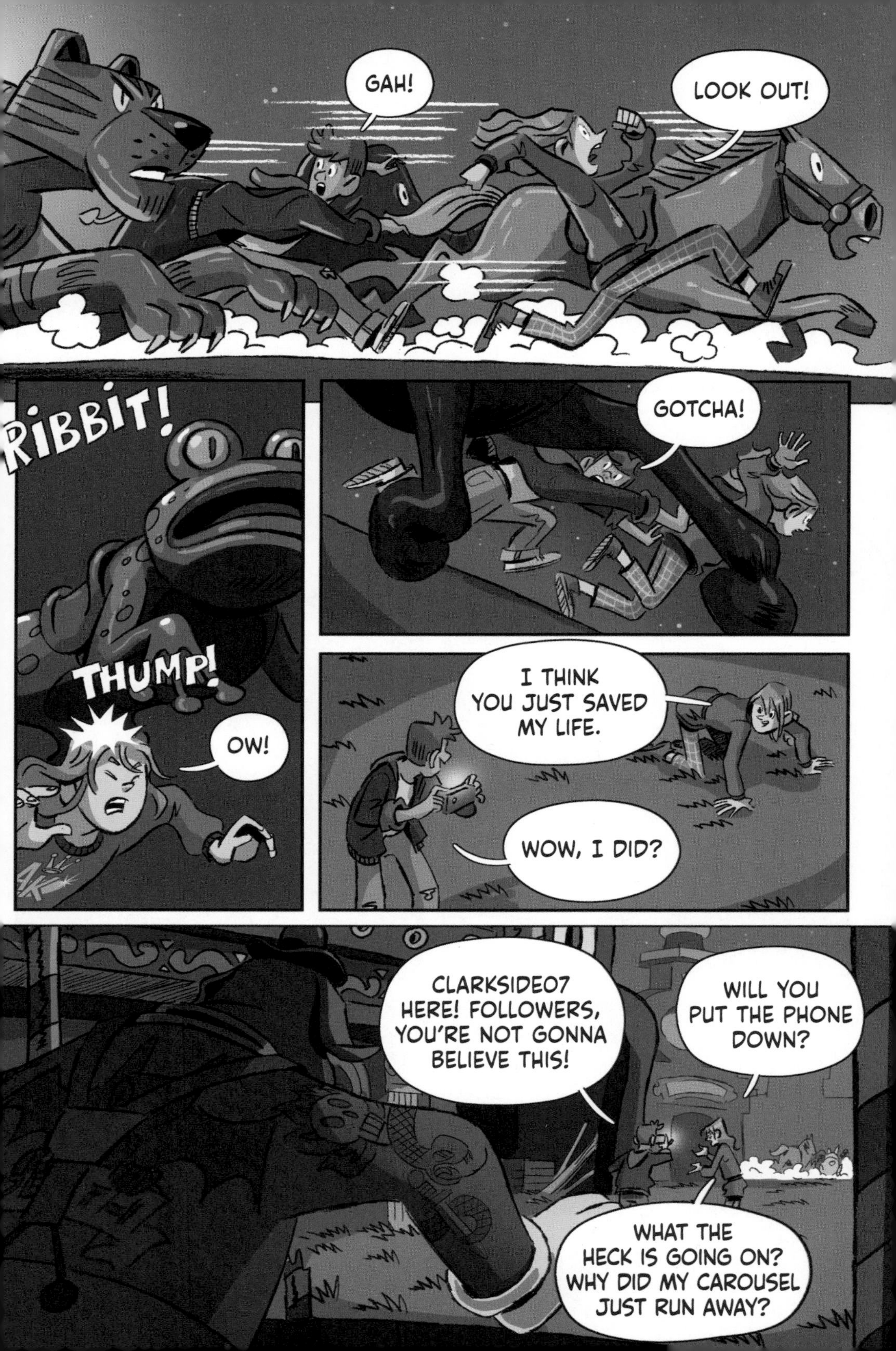
GAH!
LOOK OUT!
RIBBIT!
THUMP!
OW!
GOTCHA!
I THINK YOU JUST SAVED MY LIFE.
WOW, I DID?
CLARKSIDE07 HERE! FOLLOWERS, YOU'RE NOT GONNA BELIEVE THIS!
WILL YOU PUT THE PHONE DOWN?
WHAT THE HECK IS GOING ON? WHY DID MY CAROUSEL JUST RUN AWAY?

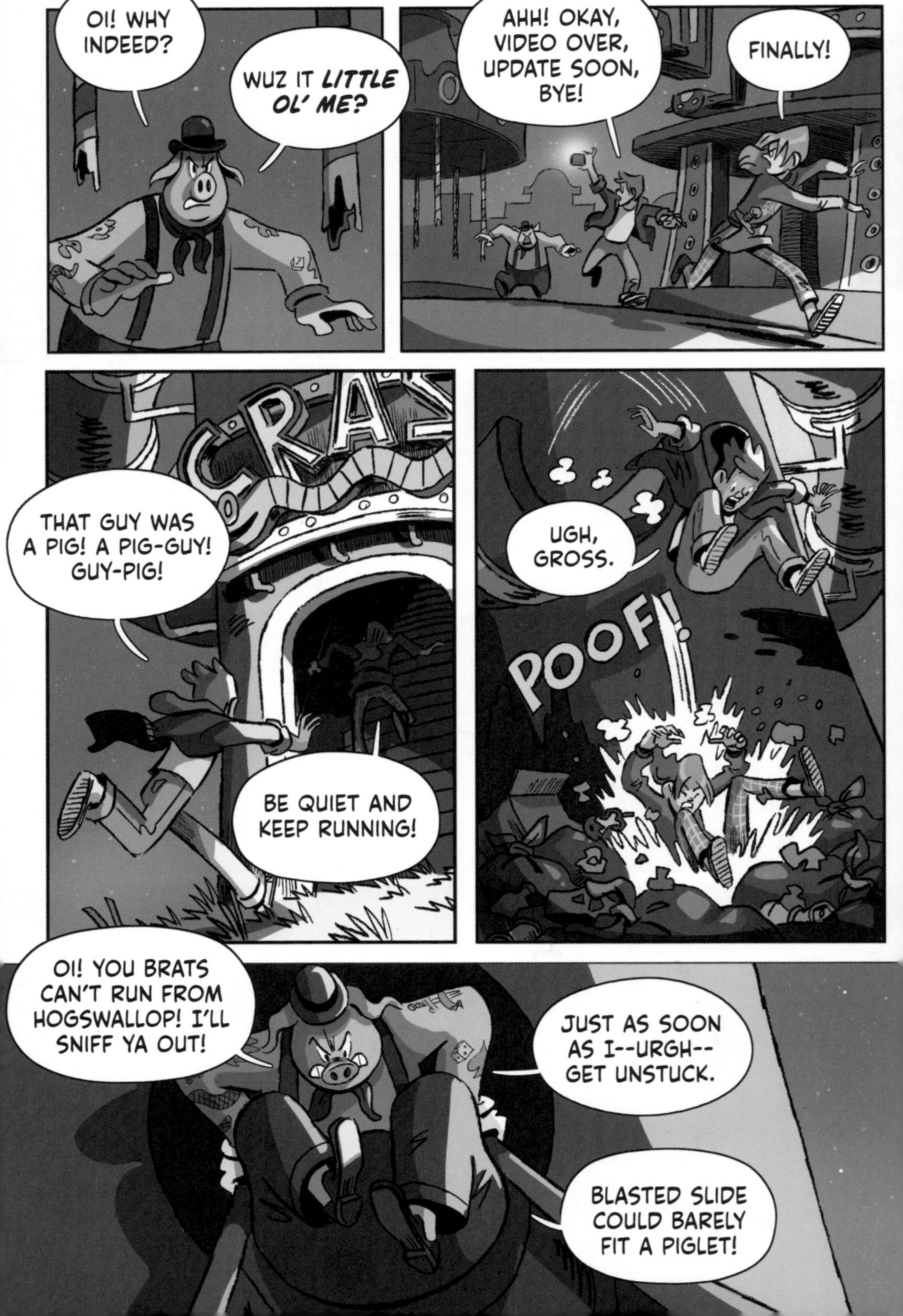
OI! WHY INDEED?
WUZ IT *LITTLE OL' ME?*
AHH! OKAY, VIDEO OVER, UPDATE SOON, BYE!
FINALLY!
THAT GUY WAS A PIG! A PIG-GUY! GUY-PIG!
BE QUIET AND KEEP RUNNING!
UGH, GROSS.
POOF!
OI! YOU BRATS CAN'T RUN FROM HOGSWALLOP! I'LL SNIFF YA OUT!
JUST AS SOON AS I--URGH-- GET UNSTUCK.
BLASTED SLIDE COULD BARELY FIT A PIGLET!

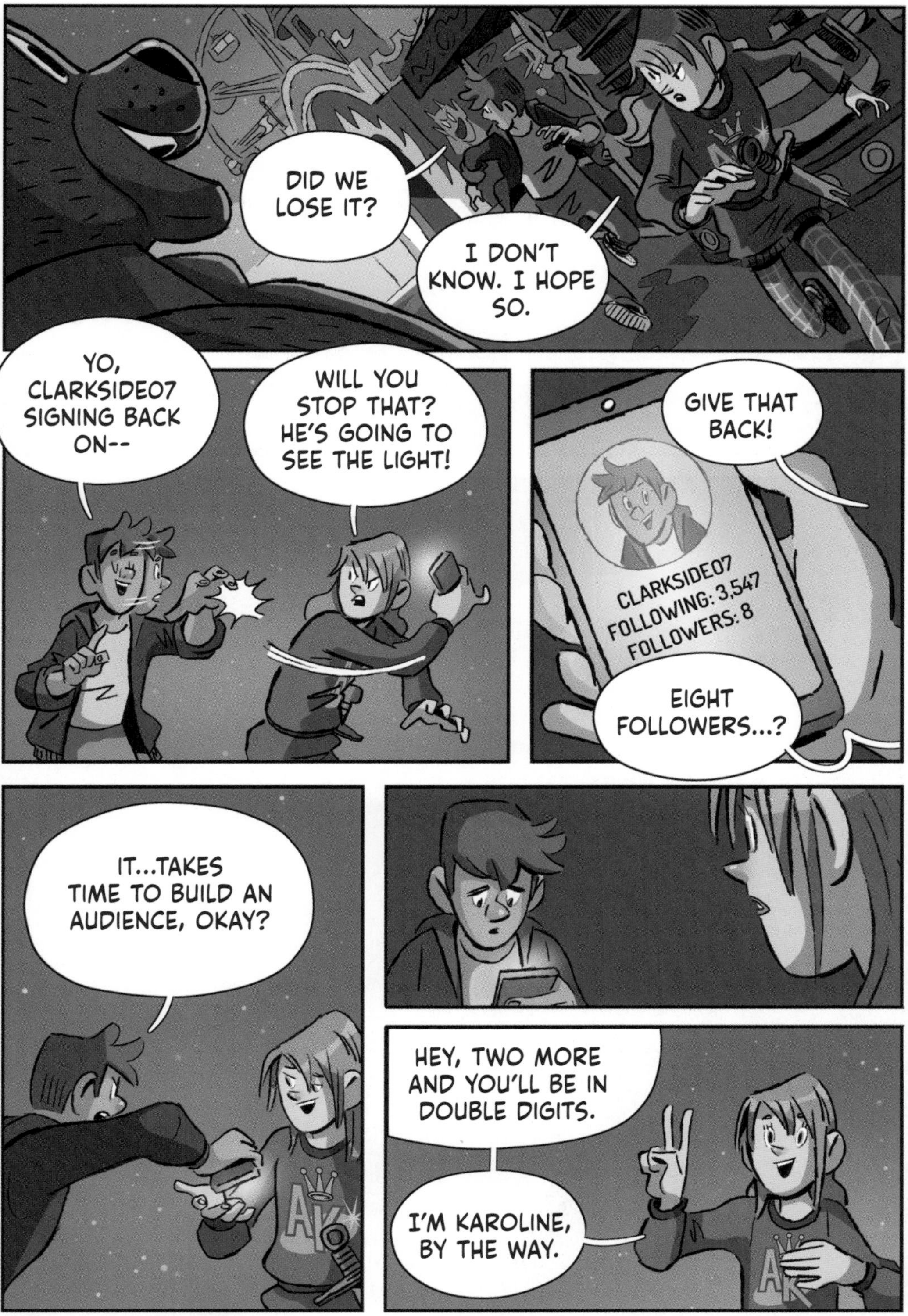
DID WE LOSE IT?
I DON'T KNOW. I HOPE SO.
YO, CLARKSIDE07 SIGNING BACK ON--
WILL YOU STOP THAT? HE'S GOING TO SEE THE LIGHT!
GIVE THAT BACK!
CLARKSIDE07
FOLLOWING: 3,547
FOLLOWERS: 8
EIGHT FOLLOWERS...?
IT...TAKES TIME TO BUILD AN AUDIENCE, OKAY?
HEY, TWO MORE AND YOU'LL BE IN DOUBLE DIGITS.
I'M KAROLINE, BY THE WAY.

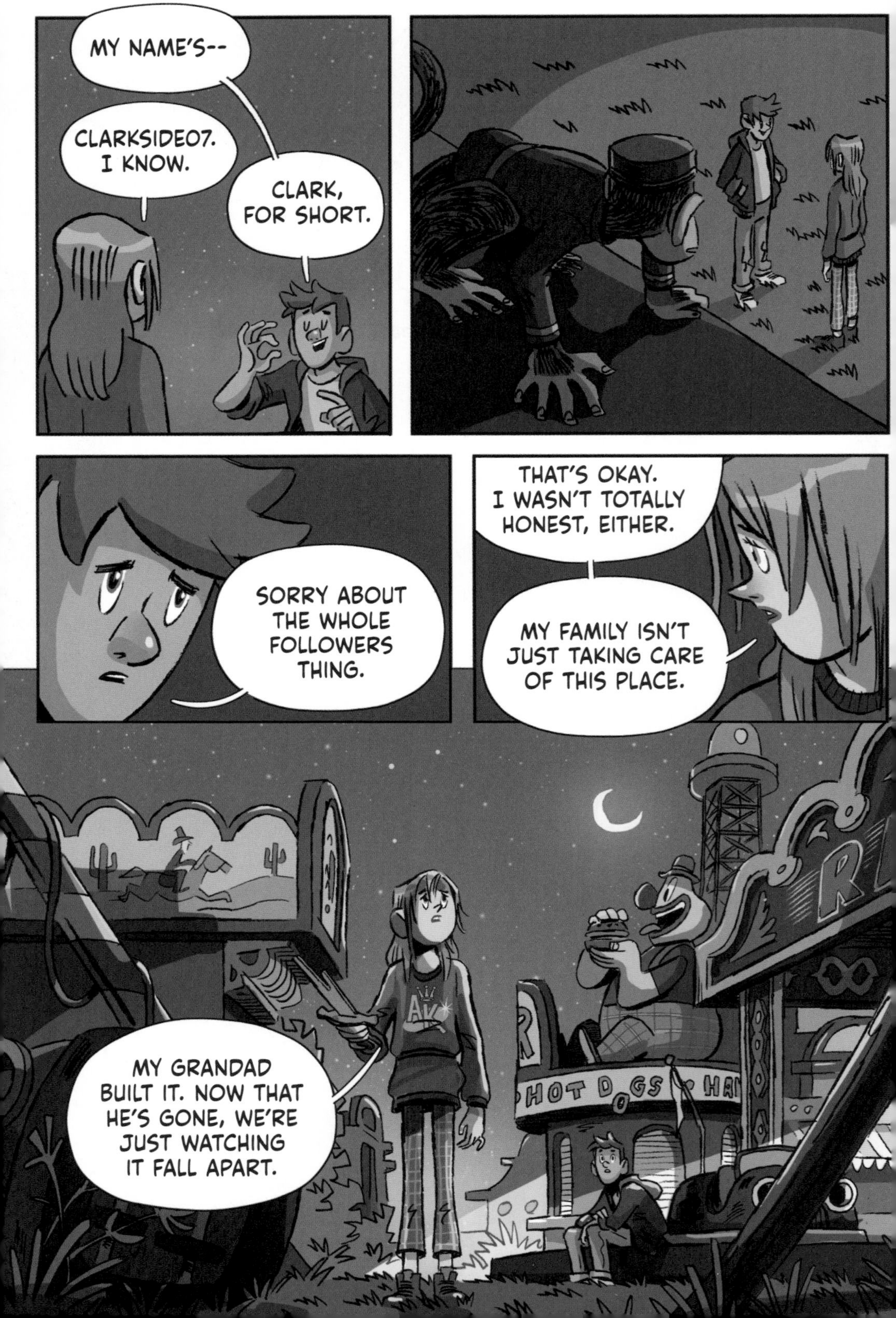
MY NAME'S--
CLARKSIDE07. I KNOW.
CLARK, FOR SHORT.
SORRY ABOUT THE WHOLE FOLLOWERS THING.
THAT'S OKAY. I WASN'T TOTALLY HONEST, EITHER.
MY FAMILY ISN'T JUST TAKING CARE OF THIS PLACE.
HOT DOGS
MY GRANDAD BUILT IT. NOW THAT HE'S GONE, WE'RE JUST WATCHING IT FALL APART.

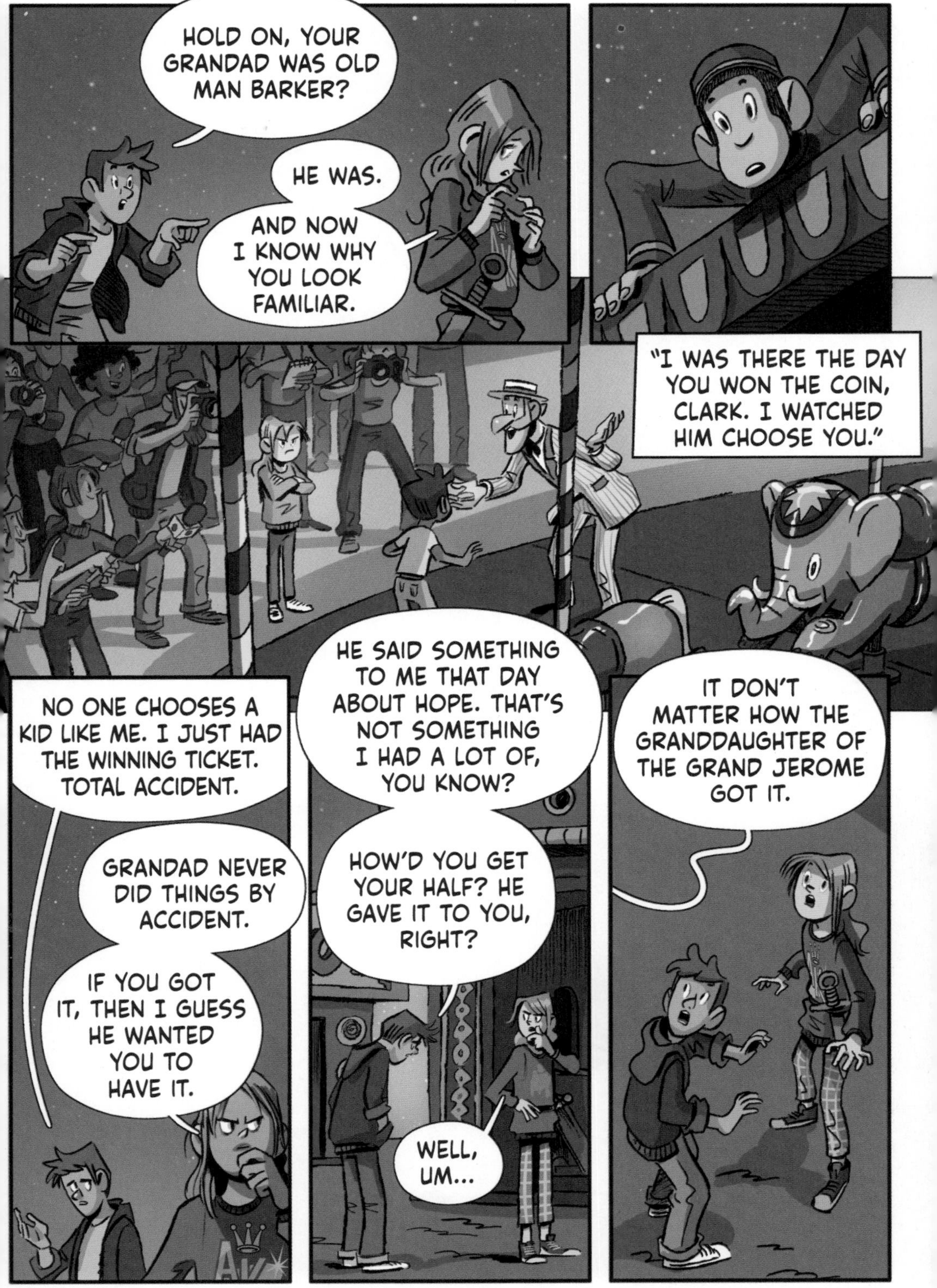
HOLD ON, YOUR GRANDAD WAS OLD MAN BARKER?
HE WAS.
AND NOW I KNOW WHY YOU LOOK FAMILIAR.
"I WAS THERE THE DAY YOU WON THE COIN, CLARK. I WATCHED HIM CHOOSE YOU."
NO ONE CHOOSES A KID LIKE ME. I JUST HAD THE WINNING TICKET. TOTAL ACCIDENT.
GRANDAD NEVER DID THINGS BY ACCIDENT.
IF YOU GOT IT, THEN I GUESS HE WANTED YOU TO HAVE IT.
HE SAID SOMETHING TO ME THAT DAY ABOUT HOPE. THAT'S NOT SOMETHING I HAD A LOT OF, YOU KNOW?
HOW'D YOU GET YOUR HALF? HE GAVE IT TO YOU, RIGHT?
WELL, UM...
IT DON'T MATTER HOW THE GRANDDAUGHTER OF THE GRAND JEROME GOT IT.

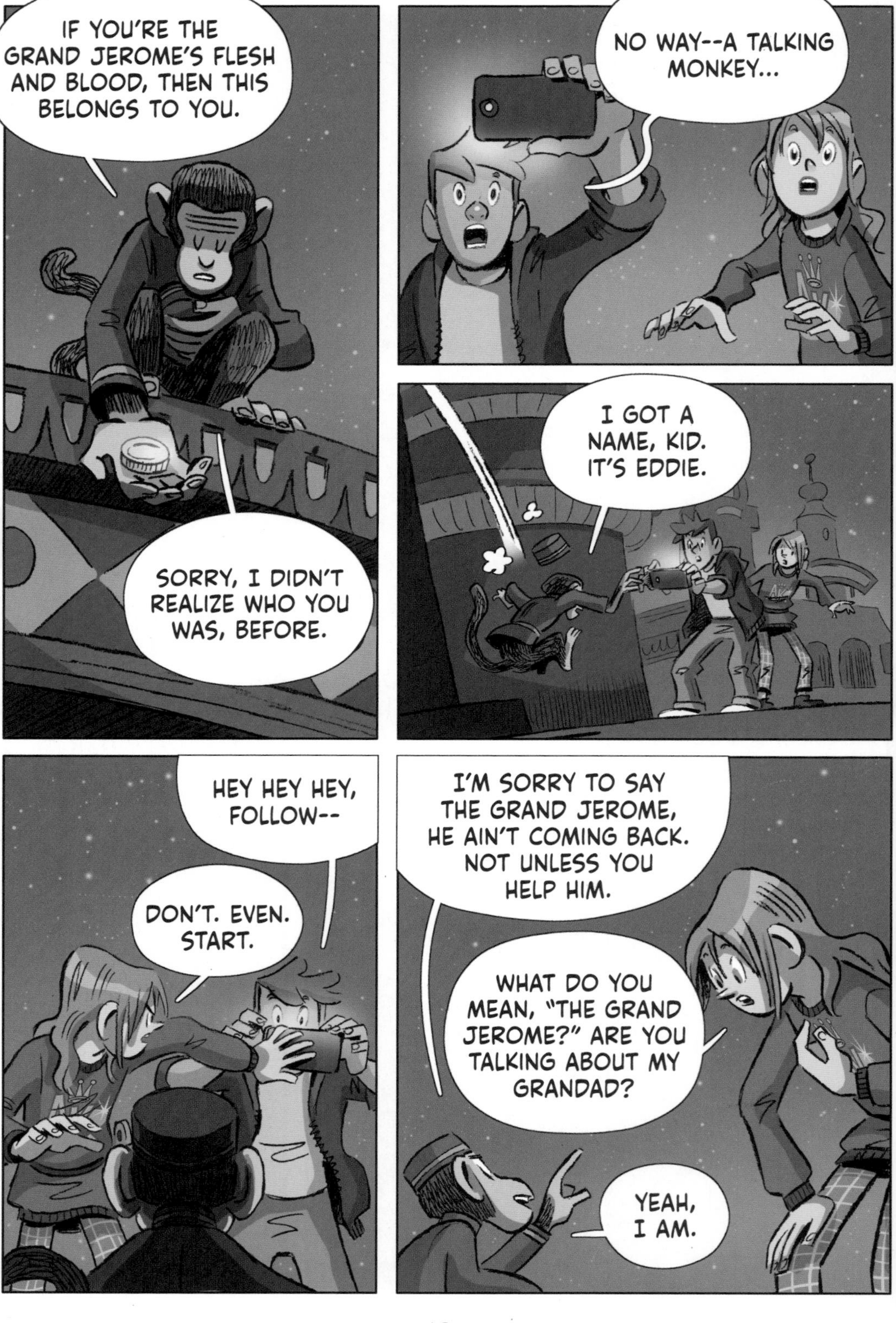
IF YOU'RE THE GRAND JEROME'S FLESH AND BLOOD, THEN THIS BELONGS TO YOU.
SORRY, I DIDN'T REALIZE WHO YOU WAS, BEFORE.
NO WAY--A TALKING MONKEY...
I GOT A NAME, KID. IT'S EDDIE.
HEY HEY HEY, FOLLOW--
DON'T. EVEN. START.
I'M SORRY TO SAY THE GRAND JEROME, HE AIN'T COMING BACK. NOT UNLESS YOU HELP HIM.
WHAT DO YOU MEAN, "THE GRAND JEROME?" ARE YOU TALKING ABOUT MY GRANDAD?
YEAH, I AM.

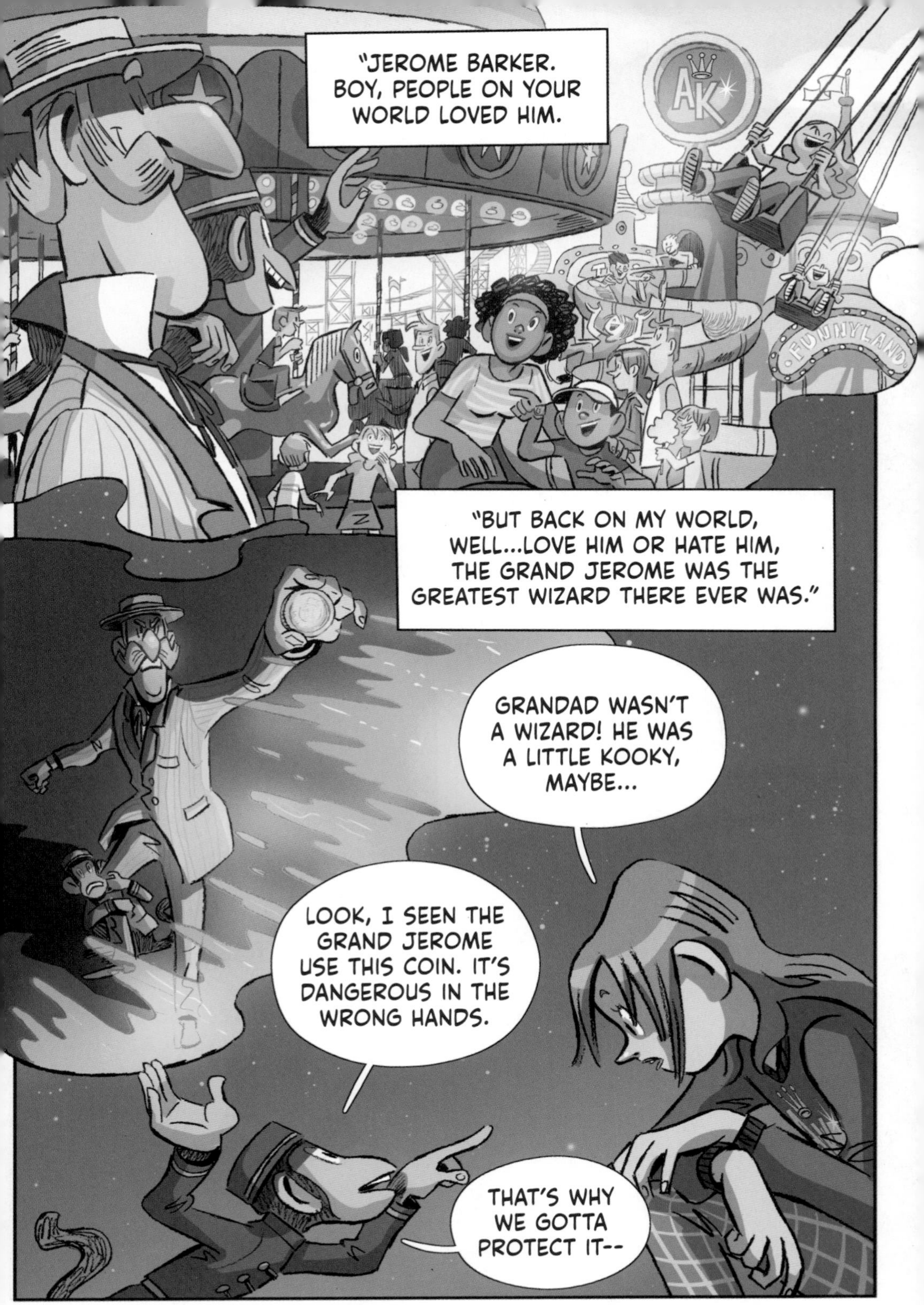
"JEROME BARKER. BOY, PEOPLE ON YOUR WORLD LOVED HIM.
AK
FUNNYLAND
"BUT BACK ON MY WORLD, WELL...LOVE HIM OR HATE HIM, THE GRAND JEROME WAS THE GREATEST WIZARD THERE EVER WAS."
GRANDAD WASN'T A WIZARD! HE WAS A LITTLE KOOKY, MAYBE...
LOOK, I SEEN THE GRAND JEROME USE THIS COIN. IT'S DANGEROUS IN THE WRONG HANDS.
THAT'S WHY WE GOTTA PROTECT IT--

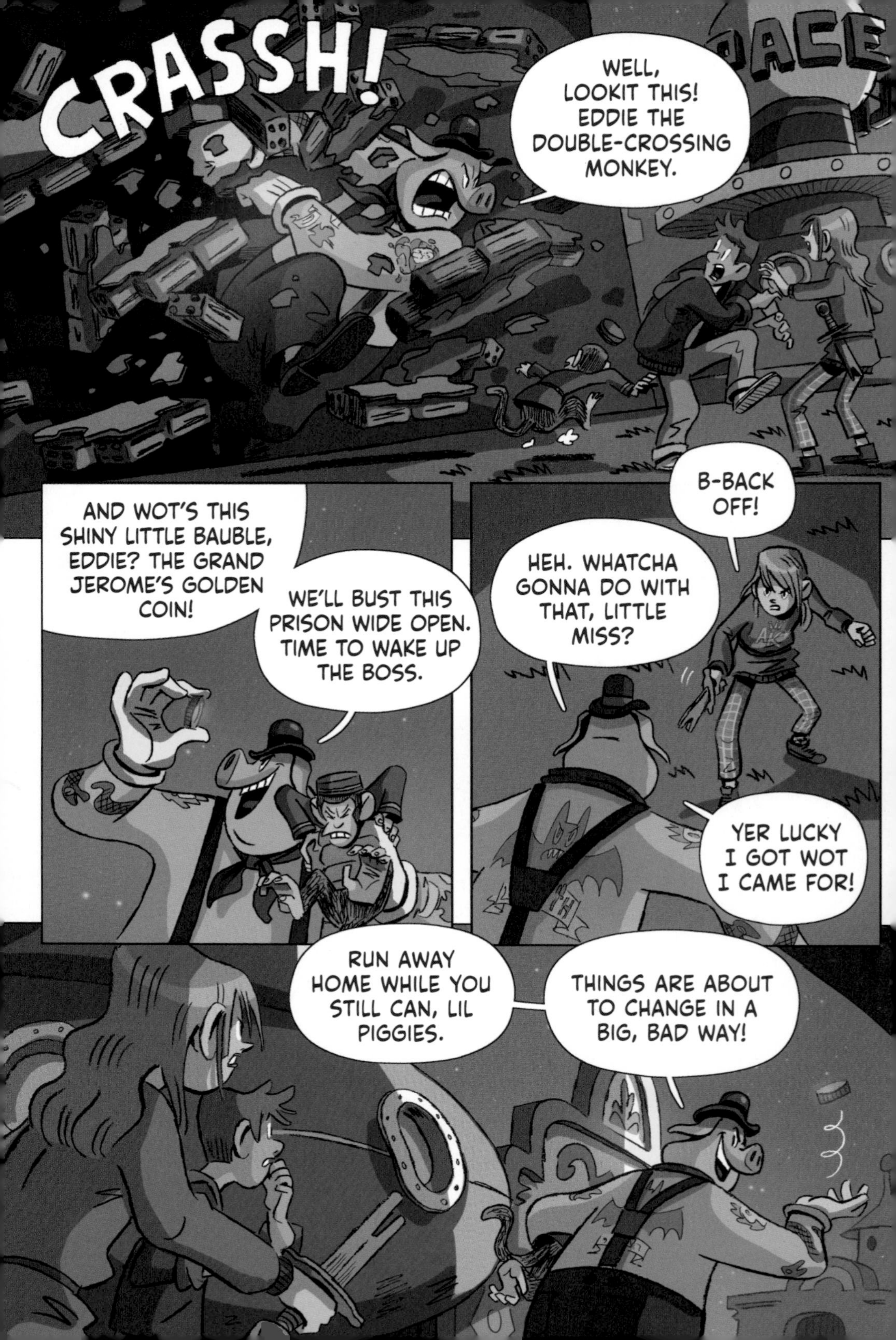
CRASSH!
WELL, LOOKIT THIS! EDDIE THE DOUBLE-CROSSING MONKEY.
AND WOT'S THIS SHINY LITTLE BAUBLE, EDDIE? THE GRAND JEROME'S GOLDEN COIN!
WE'LL BUST THIS PRISON WIDE OPEN. TIME TO WAKE UP THE BOSS.
B-BACK OFF!
HEH. WHATCHA GONNA DO WITH THAT, LITTLE MISS?
YER LUCKY I GOT WOT I CAME FOR!
RUN AWAY HOME WHILE YOU STILL CAN, LIL PIGGIES.
THINGS ARE ABOUT TO CHANGE IN A BIG, BAD WAY!

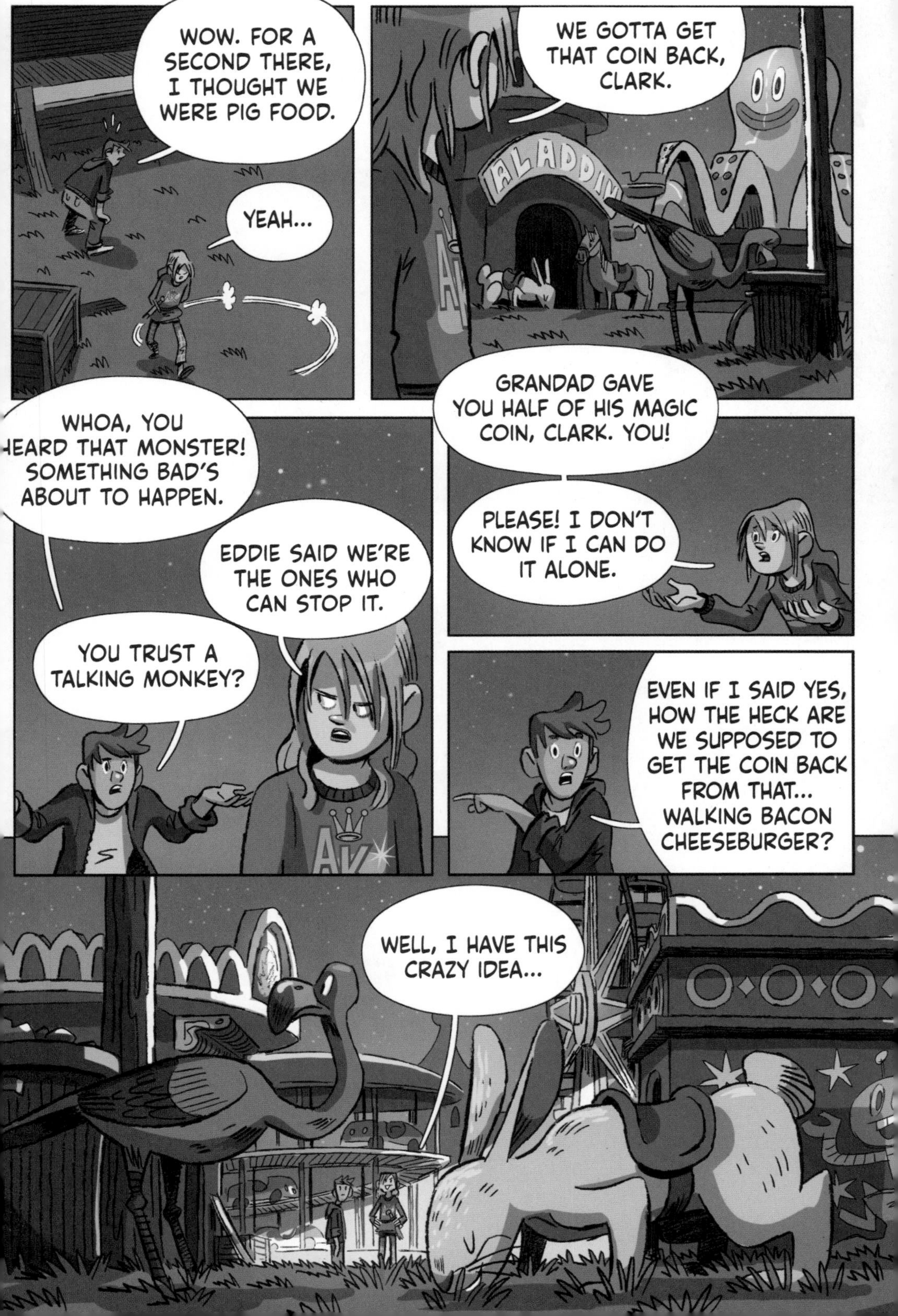
WOW. FOR A SECOND THERE, I THOUGHT WE WERE PIG FOOD.
YEAH...
WE GOTTA GET THAT COIN BACK, CLARK.
ALADDIN
WHOA, YOU HEARD THAT MONSTER! SOMETHING BAD'S ABOUT TO HAPPEN.
EDDIE SAID WE'RE THE ONES WHO CAN STOP IT.
YOU TRUST A TALKING MONKEY?
GRANDAD GAVE YOU HALF OF HIS MAGIC COIN, CLARK. YOU!
PLEASE! I DON'T KNOW IF I CAN DO IT ALONE.
EVEN IF I SAID YES, HOW THE HECK ARE WE SUPPOSED TO GET THE COIN BACK FROM THAT... WALKING BACON CHEESEBURGER?
WELL, I HAVE THIS CRAZY IDEA...

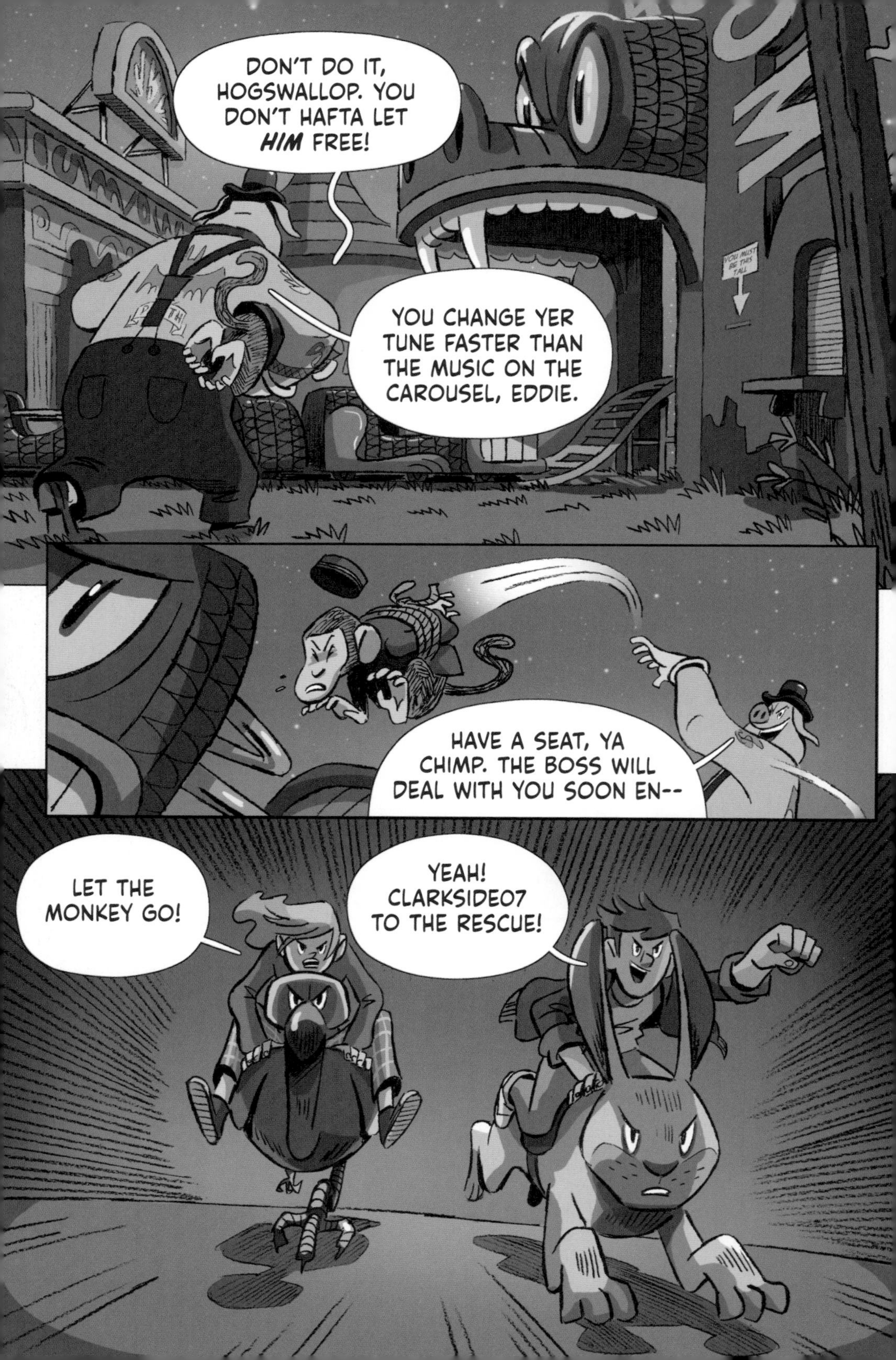
DON'T DO IT, HOGSWALLOP. YOU DON'T HAFTA LET *HIM* FREE!
YOU MUST BE THIS TALL
YOU CHANGE YER TUNE FASTER THAN THE MUSIC ON THE CAROUSEL, EDDIE.
HAVE A SEAT, YA CHIMP. THE BOSS WILL DEAL WITH YOU SOON EN--
LET THE MONKEY GO!
YEAH! CLARKSIDE07 TO THE RESCUE!

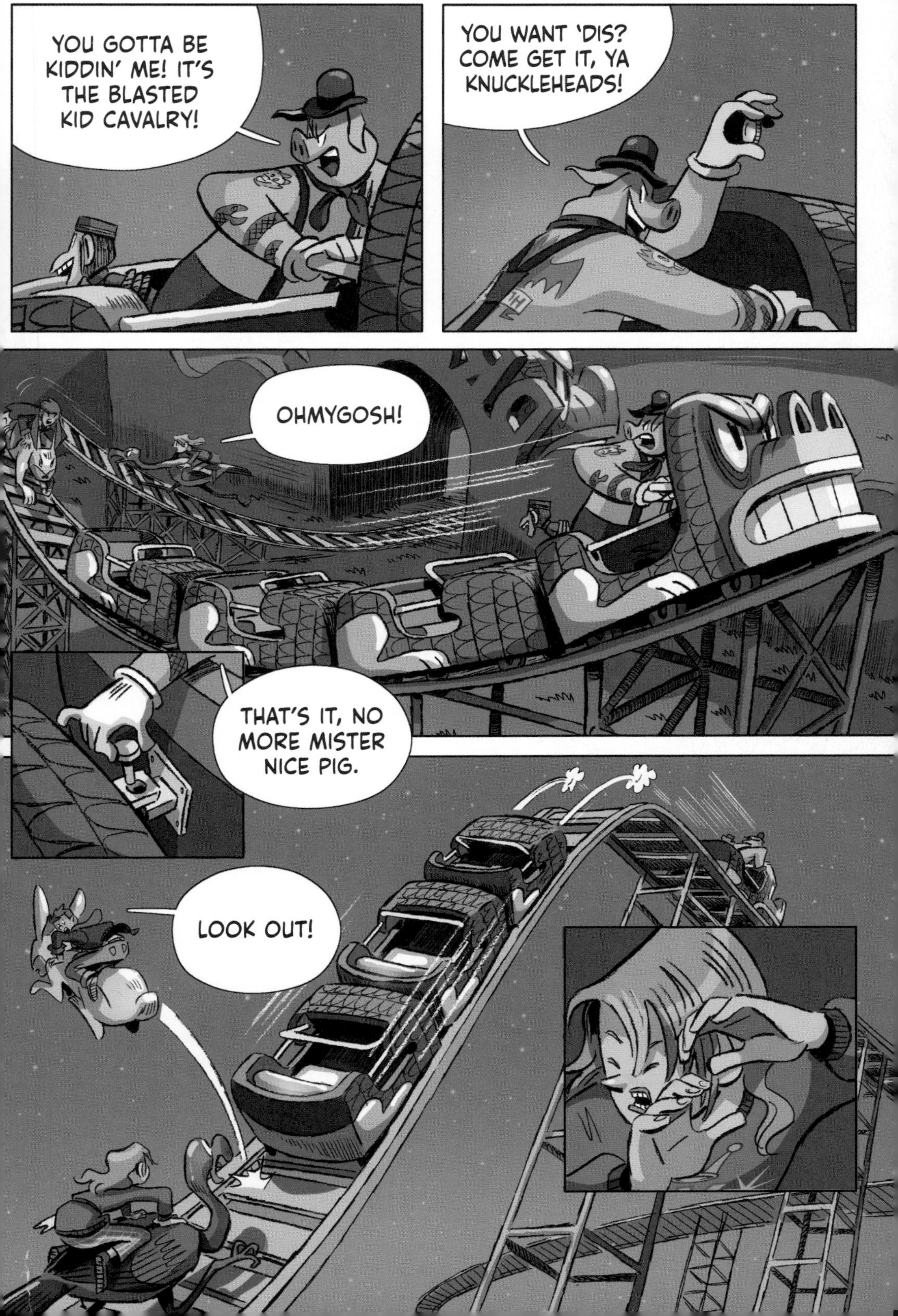
YOU GOTTA BE KIDDIN' ME! IT'S THE BLASTED KID CAVALRY!
YOU WANT 'DIS? COME GET IT, YA KNUCKLEHEADS!
OHMYGOSH!
THAT'S IT, NO MORE MISTER NICE PIG.
LOOK OUT!

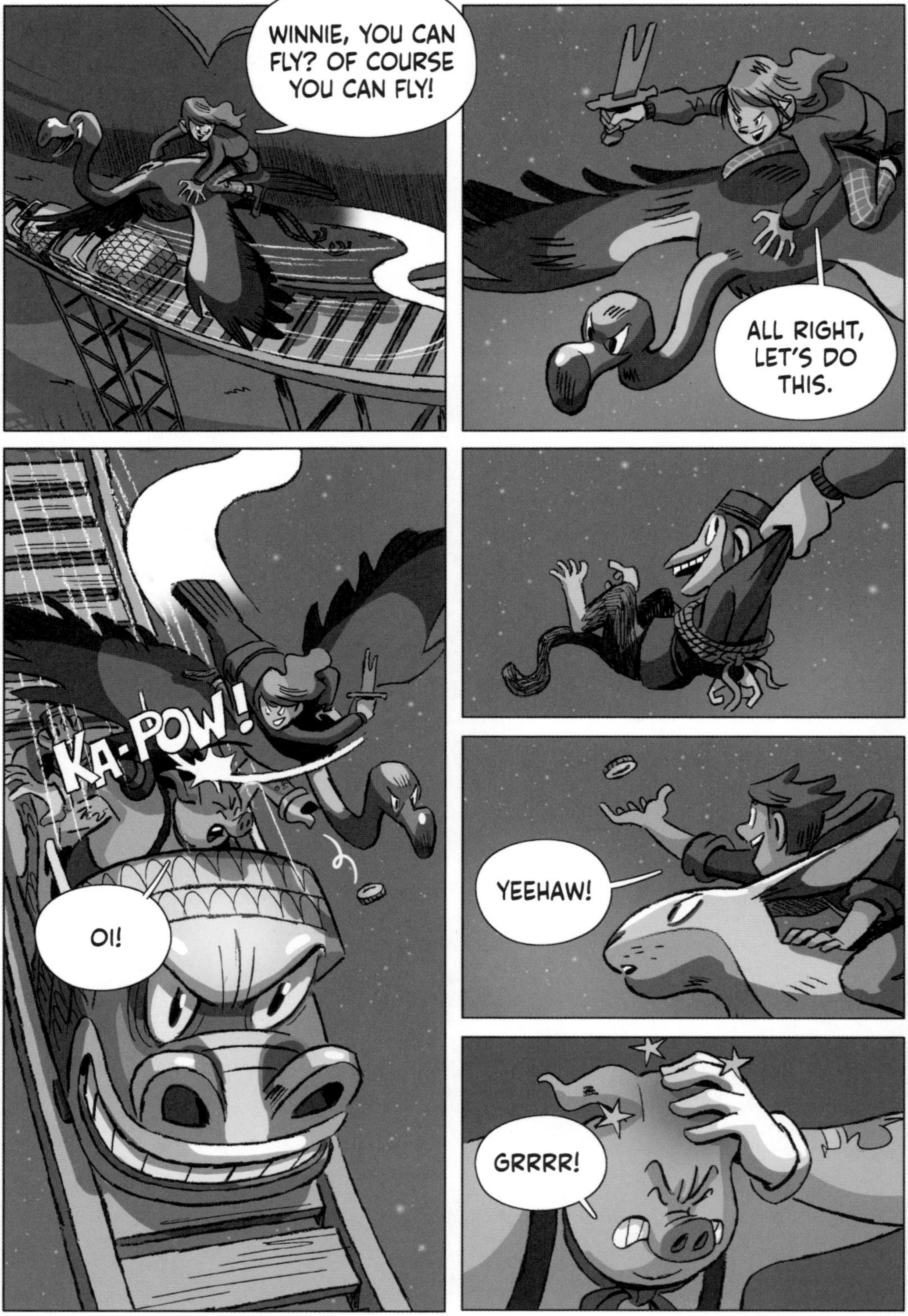

WINNIE, YOU CAN FLY? OF COURSE YOU CAN FLY!
ALL RIGHT, LET'S DO THIS.
KA-POW!
OI!
YEEHAW!
GRRRR!

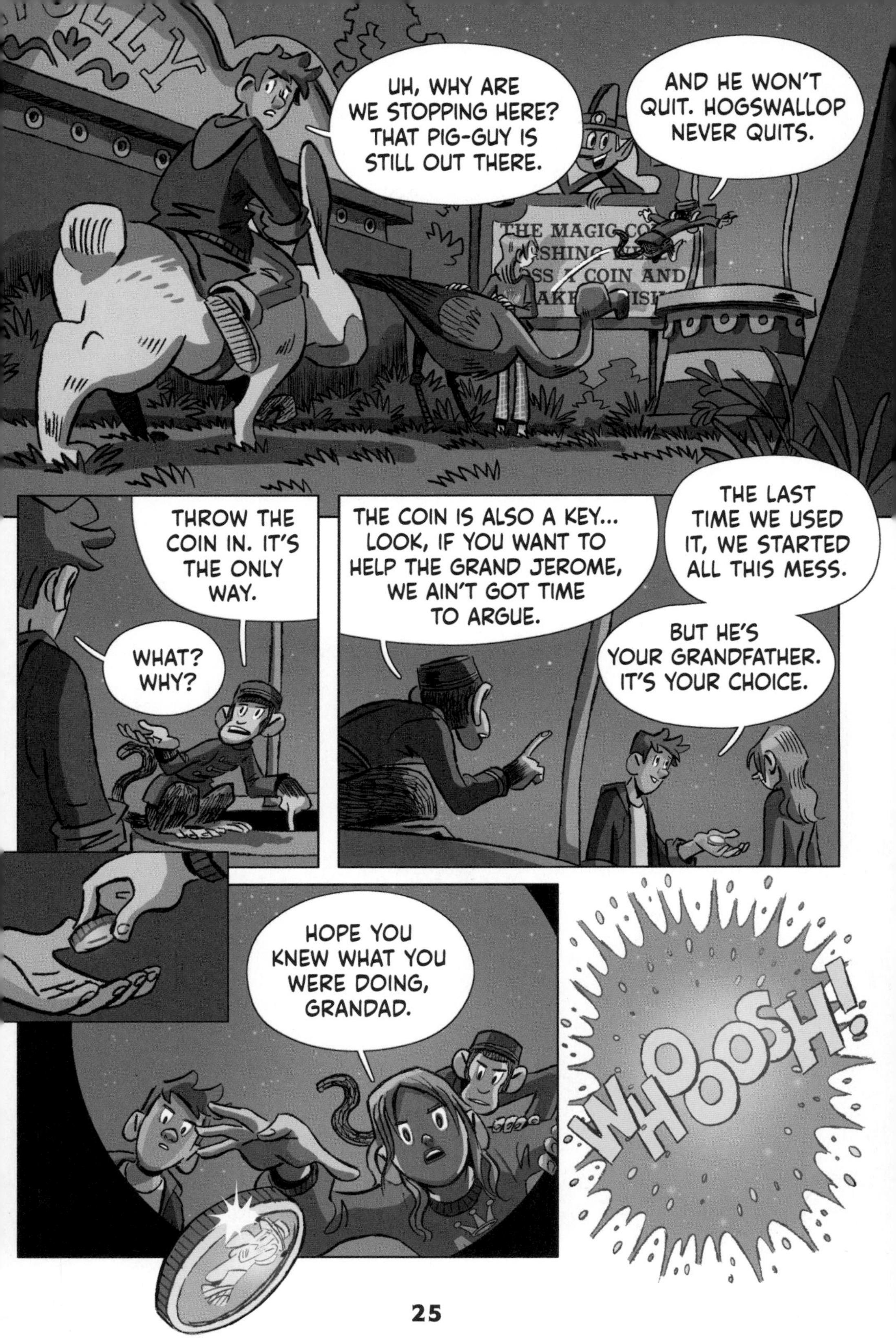
UH, WHY ARE WE STOPPING HERE? THAT PIG-GUY IS STILL OUT THERE.
AND HE WON'T QUIT. HOGSWALLOP NEVER QUITS.
THROW THE COIN IN. IT'S THE ONLY WAY.
WHAT? WHY?
THE COIN IS ALSO A KEY... LOOK, IF YOU WANT TO HELP THE GRAND JEROME, WE AIN'T GOT TIME TO ARGUE.
THE LAST TIME WE USED IT, WE STARTED ALL THIS MESS.
BUT HE'S YOUR GRANDFATHER. IT'S YOUR CHOICE.
HOPE YOU KNEW WHAT YOU WERE DOING, GRANDAD.
WHOOOSH!

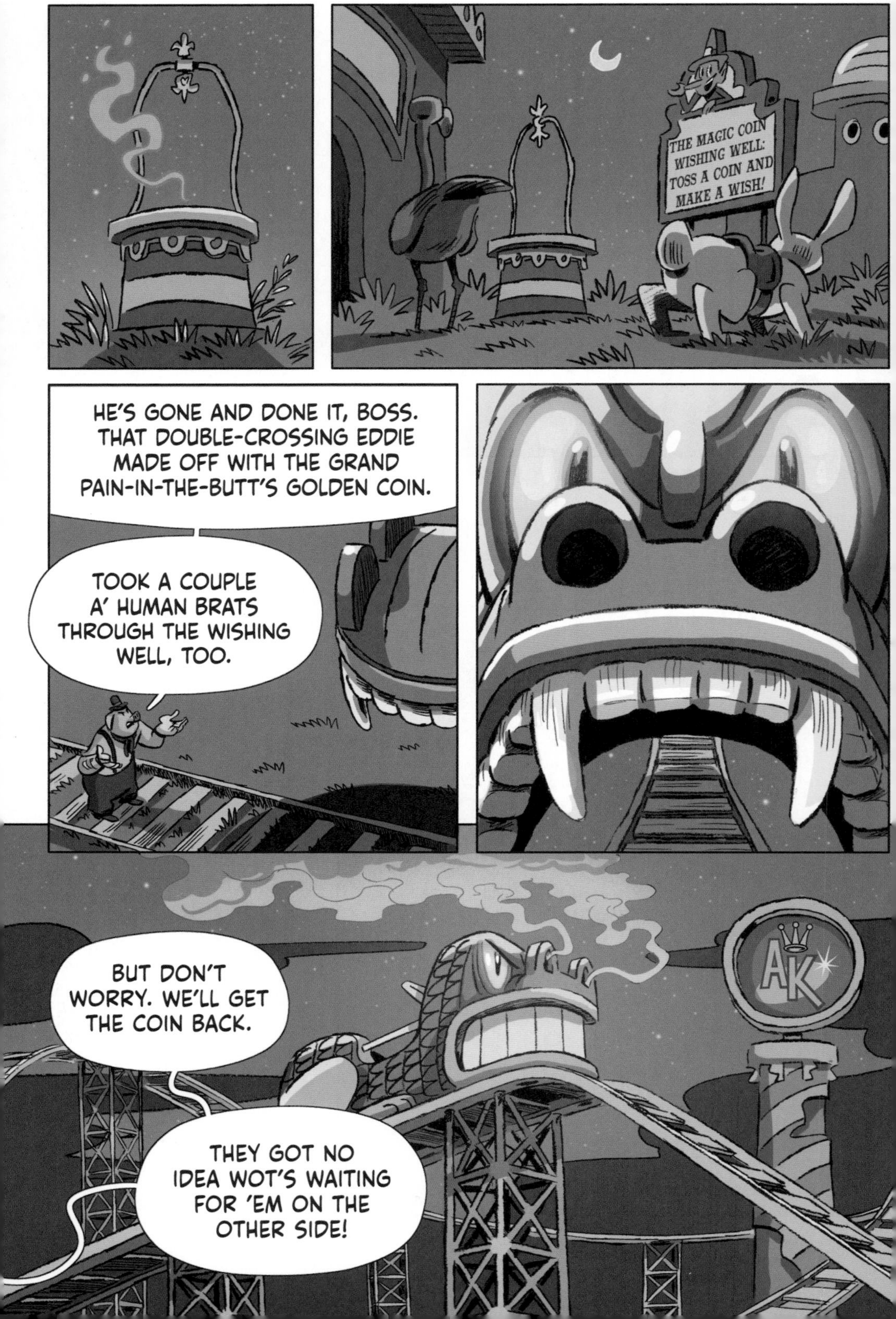
THE MAGIC COIN WISHING WELL: TOSS A COIN AND MAKE A WISH!
HE'S GONE AND DONE IT, BOSS. THAT DOUBLE-CROSSING EDDIE MADE OFF WITH THE GRAND PAIN-IN-THE-BUTT'S GOLDEN COIN.
TOOK A COUPLE A' HUMAN BRATS THROUGH THE WISHING WELL, TOO.
AK
BUT DON'T WORRY. WE'LL GET THE COIN BACK.
THEY GOT NO IDEA WOT'S WAITING FOR 'EM ON THE OTHER SIDE!

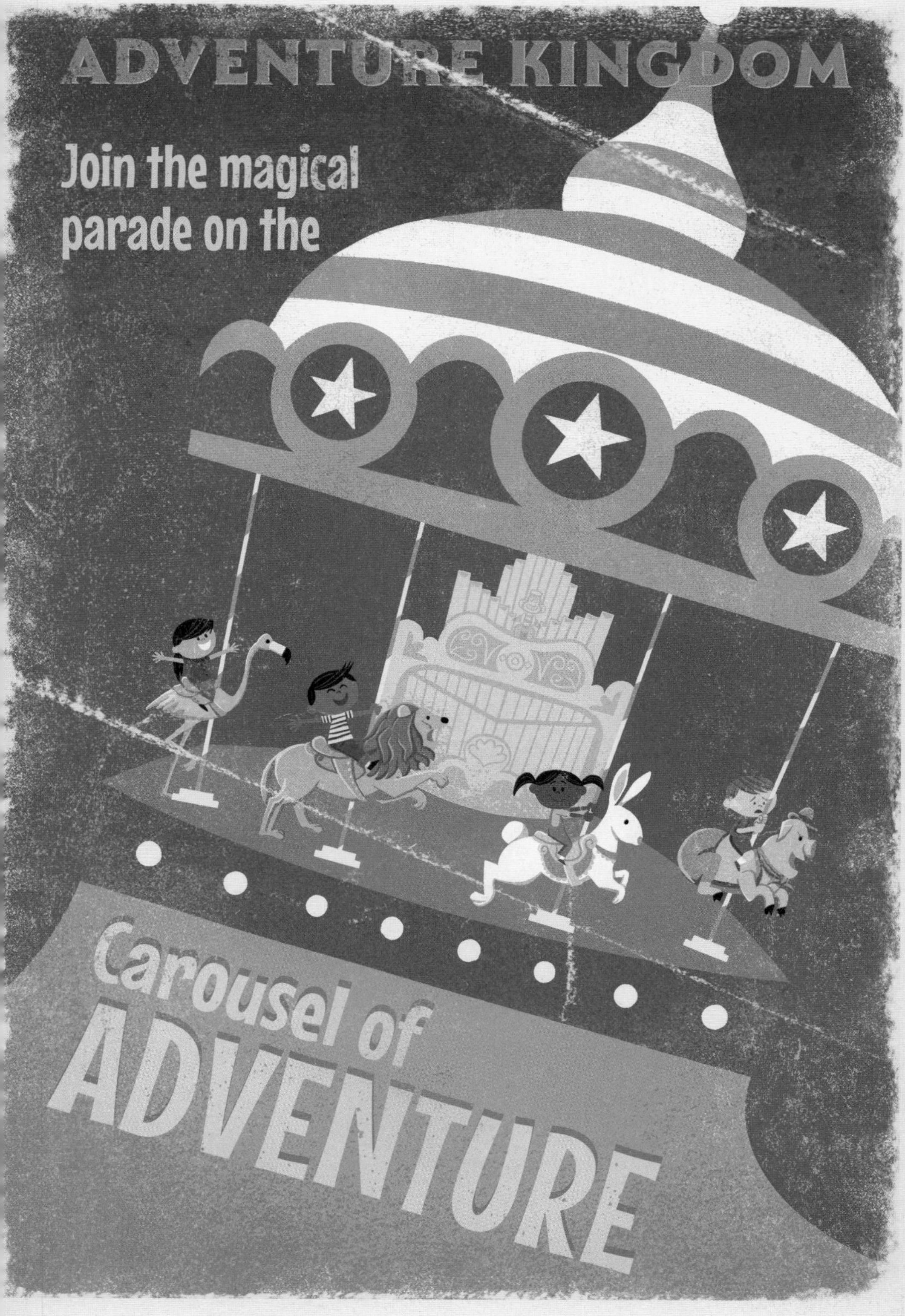
ADVENTURE KINGDOM
Join the magical parade on the
Carousel of ADVENTURE

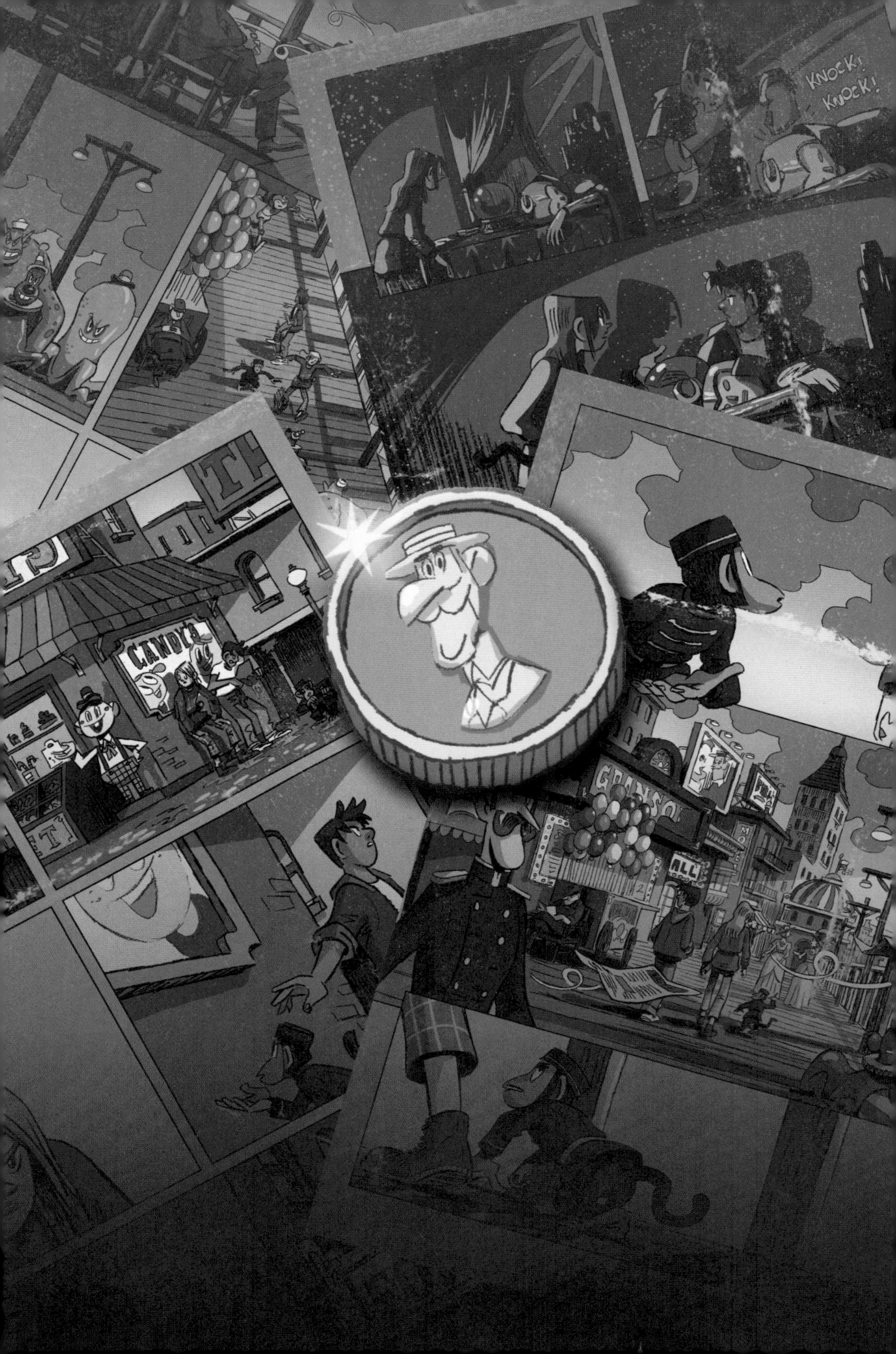
KNOCK! KNOCK!
CANDY

CHAPTER 2
FRIENDS AND FORTUNES

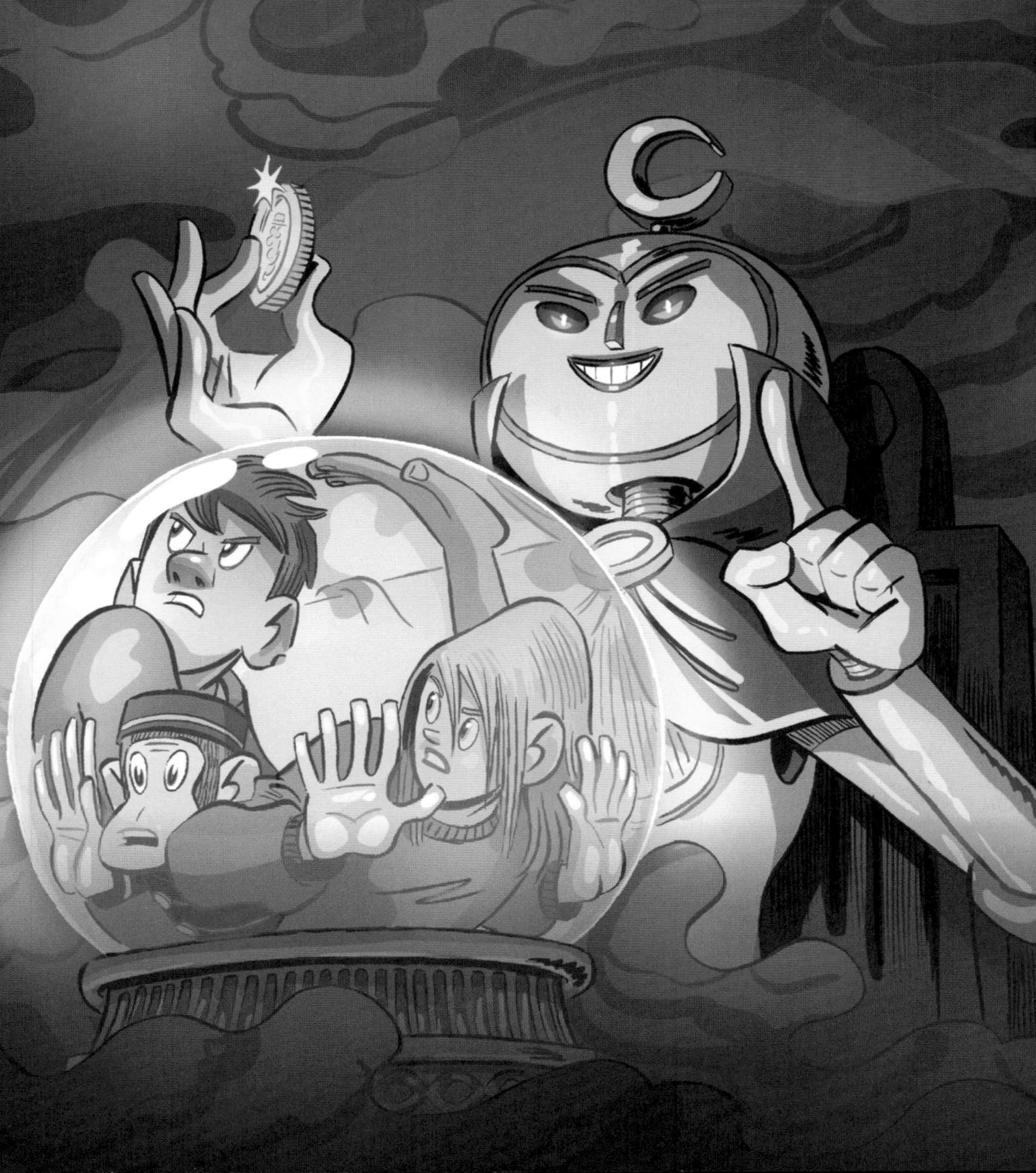

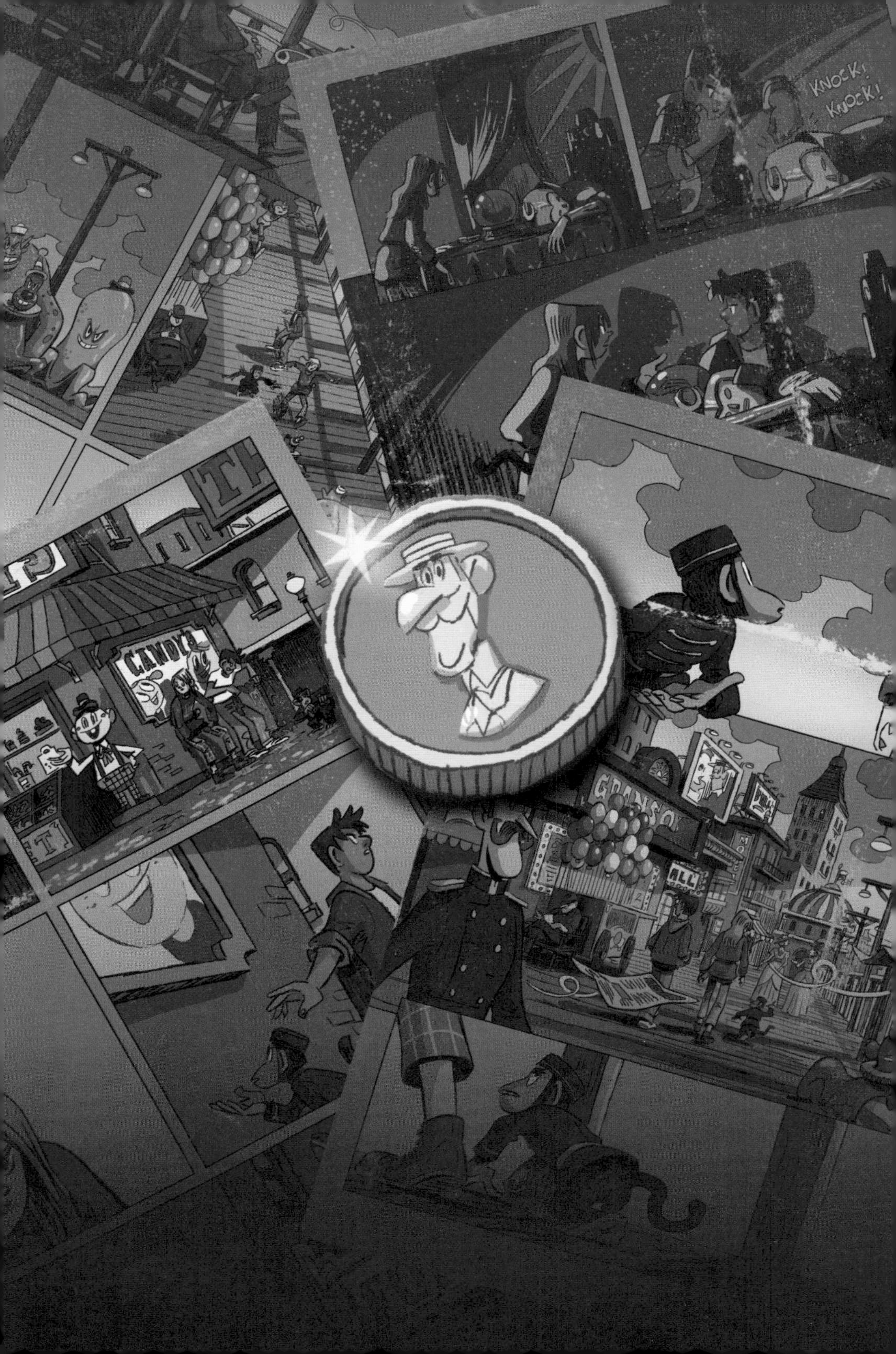
KNOCK! KNOCK!
CANDY
GRANSO
ALL

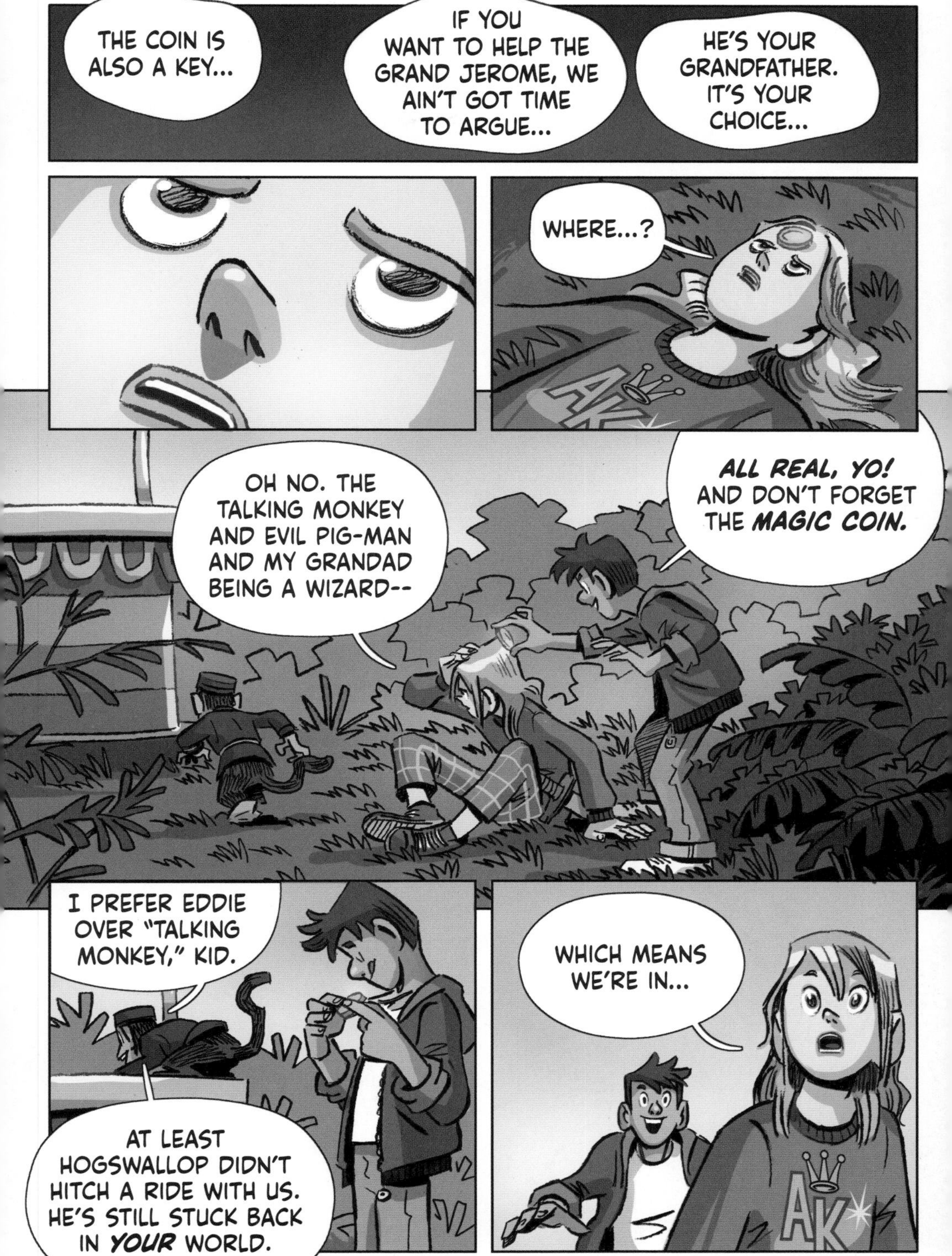
THE COIN IS ALSO A KEY...
IF YOU WANT TO HELP THE GRAND JEROME, WE AIN'T GOT TIME TO ARGUE...
HE'S YOUR GRANDFATHER. IT'S YOUR CHOICE...
WHERE...?
OH NO. THE TALKING MONKEY AND EVIL PIG-MAN AND MY GRANDAD BEING A WIZARD--
ALL REAL, YO! AND DON'T FORGET THE ***MAGIC COIN.***
I PREFER EDDIE OVER "TALKING MONKEY," KID.
AT LEAST HOGSWALLOP DIDN'T HITCH A RIDE WITH US. HE'S STILL STUCK BACK IN ***YOUR*** WORLD.
WHICH MEANS WE'RE IN...
AK
AK

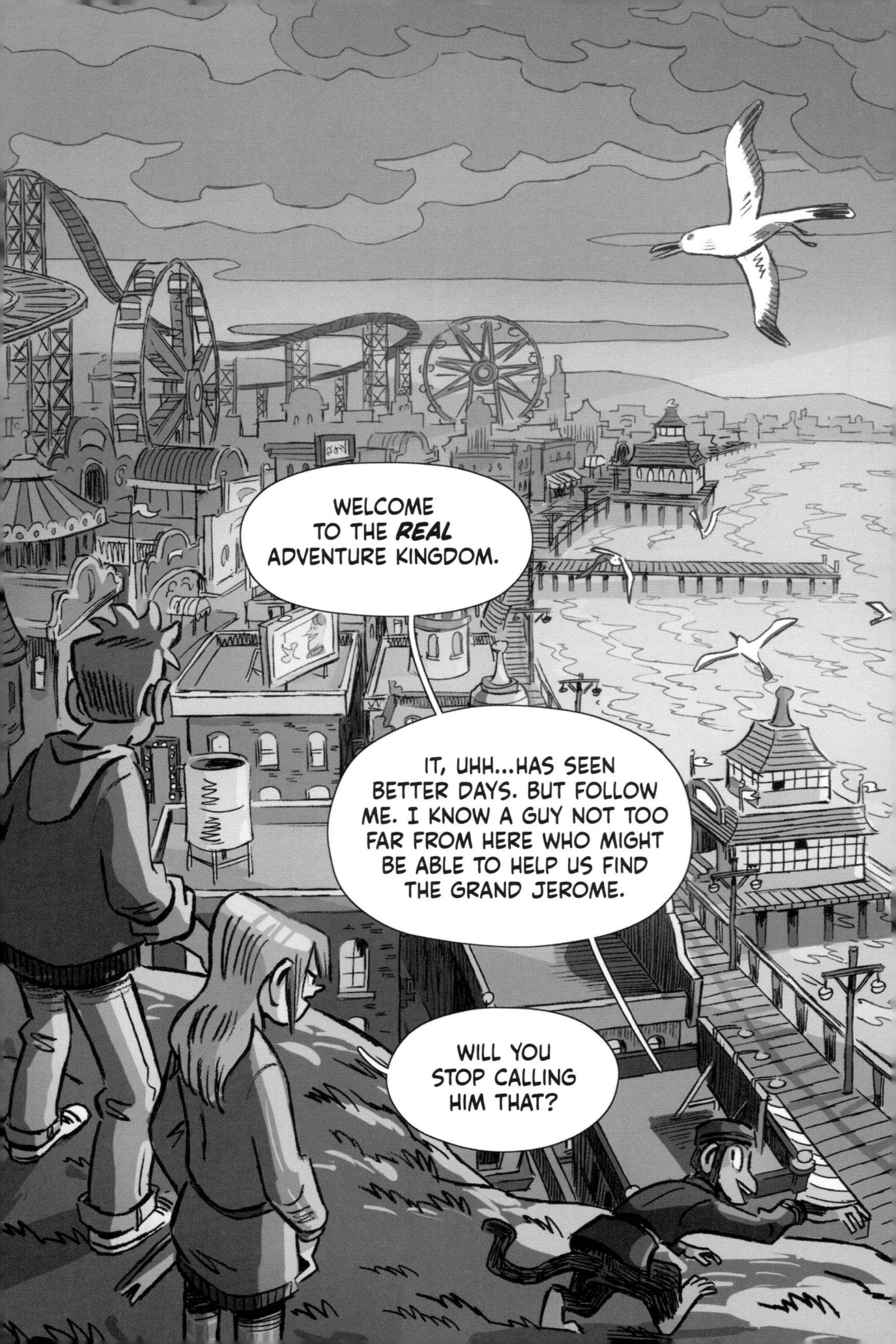
WELCOME TO THE *REAL* ADVENTURE KINGDOM.
IT, UHH...HAS SEEN BETTER DAYS. BUT FOLLOW ME. I KNOW A GUY NOT TOO FAR FROM HERE WHO MIGHT BE ABLE TO HELP US FIND THE GRAND JEROME.
WILL YOU STOP CALLING HIM THAT?

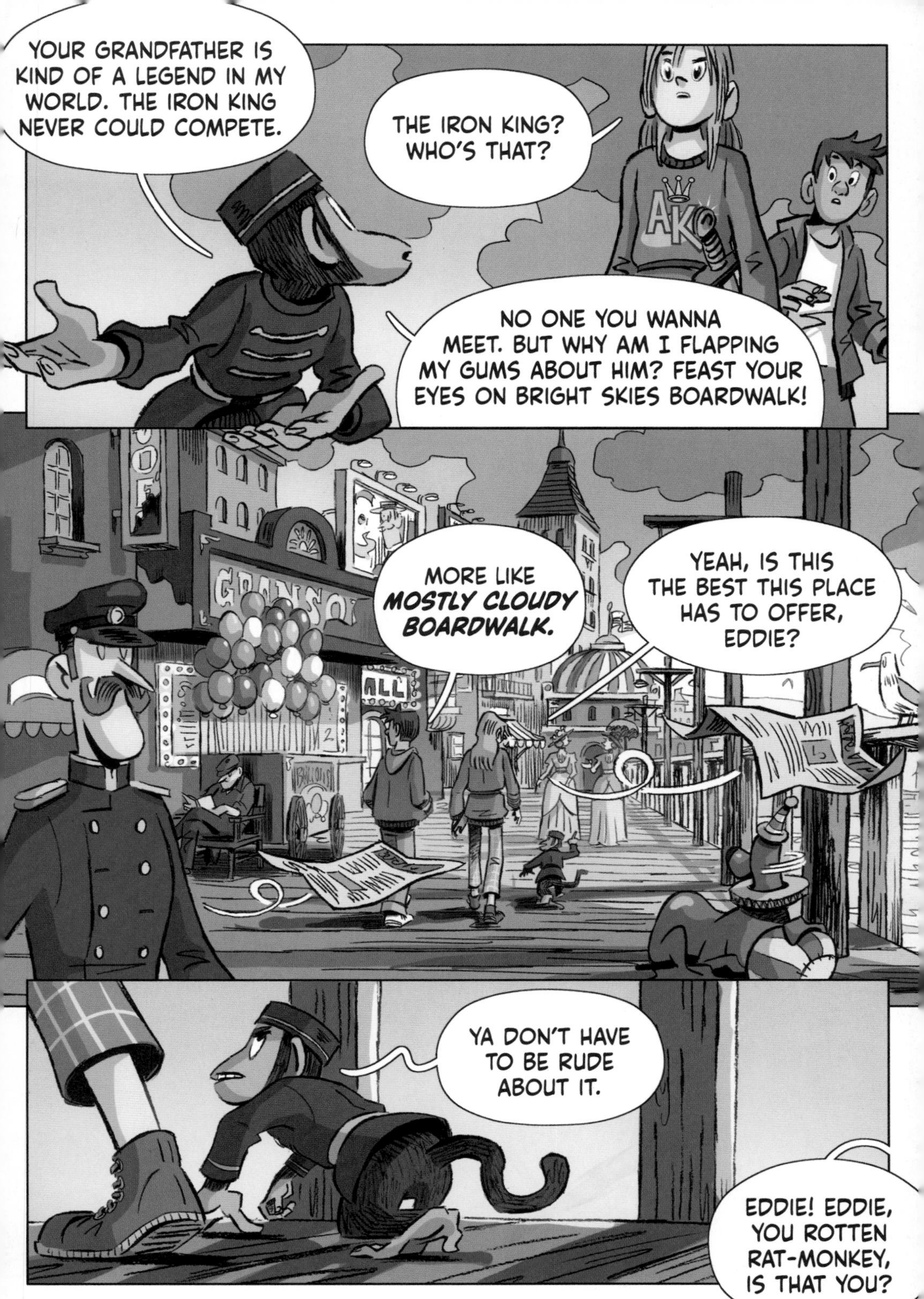
YOUR GRANDFATHER IS KIND OF A LEGEND IN MY WORLD. THE IRON KING NEVER COULD COMPETE.
THE IRON KING? WHO'S THAT?
NO ONE YOU WANNA MEET. BUT WHY AM I FLAPPING MY GUMS ABOUT HIM? FEAST YOUR EYES ON BRIGHT SKIES BOARDWALK!
MORE LIKE *MOSTLY CLOUDY BOARDWALK.*
YEAH, IS THIS THE BEST THIS PLACE HAS TO OFFER, EDDIE?
YA DON'T HAVE TO BE RUDE ABOUT IT.
EDDIE! EDDIE, YOU ROTTEN RAT-MONKEY, IS THAT YOU?

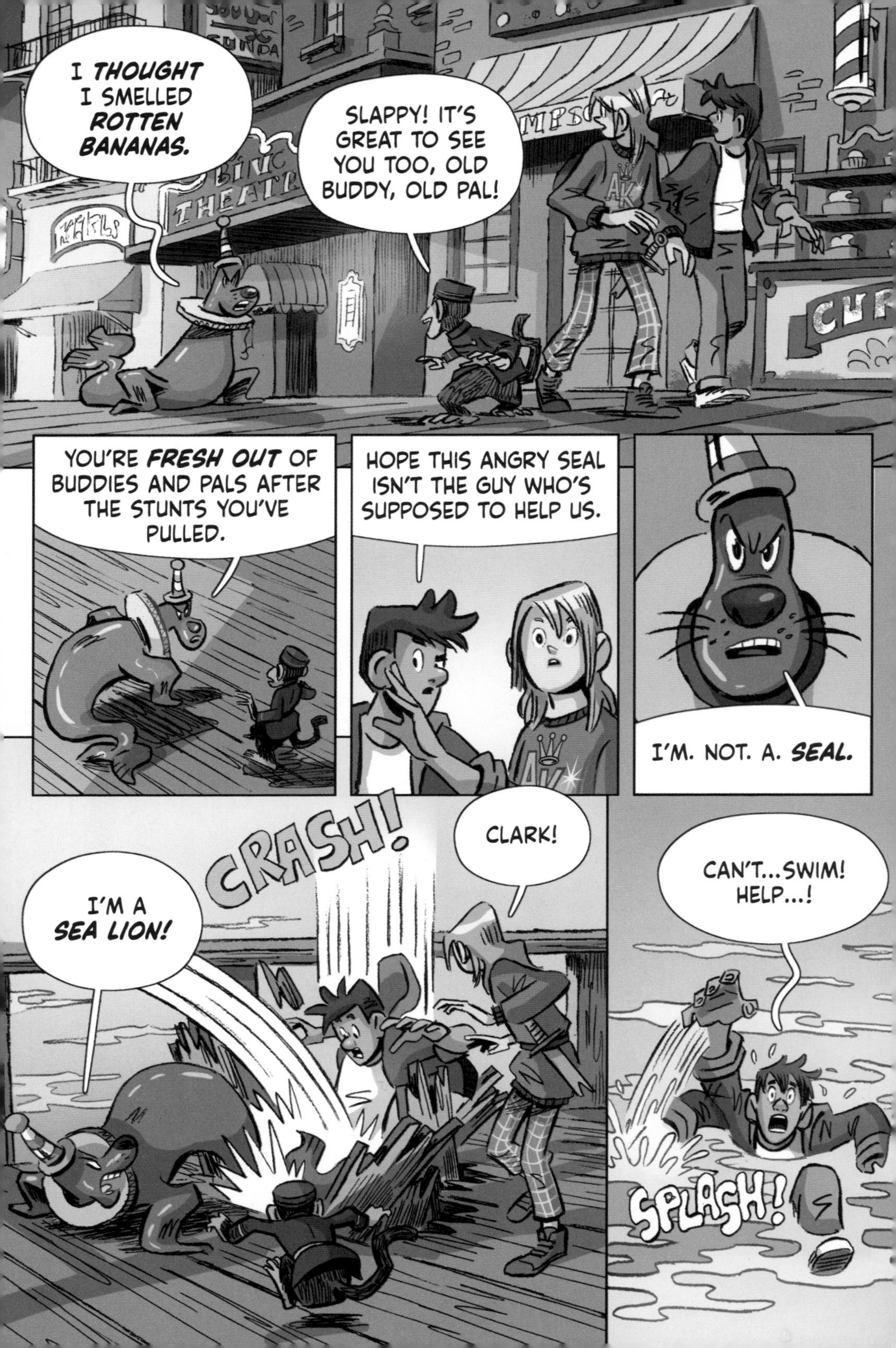
I *THOUGHT* I SMELLED ***ROTTEN BANANAS.***
SLAPPY! IT'S GREAT TO SEE YOU TOO, OLD BUDDY, OLD PAL!
YOU'RE ***FRESH OUT*** OF BUDDIES AND PALS AFTER THE STUNTS YOU'VE PULLED.
HOPE THIS ANGRY SEAL ISN'T THE GUY WHO'S SUPPOSED TO HELP US.
I'M. NOT. A. ***SEAL.***
CRASH!
I'M A ***SEA LION!***
CLARK!
CAN'T...SWIM! HELP...!
SPLASH!

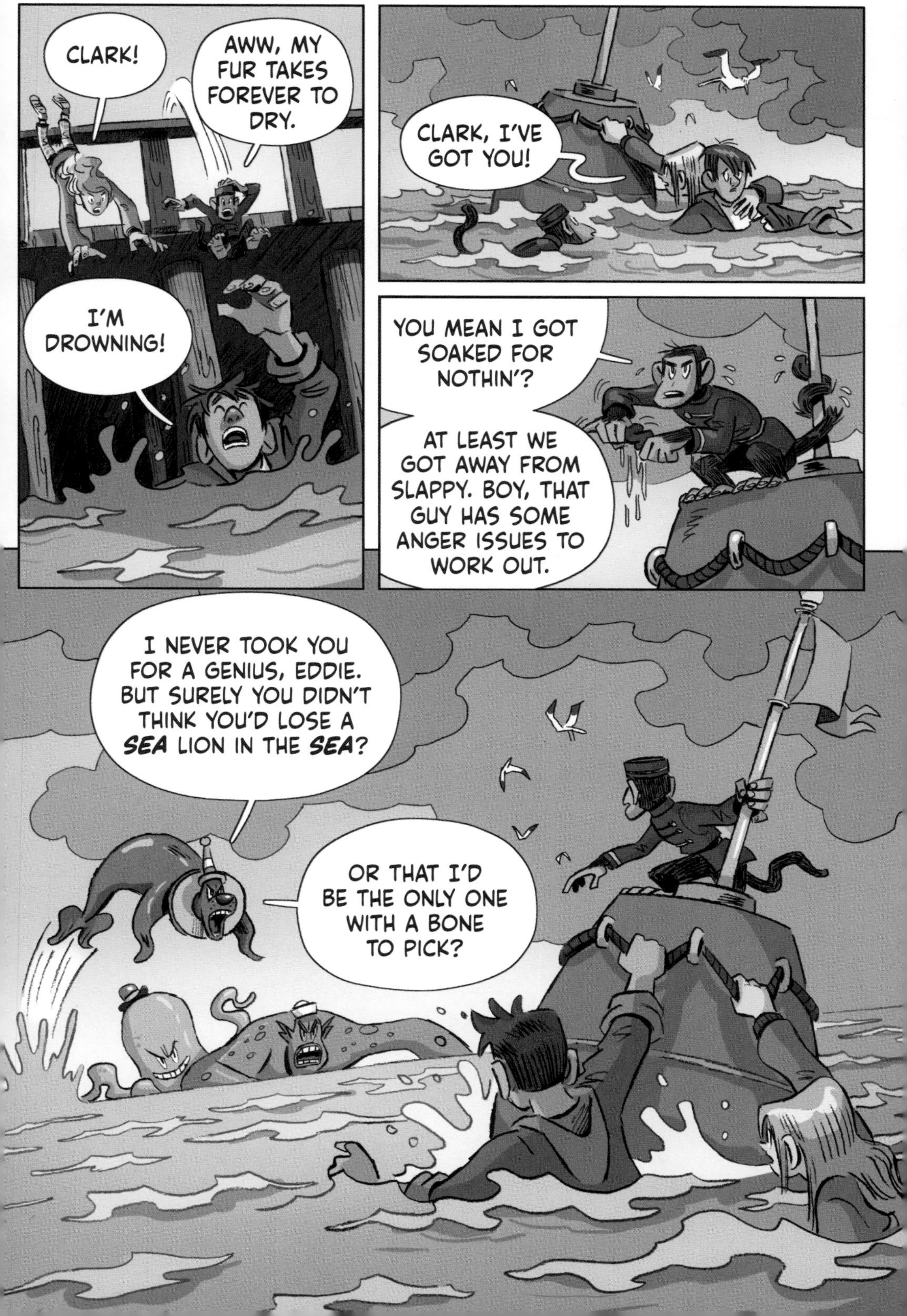
CLARK!
AWW, MY FUR TAKES FOREVER TO DRY.
I'M DROWNING!
CLARK, I'VE GOT YOU!
YOU MEAN I GOT SOAKED FOR NOTHIN'?
AT LEAST WE GOT AWAY FROM SLAPPY. BOY, THAT GUY HAS SOME ANGER ISSUES TO WORK OUT.
I NEVER TOOK YOU FOR A GENIUS, EDDIE. BUT SURELY YOU DIDN'T THINK YOU'D LOSE A *SEA* LION IN THE *SEA*?
OR THAT I'D BE THE ONLY ONE WITH A BONE TO PICK?

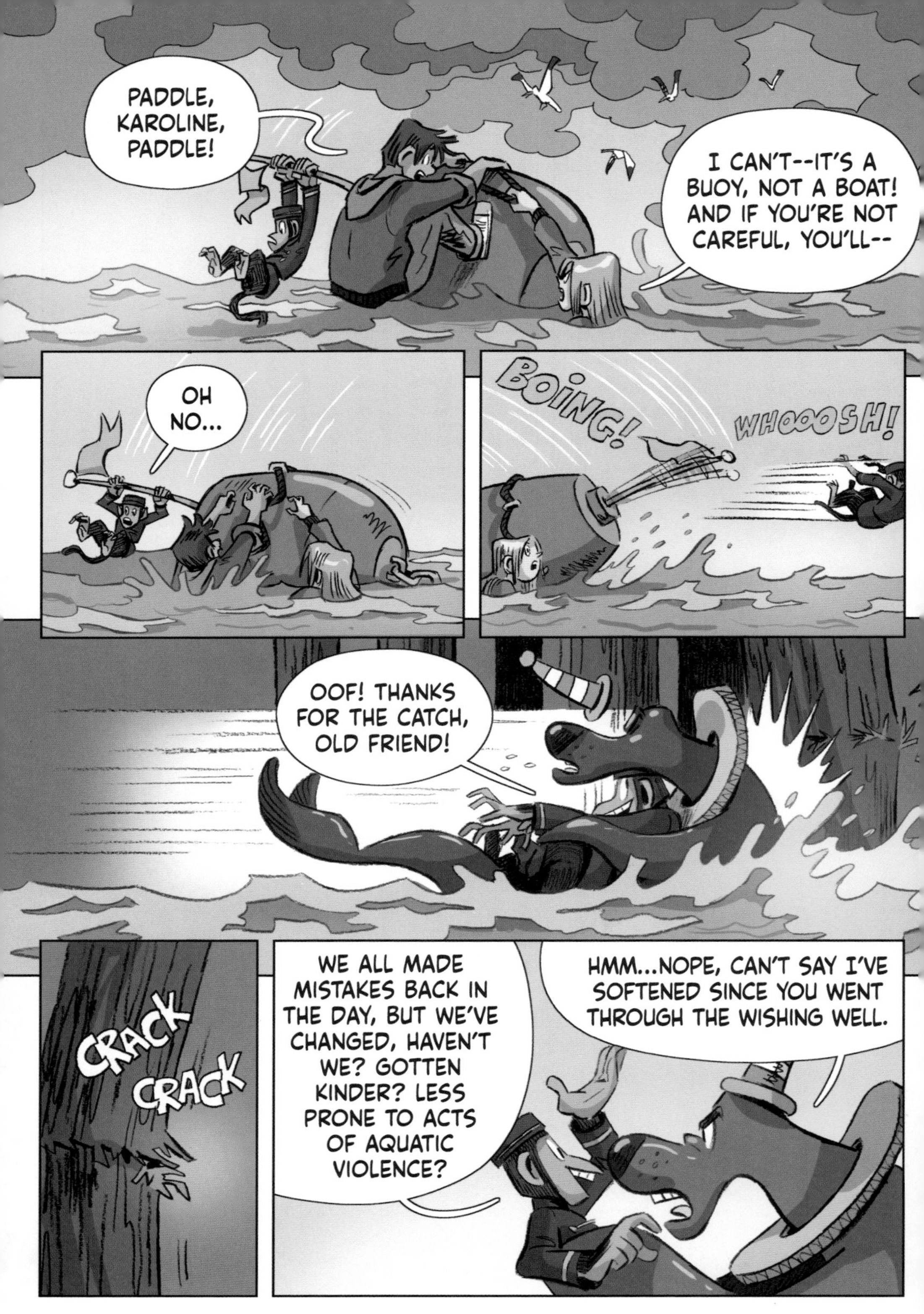
PADDLE, KAROLINE, PADDLE!
I CAN'T--IT'S A BUOY, NOT A BOAT! AND IF YOU'RE NOT CAREFUL, YOU'LL--
OH NO...
BOING!
WHOOOSH!
OOF! THANKS FOR THE CATCH, OLD FRIEND!
CRACK
CRACK
WE ALL MADE MISTAKES BACK IN THE DAY, BUT WE'VE CHANGED, HAVEN'T WE? GOTTEN KINDER? LESS PRONE TO ACTS OF AQUATIC VIOLENCE?
HMM...NOPE, CAN'T SAY I'VE SOFTENED SINCE YOU WENT THROUGH THE WISHING WELL.

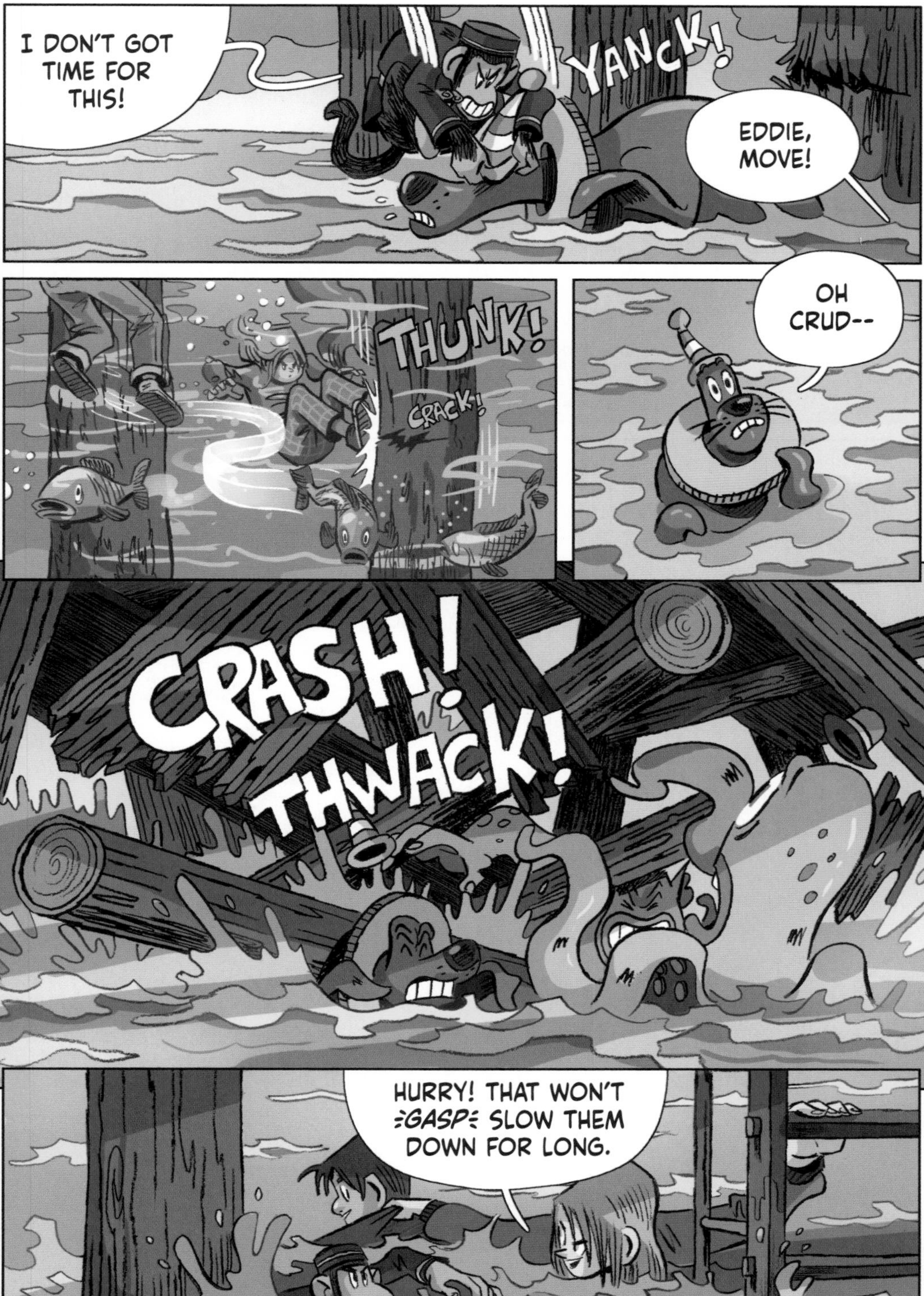
I DON'T GOT TIME FOR THIS!
YANCK!
EDDIE, MOVE!
THUNK!
CRACK!
OH CRUD--
CRASH!
THWACK!
HURRY! THAT WON'T =GASP= SLOW THEM DOWN FOR LONG.

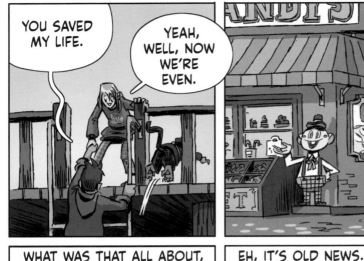

YOU SAVED MY LIFE.

YEAH, WELL, NOW WE'RE EVEN.

VERY TOUCHING. MUCH SWEETER THAN MY REUNION WITH SLAPPY.

WHAT WAS THAT ALL ABOUT, EDDIE? CLARK ALMOST *DROWNED.* WHY WAS THAT SEA LION SO MAD AT YOU?

EH, IT'S OLD NEWS. EXPLAININ' WHY SLAPPY'S LIKE THAT WOULD JUST BORE YOU. BESIDES, I KNOW THIS *OTHER* GUY WHO CAN--

NO! NO MORE OLD "FRIENDS." I BARELY SURVIVED THAT ONE.

I HAVE A NEW IDEA FOR HOW WE CAN FIND KAROLINE'S GRANDAD.

FORTUNE·T

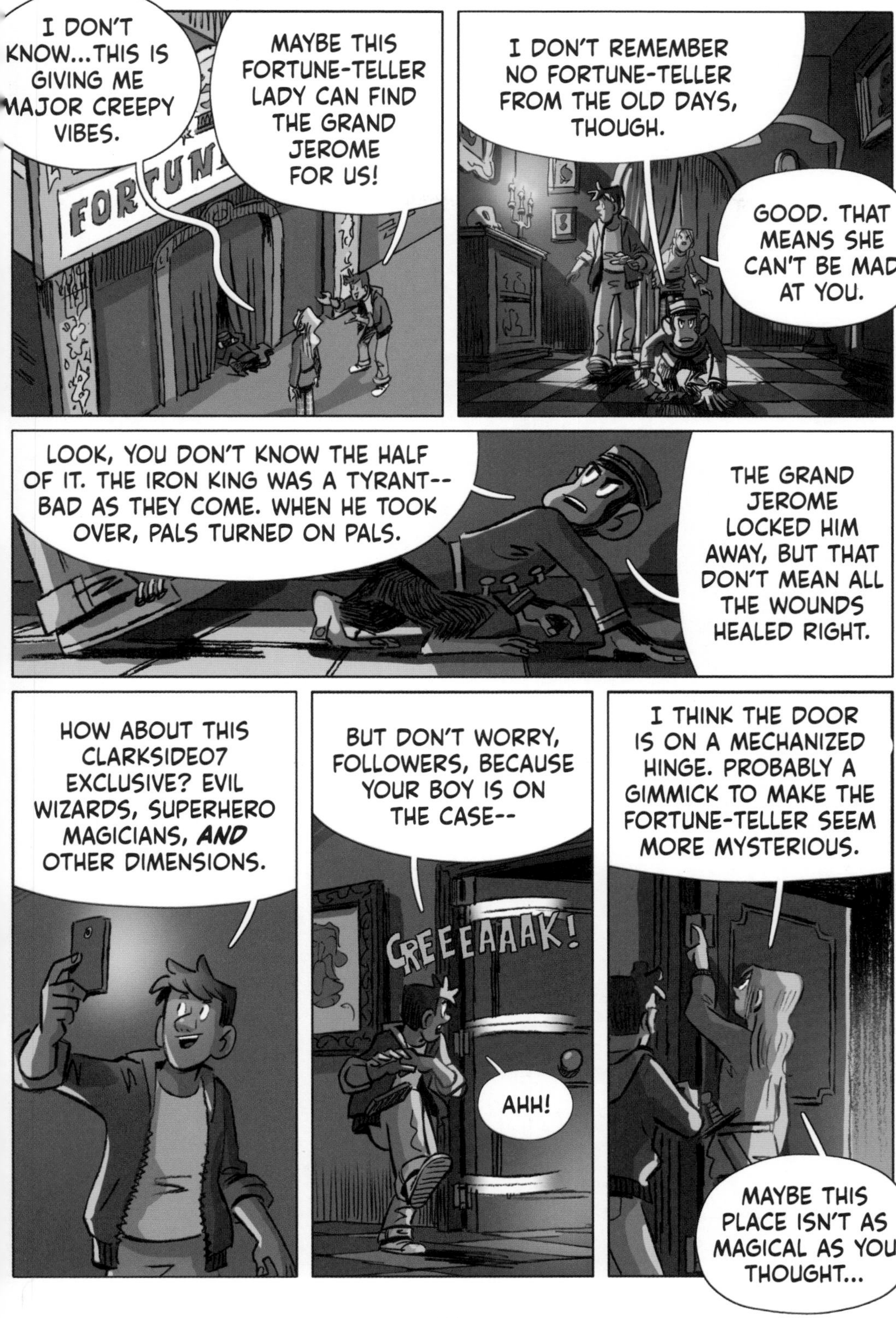
I DON'T KNOW...THIS IS GIVING ME MAJOR CREEPY VIBES.
FOR TUN
MAYBE THIS FORTUNE-TELLER LADY CAN FIND THE GRAND JEROME FOR US!
I DON'T REMEMBER NO FORTUNE-TELLER FROM THE OLD DAYS, THOUGH.
GOOD. THAT MEANS SHE CAN'T BE MAD AT YOU.
LOOK, YOU DON'T KNOW THE HALF OF IT. THE IRON KING WAS A TYRANT-- BAD AS THEY COME. WHEN HE TOOK OVER, PALS TURNED ON PALS.
THE GRAND JEROME LOCKED HIM AWAY, BUT THAT DON'T MEAN ALL THE WOUNDS HEALED RIGHT.
HOW ABOUT THIS CLARKSIDE07 EXCLUSIVE? EVIL WIZARDS, SUPERHERO MAGICIANS, ***AND*** OTHER DIMENSIONS.
BUT DON'T WORRY, FOLLOWERS, BECAUSE YOUR BOY IS ON THE CASE--
CREEEAAAK!
AHH!
I THINK THE DOOR IS ON A MECHANIZED HINGE. PROBABLY A GIMMICK TO MAKE THE FORTUNE-TELLER SEEM MORE MYSTERIOUS.
MAYBE THIS PLACE ISN'T AS MAGICAL AS YOU THOUGHT...

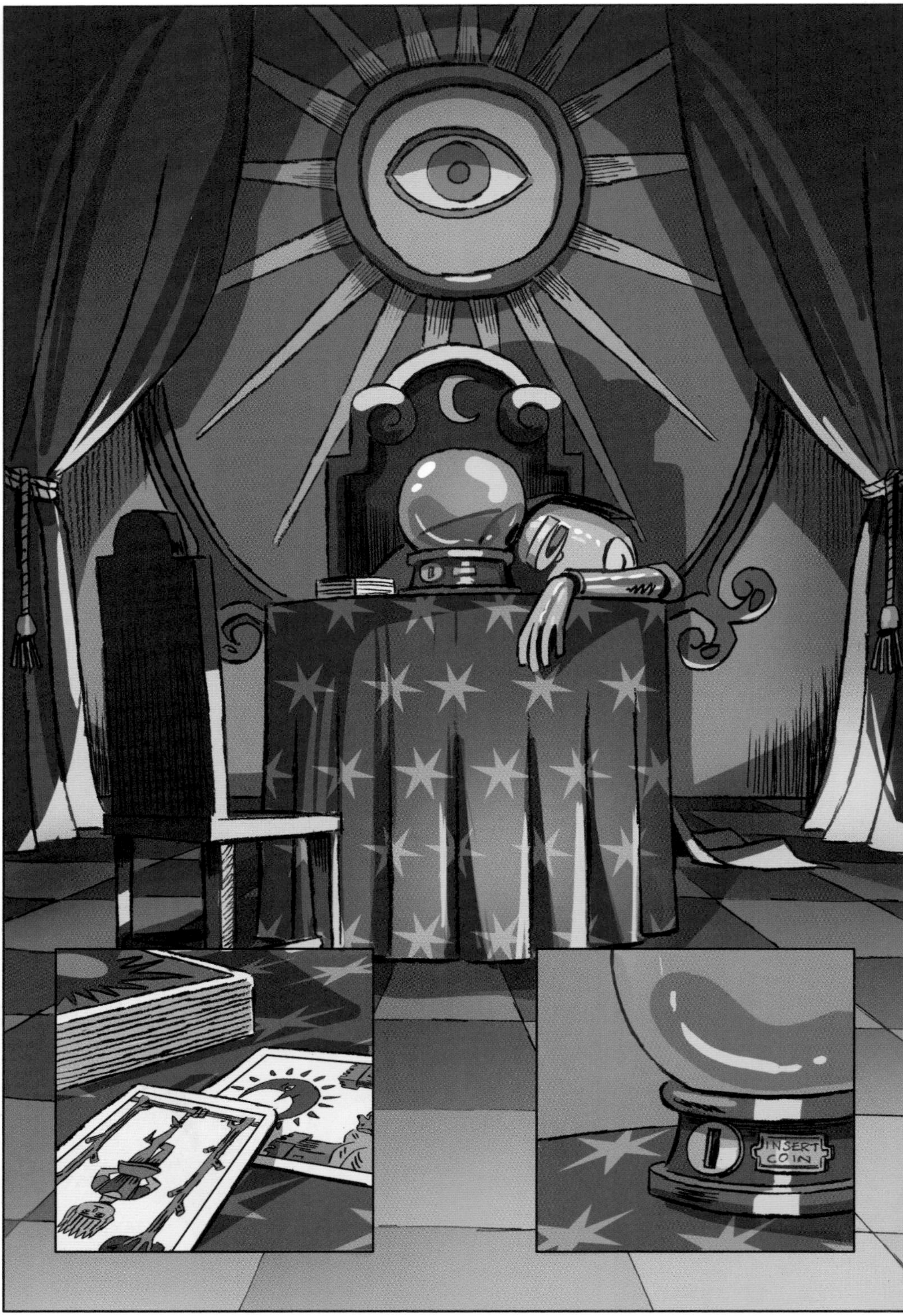
INSERT COIN

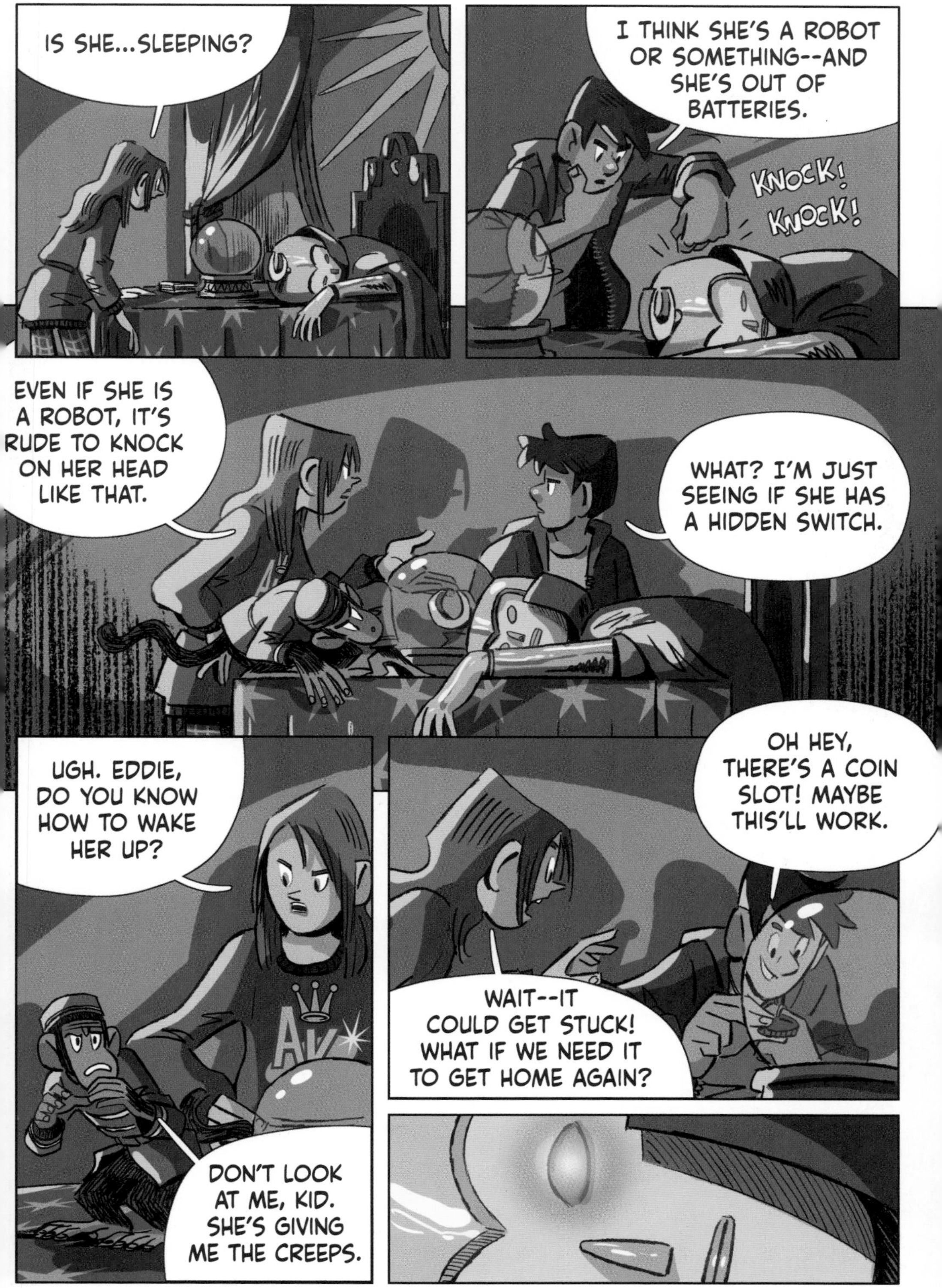
IS SHE...SLEEPING?
I THINK SHE'S A ROBOT OR SOMETHING--AND SHE'S OUT OF BATTERIES.
KNOCK! KNOCK!
EVEN IF SHE IS A ROBOT, IT'S RUDE TO KNOCK ON HER HEAD LIKE THAT.
WHAT? I'M JUST SEEING IF SHE HAS A HIDDEN SWITCH.
UGH. EDDIE, DO YOU KNOW HOW TO WAKE HER UP?
DON'T LOOK AT ME, KID. SHE'S GIVING ME THE CREEPS.
OH HEY, THERE'S A COIN SLOT! MAYBE THIS'LL WORK.
WAIT--IT COULD GET STUCK! WHAT IF WE NEED IT TO GET HOME AGAIN?

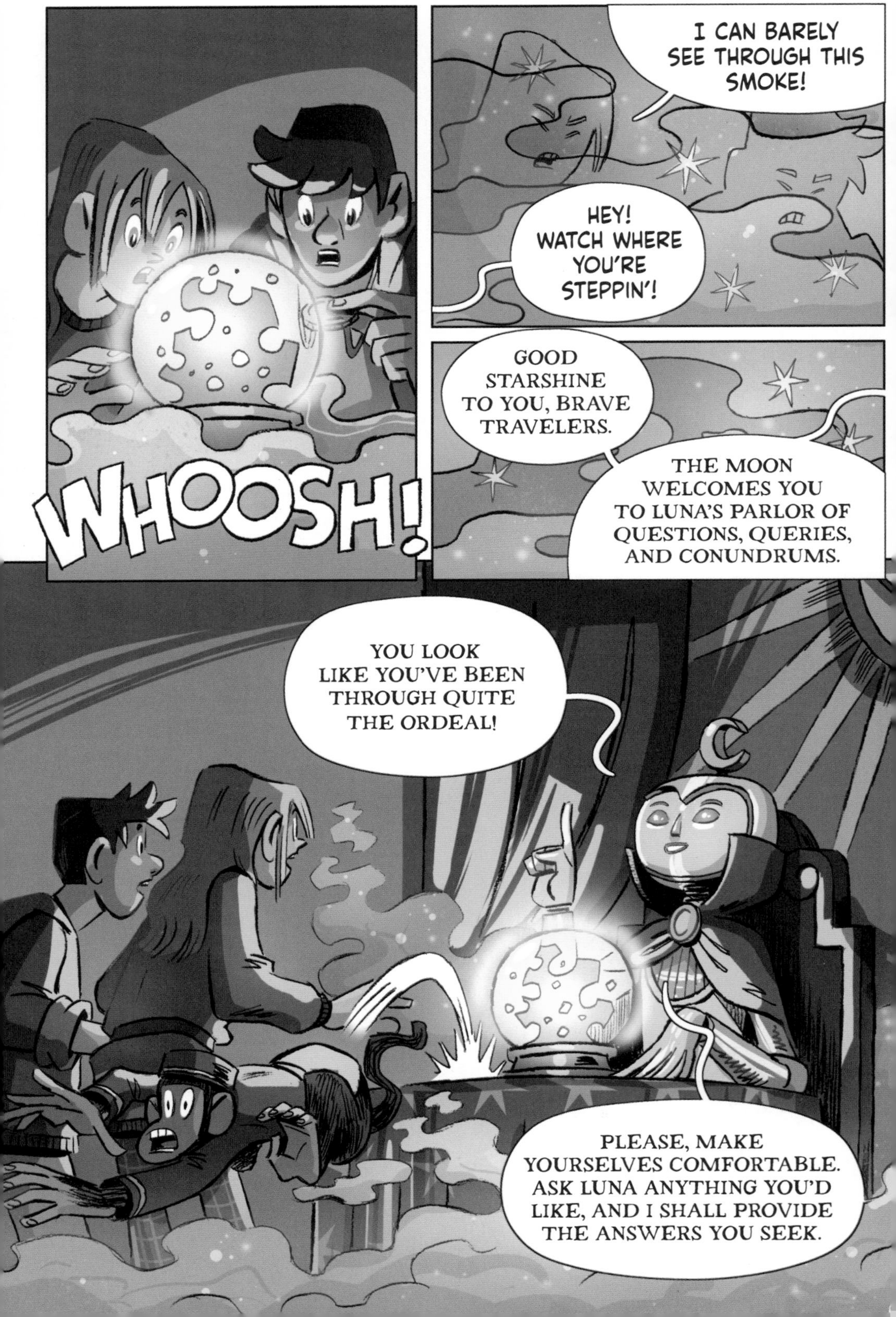
WHOOSH!
I CAN BARELY SEE THROUGH THIS SMOKE!
HEY! WATCH WHERE YOU'RE STEPPIN'!
GOOD STARSHINE TO YOU, BRAVE TRAVELERS.
THE MOON WELCOMES YOU TO LUNA'S PARLOR OF QUESTIONS, QUERIES, AND CONUNDRUMS.
YOU LOOK LIKE YOU'VE BEEN THROUGH QUITE THE ORDEAL!
PLEASE, MAKE YOURSELVES COMFORTABLE. ASK LUNA ANYTHING YOU'D LIKE, AND I SHALL PROVIDE THE ANSWERS YOU SEEK.

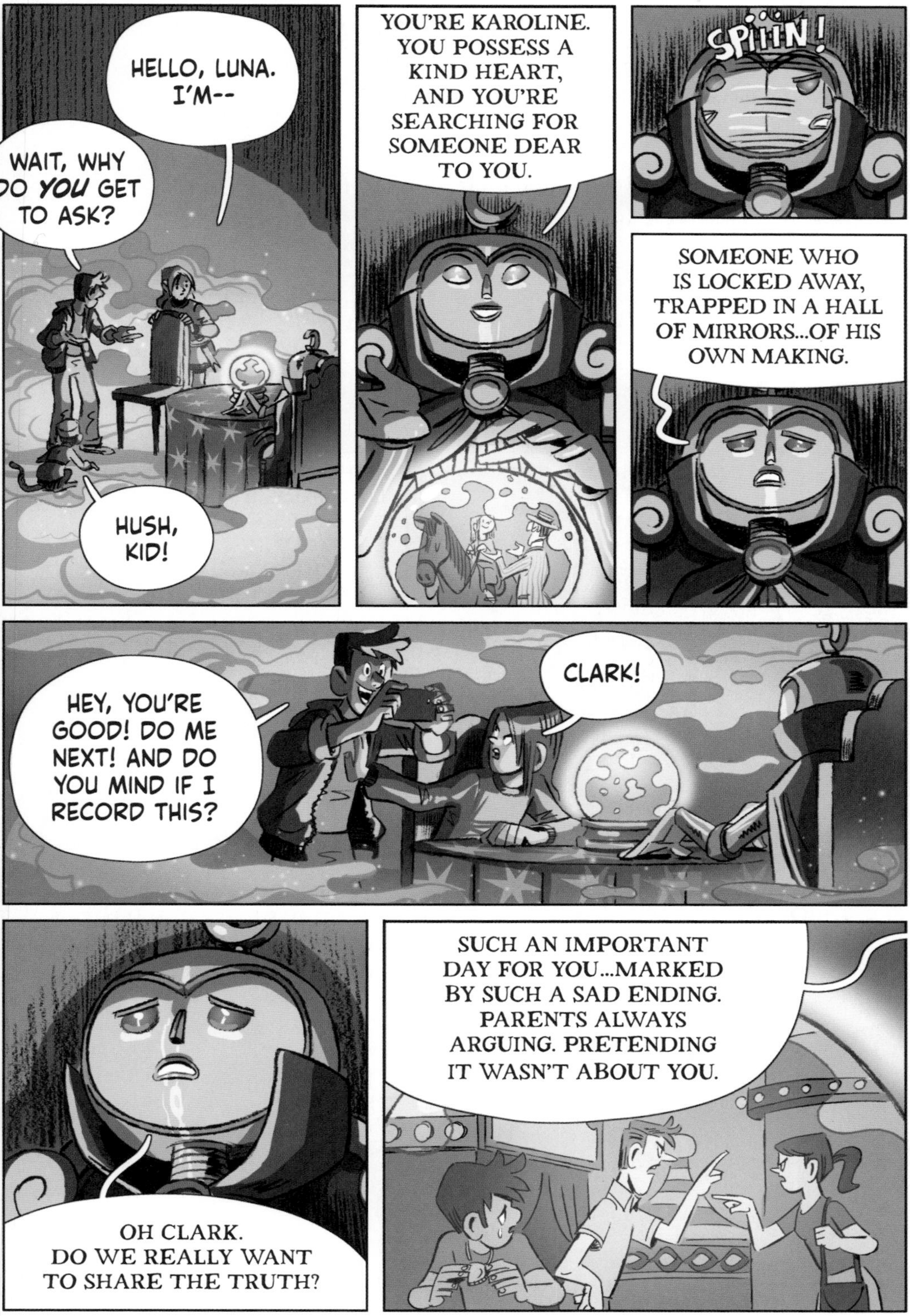
HELLO, LUNA. I'M--
WAIT, WHY DO *YOU* GET TO ASK?
HUSH, KID!
YOU'RE KAROLINE. YOU POSSESS A KIND HEART, AND YOU'RE SEARCHING FOR SOMEONE DEAR TO YOU.
SPIIIN!
SOMEONE WHO IS LOCKED AWAY, TRAPPED IN A HALL OF MIRRORS...OF HIS OWN MAKING.
HEY, YOU'RE GOOD! DO ME NEXT! AND DO YOU MIND IF I RECORD THIS?
CLARK!
OH CLARK. DO WE REALLY WANT TO SHARE THE TRUTH?
SUCH AN IMPORTANT DAY FOR YOU...MARKED BY SUCH A SAD ENDING. PARENTS ALWAYS ARGUING. PRETENDING IT WASN'T ABOUT YOU.

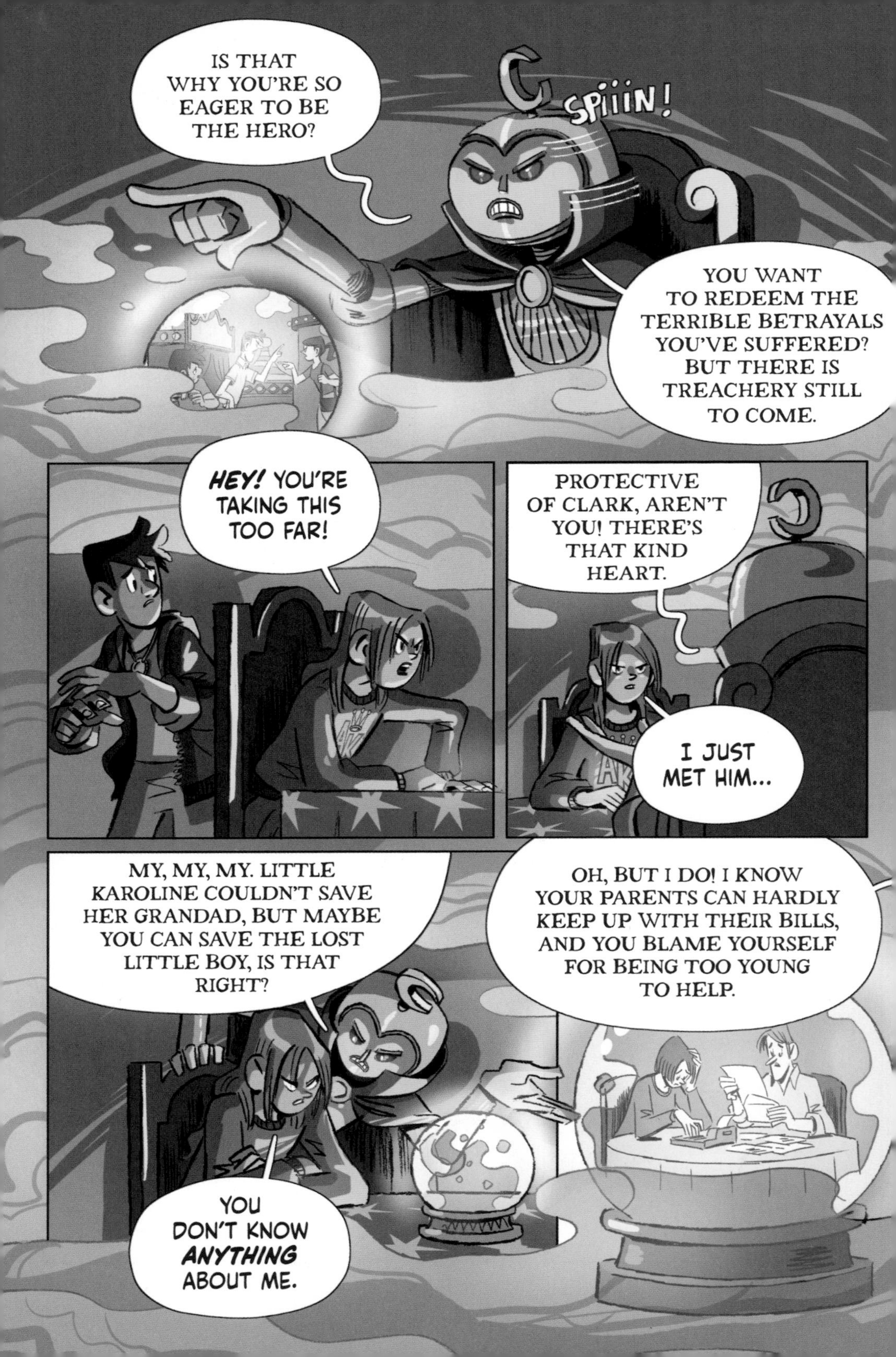
IS THAT WHY YOU'RE SO EAGER TO BE THE HERO?
SPIIIN!
YOU WANT TO REDEEM THE TERRIBLE BETRAYALS YOU'VE SUFFERED? BUT THERE IS TREACHERY STILL TO COME.
HEY! YOU'RE TAKING THIS TOO FAR!
PROTECTIVE OF CLARK, AREN'T YOU! THERE'S THAT KIND HEART.
I JUST MET HIM...
MY, MY, MY. LITTLE KAROLINE COULDN'T SAVE HER GRANDAD, BUT MAYBE YOU CAN SAVE THE LOST LITTLE BOY, IS THAT RIGHT?
YOU DON'T KNOW ANYTHING ABOUT ME.
OH, BUT I DO! I KNOW YOUR PARENTS CAN HARDLY KEEP UP WITH THEIR BILLS, AND YOU BLAME YOURSELF FOR BEING TOO YOUNG TO HELP.

NOW YOU'RE AFRAID BECAUSE YOU KNOW THAT YOU'LL LET EVERYONE DOWN AGAIN. LIKE YOU *ALWAYS* DO, KAROLINE.

YOUR LITTLE HEAD IS SO FULL OF WORRIES.

I KNEW THIS SHAM PSYCHIC WAS BAD NEWS. GONNA SMASH THAT CRYSTAL BALL AND AIR THIS JOINT OUT!

NOT SO FAST, LITTLE TURNCOAT. I KNOW ALL OF *YOUR* SECRETS, TOO.

YIKES!

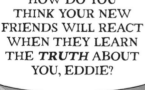

HOW DO YOU THINK YOUR NEW FRIENDS WILL REACT WHEN THEY LEARN THE *TRUTH* ABOUT YOU, EDDIE?

SPiiiN!

DO YOU THINK KAROLINE WILL STILL TRUST YOU? THAT CLARK CAN HANDLE ANOTHER *BETRAYAL*?

ENOUGH!

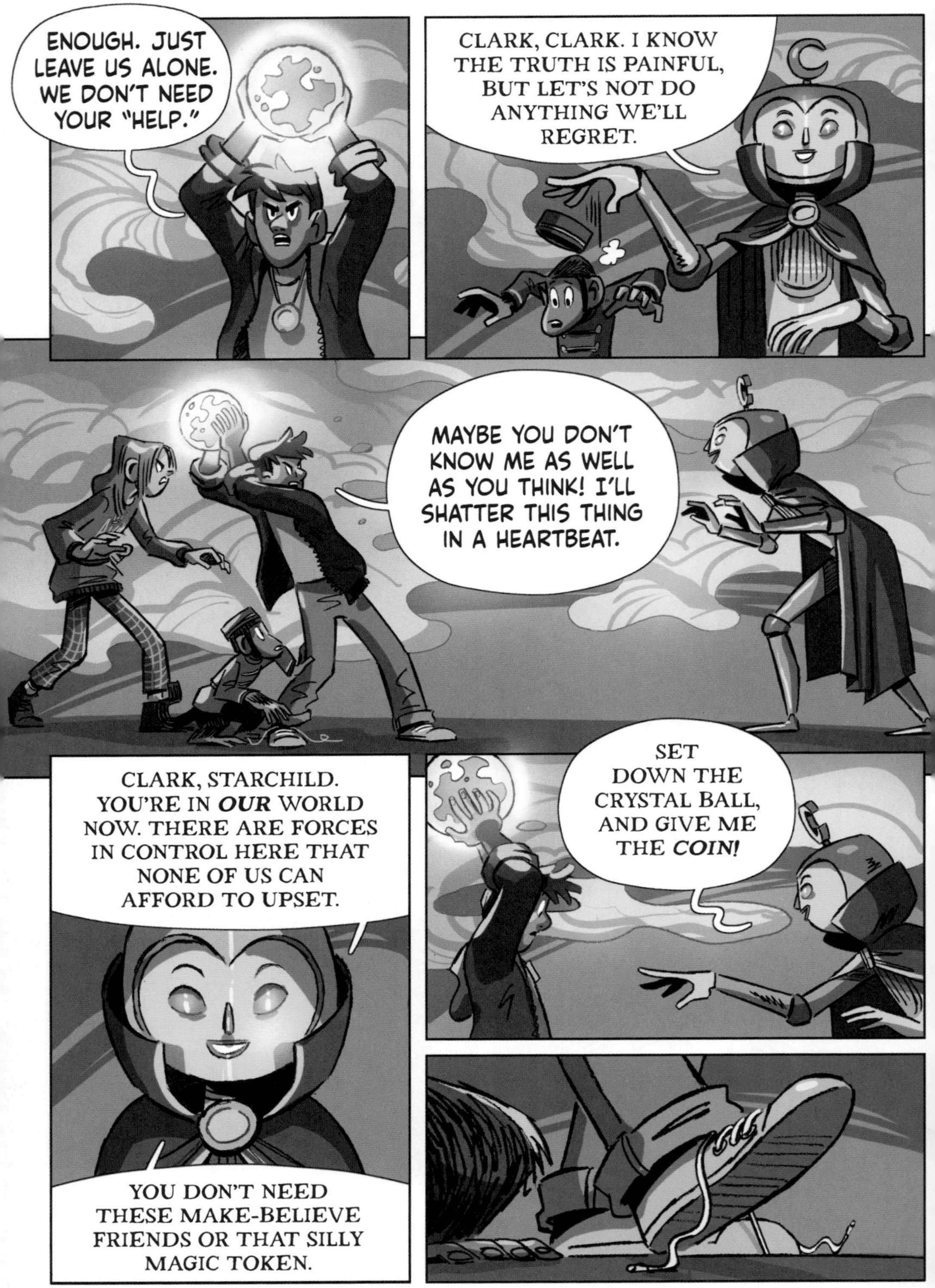
ENOUGH. JUST LEAVE US ALONE. WE DON'T NEED YOUR "HELP."
CLARK, CLARK. I KNOW THE TRUTH IS PAINFUL, BUT LET'S NOT DO ANYTHING WE'LL REGRET.
MAYBE YOU DON'T KNOW ME AS WELL AS YOU THINK! I'LL SHATTER THIS THING IN A HEARTBEAT.
CLARK, STARCHILD. YOU'RE IN *OUR* WORLD NOW. THERE ARE FORCES IN CONTROL HERE THAT NONE OF US CAN AFFORD TO UPSET.
YOU DON'T NEED THESE MAKE-BELIEVE FRIENDS OR THAT SILLY MAGIC TOKEN.
SET DOWN THE CRYSTAL BALL, AND GIVE ME THE *COIN!*

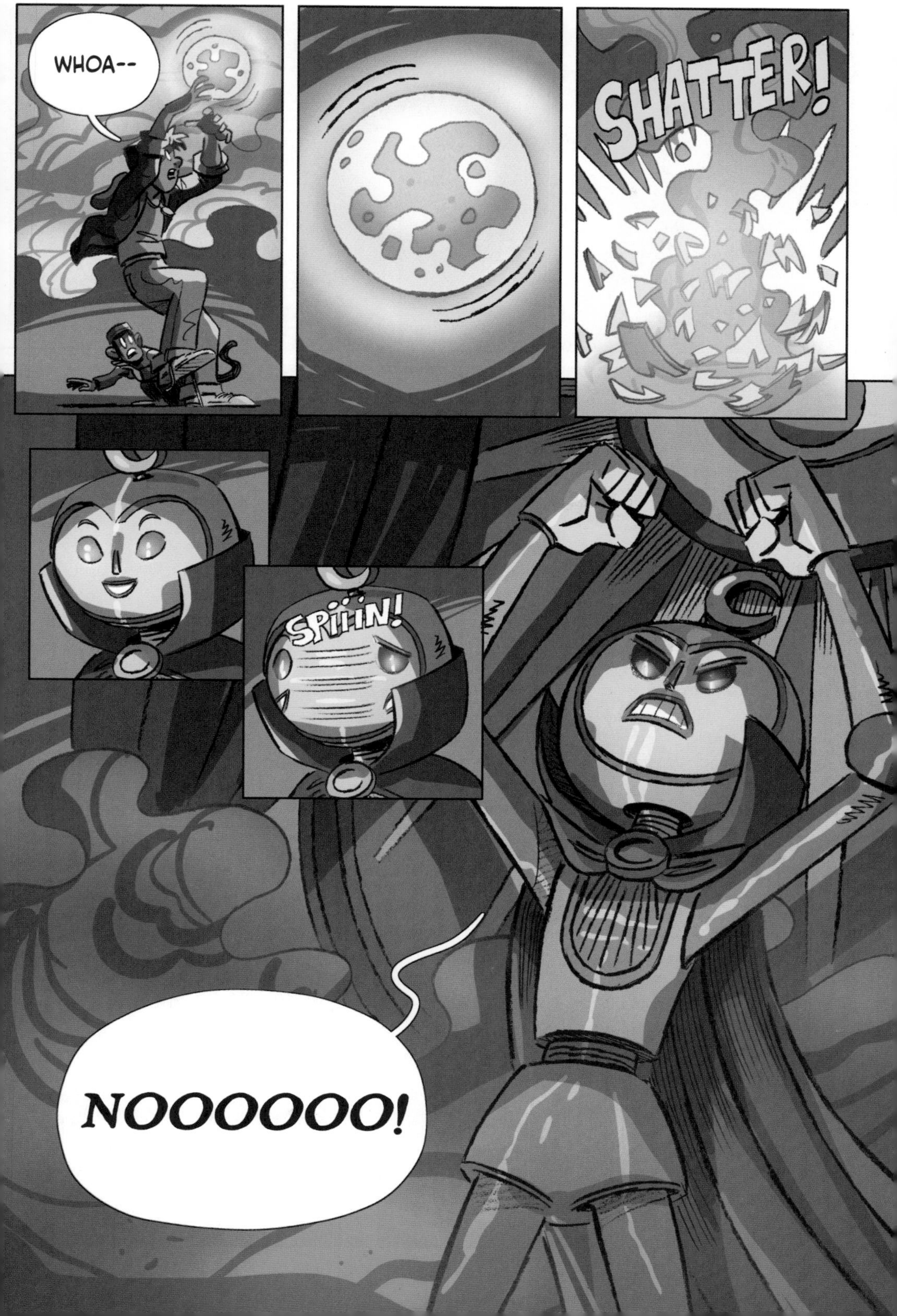
WHOA--
SHATTER!
SPIIIN!
NOOOOOO!

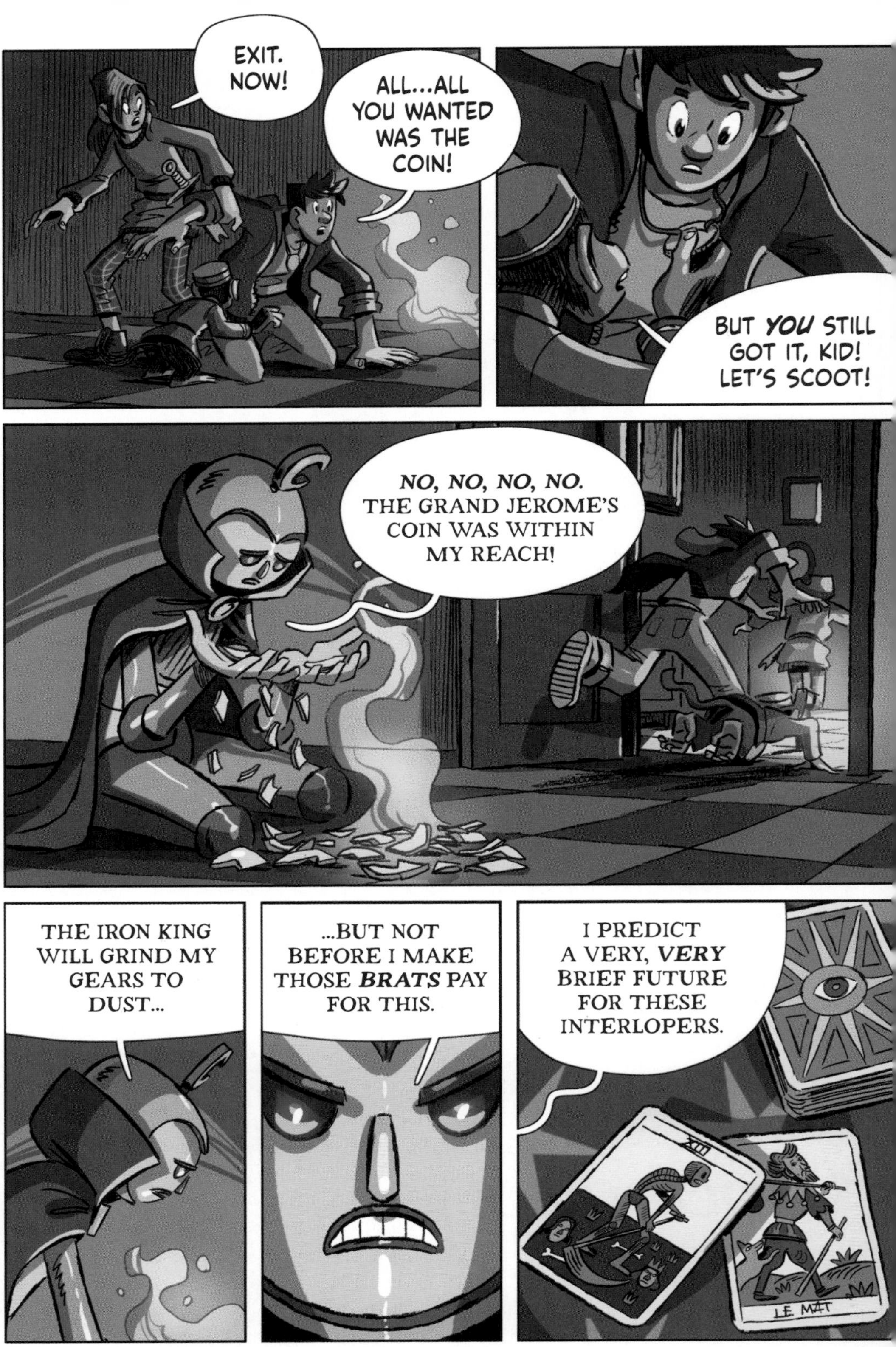
EXIT. NOW!
ALL...ALL YOU WANTED WAS THE COIN!
BUT *YOU* STILL GOT IT, KID! LET'S SCOOT!
NO, NO, NO, NO. THE GRAND JEROME'S COIN WAS WITHIN MY REACH!
THE IRON KING WILL GRIND MY GEARS TO DUST...
...BUT NOT BEFORE I MAKE THOSE ***BRATS*** PAY FOR THIS.
I PREDICT A VERY, ***VERY*** BRIEF FUTURE FOR THESE INTERLOPERS.
XIII
LE MAT

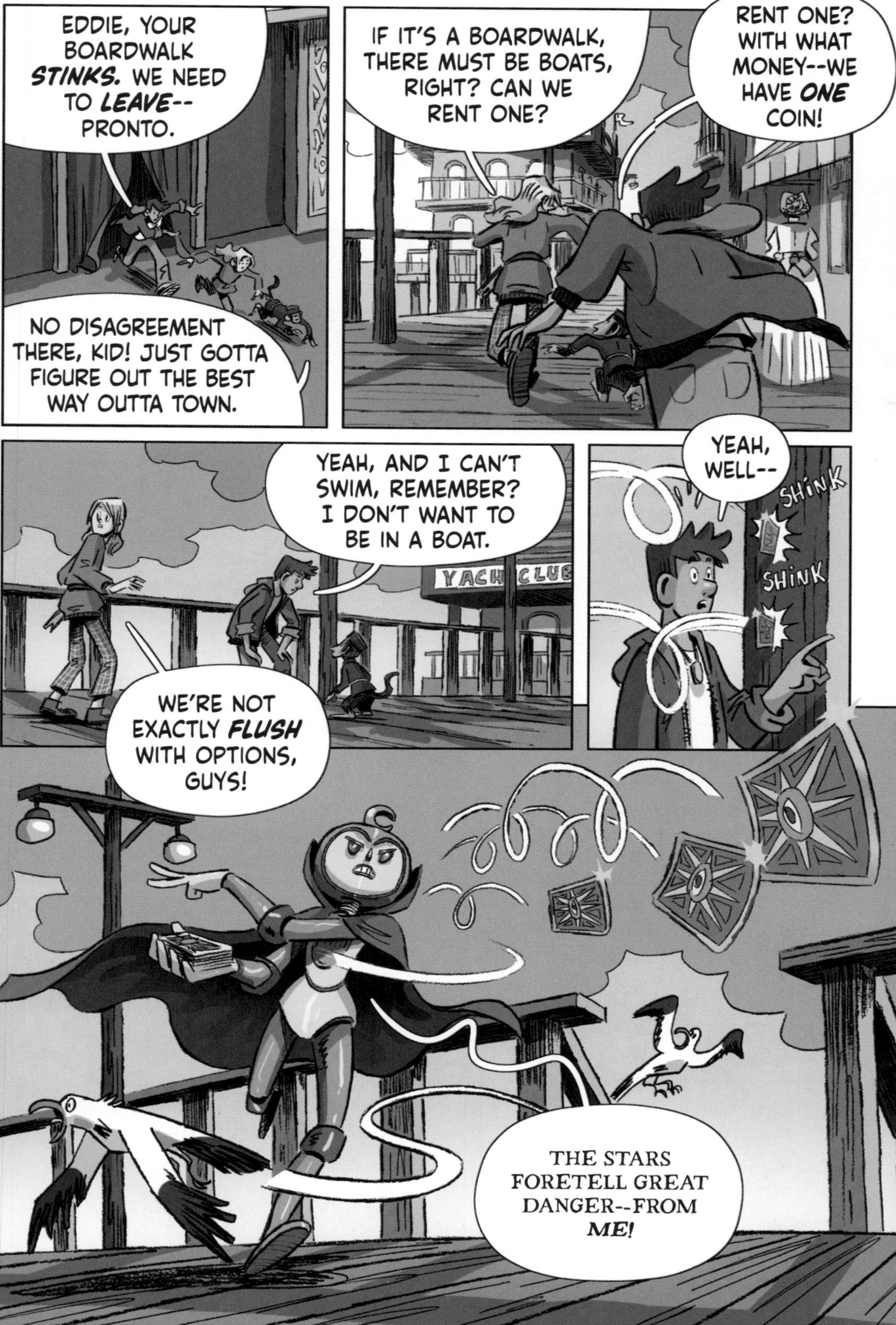
EDDIE, YOUR BOARDWALK STINKS. WE NEED TO LEAVE-- PRONTO.
NO DISAGREEMENT THERE, KID! JUST GOTTA FIGURE OUT THE BEST WAY OUTTA TOWN.
IF IT'S A BOARDWALK, THERE MUST BE BOATS, RIGHT? CAN WE RENT ONE?
RENT ONE? WITH WHAT MONEY--WE HAVE ONE COIN!
YEAH, AND I CAN'T SWIM, REMEMBER? I DON'T WANT TO BE IN A BOAT.
YACHT CLUB
WE'RE NOT EXACTLY FLUSH WITH OPTIONS, GUYS!
YEAH, WELL--
SHINK
SHINK
THE STARS FORETELL GREAT DANGER--FROM ME!

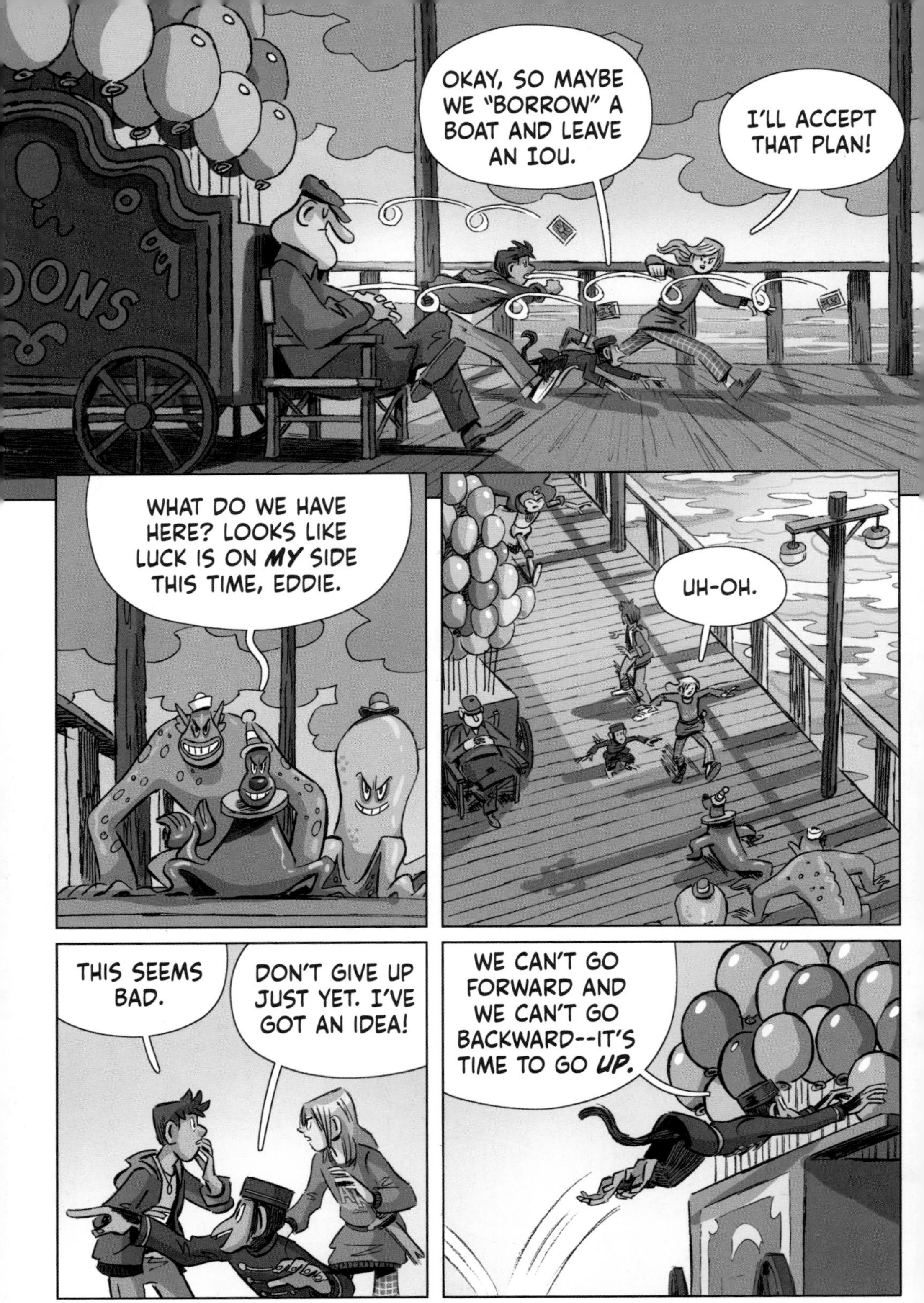
OKAY, SO MAYBE WE "BORROW" A BOAT AND LEAVE AN IOU.
I'LL ACCEPT THAT PLAN!
OONS
WHAT DO WE HAVE HERE? LOOKS LIKE LUCK IS ON ***MY*** SIDE THIS TIME, EDDIE.
UH-OH.
THIS SEEMS BAD.
DON'T GIVE UP JUST YET. I'VE GOT AN IDEA!
WE CAN'T GO FORWARD AND WE CAN'T GO BACKWARD--IT'S TIME TO GO ***UP.***

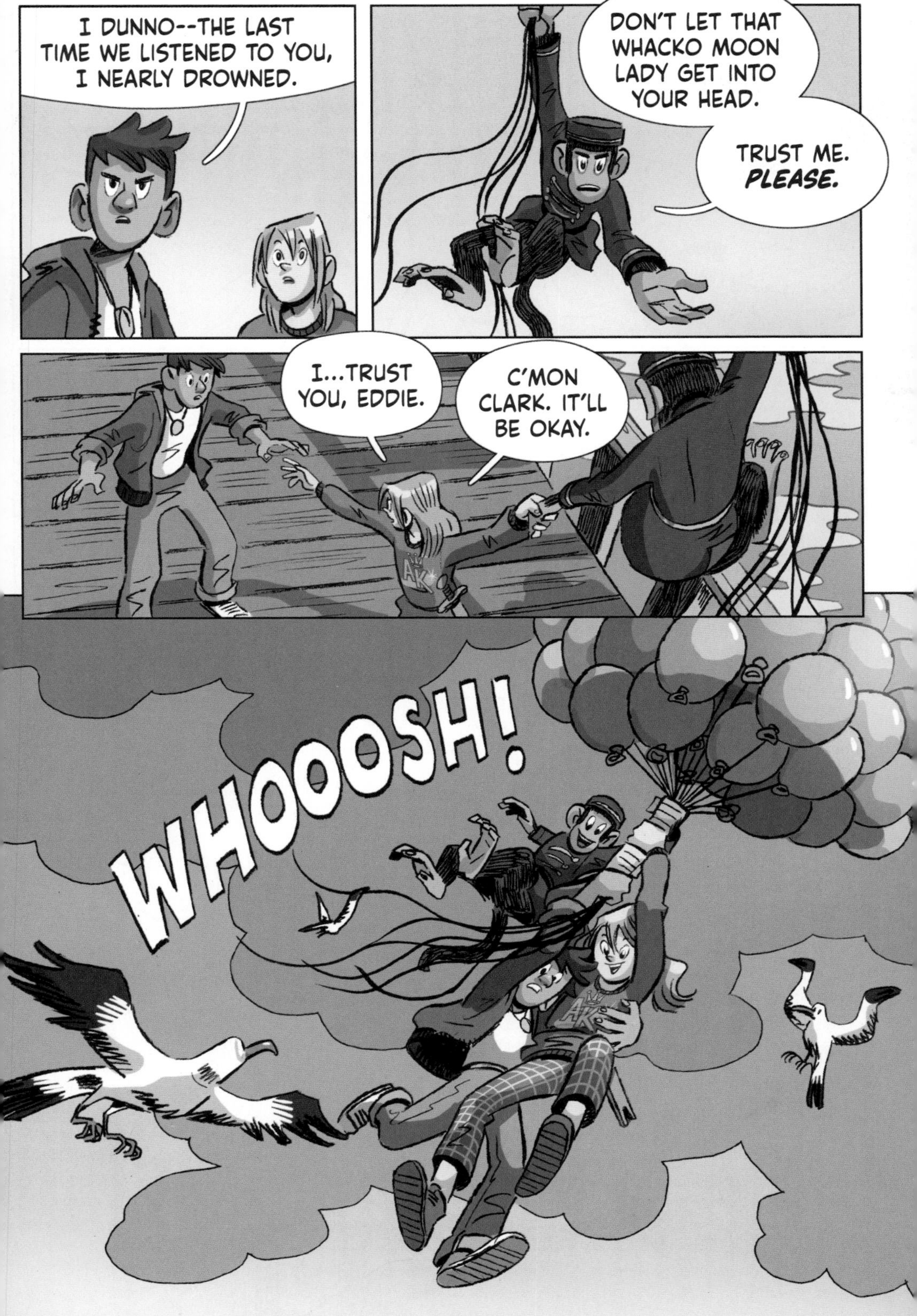
I DUNNO--THE LAST TIME WE LISTENED TO YOU, I NEARLY DROWNED.
DON'T LET THAT WHACKO MOON LADY GET INTO YOUR HEAD.
TRUST ME. *PLEASE.*
I...TRUST YOU, EDDIE.
C'MON CLARK. IT'LL BE OKAY.
WHOOOSH!

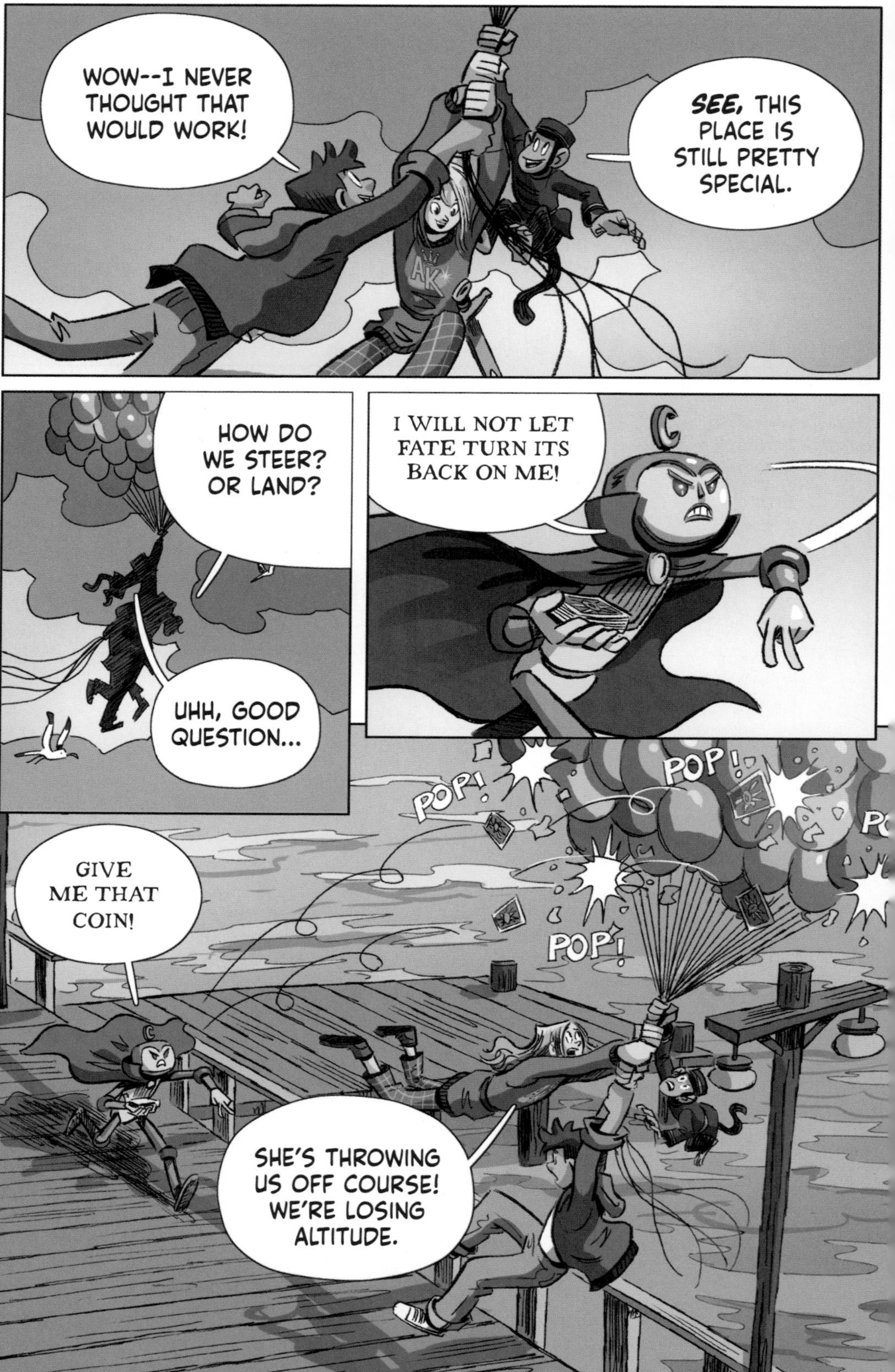
WOW--I NEVER THOUGHT THAT WOULD WORK!
SEE, THIS PLACE IS STILL PRETTY SPECIAL.
HOW DO WE STEER? OR LAND?
UHH, GOOD QUESTION...
I WILL NOT LET FATE TURN ITS BACK ON ME!
POP!
POP!
POP!
GIVE ME THAT COIN!
SHE'S THROWING US OFF COURSE! WE'RE LOSING ALTITUDE.

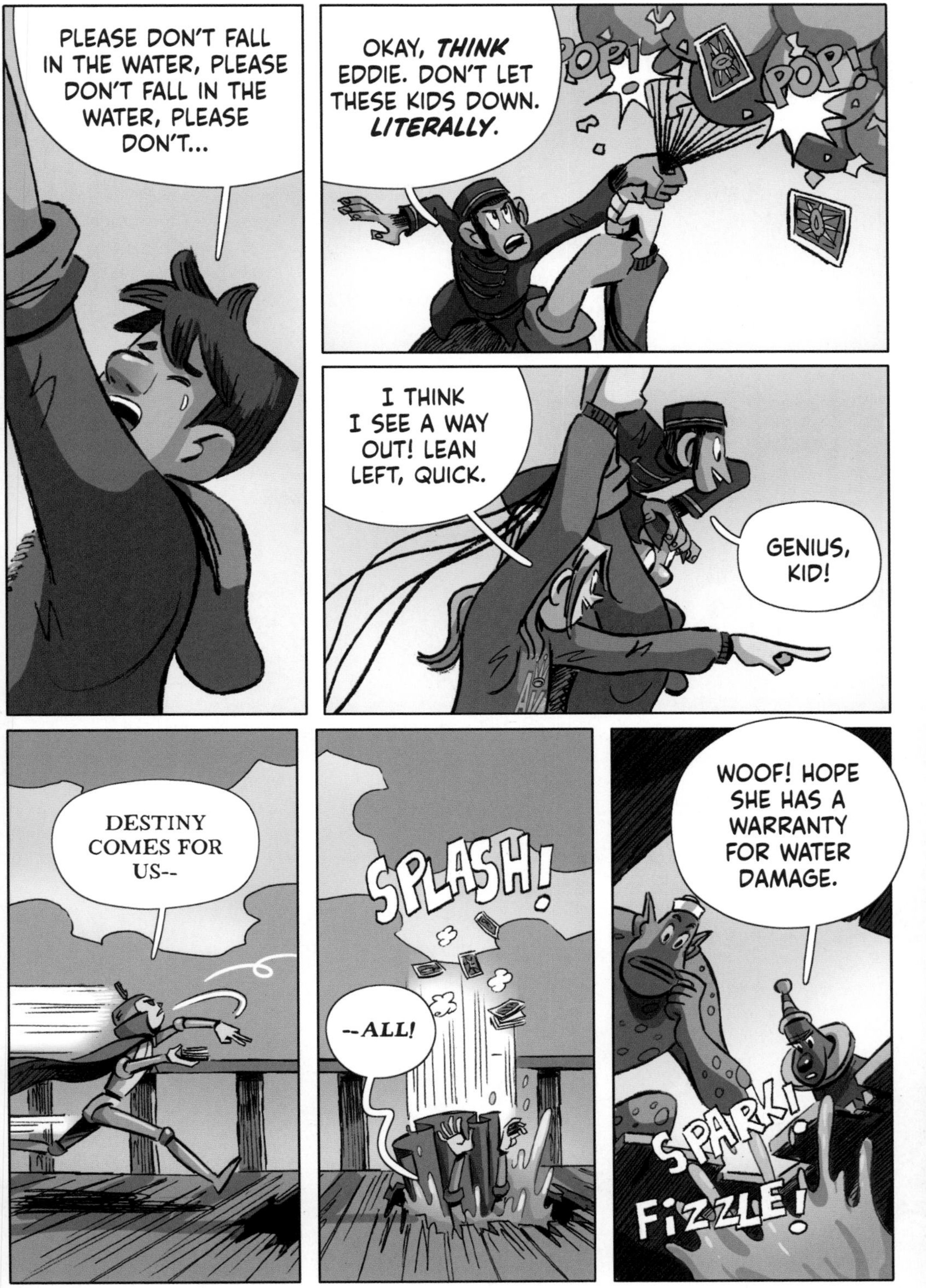
PLEASE DON'T FALL IN THE WATER, PLEASE DON'T FALL IN THE WATER, PLEASE DON'T...
OKAY, *THINK* EDDIE. DON'T LET THESE KIDS DOWN. ***LITERALLY***.
POP!
POP!
I THINK I SEE A WAY OUT! LEAN LEFT, QUICK.
GENIUS, KID!
DESTINY COMES FOR US--
SPLASH!
--ALL!
WOOF! HOPE SHE HAS A WARRANTY FOR WATER DAMAGE.
SPARK!
FIZZLE!

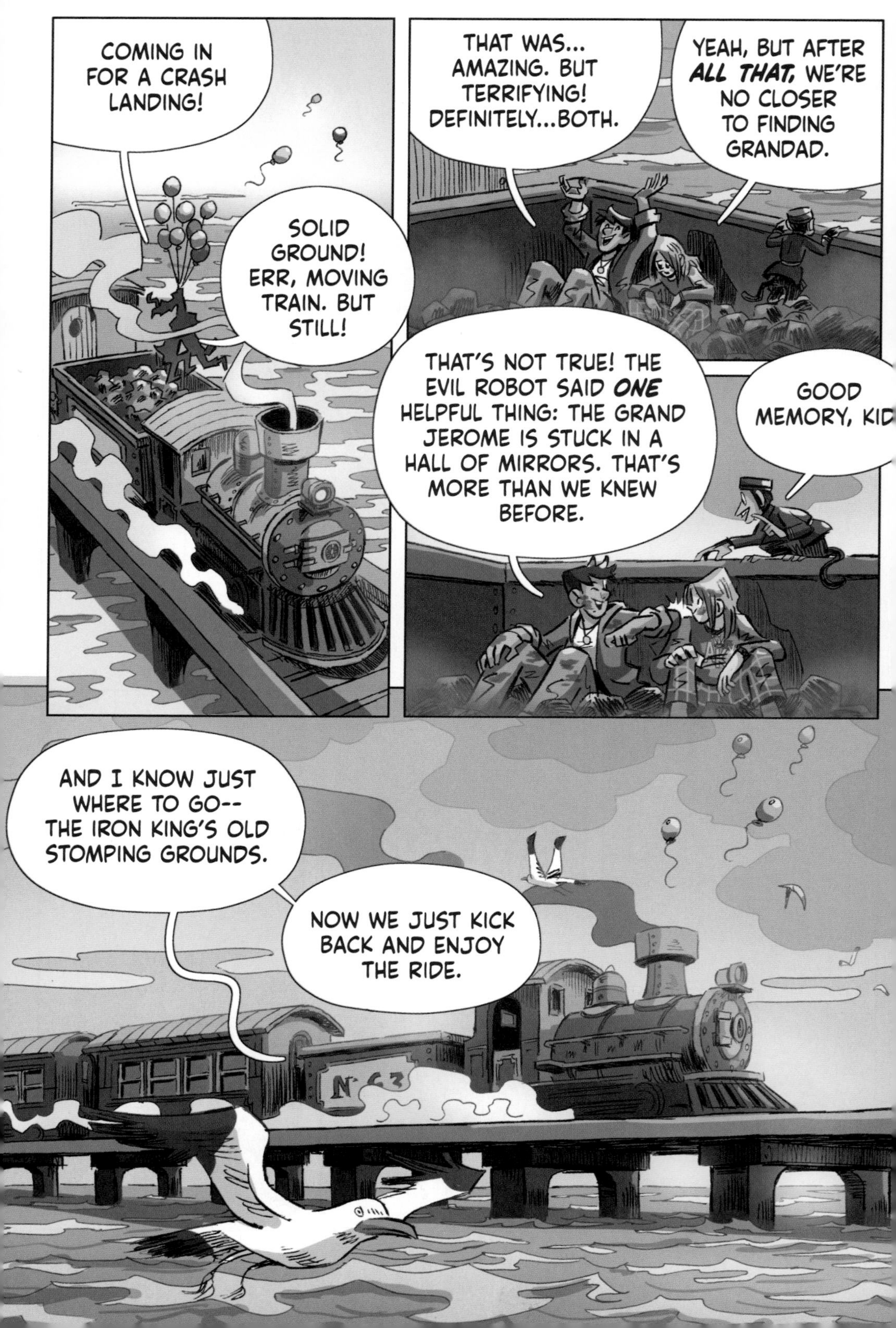
COMING IN FOR A CRASH LANDING!
SOLID GROUND! ERR, MOVING TRAIN. BUT STILL!
THAT WAS... AMAZING. BUT TERRIFYING! DEFINITELY...BOTH.
YEAH, BUT AFTER ALL THAT, WE'RE NO CLOSER TO FINDING GRANDAD.
THAT'S NOT TRUE! THE EVIL ROBOT SAID ONE HELPFUL THING: THE GRAND JEROME IS STUCK IN A HALL OF MIRRORS. THAT'S MORE THAN WE KNEW BEFORE.
GOOD MEMORY, KID
AND I KNOW JUST WHERE TO GO-- THE IRON KING'S OLD STOMPING GROUNDS.
NOW WE JUST KICK BACK AND ENJOY THE RIDE.

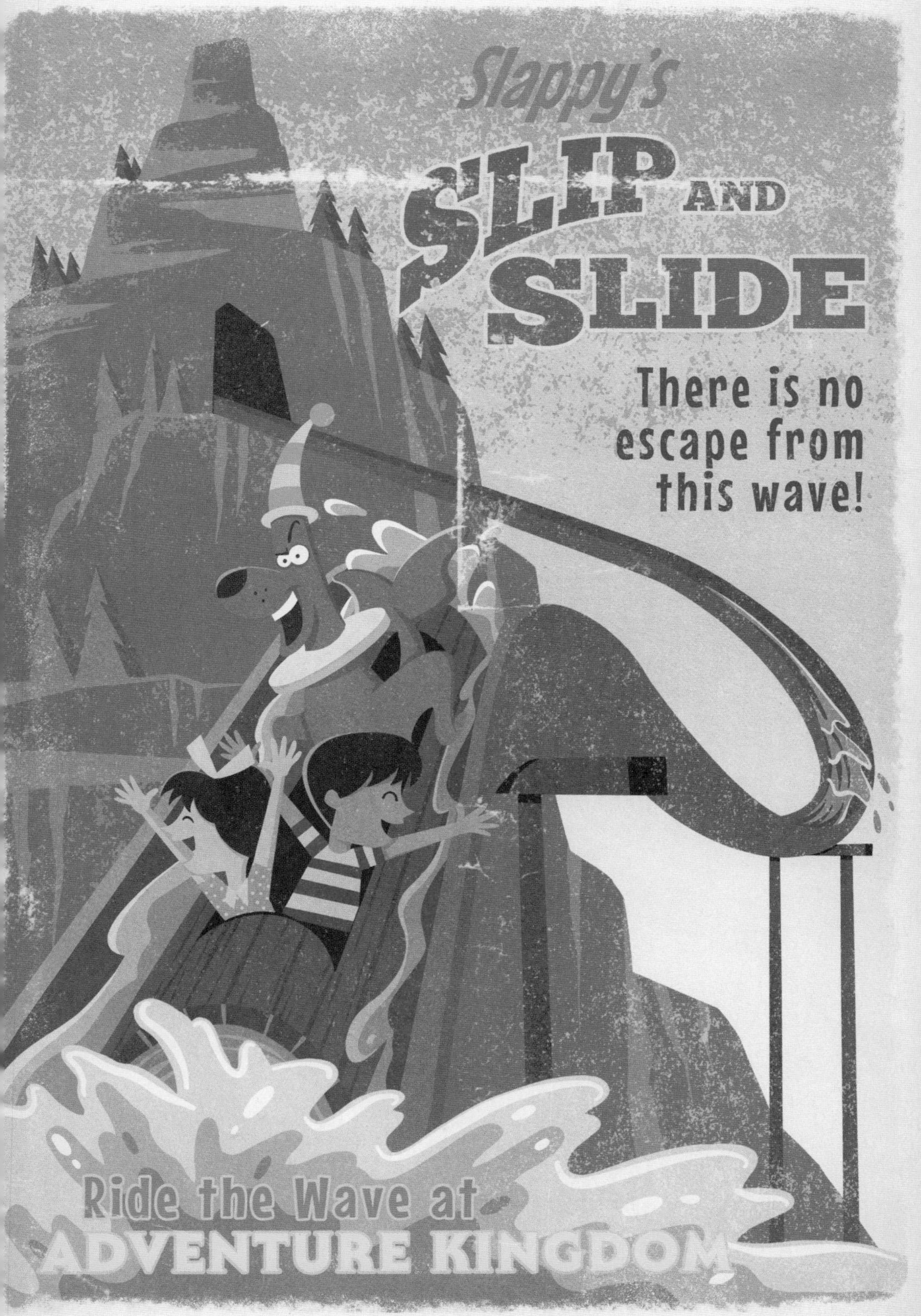
Slappy's
SLIP AND
SLIDE
There is no
escape from
this wave!
Ride the Wave at
ADVENTURE KINGDOM

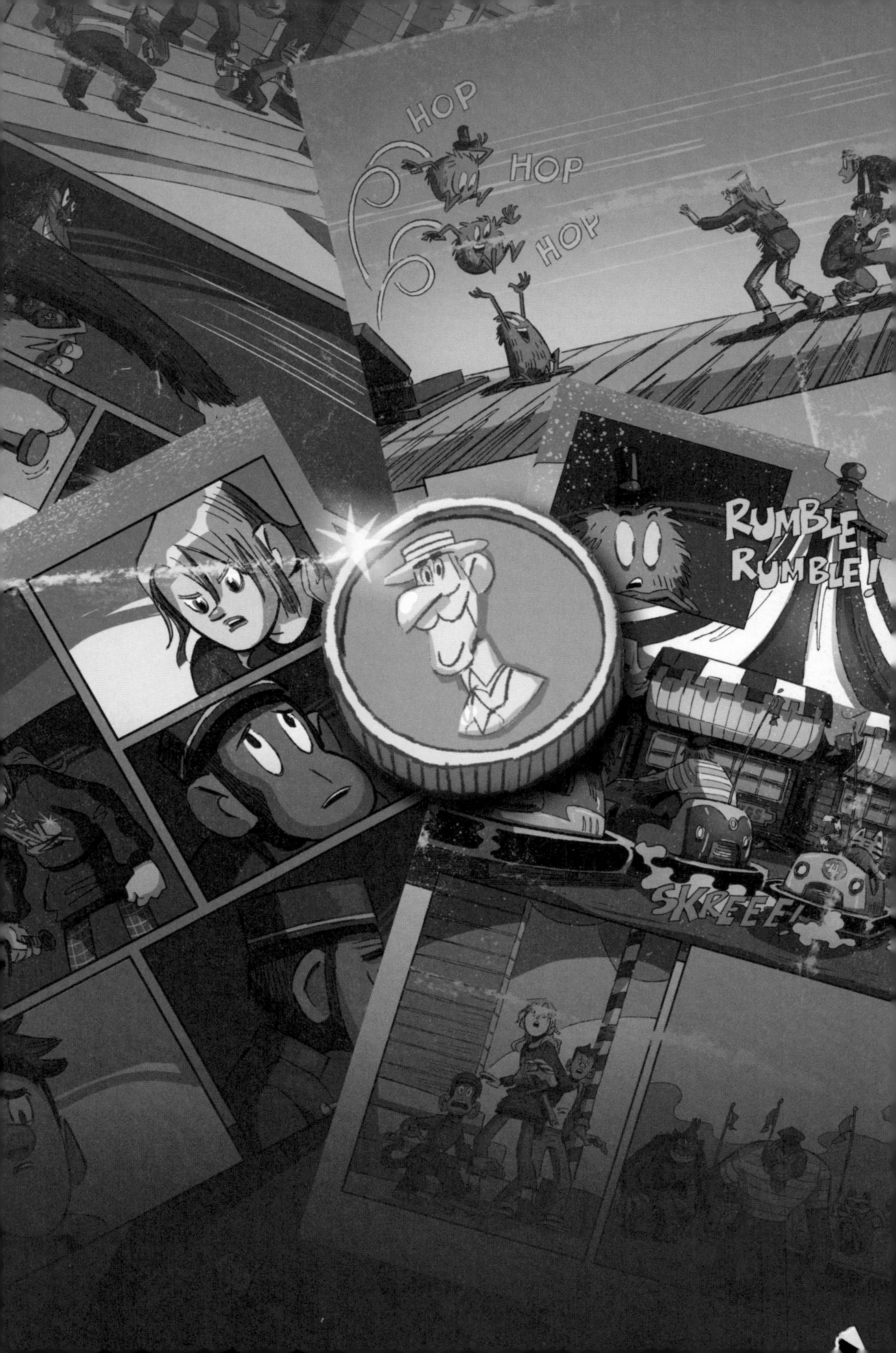
HOP
HOP
HOP
RUMBLE
RUMBLE!
SKREEEE!

CHAPTER 3
TRAINS, TAILS, AND TRAITORS!

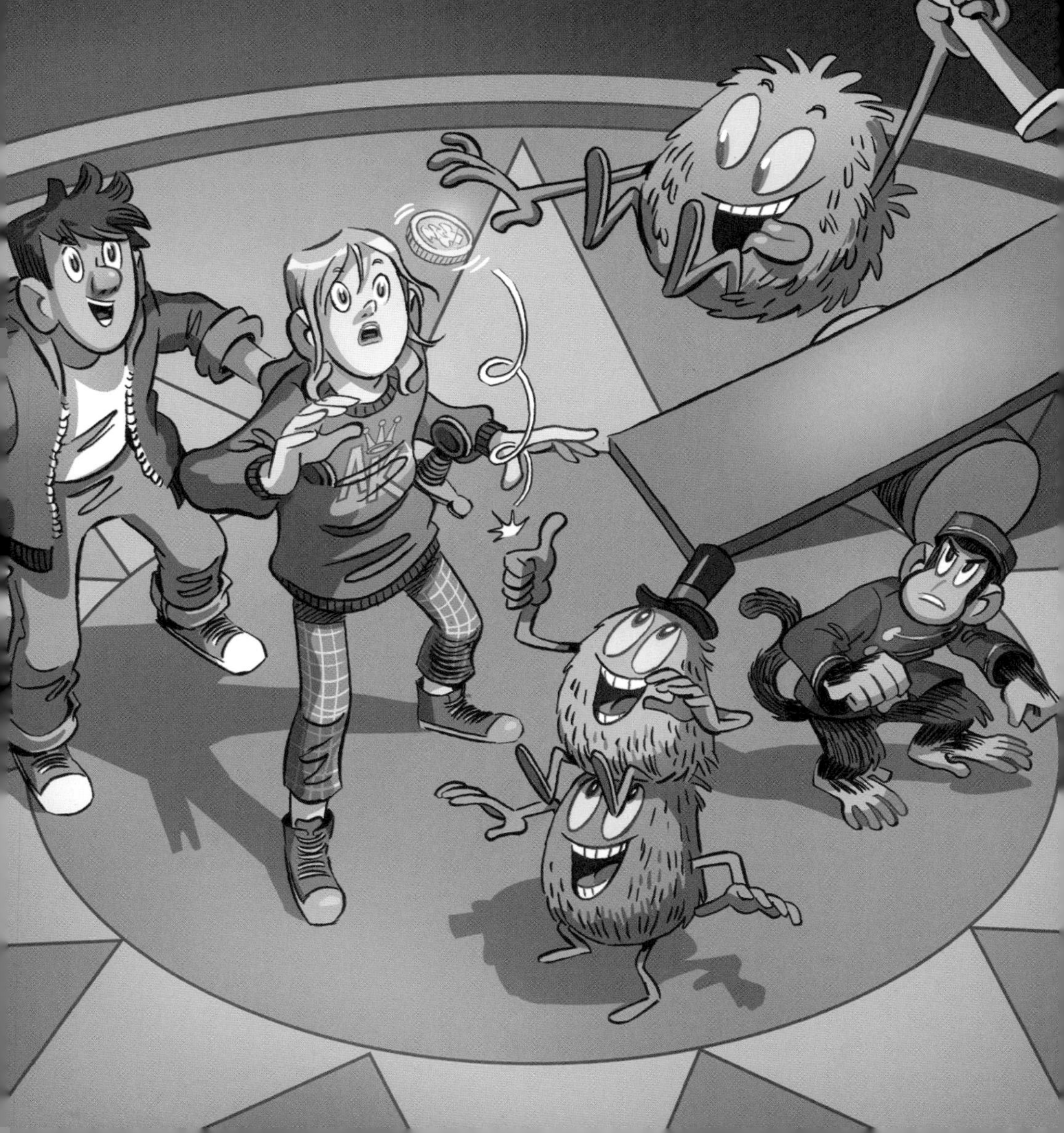

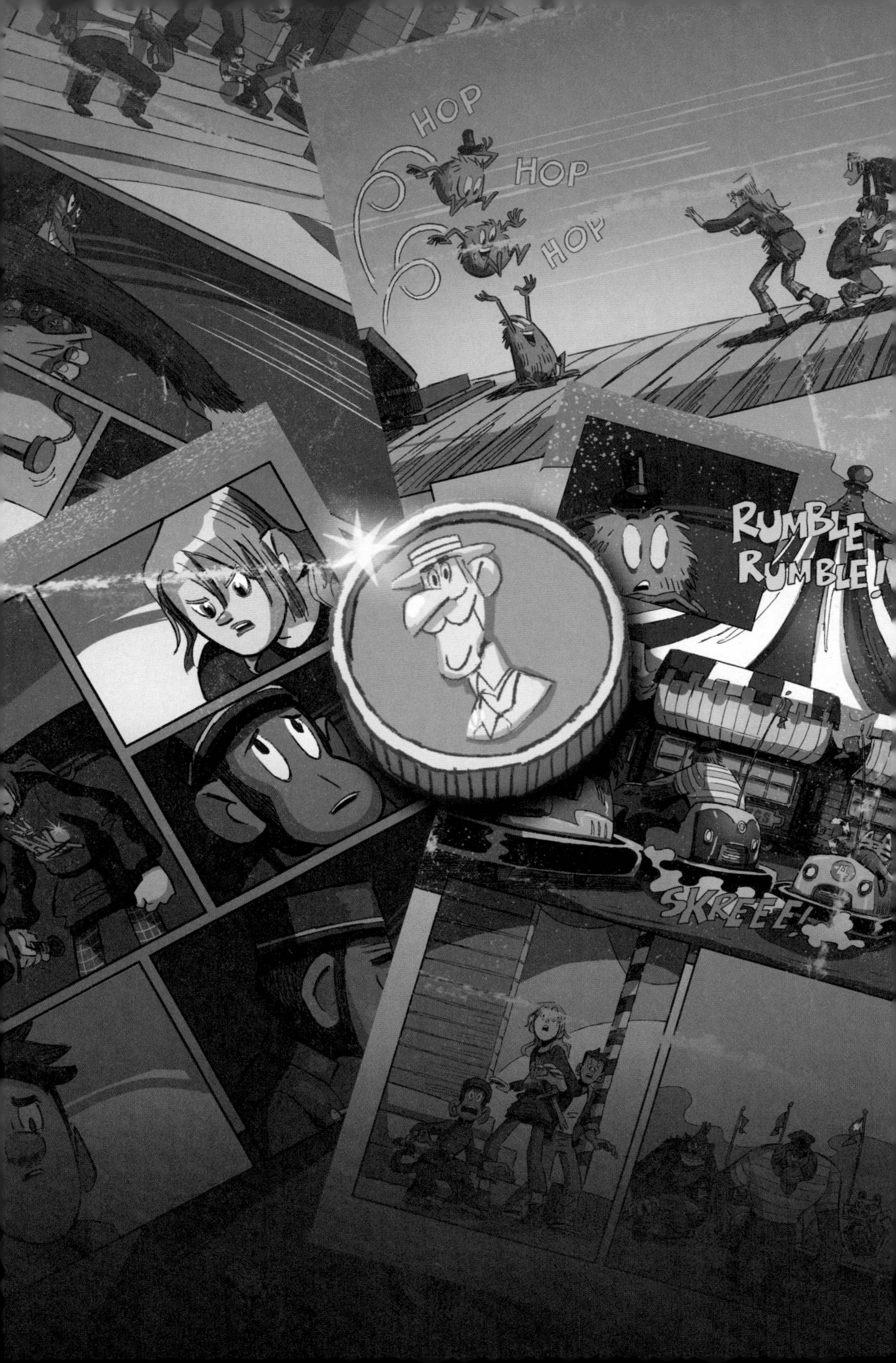
HOP
HOP
HOP
RUMBLE
RUMBLE!
SKREEEE!

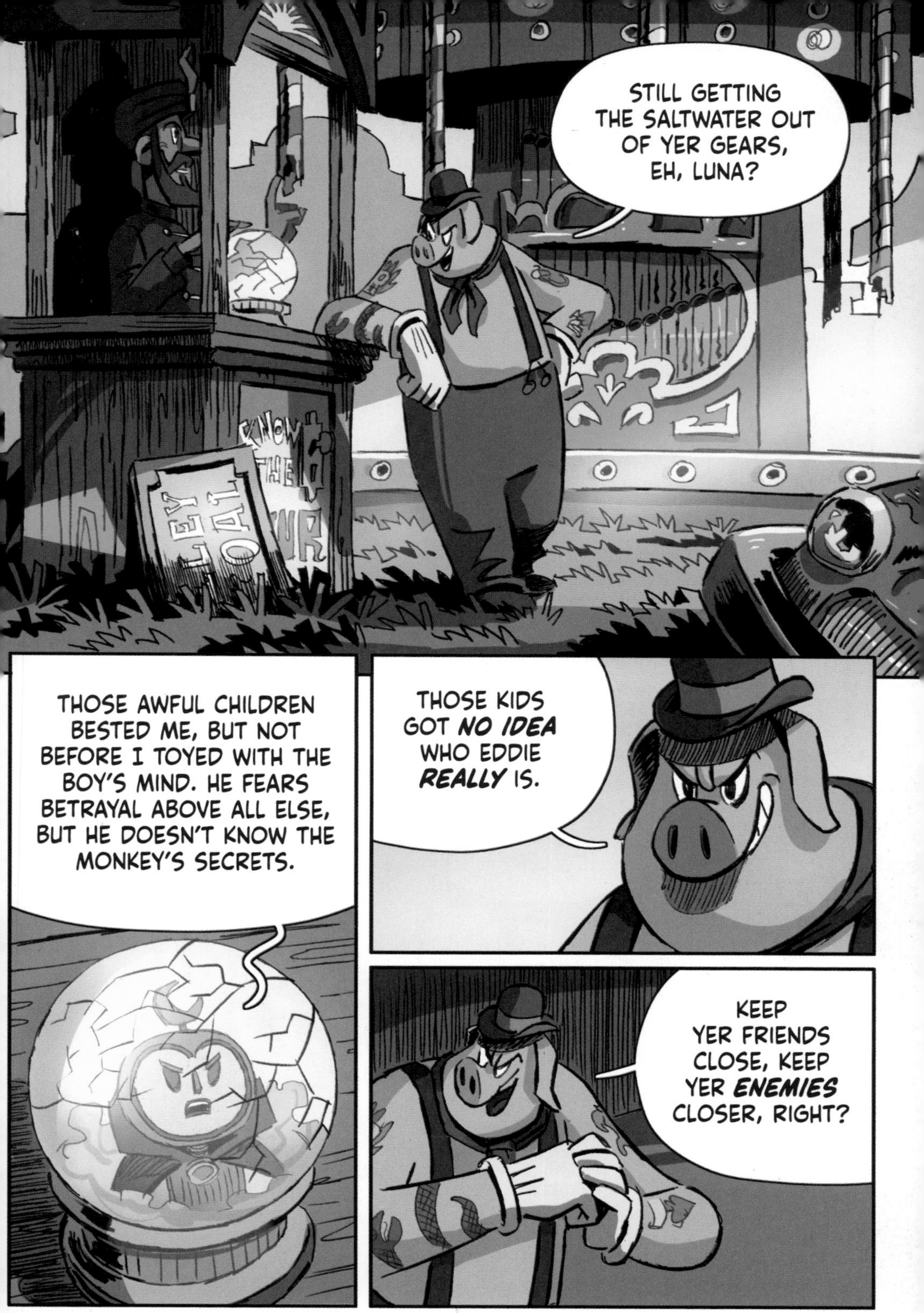
STILL GETTING THE SALTWATER OUT OF YER GEARS, EH, LUNA?
THOSE AWFUL CHILDREN BESTED ME, BUT NOT BEFORE I TOYED WITH THE BOY'S MIND. HE FEARS BETRAYAL ABOVE ALL ELSE, BUT HE DOESN'T KNOW THE MONKEY'S SECRETS.
THOSE KIDS GOT ***NO IDEA*** WHO EDDIE ***REALLY*** IS.
KEEP YER FRIENDS CLOSE, KEEP YER ***ENEMIES*** CLOSER, RIGHT?

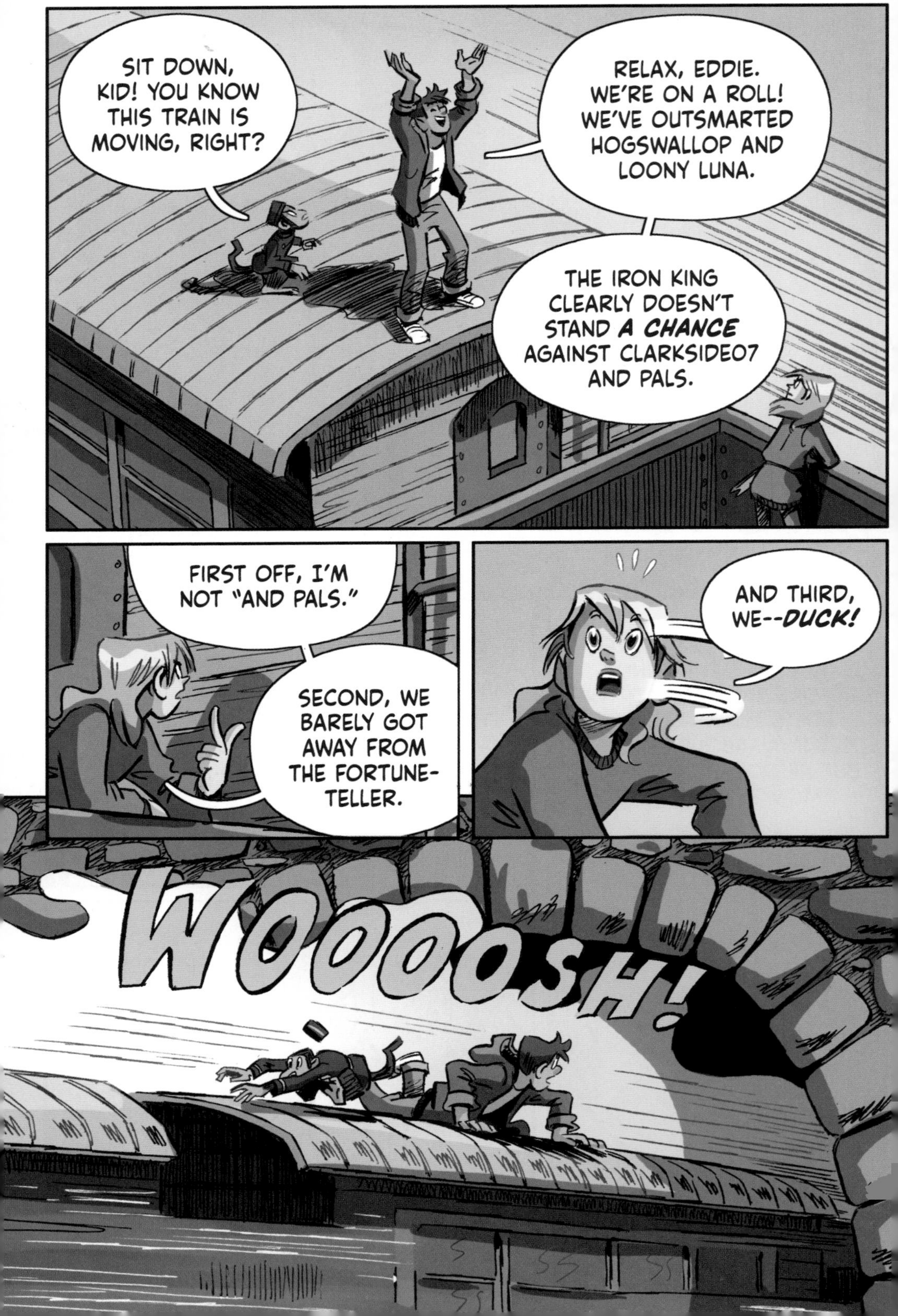
SIT DOWN, KID! YOU KNOW THIS TRAIN IS MOVING, RIGHT?
RELAX, EDDIE. WE'RE ON A ROLL! WE'VE OUTSMARTED HOGSWALLOP AND LOONY LUNA.
THE IRON KING CLEARLY DOESN'T STAND *A CHANCE* AGAINST CLARKSIDE07 AND PALS.
FIRST OFF, I'M NOT "AND PALS."
SECOND, WE BARELY GOT AWAY FROM THE FORTUNE-TELLER.
AND THIRD, WE--*DUCK!*
WOOOOSH!

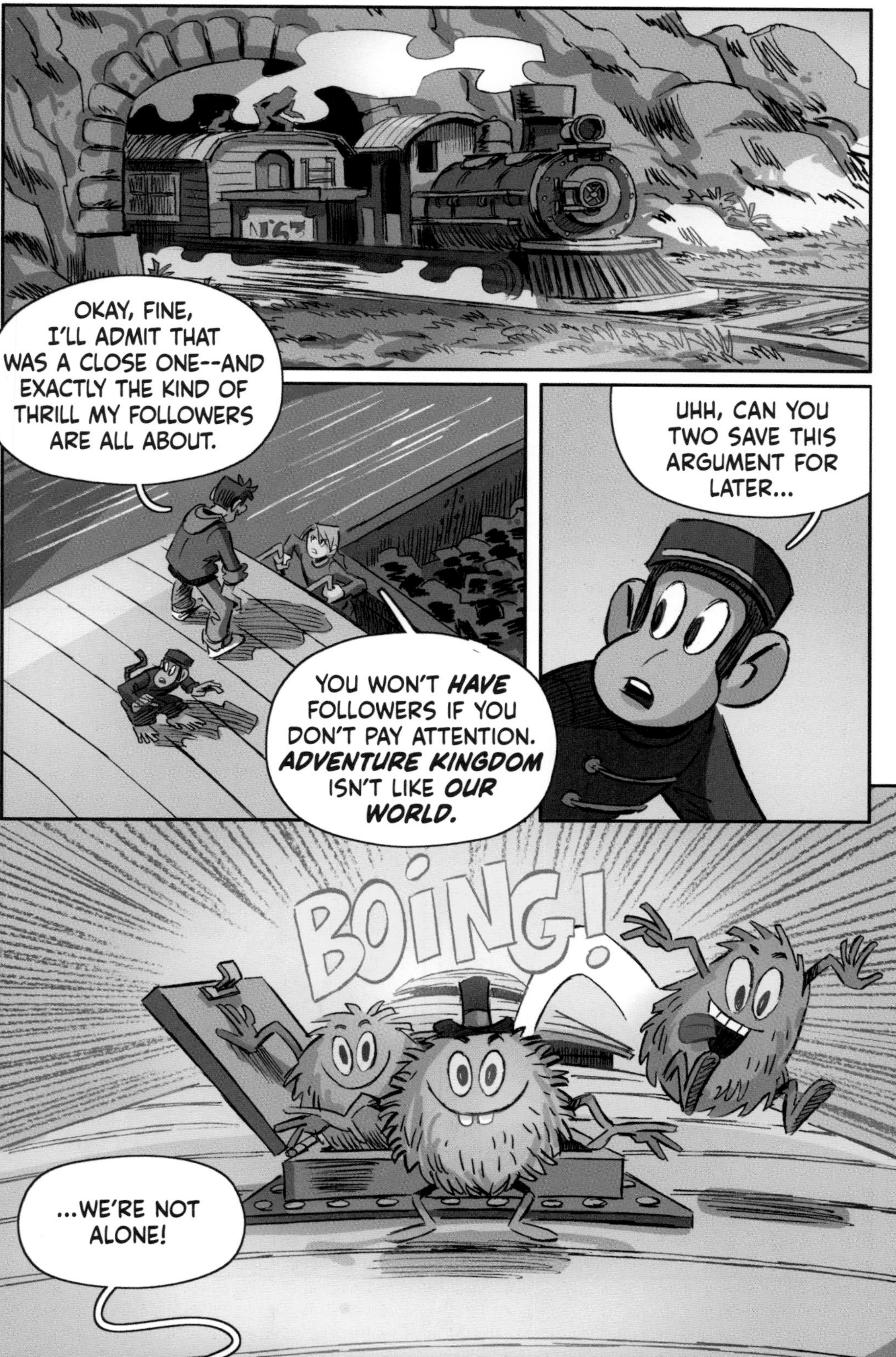
OKAY, FINE, I'LL ADMIT THAT WAS A CLOSE ONE--AND EXACTLY THE KIND OF THRILL MY FOLLOWERS ARE ALL ABOUT.
YOU WON'T ***HAVE*** FOLLOWERS IF YOU DON'T PAY ATTENTION. ***ADVENTURE KINGDOM*** ISN'T LIKE ***OUR WORLD.***
UHH, CAN YOU TWO SAVE THIS ARGUMENT FOR LATER...
BOING!
...WE'RE NOT ALONE!

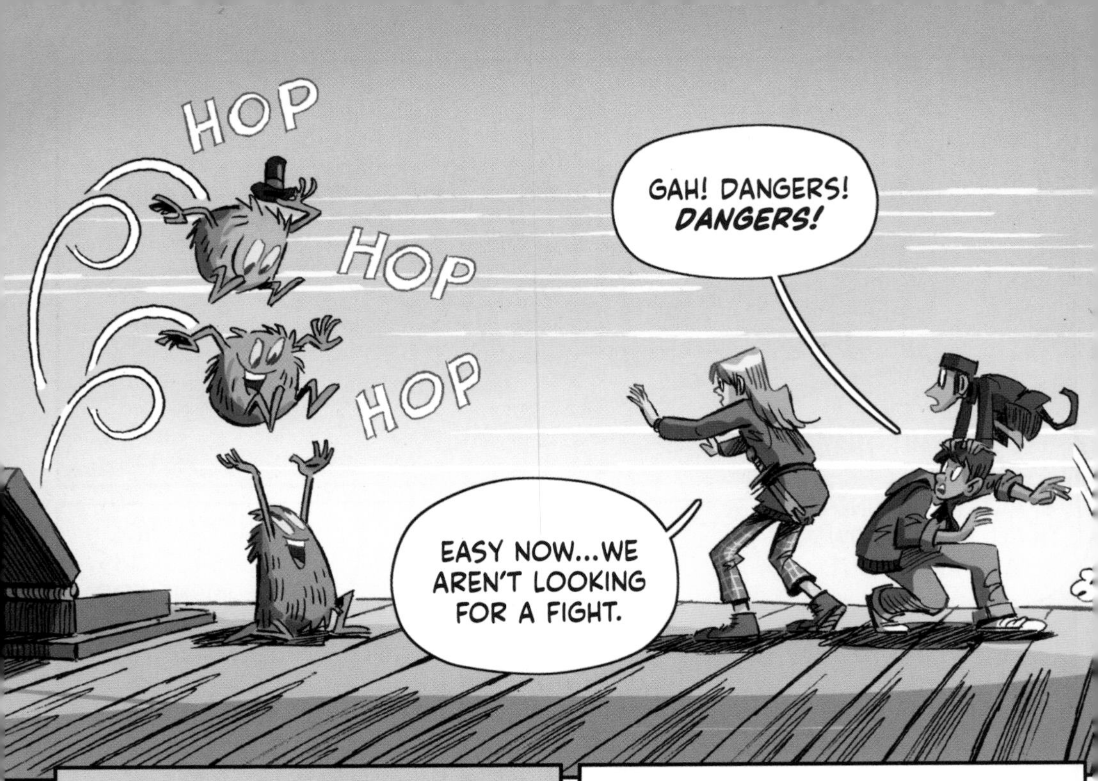
HOP
HOP
HOP
GAH! DANGERS! *DANGERS!*
EASY NOW...WE AREN'T LOOKING FOR A FIGHT.

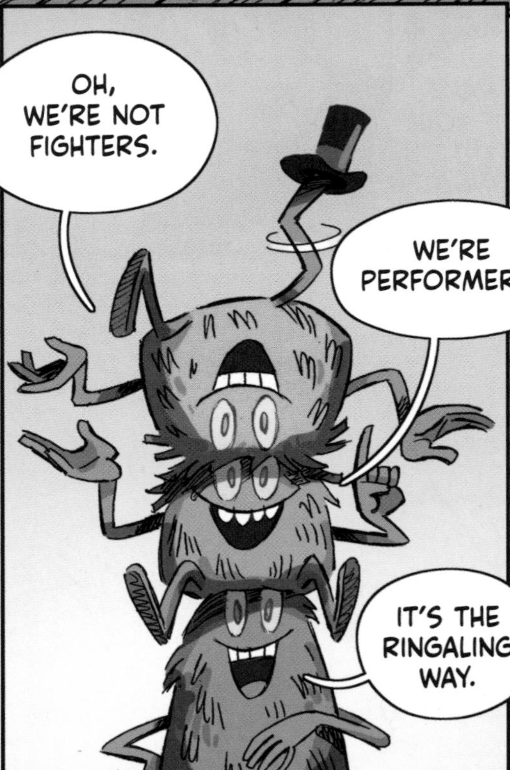
OH, WE'RE NOT FIGHTERS.
WE'RE PERFORMERS!
IT'S THE RINGALING WAY.

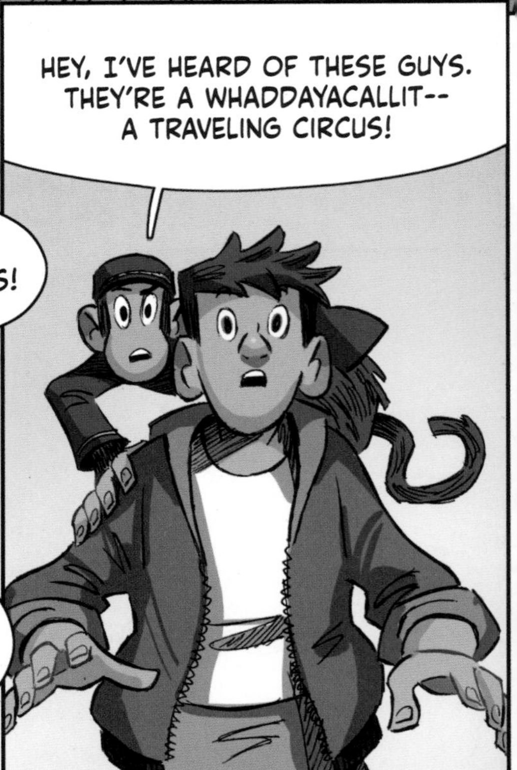
HEY, I'VE HEARD OF THESE GUYS. THEY'RE A WHADDAYACALLIT-- A TRAVELING CIRCUS!

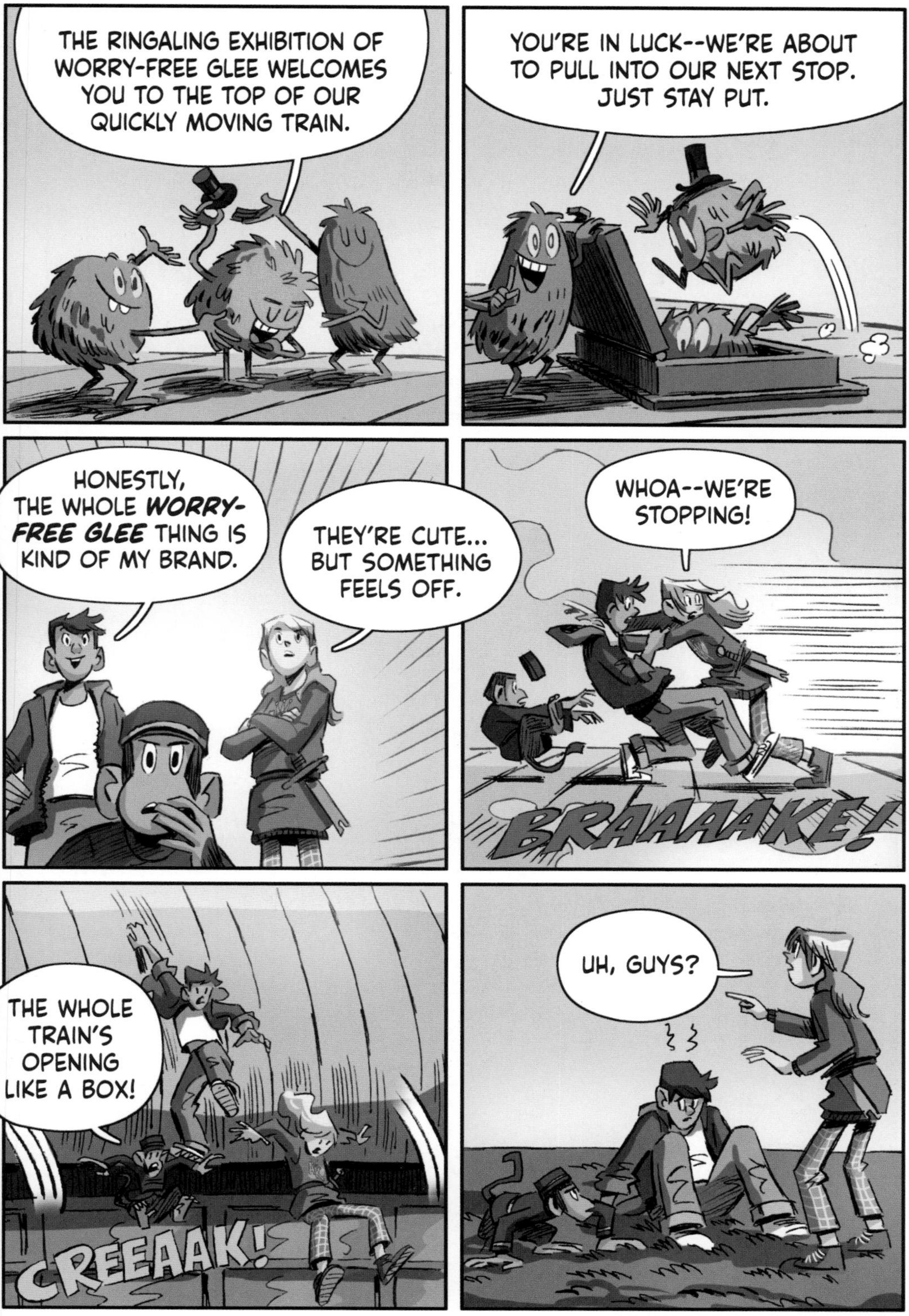
THE RINGALING EXHIBITION OF WORRY-FREE GLEE WELCOMES YOU TO THE TOP OF OUR QUICKLY MOVING TRAIN.
YOU'RE IN LUCK--WE'RE ABOUT TO PULL INTO OUR NEXT STOP. JUST STAY PUT.
HONESTLY, THE WHOLE ***WORRY-FREE GLEE*** THING IS KIND OF MY BRAND.
THEY'RE CUTE... BUT SOMETHING FEELS OFF.
WHOA--WE'RE STOPPING!
BRAAAAKE!
THE WHOLE TRAIN'S OPENING LIKE A BOX!
CREEAAK!
UH, GUYS?

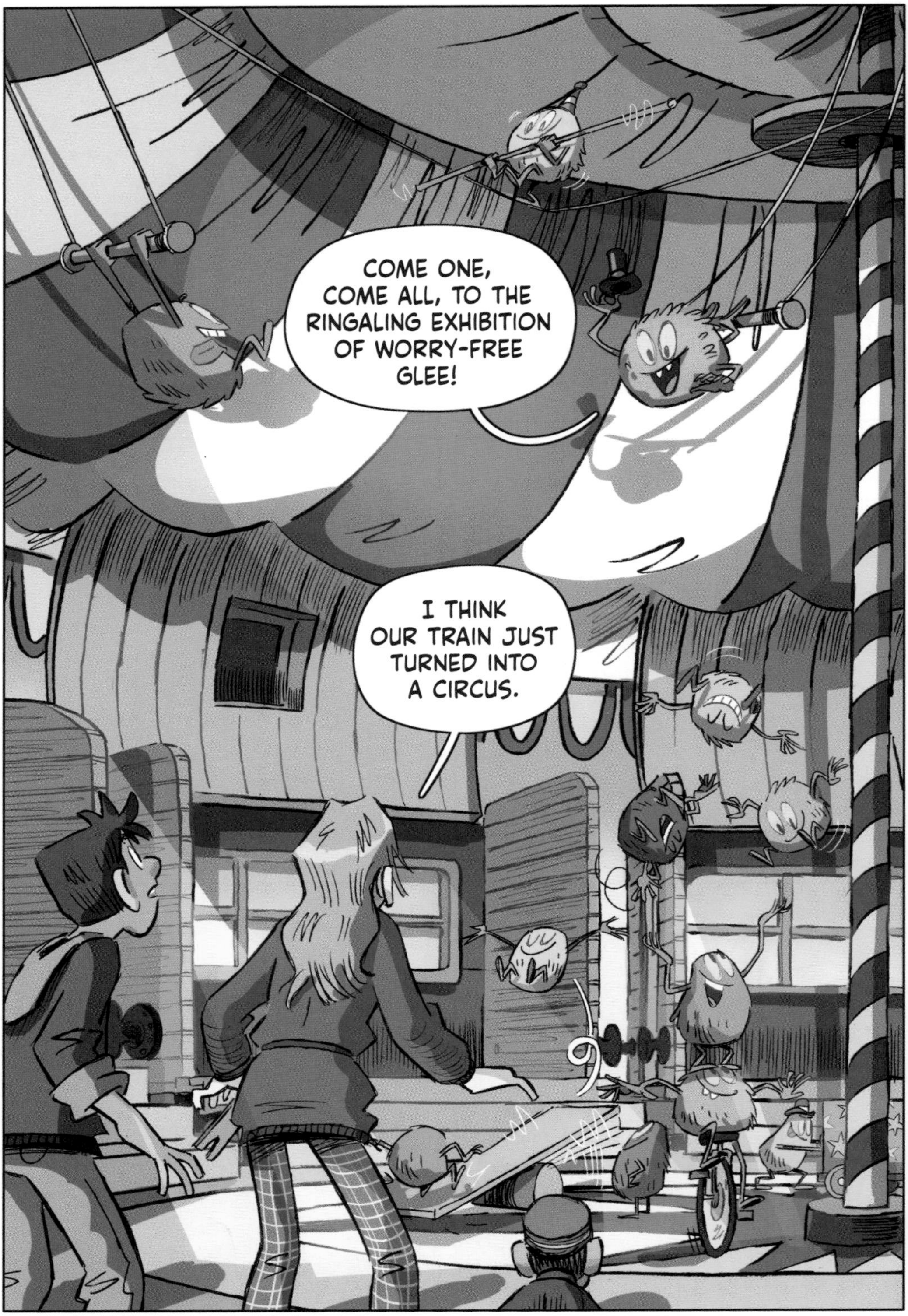
COME ONE, COME ALL, TO THE RINGALING EXHIBITION OF WORRY-FREE GLEE!
I THINK OUR TRAIN JUST TURNED INTO A CIRCUS.

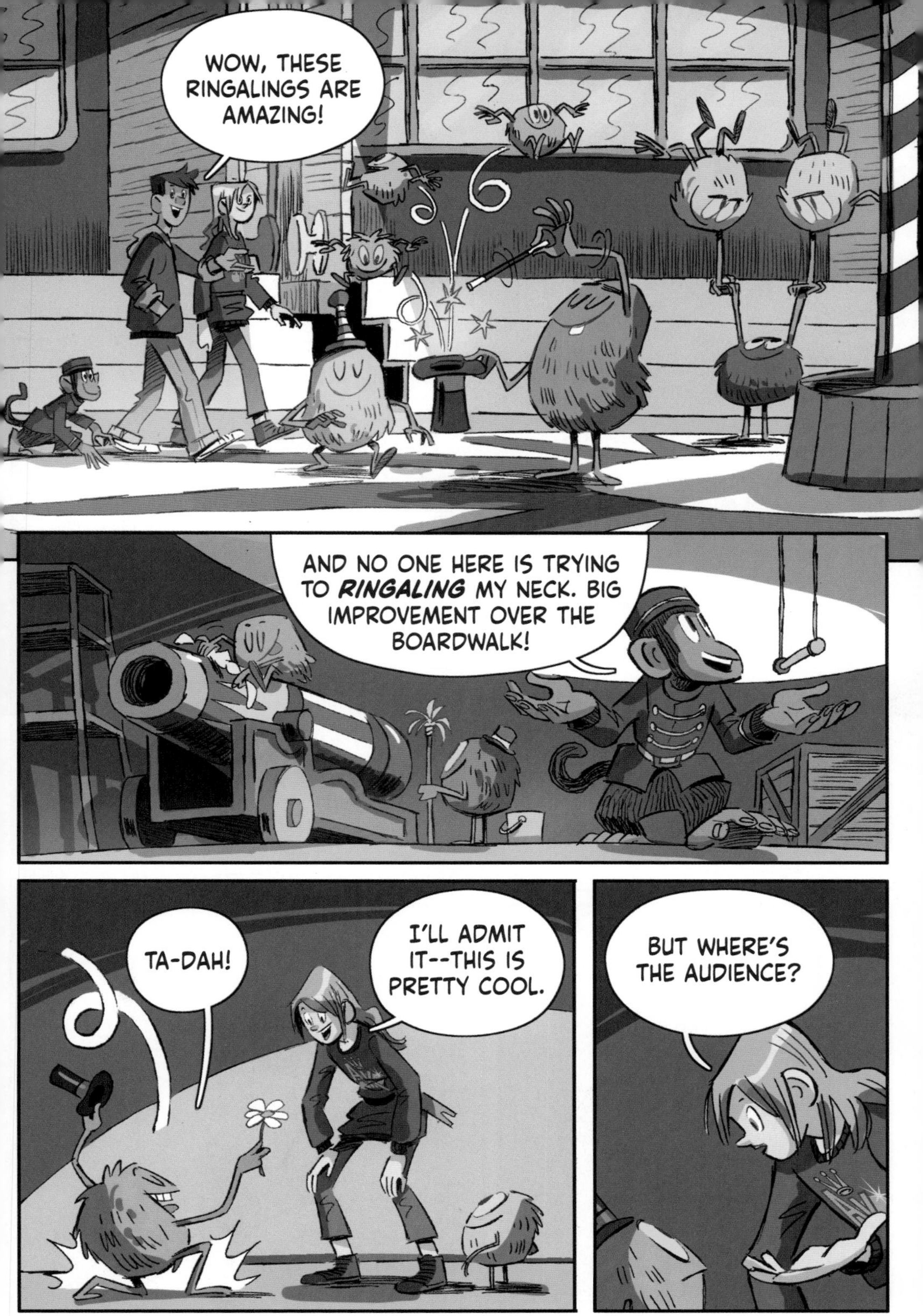
WOW, THESE RINGALINGS ARE AMAZING!
AND NO ONE HERE IS TRYING TO *RINGALING* MY NECK. BIG IMPROVEMENT OVER THE BOARDWALK!
TA-DAH!
I'LL ADMIT IT--THIS IS PRETTY COOL.
BUT WHERE'S THE AUDIENCE?

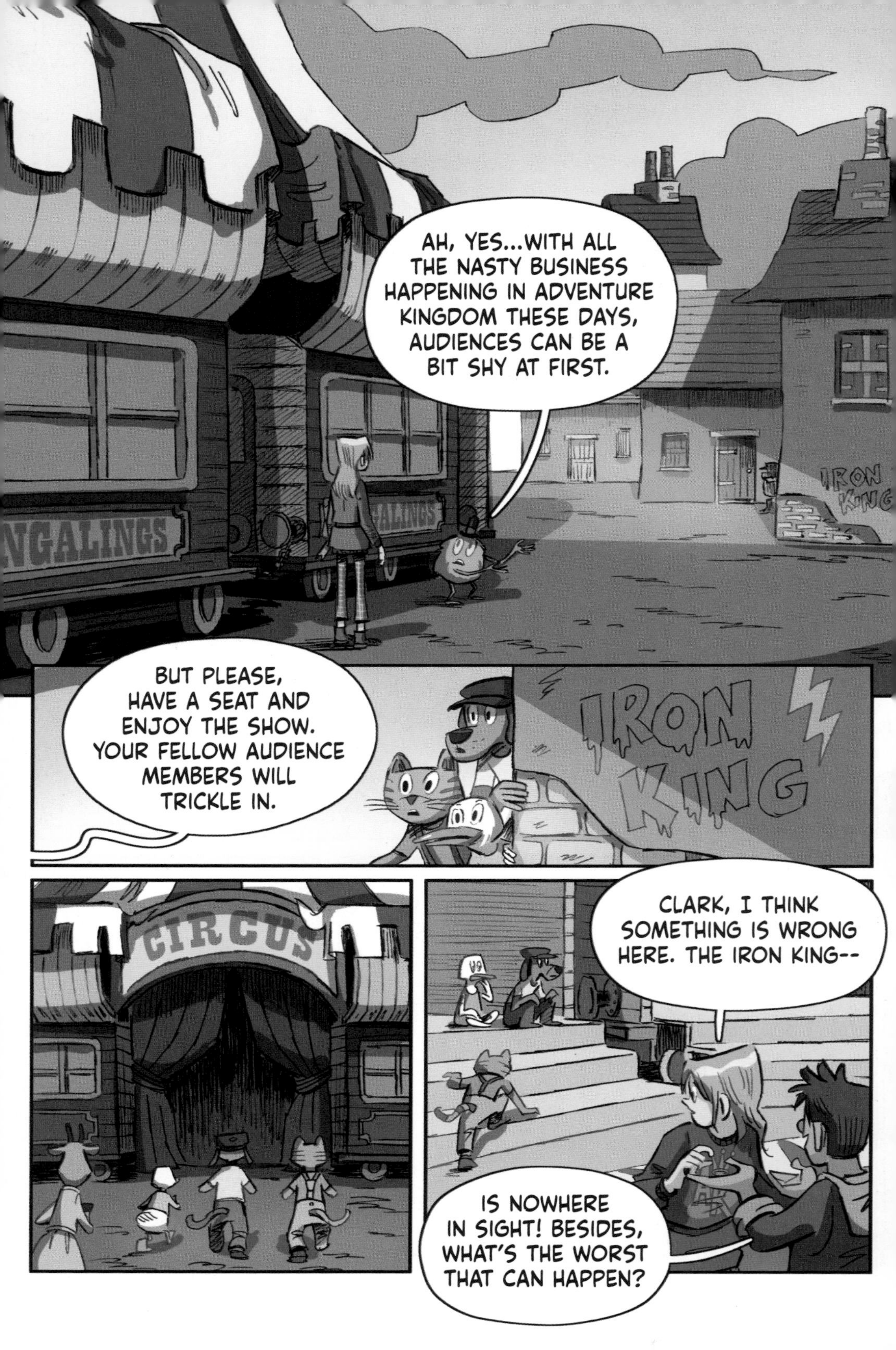
AH, YES...WITH ALL THE NASTY BUSINESS HAPPENING IN ADVENTURE KINGDOM THESE DAYS, AUDIENCES CAN BE A BIT SHY AT FIRST.
NGALINGS
GALINGS
IRON KING
BUT PLEASE, HAVE A SEAT AND ENJOY THE SHOW. YOUR FELLOW AUDIENCE MEMBERS WILL TRICKLE IN.
IRON KING
CIRCUS
CLARK, I THINK SOMETHING IS WRONG HERE. THE IRON KING--
IS NOWHERE IN SIGHT! BESIDES, WHAT'S THE WORST THAT CAN HAPPEN?

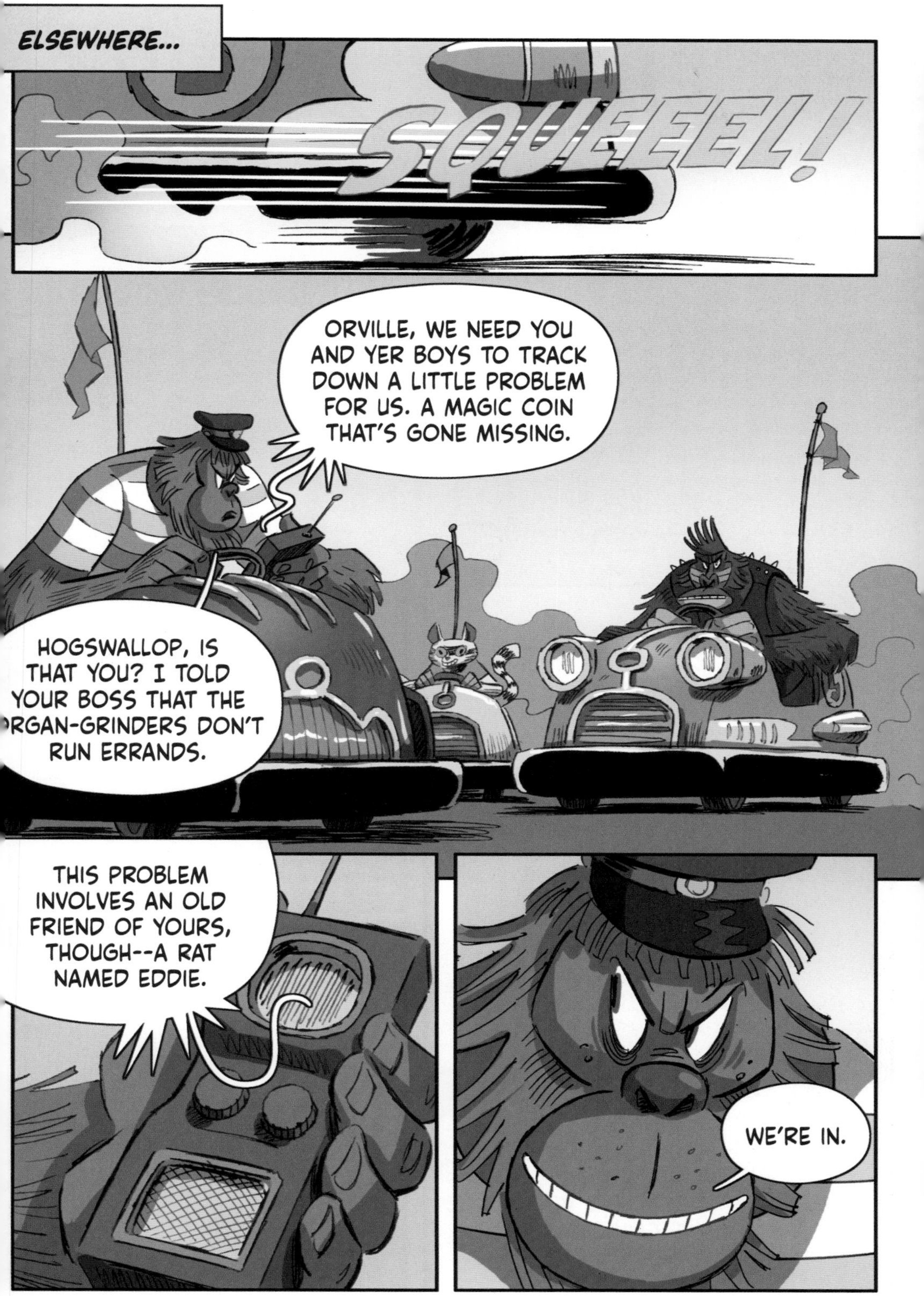
ELSEWHERE...
SQUEEEEL!
ORVILLE, WE NEED YOU AND YER BOYS TO TRACK DOWN A LITTLE PROBLEM FOR US. A MAGIC COIN THAT'S GONE MISSING.
HOGSWALLOP, IS THAT YOU? I TOLD YOUR BOSS THAT THE RGAN-GRINDERS DON'T RUN ERRANDS.
THIS PROBLEM INVOLVES AN OLD FRIEND OF YOURS, THOUGH--A RAT NAMED EDDIE.
WE'RE IN.

EDDIE, ALL THESE VILLAGERS LOOK... SCARED.

WELCOME TO LIFE UNDER THE IRON KING, KID. CAN'T EVEN ENJOY A SHOW WITHOUT WORRYING ABOUT WHO'LL CRASH IT.

ERR...DID YOU MENTION THE IRON KING?

YES! WE'RE LOOKING FOR THE GRAND JEROME, AND A--WELL, ACTUALLY A PRETTY EVIL ROBOT SAID WE COULD FIND HIM IN A HALL OF MIRRORS.

SHH! THE RINGALINGS DON'T PICK SIDES.

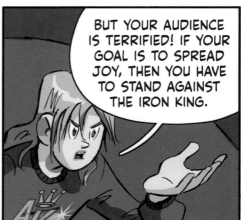

BUT YOUR AUDIENCE IS TERRIFIED! IF YOUR GOAL IS TO SPREAD JOY, THEN YOU HAVE TO STAND AGAINST THE IRON KING.

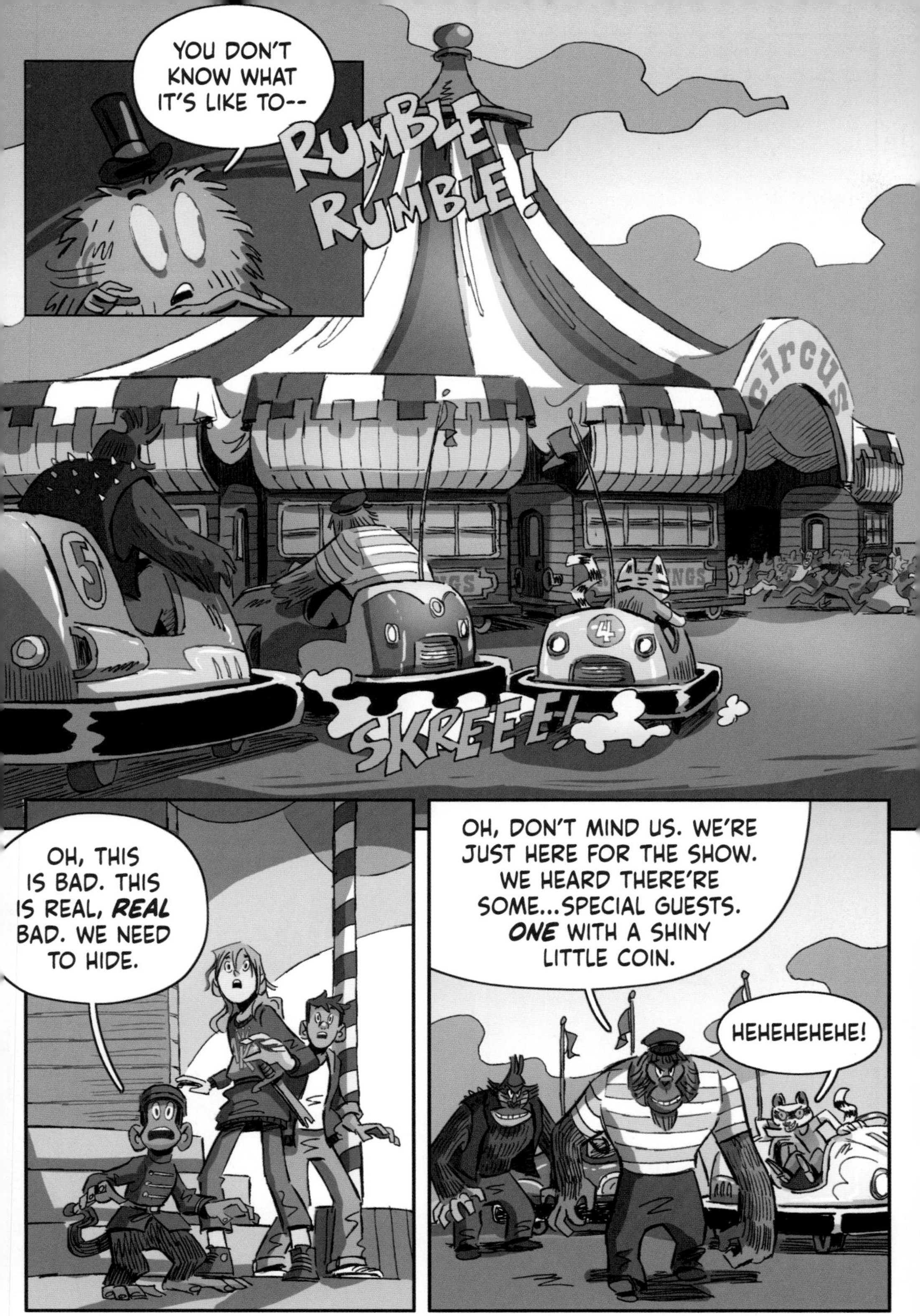
YOU DON'T KNOW WHAT IT'S LIKE TO--
RUMBLE RUMBLE!
SKREEEE!
OH, THIS IS BAD. THIS IS REAL, *REAL* BAD. WE NEED TO HIDE.
OH, DON'T MIND US. WE'RE JUST HERE FOR THE SHOW. WE HEARD THERE'RE SOME...SPECIAL GUESTS. *ONE* WITH A SHINY LITTLE COIN.
HEHEHEHEHE!

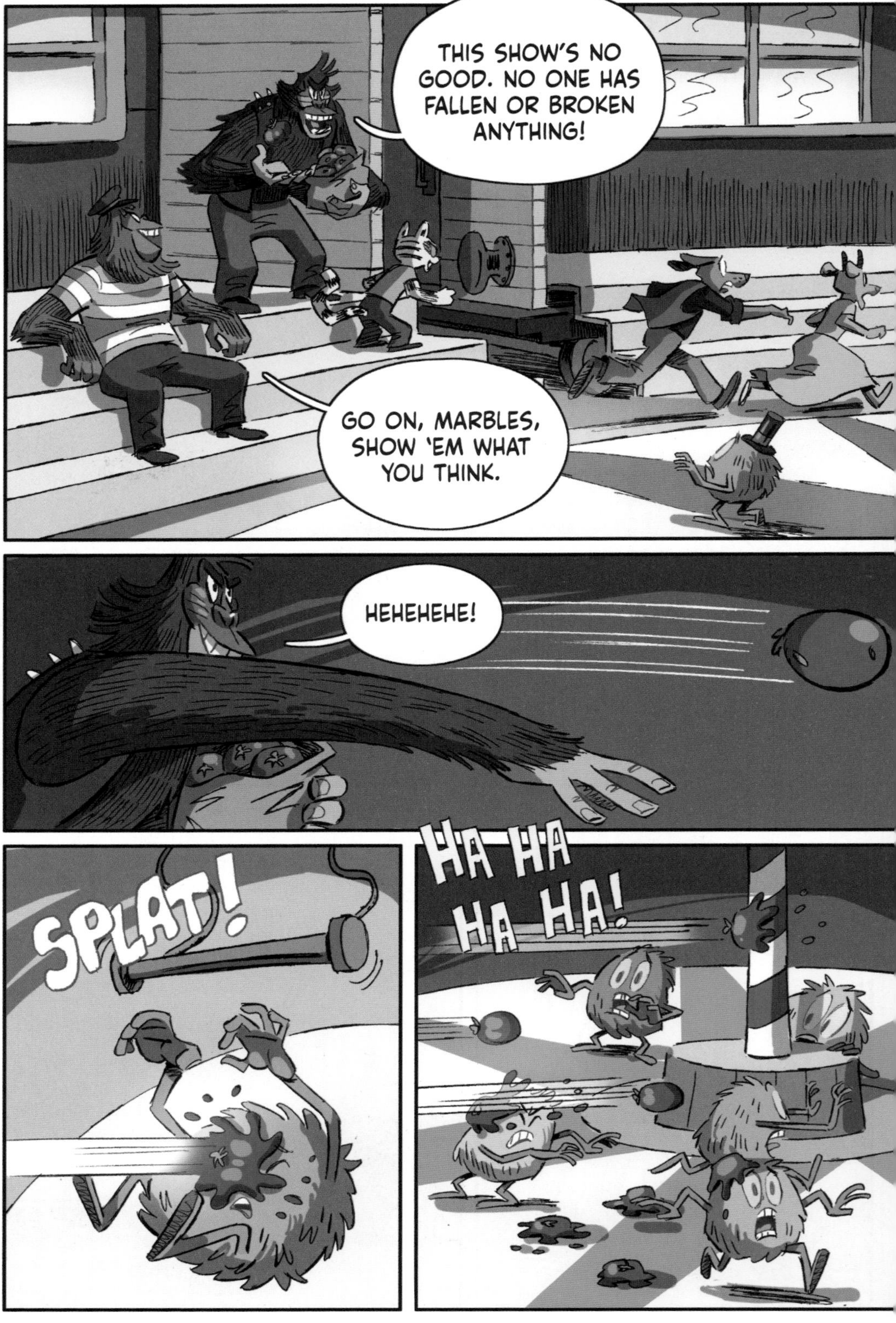
THIS SHOW'S NO GOOD. NO ONE HAS FALLEN OR BROKEN ANYTHING!
GO ON, MARBLES, SHOW 'EM WHAT YOU THINK.
HEHEHEHE!
SPLAT!
HA HA HA HA!

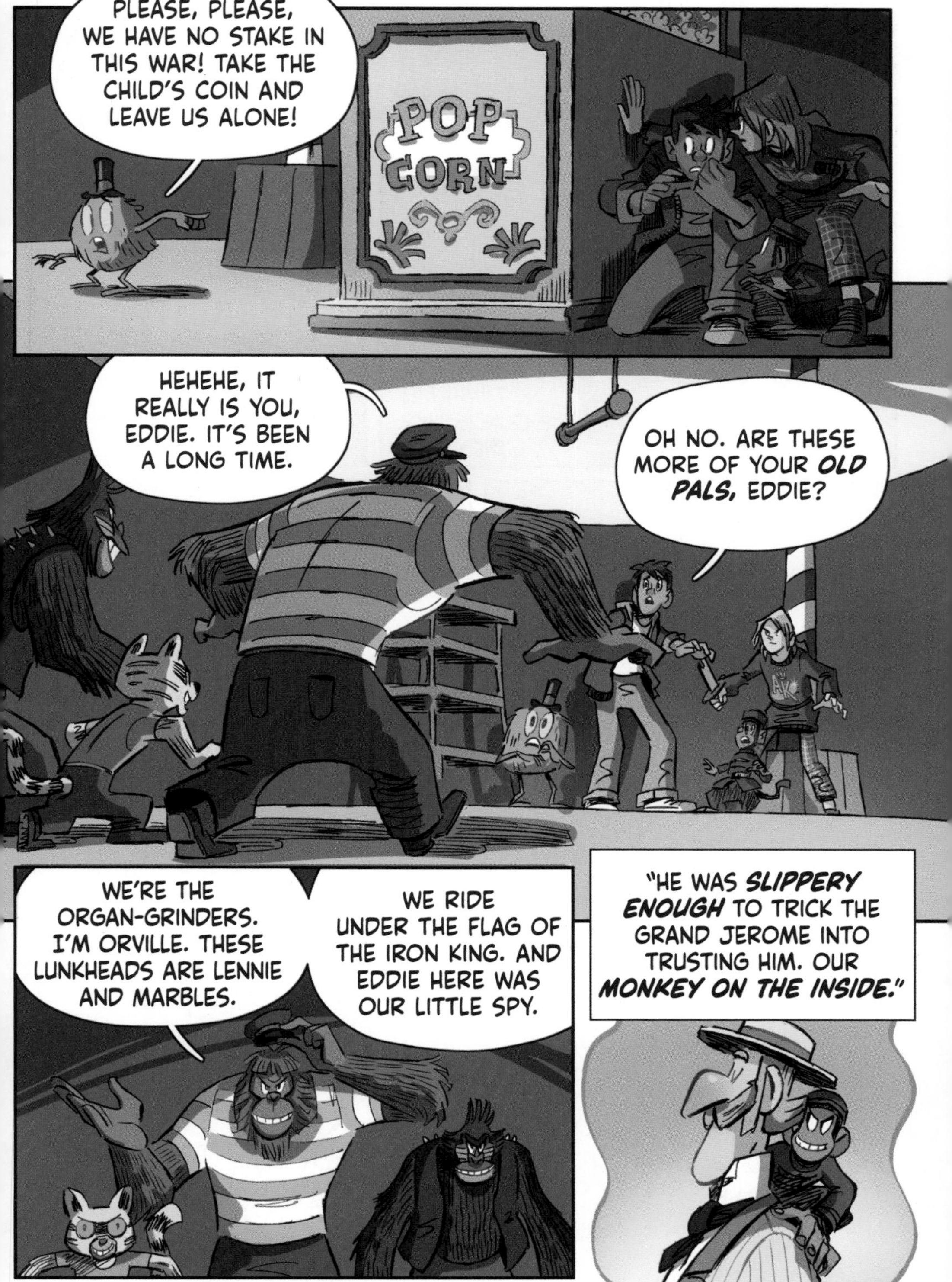
PLEASE, PLEASE, WE HAVE NO STAKE IN THIS WAR! TAKE THE CHILD'S COIN AND LEAVE US ALONE!
POP CORN
HEHEHE, IT REALLY IS YOU, EDDIE. IT'S BEEN A LONG TIME.
OH NO. ARE THESE MORE OF YOUR *OLD PALS,* EDDIE?
WE'RE THE ORGAN-GRINDERS. I'M ORVILLE. THESE LUNKHEADS ARE LENNIE AND MARBLES.
WE RIDE UNDER THE FLAG OF THE IRON KING. AND EDDIE HERE WAS OUR LITTLE SPY.
"HE WAS *SLIPPERY ENOUGH* TO TRICK THE GRAND JEROME INTO TRUSTING HIM. OUR *MONKEY ON THE INSIDE.*"

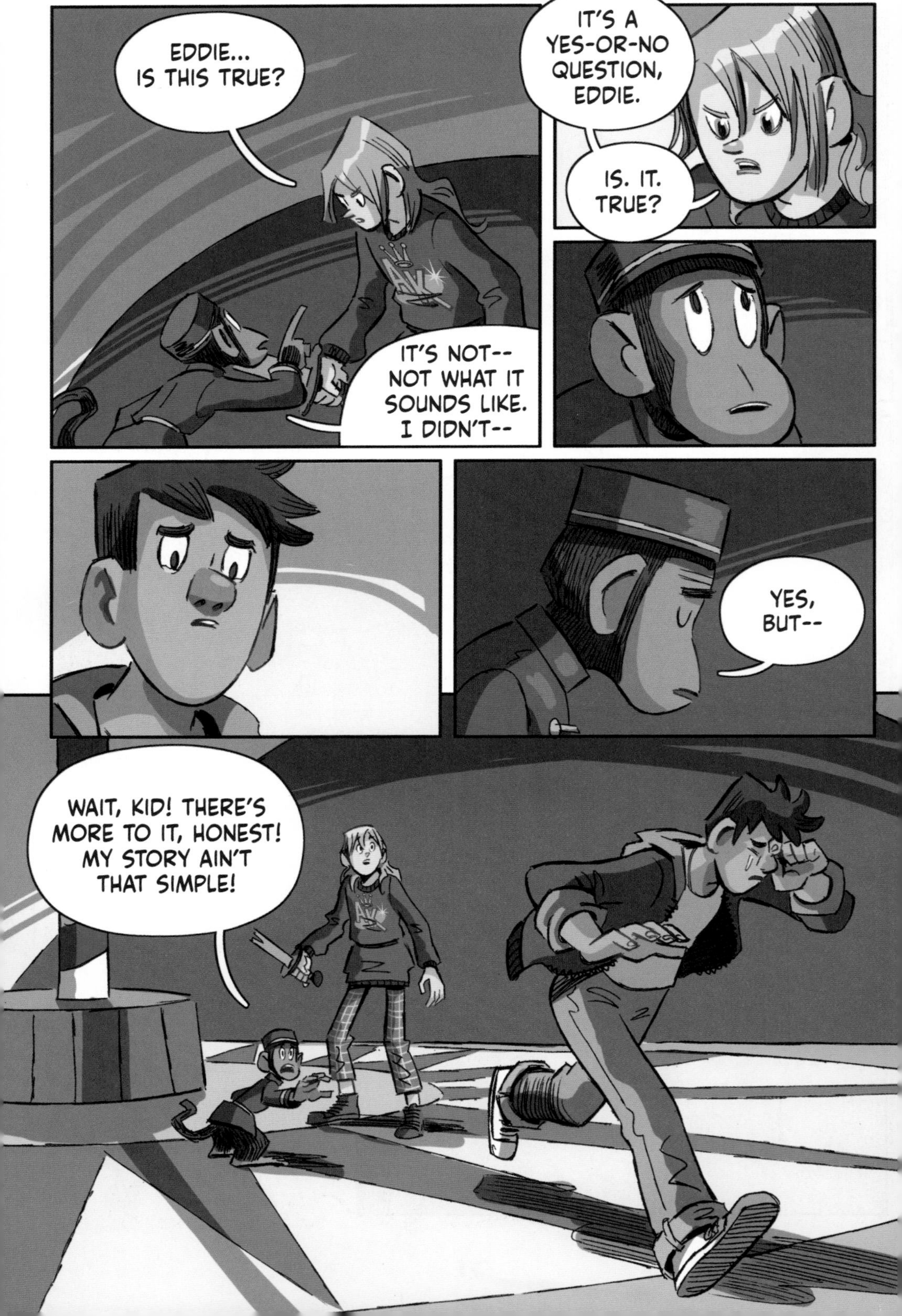
EDDIE... IS THIS TRUE?
IT'S NOT-- NOT WHAT IT SOUNDS LIKE. I DIDN'T--
IT'S A YES-OR-NO QUESTION, EDDIE.
IS. IT. TRUE?
YES, BUT--
WAIT, KID! THERE'S MORE TO IT, HONEST! MY STORY AIN'T THAT SIMPLE!

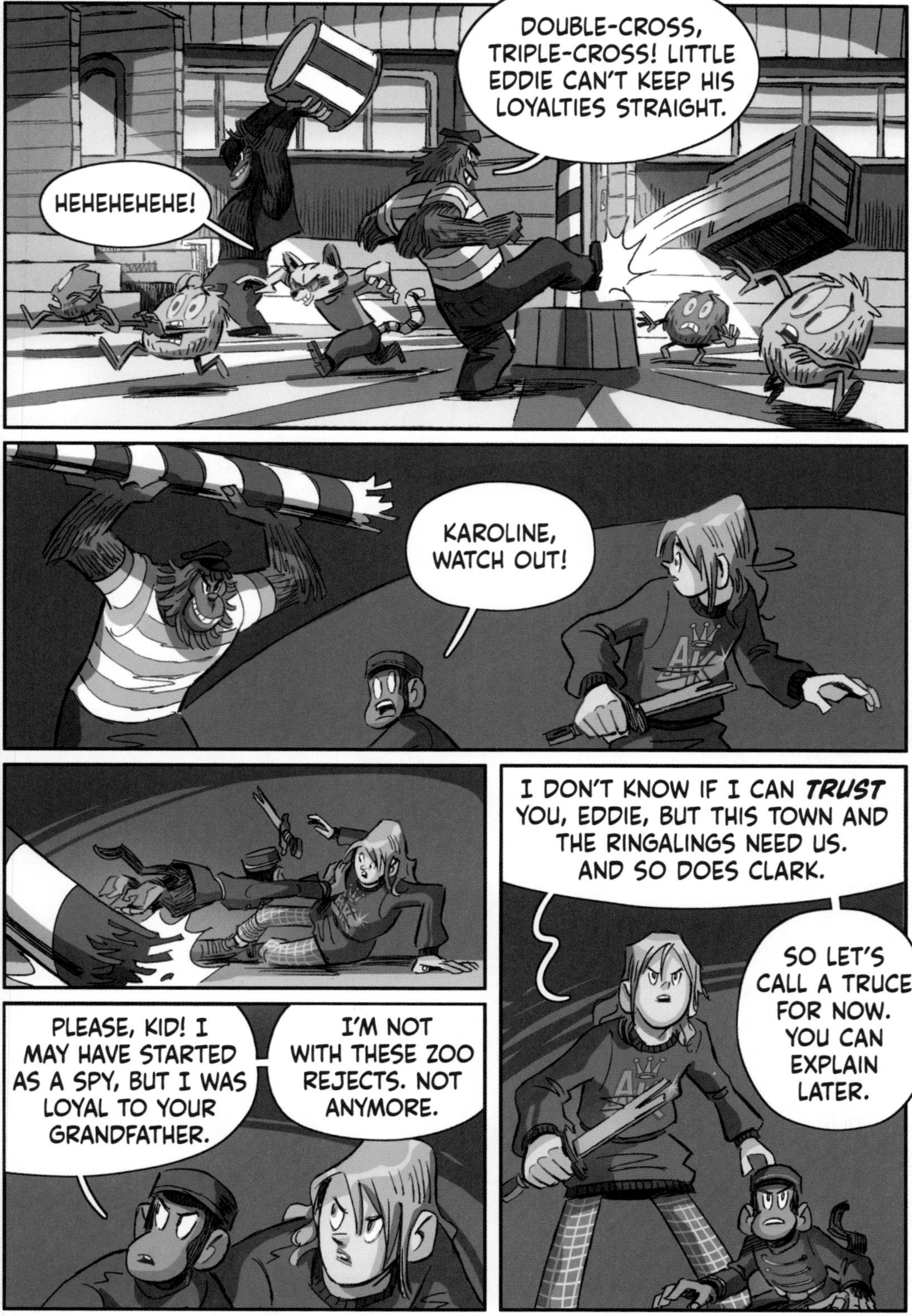
DOUBLE-CROSS, TRIPLE-CROSS! LITTLE EDDIE CAN'T KEEP HIS LOYALTIES STRAIGHT.
HEHEHEHEHE!
KAROLINE, WATCH OUT!
I DON'T KNOW IF I CAN *TRUST* YOU, EDDIE, BUT THIS TOWN AND THE RINGALINGS NEED US. AND SO DOES CLARK.
SO LET'S CALL A TRUCE FOR NOW. YOU CAN EXPLAIN LATER.
PLEASE, KID! I MAY HAVE STARTED AS A SPY, BUT I WAS LOYAL TO YOUR GRANDFATHER.
I'M NOT WITH THESE ZOO REJECTS. NOT ANYMORE.

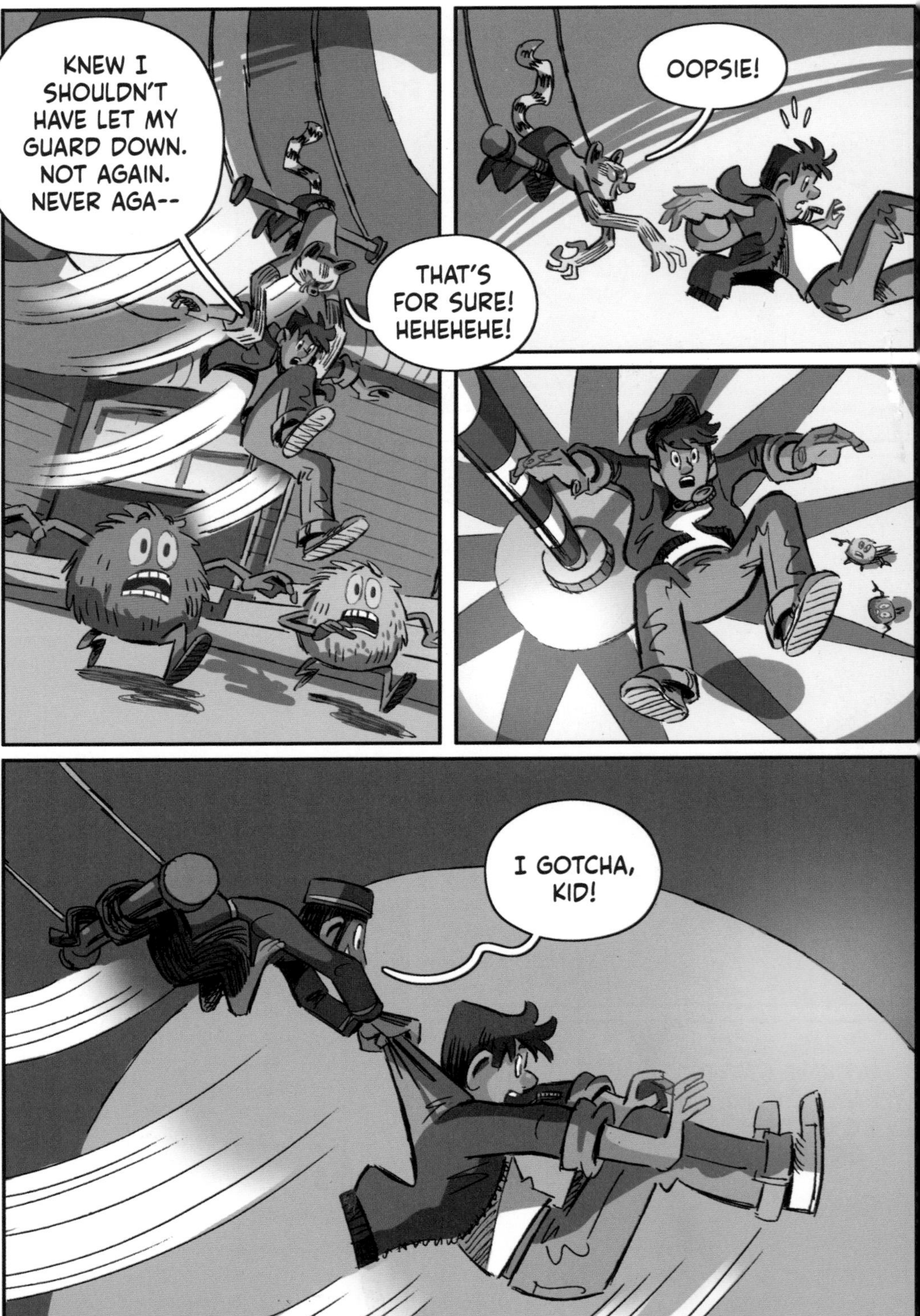
KNEW I SHOULDN'T HAVE LET MY GUARD DOWN. NOT AGAIN. NEVER AGA--
THAT'S FOR SURE! HEHEHEHE!
OOPSIE!
I GOTCHA, KID!

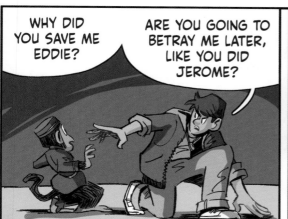

WHY DID YOU SAVE ME EDDIE?

ARE YOU GOING TO BETRAY ME LATER, LIKE YOU DID JEROME?

I DIDN'T BETRAY THE GRAND JEROME, KID.

I BETRAYED *THESE GOONS.*

WHO'RE YOU CALLING *A GOON,* EDDIE?

FZZZZ...

OH NO...

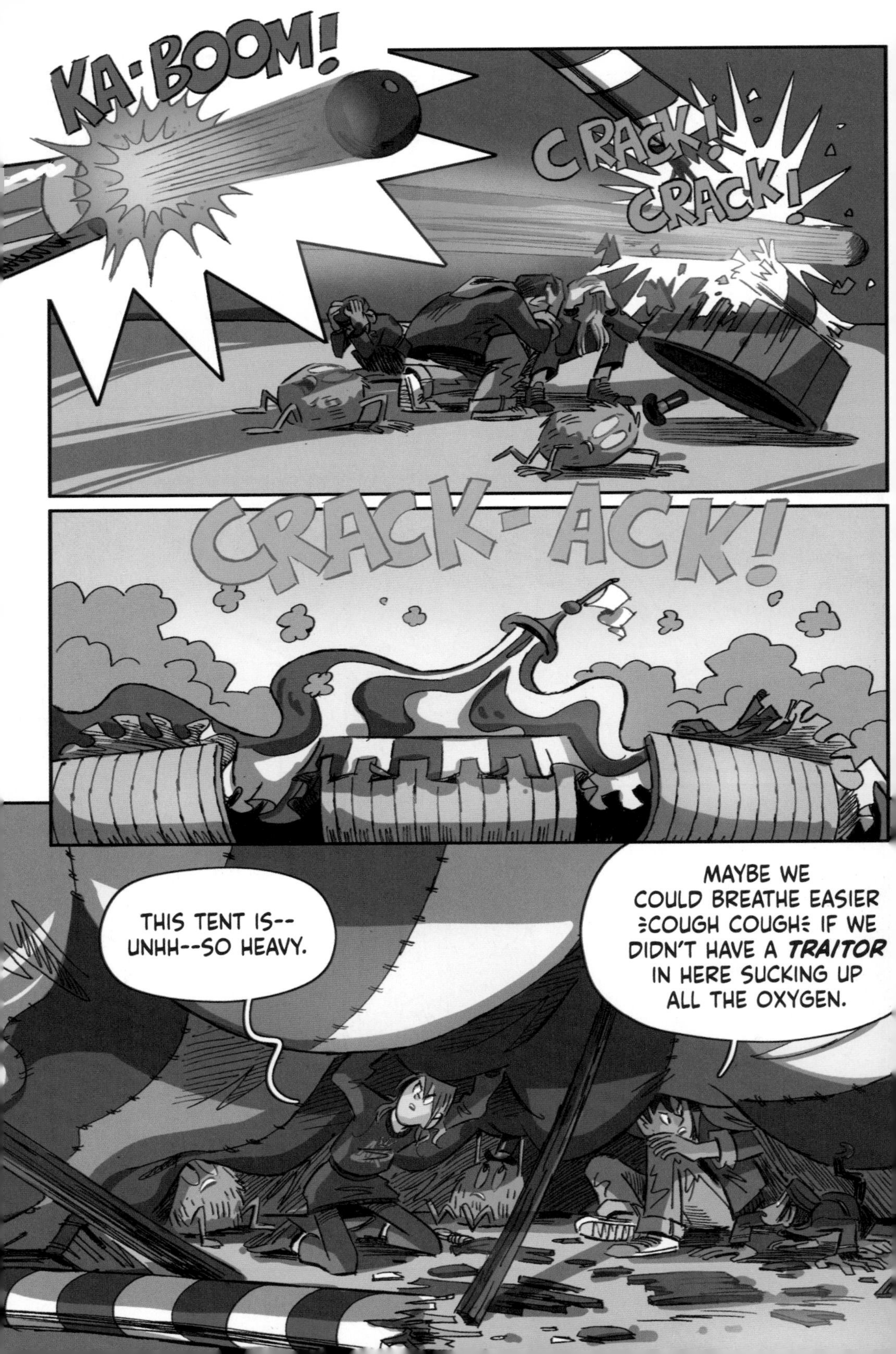
KA-BOOM!
CRACK! CRACK!
CRACK-ACK!
THIS TENT IS-- UNHH--SO HEAVY.
MAYBE WE COULD BREATHE EASIER ≑COUGH COUGH≑ IF WE DIDN'T HAVE A *TRAITOR* IN HERE SUCKING UP ALL THE OXYGEN.

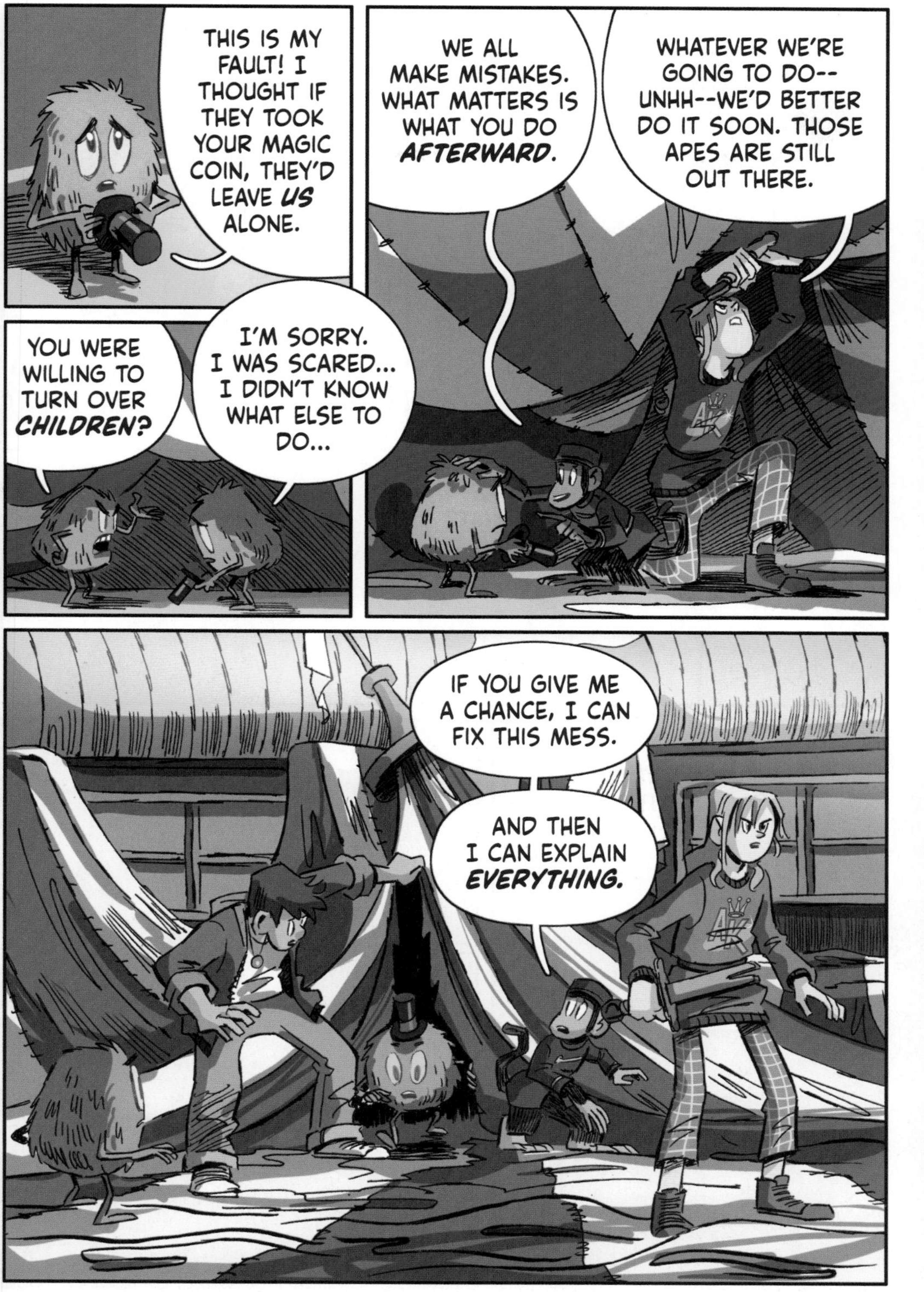
THIS IS MY FAULT! I THOUGHT IF THEY TOOK YOUR MAGIC COIN, THEY'D LEAVE *US* ALONE.
WE ALL MAKE MISTAKES. WHAT MATTERS IS WHAT YOU DO *AFTERWARD*.
WHATEVER WE'RE GOING TO DO-- UNHH--WE'D BETTER DO IT SOON. THOSE APES ARE STILL OUT THERE.
YOU WERE WILLING TO TURN OVER *CHILDREN?*
I'M SORRY. I WAS SCARED... I DIDN'T KNOW WHAT ELSE TO DO...
IF YOU GIVE ME A CHANCE, I CAN FIX THIS MESS.
AND THEN I CAN EXPLAIN *EVERYTHING.*

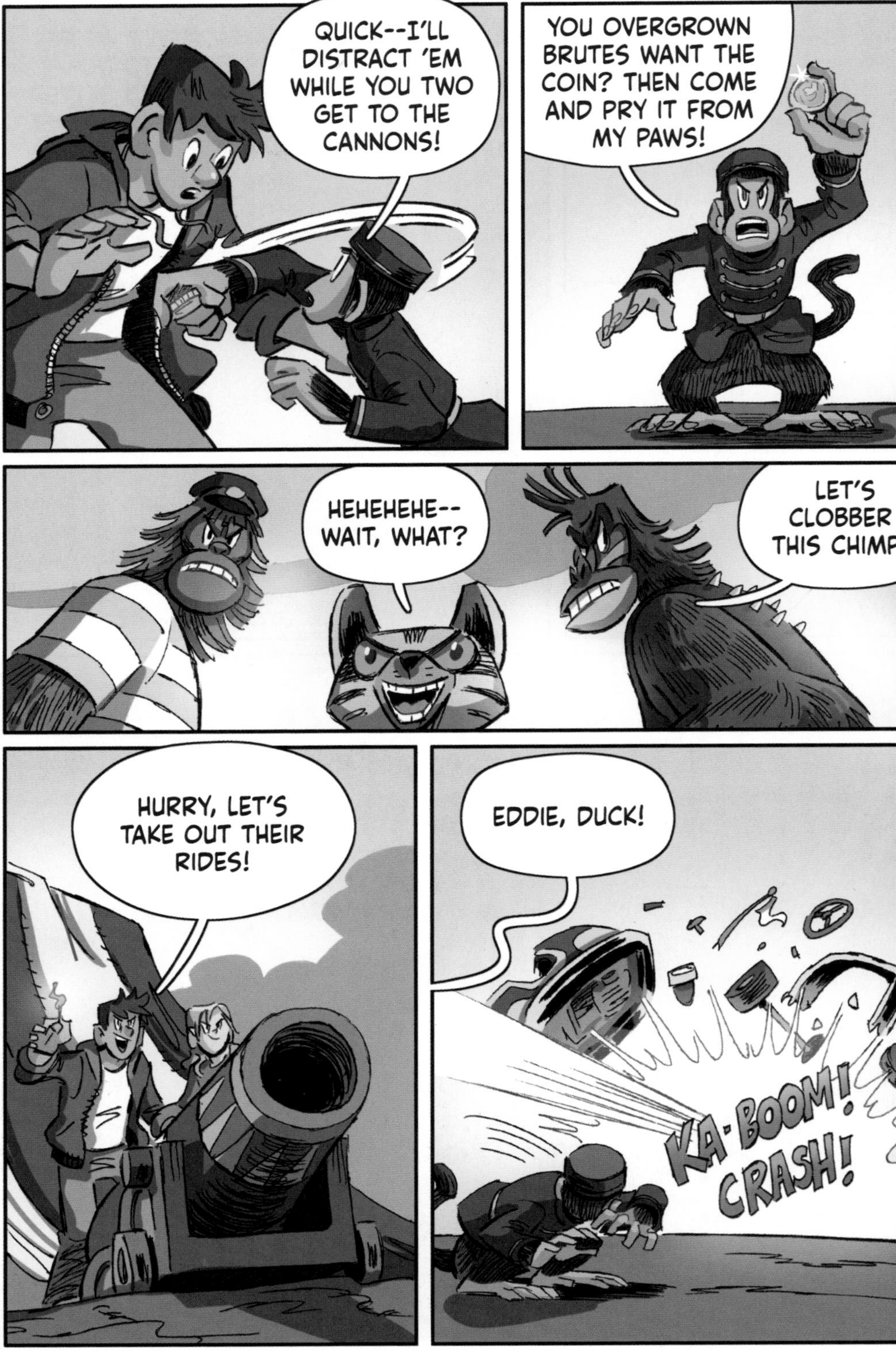
QUICK--I'LL DISTRACT 'EM WHILE YOU TWO GET TO THE CANNONS!
YOU OVERGROWN BRUTES WANT THE COIN? THEN COME AND PRY IT FROM MY PAWS!
HEHEHEHE-- WAIT, WHAT?
LET'S CLOBBER THIS CHIMP!
HURRY, LET'S TAKE OUT THEIR RIDES!
EDDIE, DUCK!
KA-BOOM!
CRASH!

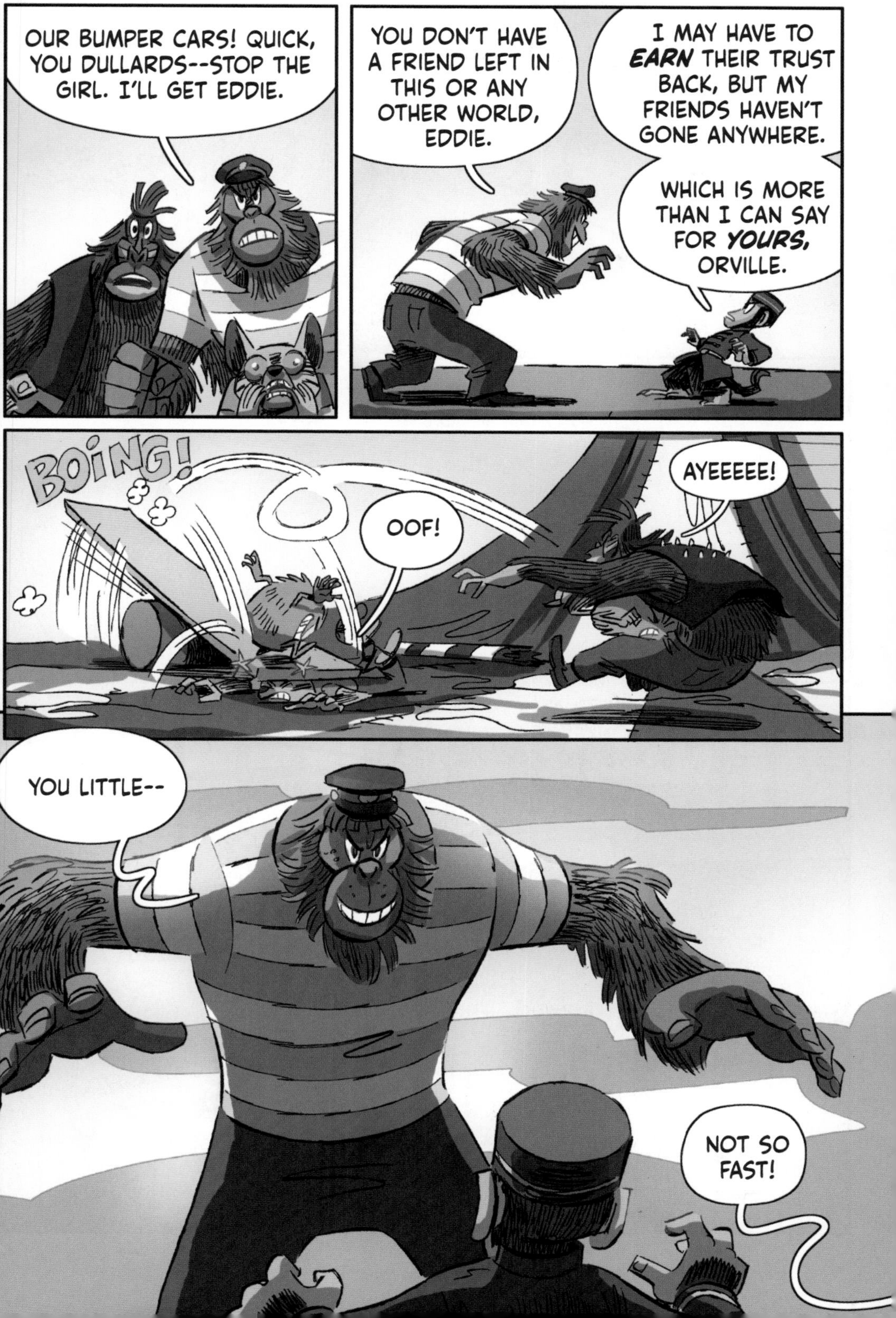

OUR BUMPER CARS! QUICK, YOU DULLARDS--STOP THE GIRL. I'LL GET EDDIE.
YOU DON'T HAVE A FRIEND LEFT IN THIS OR ANY OTHER WORLD, EDDIE.
I MAY HAVE TO ***EARN*** THEIR TRUST BACK, BUT MY FRIENDS HAVEN'T GONE ANYWHERE.
WHICH IS MORE THAN I CAN SAY FOR ***YOURS,*** ORVILLE.
BOING!
OOF!
AYEEEEE!
YOU LITTLE--
NOT SO FAST!

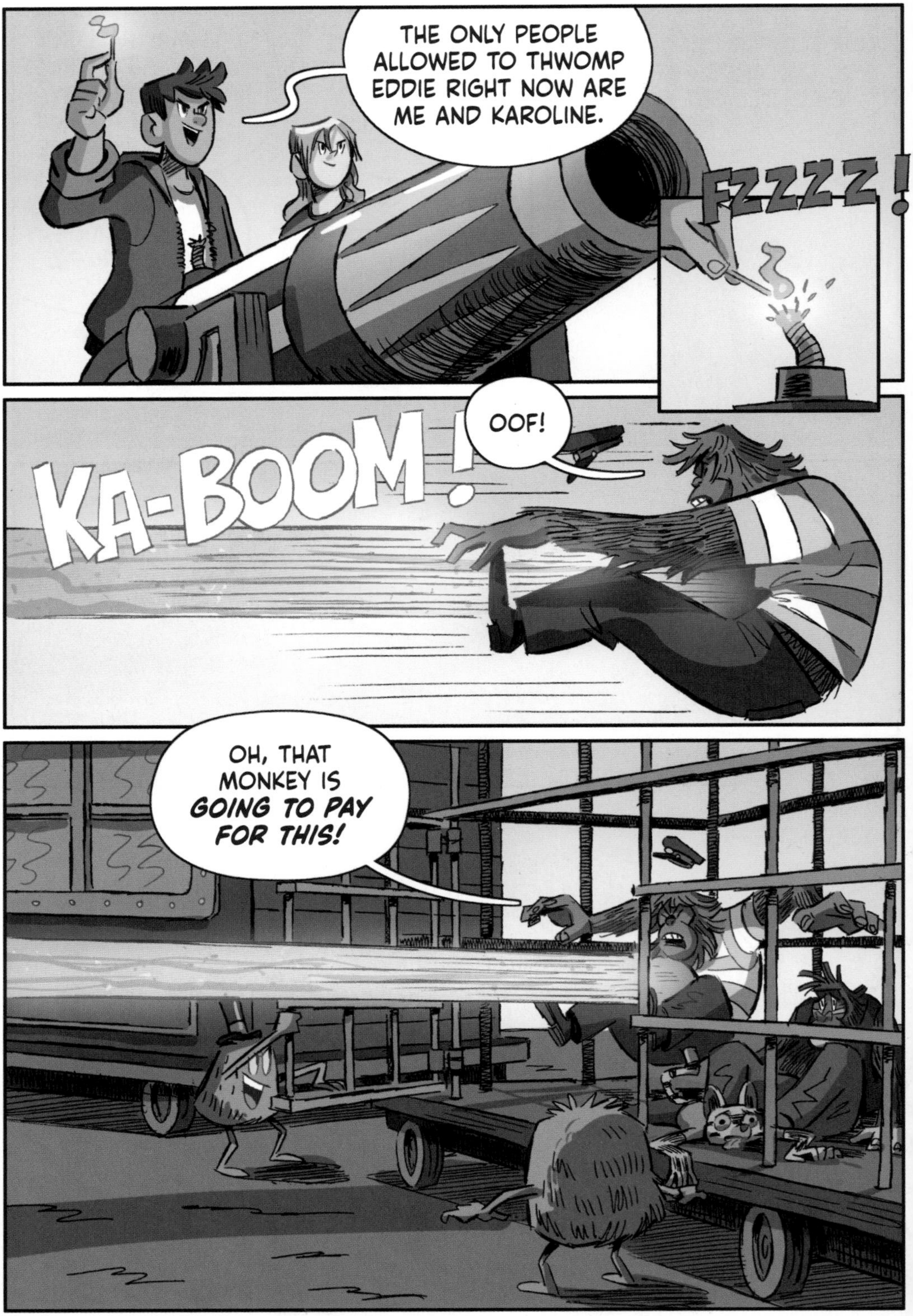
THE ONLY PEOPLE ALLOWED TO THWOMP EDDIE RIGHT NOW ARE ME AND KAROLINE.
FZZZZ!
KA-BOOM!
OOF!
OH, THAT MONKEY IS *GOING TO PAY FOR THIS!*

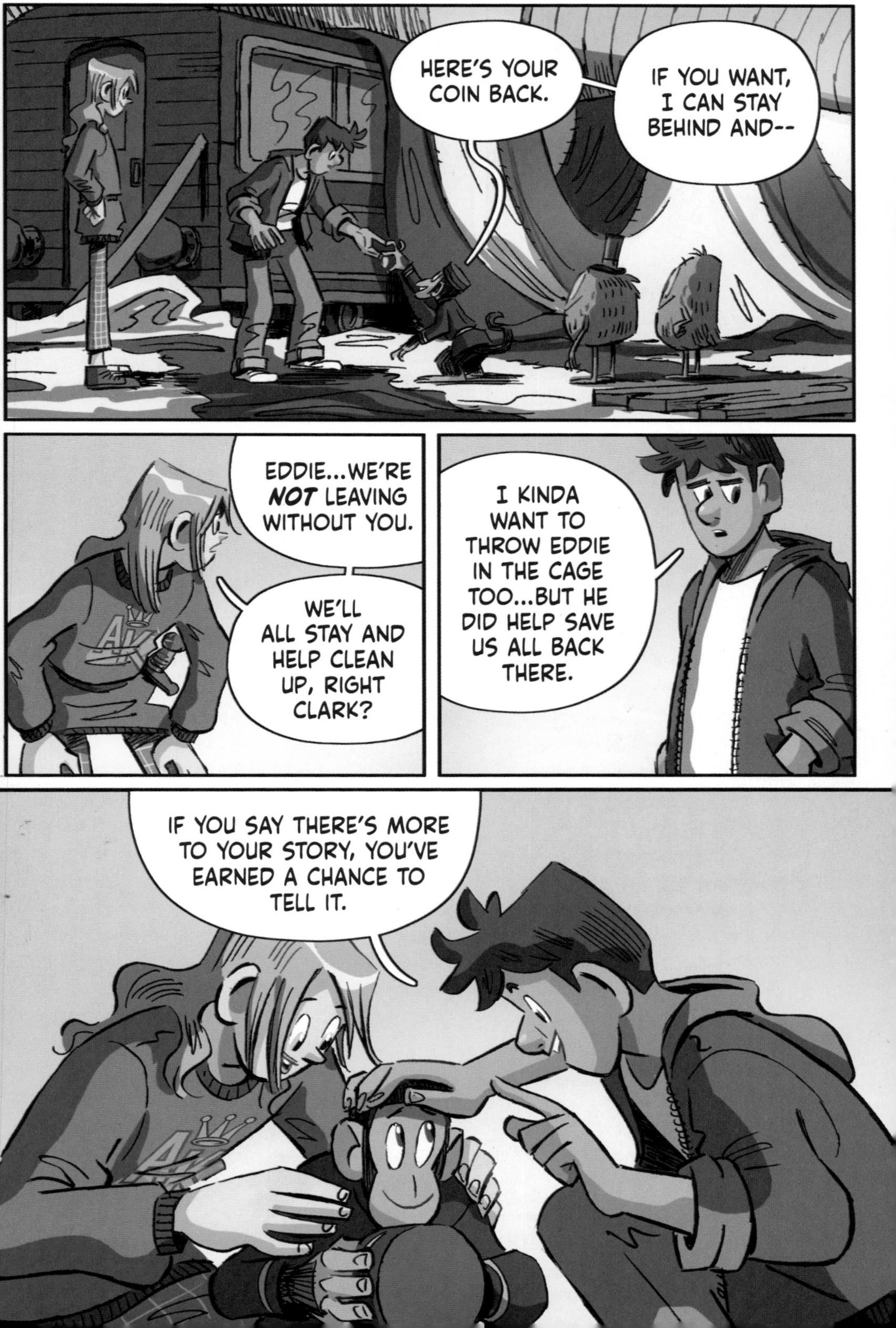
HERE'S YOUR COIN BACK.
IF YOU WANT, I CAN STAY BEHIND AND--
EDDIE...WE'RE **NOT** LEAVING WITHOUT YOU.
WE'LL ALL STAY AND HELP CLEAN UP, RIGHT CLARK?
I KINDA WANT TO THROW EDDIE IN THE CAGE TOO...BUT HE DID HELP SAVE US ALL BACK THERE.
IF YOU SAY THERE'S MORE TO YOUR STORY, YOU'VE EARNED A CHANCE TO TELL IT.

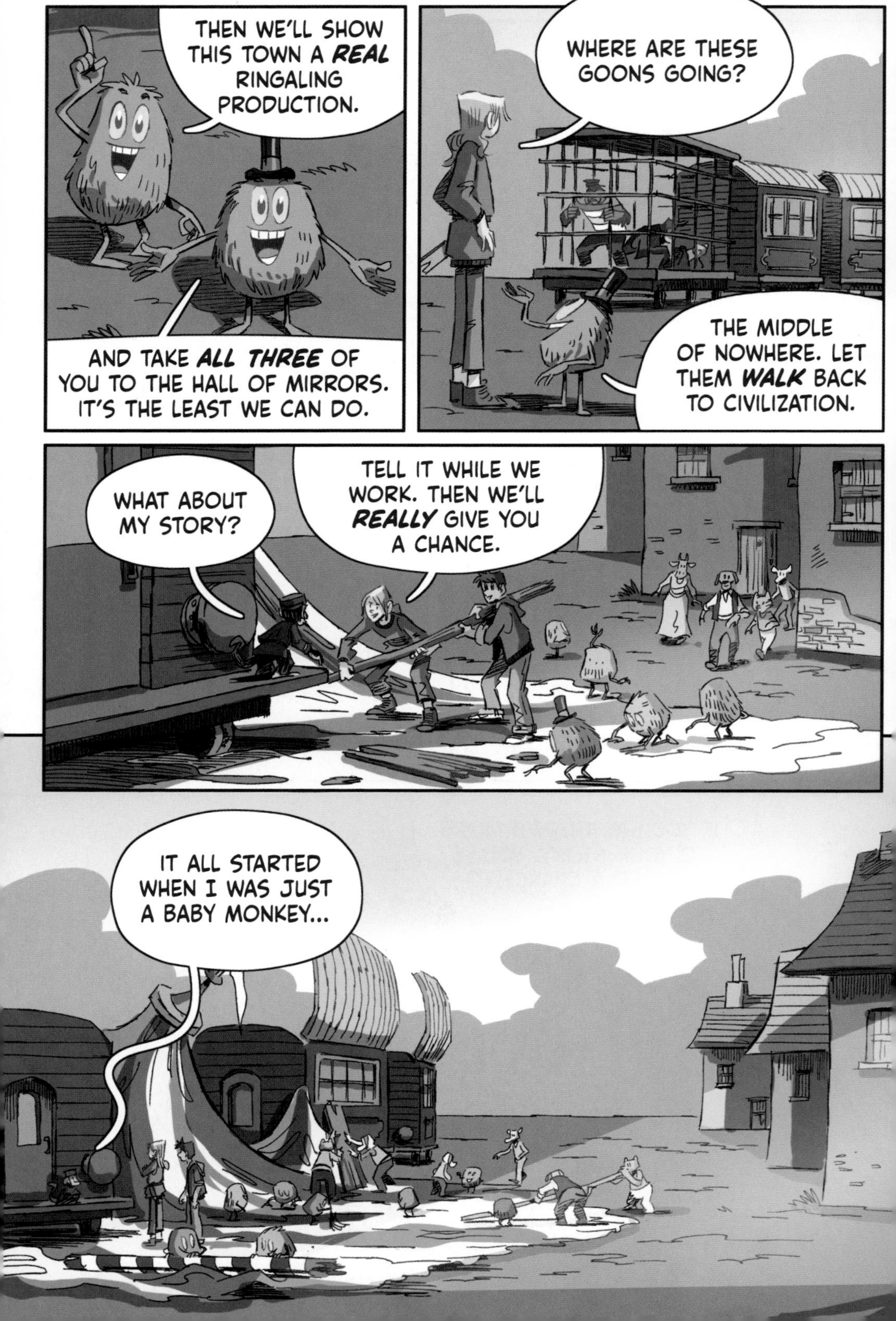
THEN WE'LL SHOW THIS TOWN A *REAL* RINGALING PRODUCTION.
AND TAKE *ALL THREE* OF YOU TO THE HALL OF MIRRORS. IT'S THE LEAST WE CAN DO.
WHERE ARE THESE GOONS GOING?
THE MIDDLE OF NOWHERE. LET THEM *WALK* BACK TO CIVILIZATION.
WHAT ABOUT MY STORY?
TELL IT WHILE WE WORK. THEN WE'LL *REALLY* GIVE YOU A CHANCE.
IT ALL STARTED WHEN I WAS JUST A BABY MONKEY...

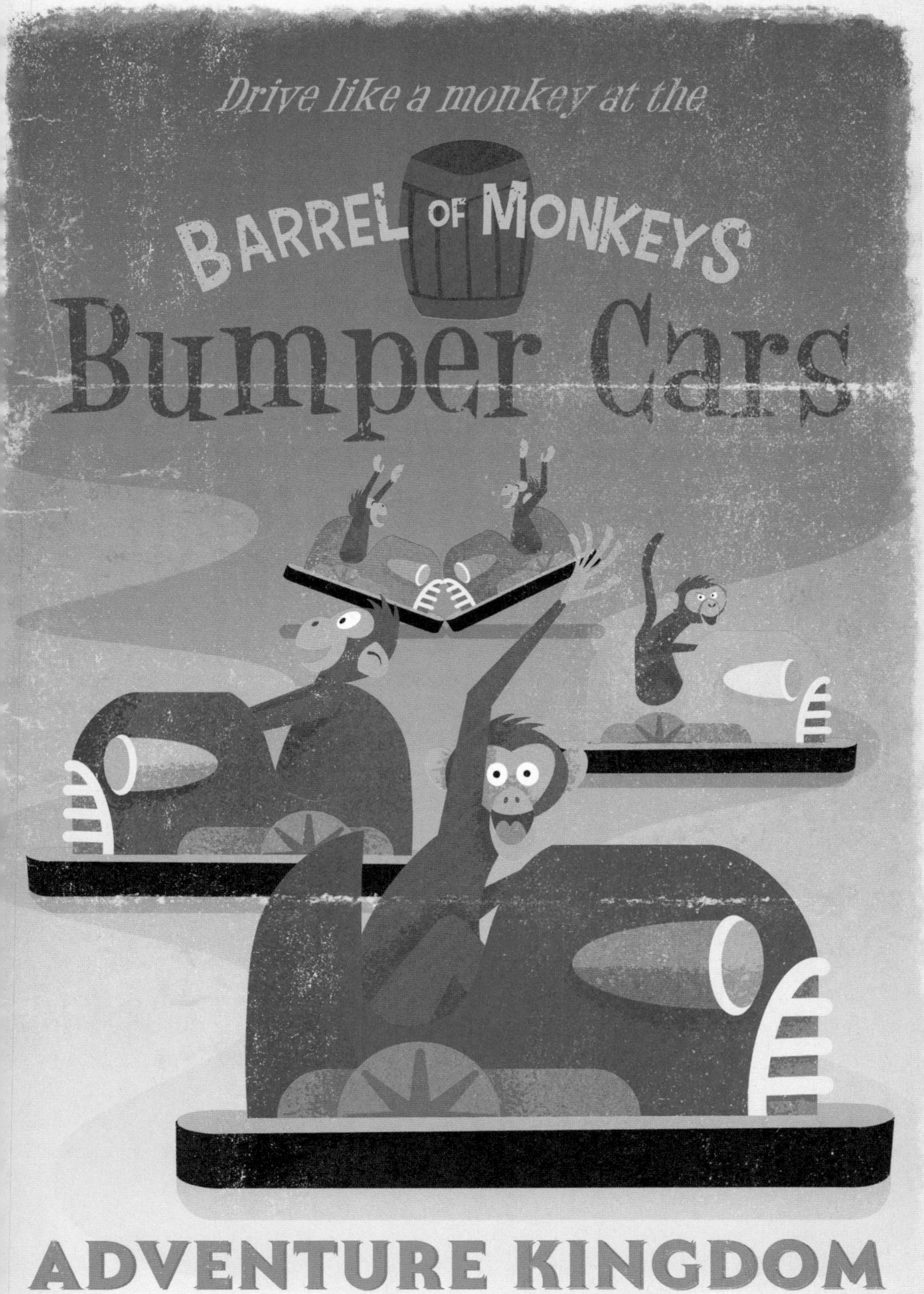
Drive like a monkey at the
BARREL OF MONKEYS
Bumper Cars
ADVENTURE KINGDOM

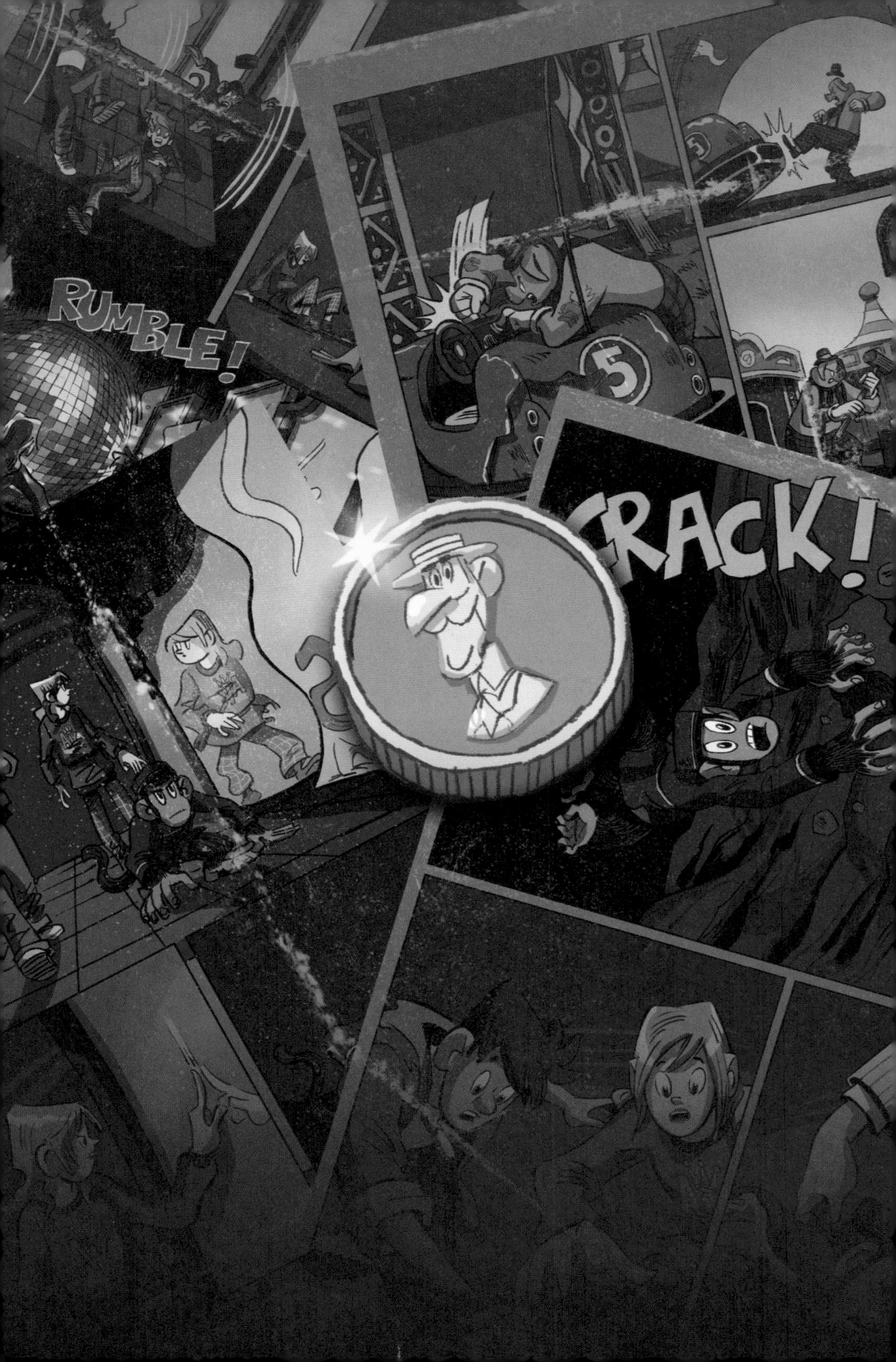
RUMBLE!
CRACK!

CHAPTER 4
MIRED IN THE MIRROR MAZE

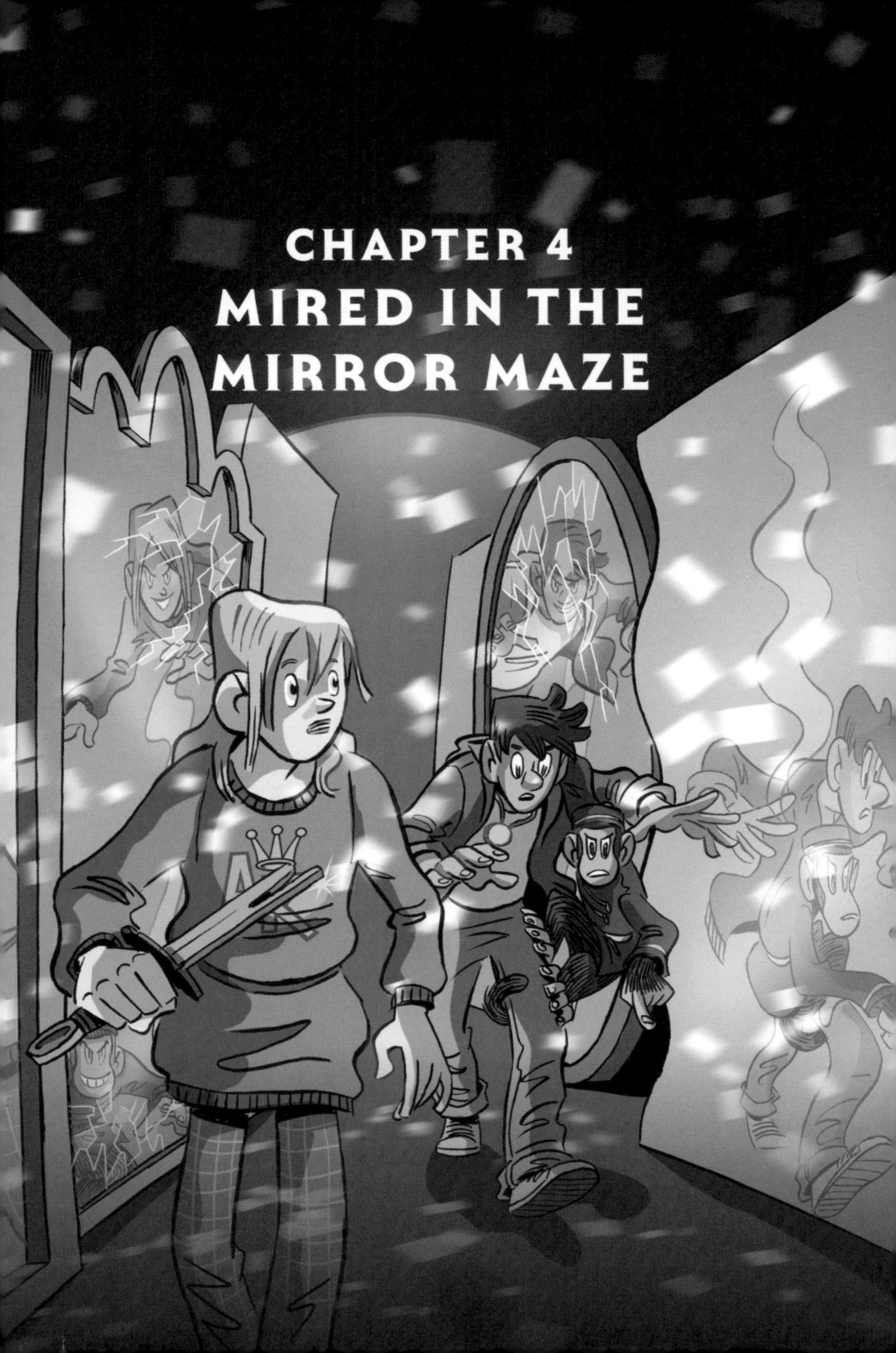

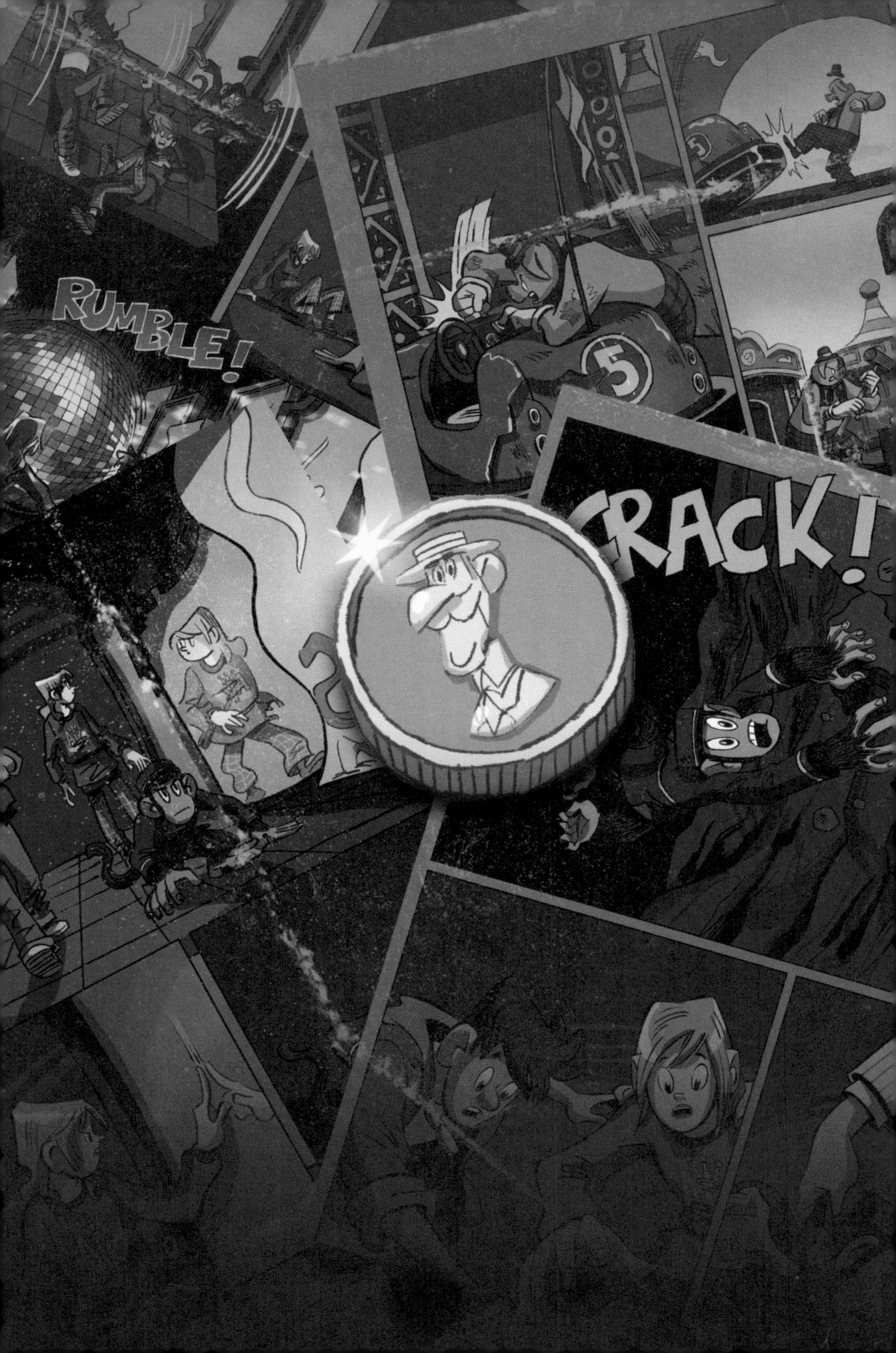
RUMBLE!
CRACK!

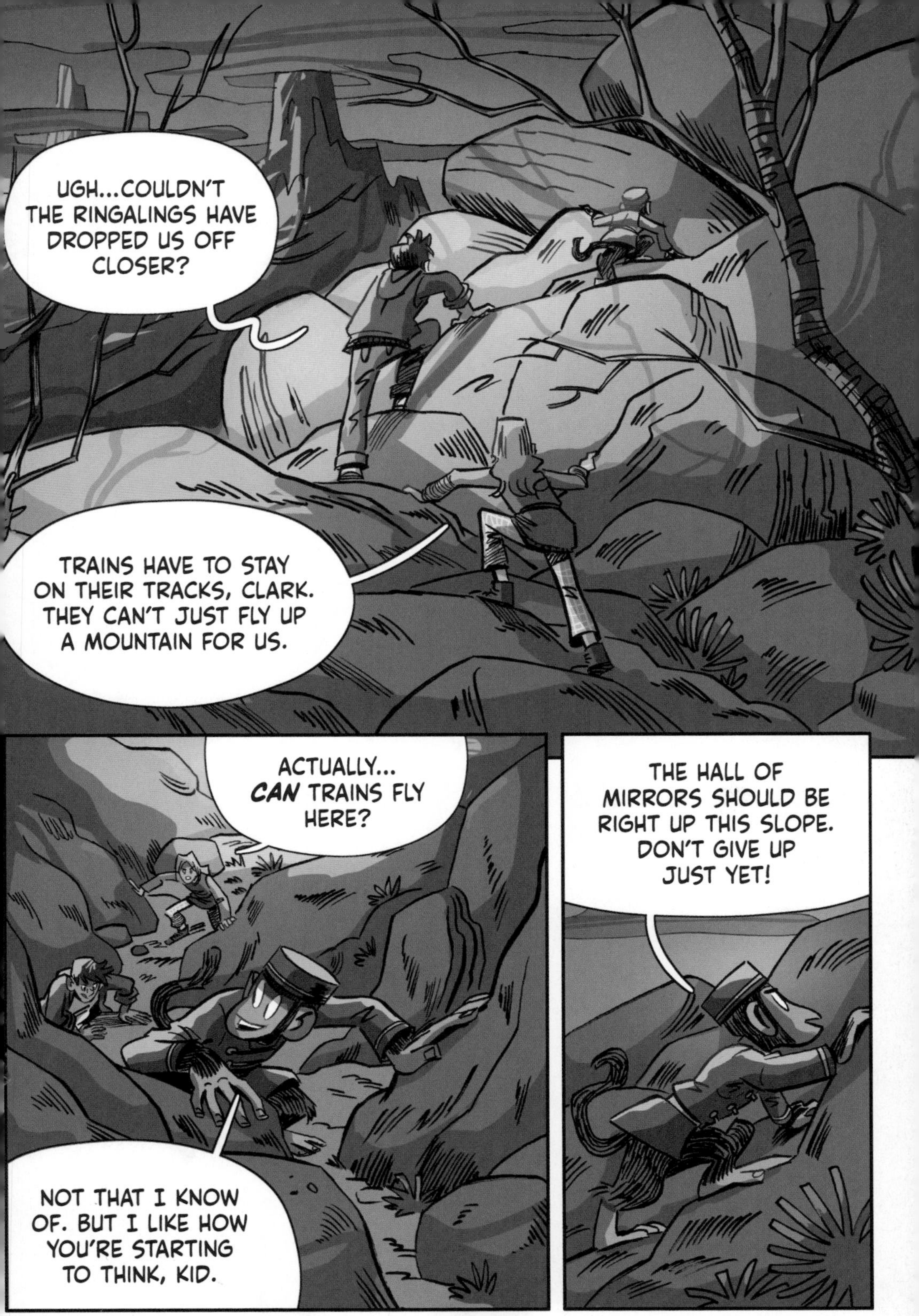
UGH...COULDN'T THE RINGALINGS HAVE DROPPED US OFF CLOSER?
TRAINS HAVE TO STAY ON THEIR TRACKS, CLARK. THEY CAN'T JUST FLY UP A MOUNTAIN FOR US.
ACTUALLY... *CAN* TRAINS FLY HERE?
NOT THAT I KNOW OF. BUT I LIKE HOW YOU'RE STARTING TO THINK, KID.
THE HALL OF MIRRORS SHOULD BE RIGHT UP THIS SLOPE. DON'T GIVE UP JUST YET!

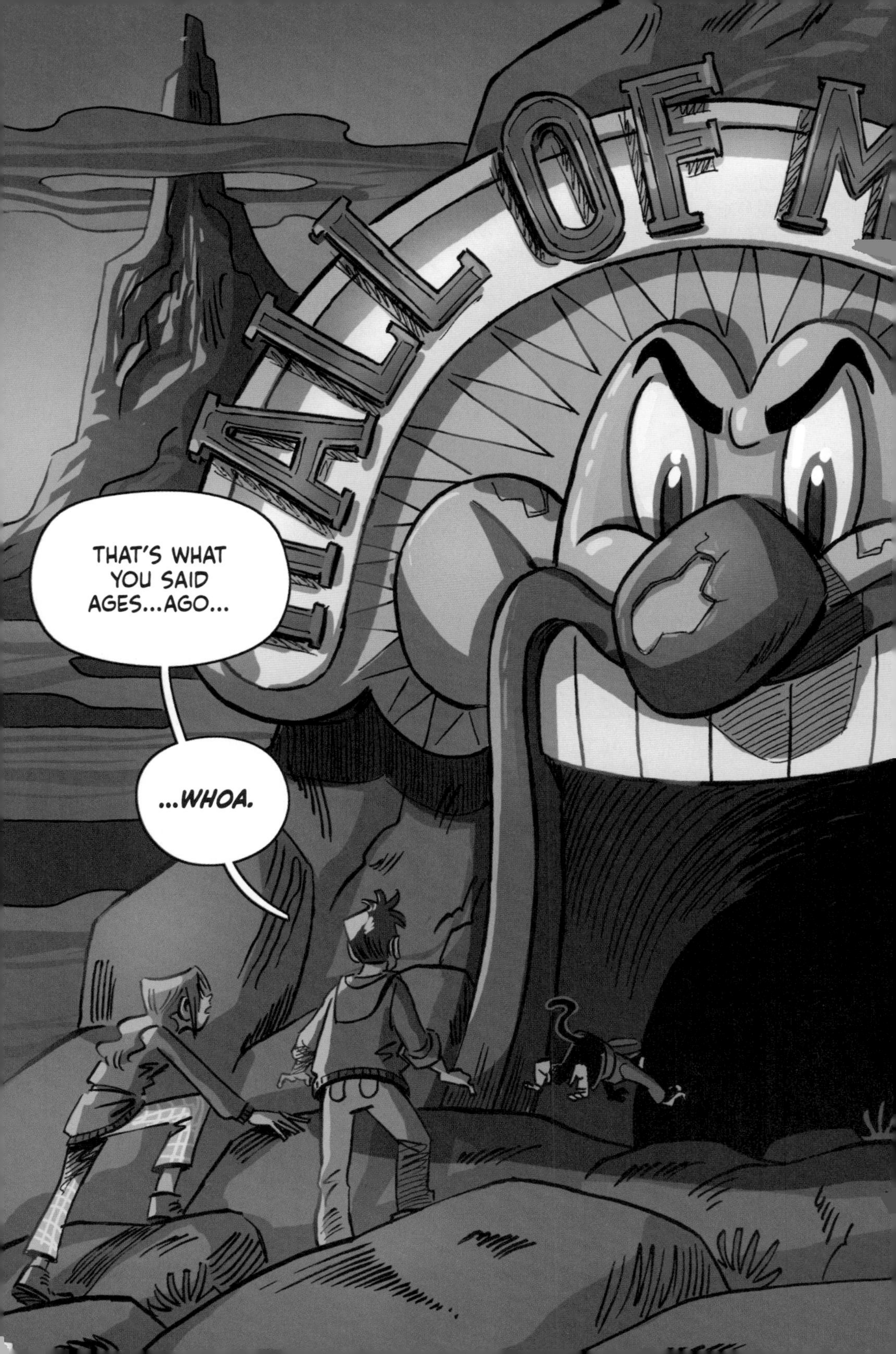
HALL OF M
THAT'S WHAT YOU SAID AGES...AGO...
...WHOA.

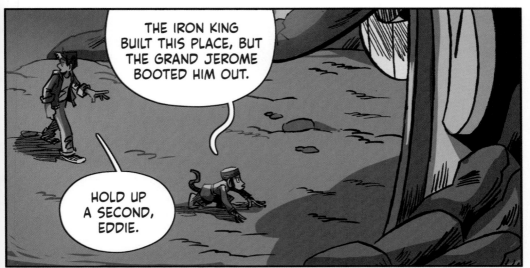

THE IRON KING BUILT THIS PLACE, BUT THE GRAND JEROME BOOTED HIM OUT.

HOLD UP A SECOND, EDDIE.

WHATEVER WE FIND IN THERE WITH YOUR GRANDAD, I'LL BE RIGHT BY YOUR SIDE...

...AND SO WILL EDDIE.

CLARK'S RIGHT, BUT IF YOU TWO DON'T PUT SOME PEP IN YOUR STEP, I'M GOING TO BE IN THERE *ALONE.*

WE'RE COMING, WE'RE COMING. DON'T GET YOUR LITTLE MONKEY TAIL IN A TWIST.

I'M GLAD YOU AND CLARK ARE SUCH PALS, BUT DO YOU GOTTA SOUND LIKE HIM NOW, TOO?

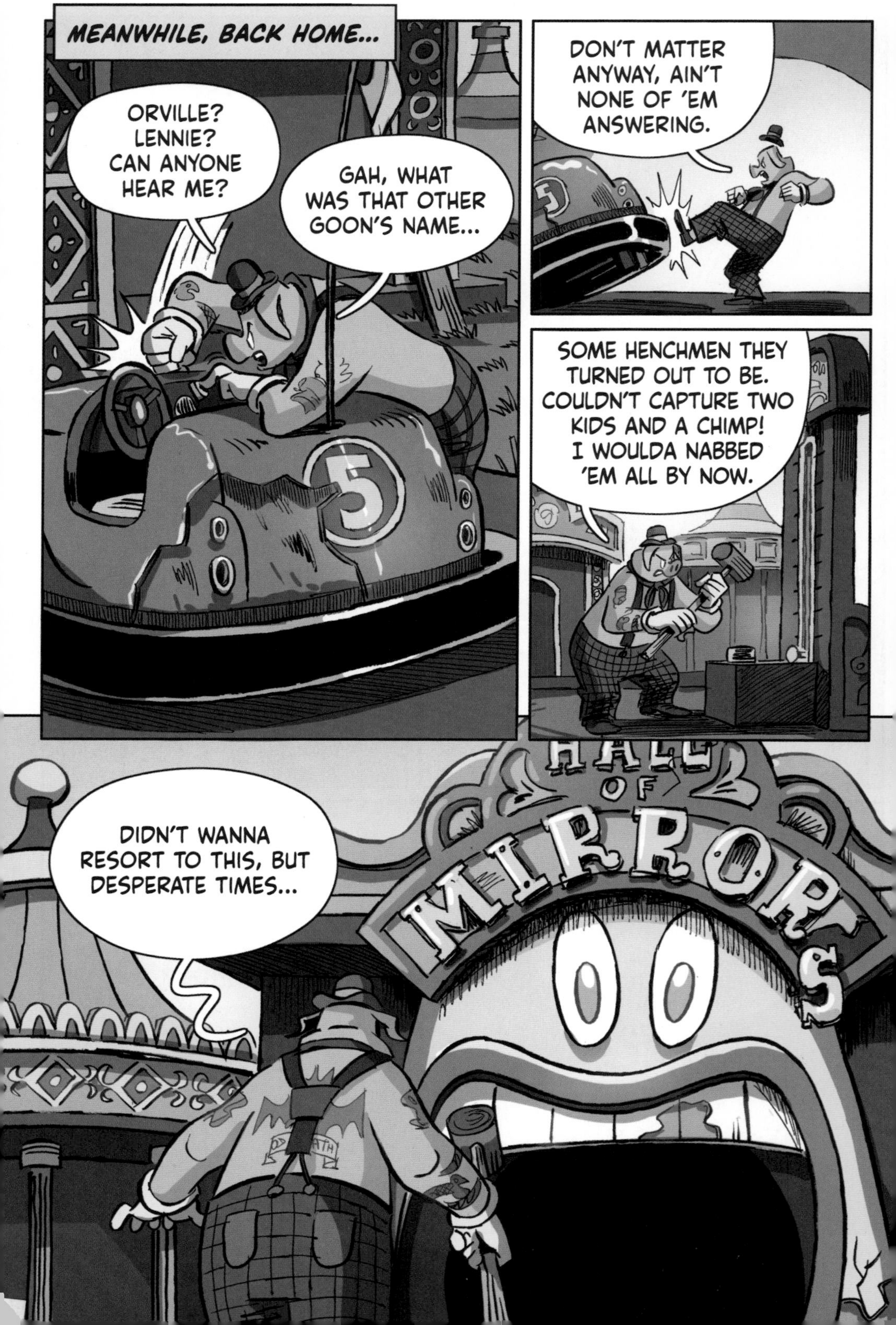
MEANWHILE, BACK HOME...
ORVILLE? LENNIE? CAN ANYONE HEAR ME?
GAH, WHAT WAS THAT OTHER GOON'S NAME...
5
DON'T MATTER ANYWAY, AIN'T NONE OF 'EM ANSWERING.
SOME HENCHMEN THEY TURNED OUT TO BE. COULDN'T CAPTURE TWO KIDS AND A CHIMP! I WOULDA NABBED 'EM ALL BY NOW.
DIDN'T WANNA RESORT TO THIS, BUT DESPERATE TIMES...
OF
MIRRORS

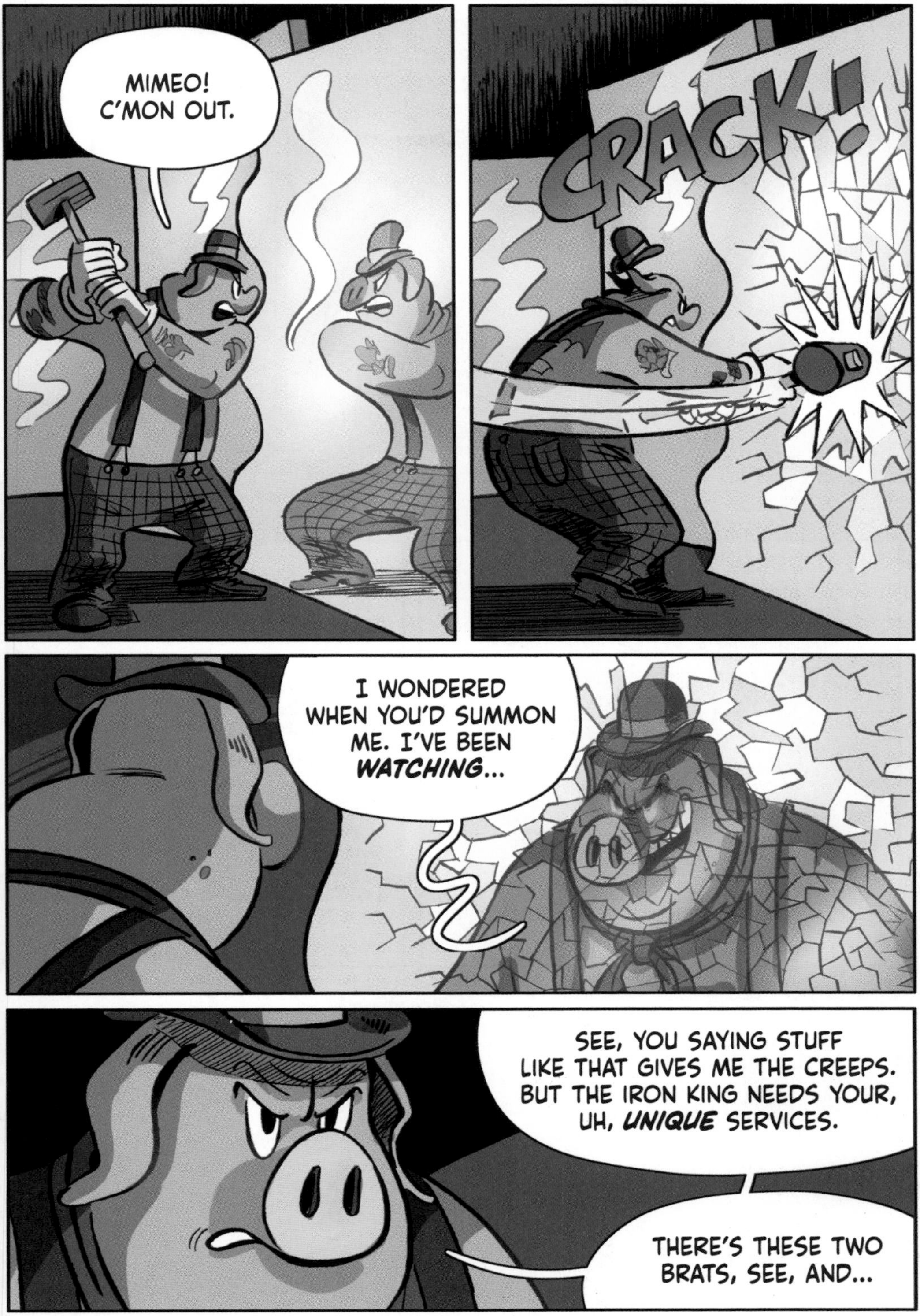

MIMEO! C'MON OUT.
CRACK!
I WONDERED WHEN YOU'D SUMMON ME. I'VE BEEN *WATCHING*...
SEE, YOU SAYING STUFF LIKE THAT GIVES ME THE CREEPS. BUT THE IRON KING NEEDS YOUR, UH, *UNIQUE* SERVICES.
THERE'S THESE TWO BRATS, SEE, AND...

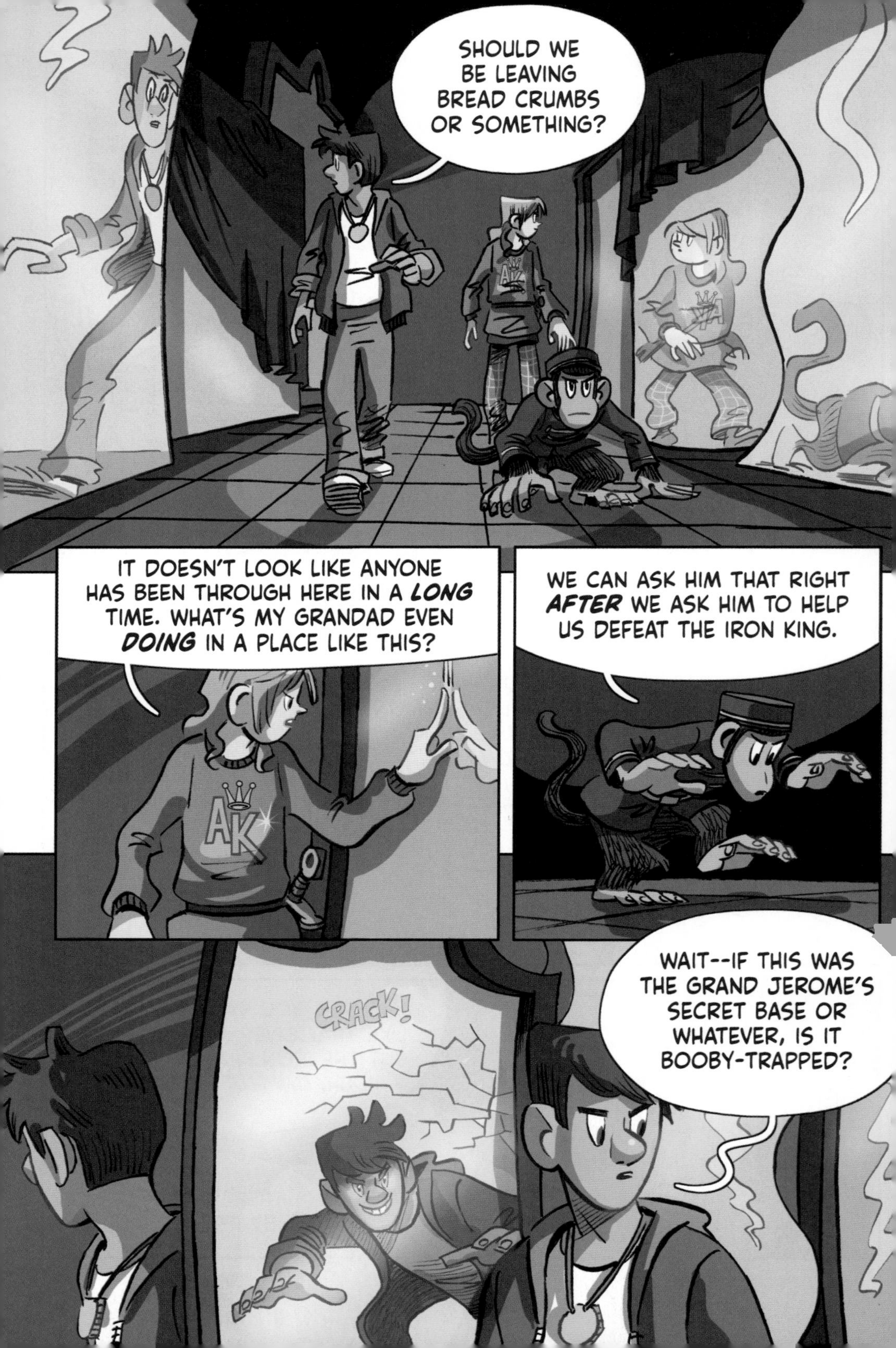
SHOULD WE BE LEAVING BREAD CRUMBS OR SOMETHING?
IT DOESN'T LOOK LIKE ANYONE HAS BEEN THROUGH HERE IN A LONG TIME. WHAT'S MY GRANDAD EVEN DOING IN A PLACE LIKE THIS?
WE CAN ASK HIM THAT RIGHT AFTER WE ASK HIM TO HELP US DEFEAT THE IRON KING.
AK
CRACK!
WAIT--IF THIS WAS THE GRAND JEROME'S SECRET BASE OR WHATEVER, IS IT BOOBY-TRAPPED?

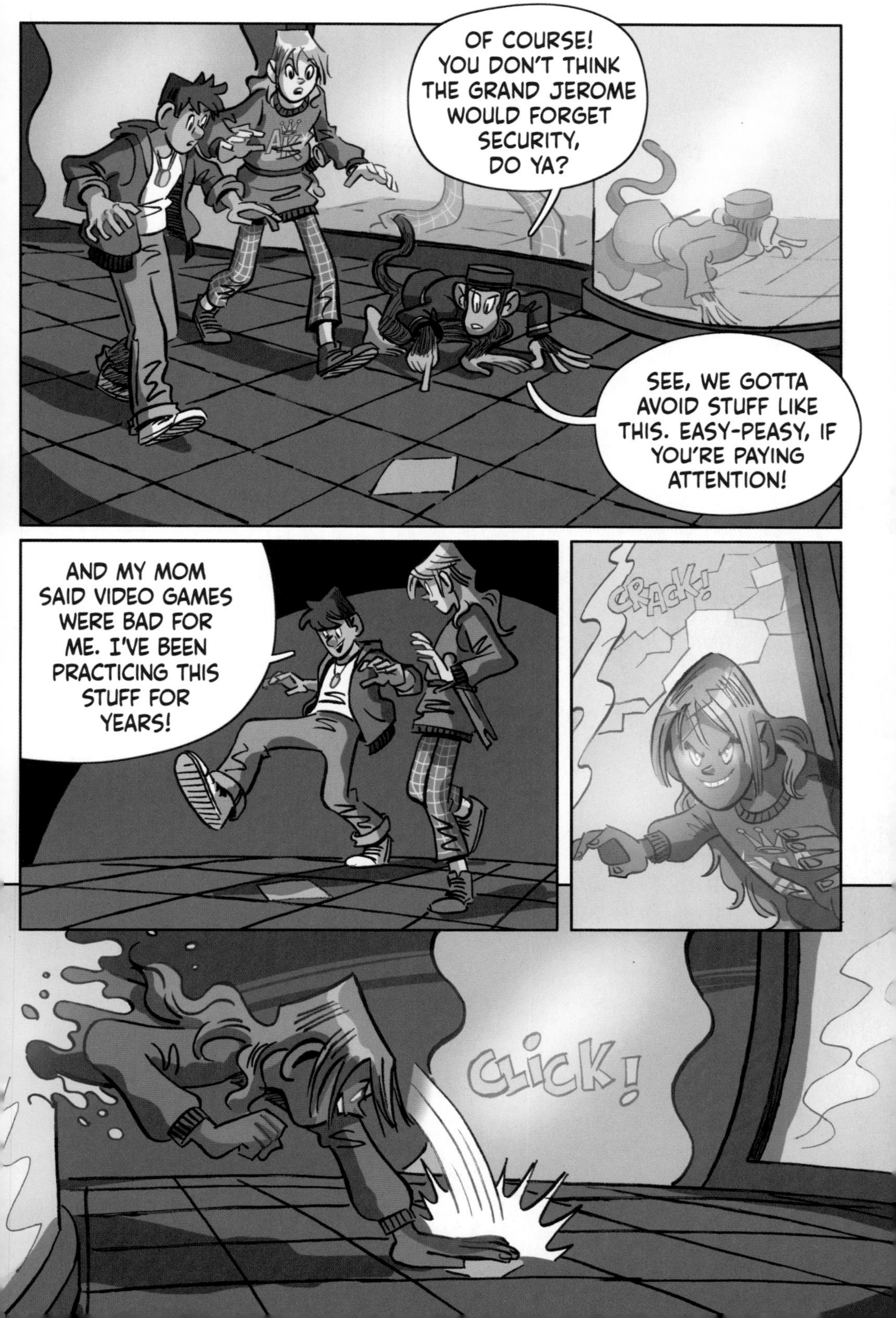
OF COURSE! YOU DON'T THINK THE GRAND JEROME WOULD FORGET SECURITY, DO YA?
SEE, WE GOTTA AVOID STUFF LIKE THIS. EASY-PEASY, IF YOU'RE PAYING ATTENTION!
AND MY MOM SAID VIDEO GAMES WERE BAD FOR ME. I'VE BEEN PRACTICING THIS STUFF FOR YEARS!
CRACK!
CLICK!

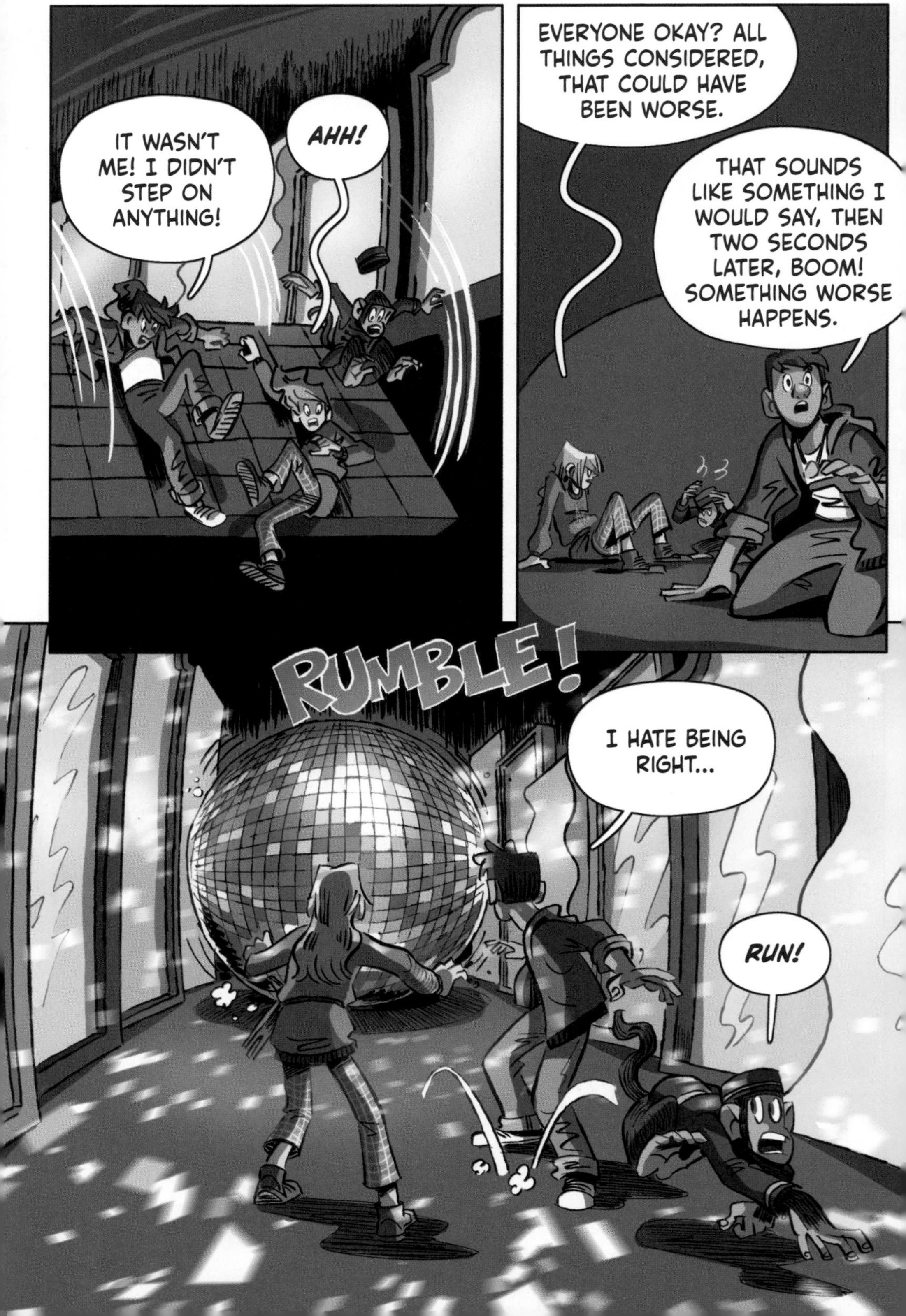
IT WASN'T ME! I DIDN'T STEP ON ANYTHING!
AHH!
EVERYONE OKAY? ALL THINGS CONSIDERED, THAT COULD HAVE BEEN WORSE.
THAT SOUNDS LIKE SOMETHING I WOULD SAY, THEN TWO SECONDS LATER, BOOM! SOMETHING WORSE HAPPENS.
RUMBLE!
I HATE BEING RIGHT...
RUN!

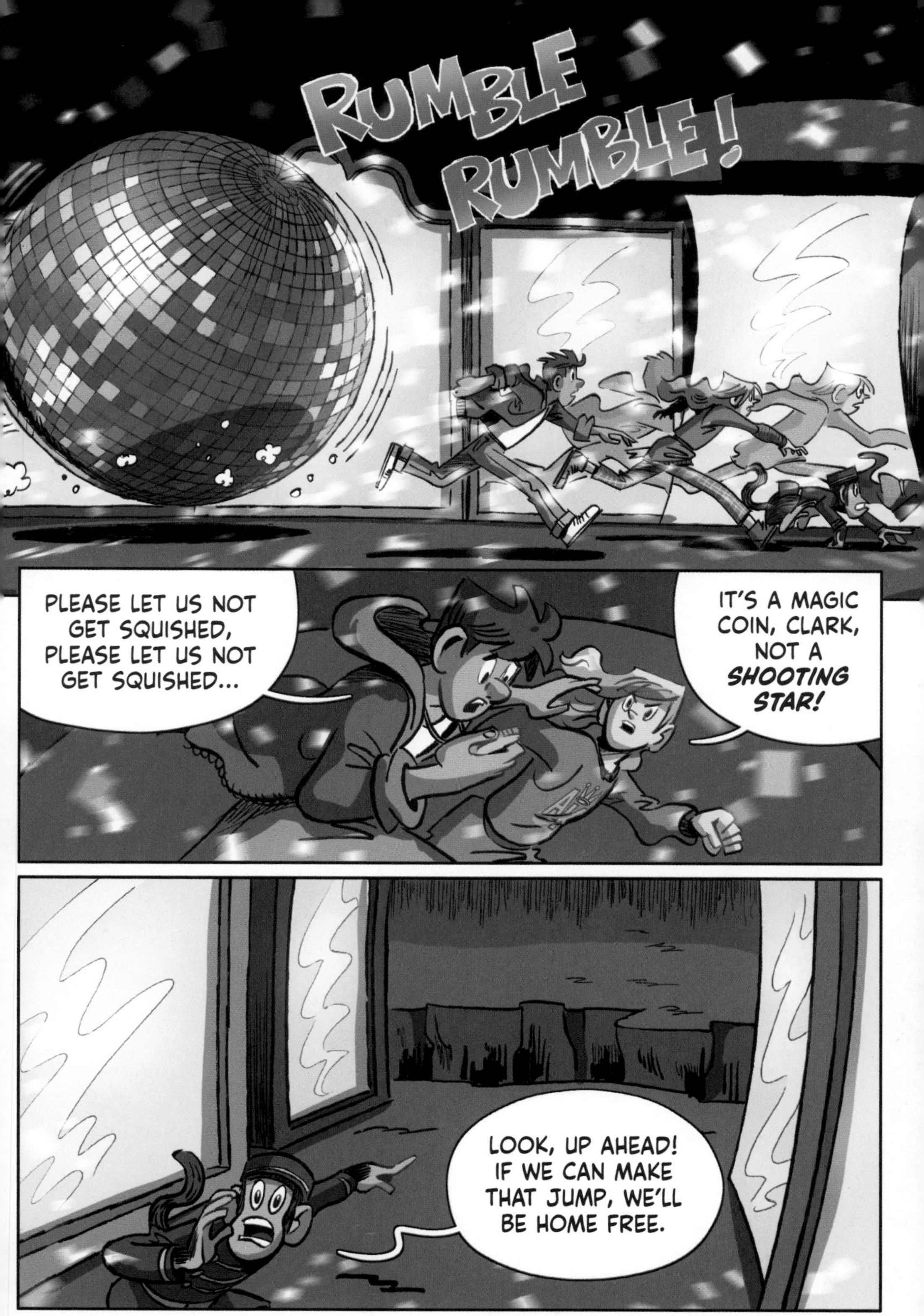

RUMBLE RUMBLE!
PLEASE LET US NOT GET SQUISHED, PLEASE LET US NOT GET SQUISHED...
IT'S A MAGIC COIN, CLARK, NOT A *SHOOTING STAR!*
LOOK, UP AHEAD! IF WE CAN MAKE THAT JUMP, WE'LL BE HOME FREE.

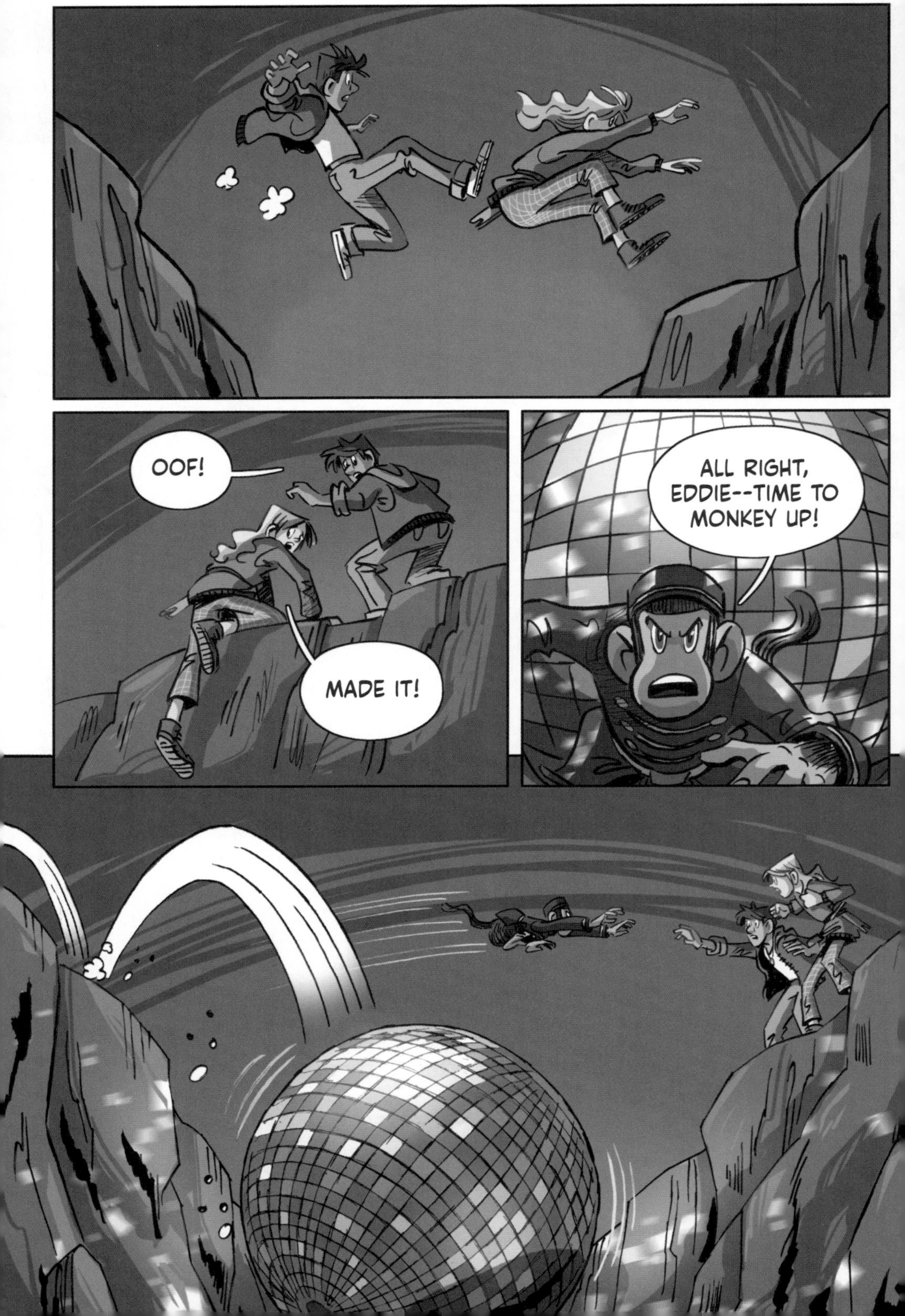
OOF!
MADE IT!
ALL RIGHT, EDDIE--TIME TO MONKEY UP!

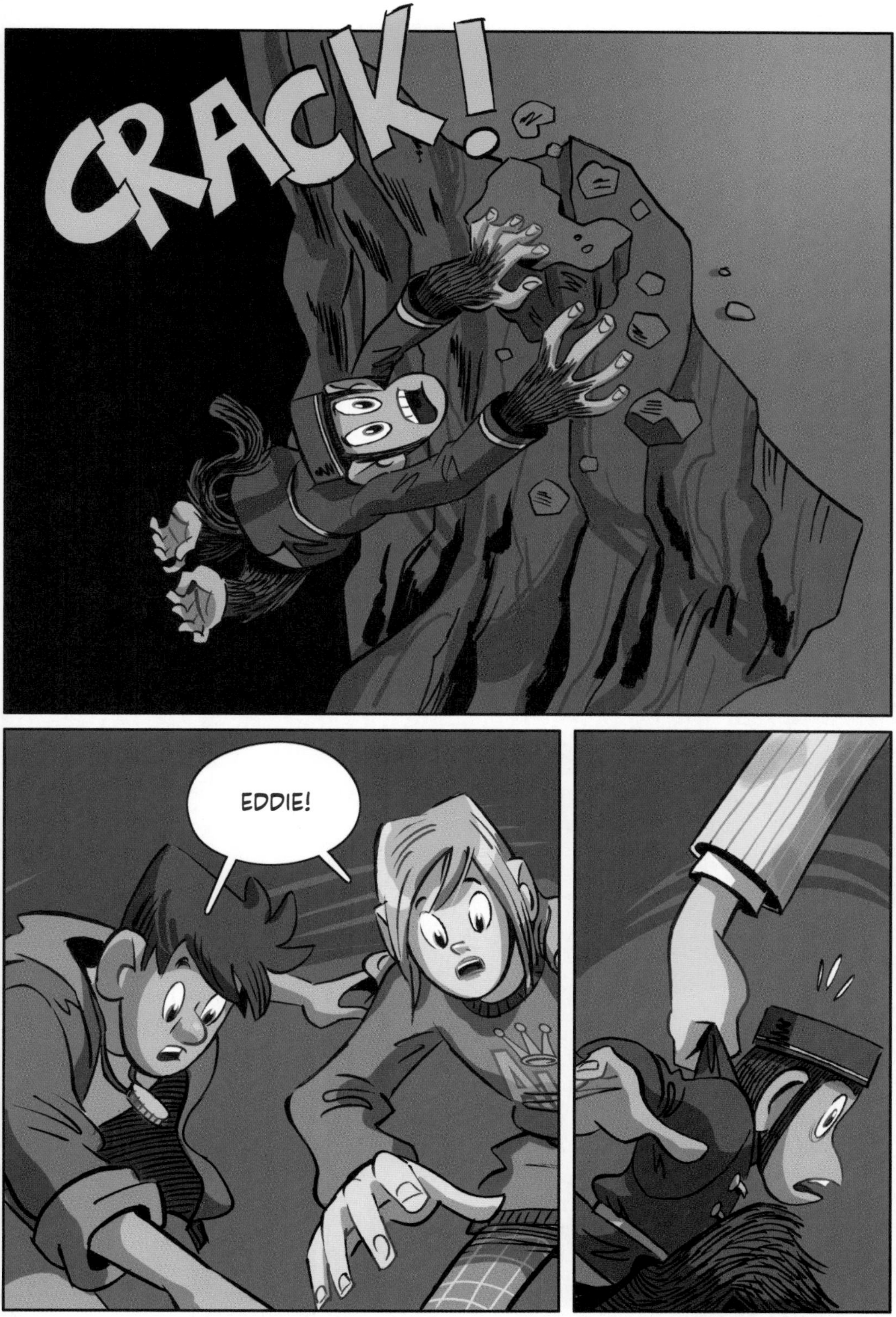
CRACK!
EDDIE!

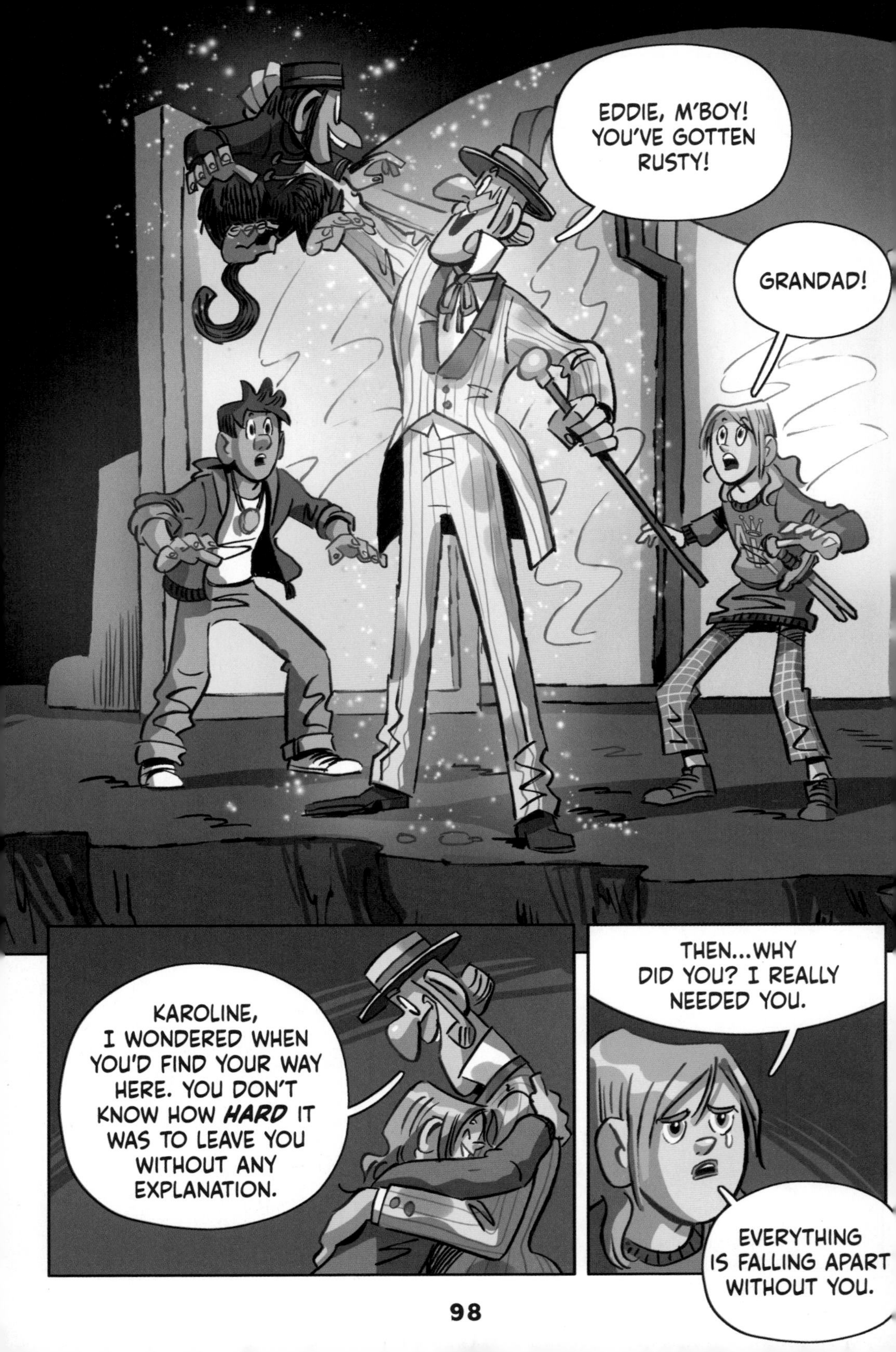

EDDIE, M'BOY! YOU'VE GOTTEN RUSTY!
GRANDAD!
KAROLINE, I WONDERED WHEN YOU'D FIND YOUR WAY HERE. YOU DON'T KNOW HOW ***HARD*** IT WAS TO LEAVE YOU WITHOUT ANY EXPLANATION.
THEN...WHY DID YOU? I REALLY NEEDED YOU.
EVERYTHING IS FALLING APART WITHOUT YOU.

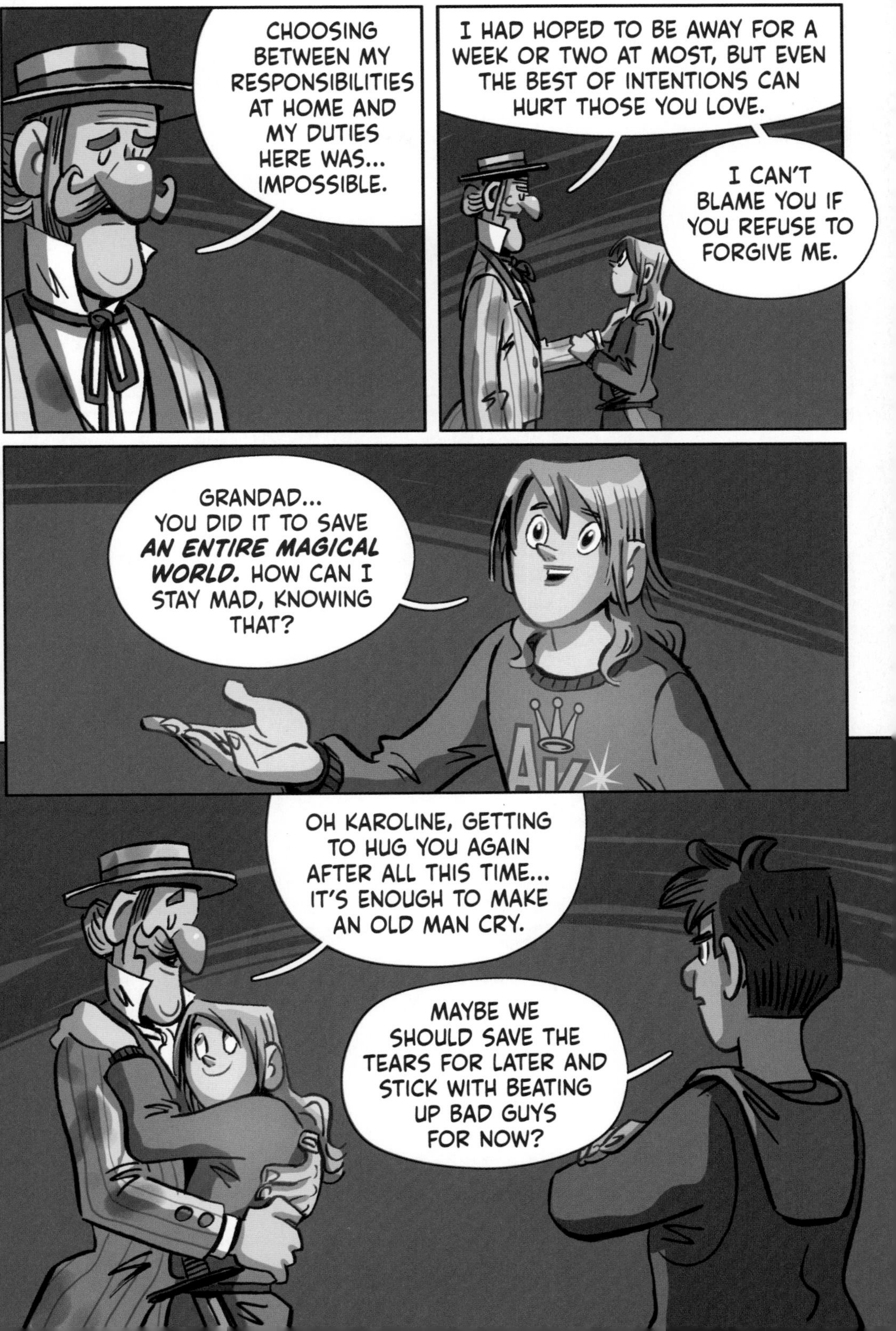
CHOOSING BETWEEN MY RESPONSIBILITIES AT HOME AND MY DUTIES HERE WAS... IMPOSSIBLE.
I HAD HOPED TO BE AWAY FOR A WEEK OR TWO AT MOST, BUT EVEN THE BEST OF INTENTIONS CAN HURT THOSE YOU LOVE.
I CAN'T BLAME YOU IF YOU REFUSE TO FORGIVE ME.
GRANDAD... YOU DID IT TO SAVE ***AN ENTIRE MAGICAL WORLD.*** HOW CAN I STAY MAD, KNOWING THAT?
OH KAROLINE, GETTING TO HUG YOU AGAIN AFTER ALL THIS TIME... IT'S ENOUGH TO MAKE AN OLD MAN CRY.
MAYBE WE SHOULD SAVE THE TEARS FOR LATER AND STICK WITH BEATING UP BAD GUYS FOR NOW?

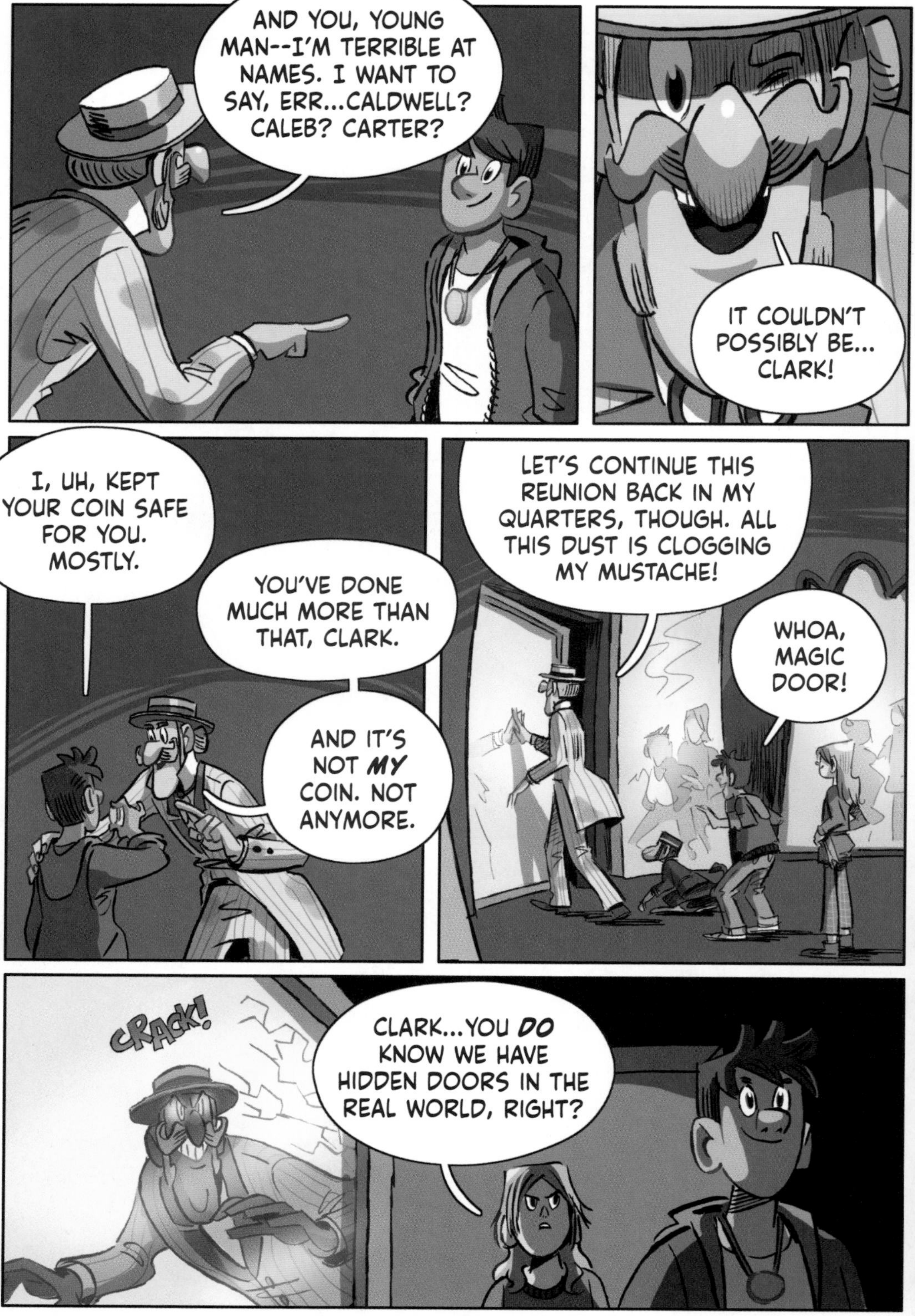
AND YOU, YOUNG MAN--I'M TERRIBLE AT NAMES. I WANT TO SAY, ERR...CALDWELL? CALEB? CARTER?
IT COULDN'T POSSIBLY BE... CLARK!
I, UH, KEPT YOUR COIN SAFE FOR YOU. MOSTLY.
YOU'VE DONE MUCH MORE THAN THAT, CLARK.
AND IT'S NOT *MY* COIN. NOT ANYMORE.
LET'S CONTINUE THIS REUNION BACK IN MY QUARTERS, THOUGH. ALL THIS DUST IS CLOGGING MY MUSTACHE!
WHOA, MAGIC DOOR!
CRACK!
CLARK...YOU ***DO*** KNOW WE HAVE HIDDEN DOORS IN THE REAL WORLD, RIGHT?

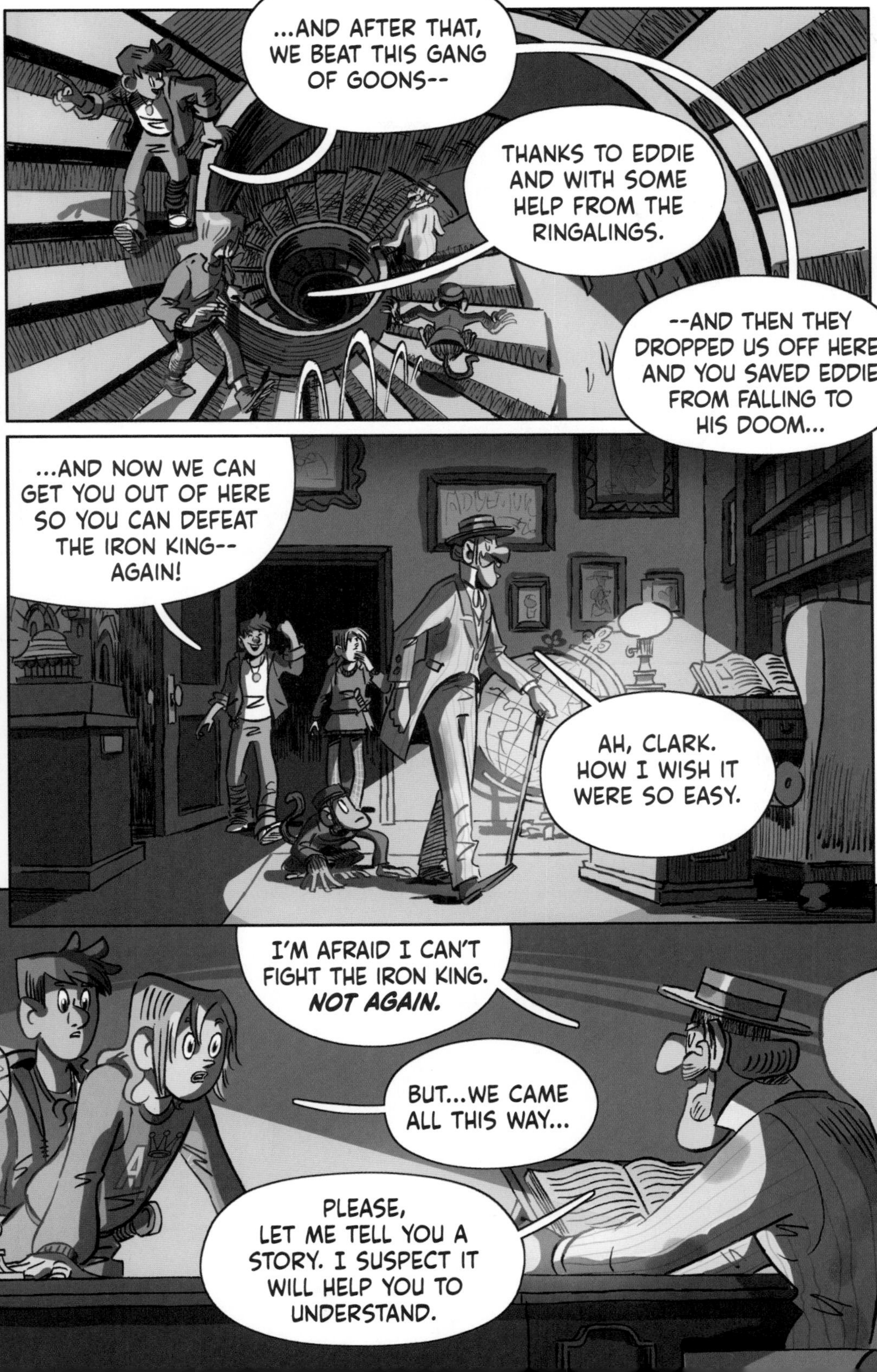
...AND AFTER THAT, WE BEAT THIS GANG OF GOONS--
THANKS TO EDDIE AND WITH SOME HELP FROM THE RINGALINGS.
--AND THEN THEY DROPPED US OFF HERE, AND YOU SAVED EDDIE FROM FALLING TO HIS DOOM...
...AND NOW WE CAN GET YOU OUT OF HERE SO YOU CAN DEFEAT THE IRON KING-- AGAIN!
AH, CLARK. HOW I WISH IT WERE SO EASY.
I'M AFRAID I CAN'T FIGHT THE IRON KING. NOT AGAIN.
BUT...WE CAME ALL THIS WAY...
PLEASE, LET ME TELL YOU A STORY. I SUSPECT IT WILL HELP YOU TO UNDERSTAND.

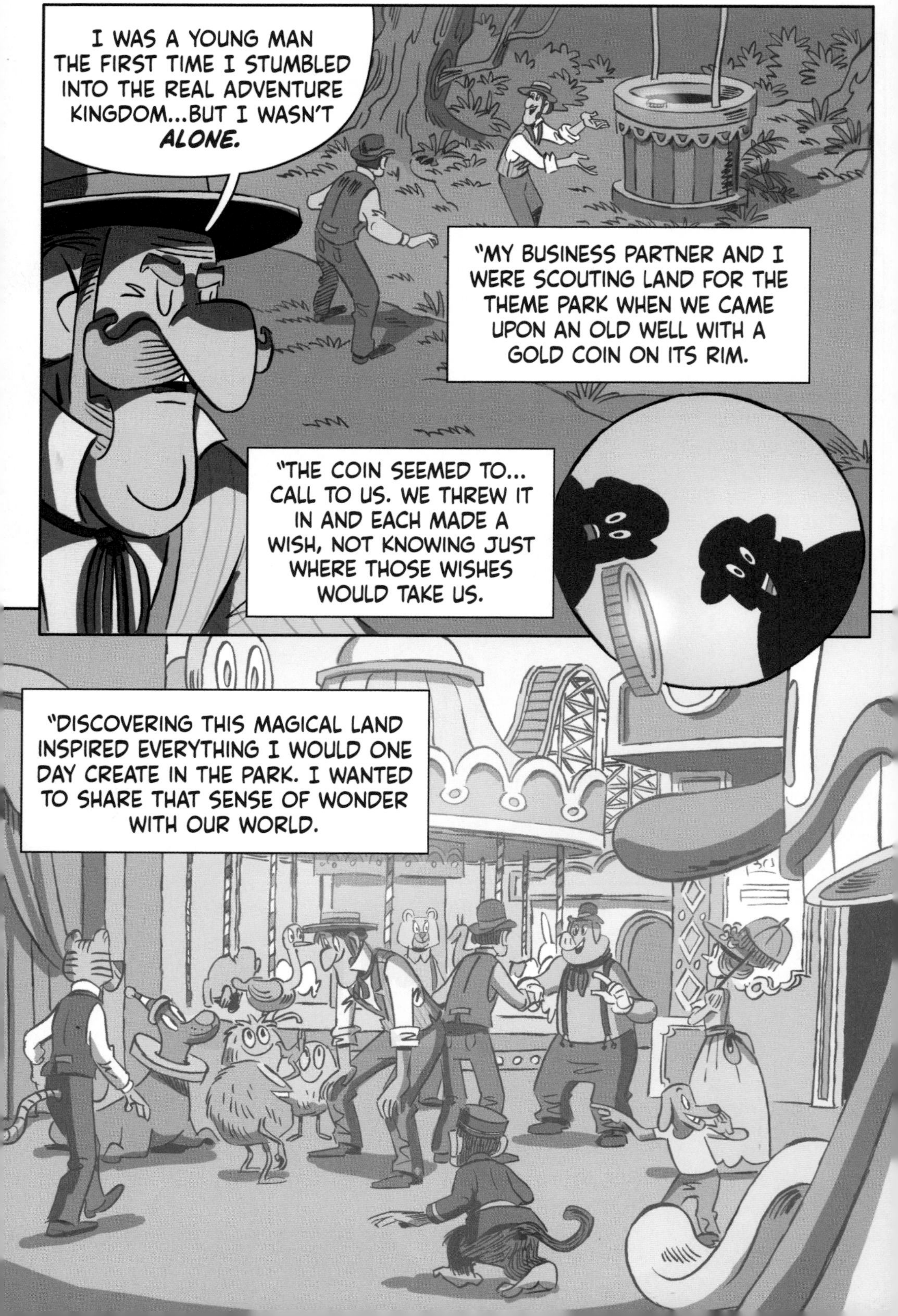

I WAS A YOUNG MAN THE FIRST TIME I STUMBLED INTO THE REAL ADVENTURE KINGDOM...BUT I WASN'T *ALONE.*
"MY BUSINESS PARTNER AND I WERE SCOUTING LAND FOR THE THEME PARK WHEN WE CAME UPON AN OLD WELL WITH A GOLD COIN ON ITS RIM.
"THE COIN SEEMED TO... CALL TO US. WE THREW IT IN AND EACH MADE A WISH, NOT KNOWING JUST WHERE THOSE WISHES WOULD TAKE US.
"DISCOVERING THIS MAGICAL LAND INSPIRED EVERYTHING I WOULD ONE DAY CREATE IN THE PARK. I WANTED TO SHARE THAT SENSE OF WONDER WITH OUR WORLD.

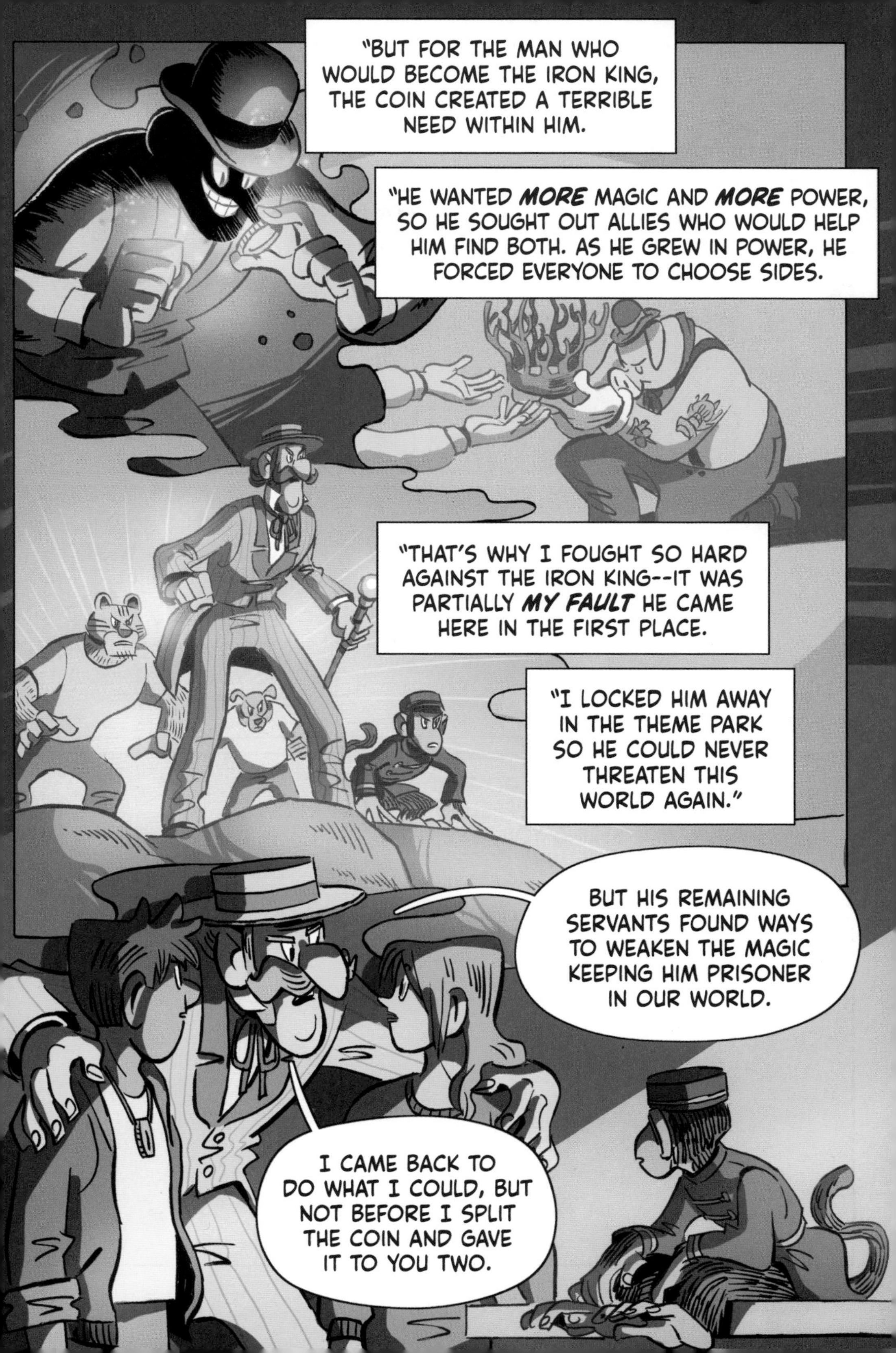
"BUT FOR THE MAN WHO WOULD BECOME THE IRON KING, THE COIN CREATED A TERRIBLE NEED WITHIN HIM.
"HE WANTED *MORE* MAGIC AND *MORE* POWER, SO HE SOUGHT OUT ALLIES WHO WOULD HELP HIM FIND BOTH. AS HE GREW IN POWER, HE FORCED EVERYONE TO CHOOSE SIDES.
"THAT'S WHY I FOUGHT SO HARD AGAINST THE IRON KING--IT WAS PARTIALLY *MY FAULT* HE CAME HERE IN THE FIRST PLACE.
"I LOCKED HIM AWAY IN THE THEME PARK SO HE COULD NEVER THREATEN THIS WORLD AGAIN."
BUT HIS REMAINING SERVANTS FOUND WAYS TO WEAKEN THE MAGIC KEEPING HIM PRISONER IN OUR WORLD.
I CAME BACK TO DO WHAT I COULD, BUT NOT BEFORE I SPLIT THE COIN AND GAVE IT TO YOU TWO.

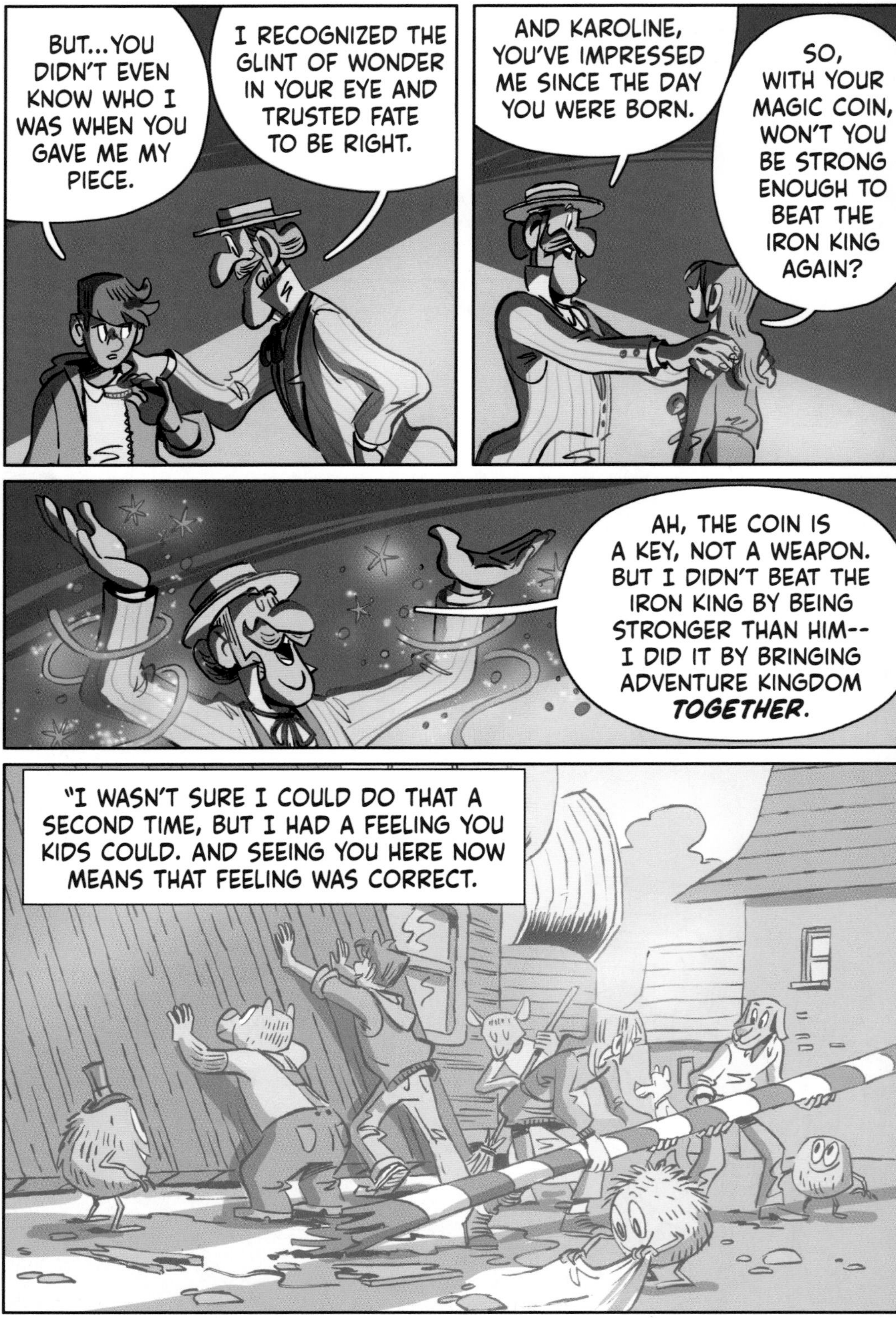
BUT...YOU DIDN'T EVEN KNOW WHO I WAS WHEN YOU GAVE ME MY PIECE.
I RECOGNIZED THE GLINT OF WONDER IN YOUR EYE AND TRUSTED FATE TO BE RIGHT.
AND KAROLINE, YOU'VE IMPRESSED ME SINCE THE DAY YOU WERE BORN.
SO, WITH YOUR MAGIC COIN, WON'T YOU BE STRONG ENOUGH TO BEAT THE IRON KING AGAIN?
AH, THE COIN IS A KEY, NOT A WEAPON. BUT I DIDN'T BEAT THE IRON KING BY BEING STRONGER THAN HIM-- I DID IT BY BRINGING ADVENTURE KINGDOM ***TOGETHER***.
"I WASN'T SURE I COULD DO THAT A SECOND TIME, BUT I HAD A FEELING YOU KIDS COULD. AND SEEING YOU HERE NOW MEANS THAT FEELING WAS CORRECT.

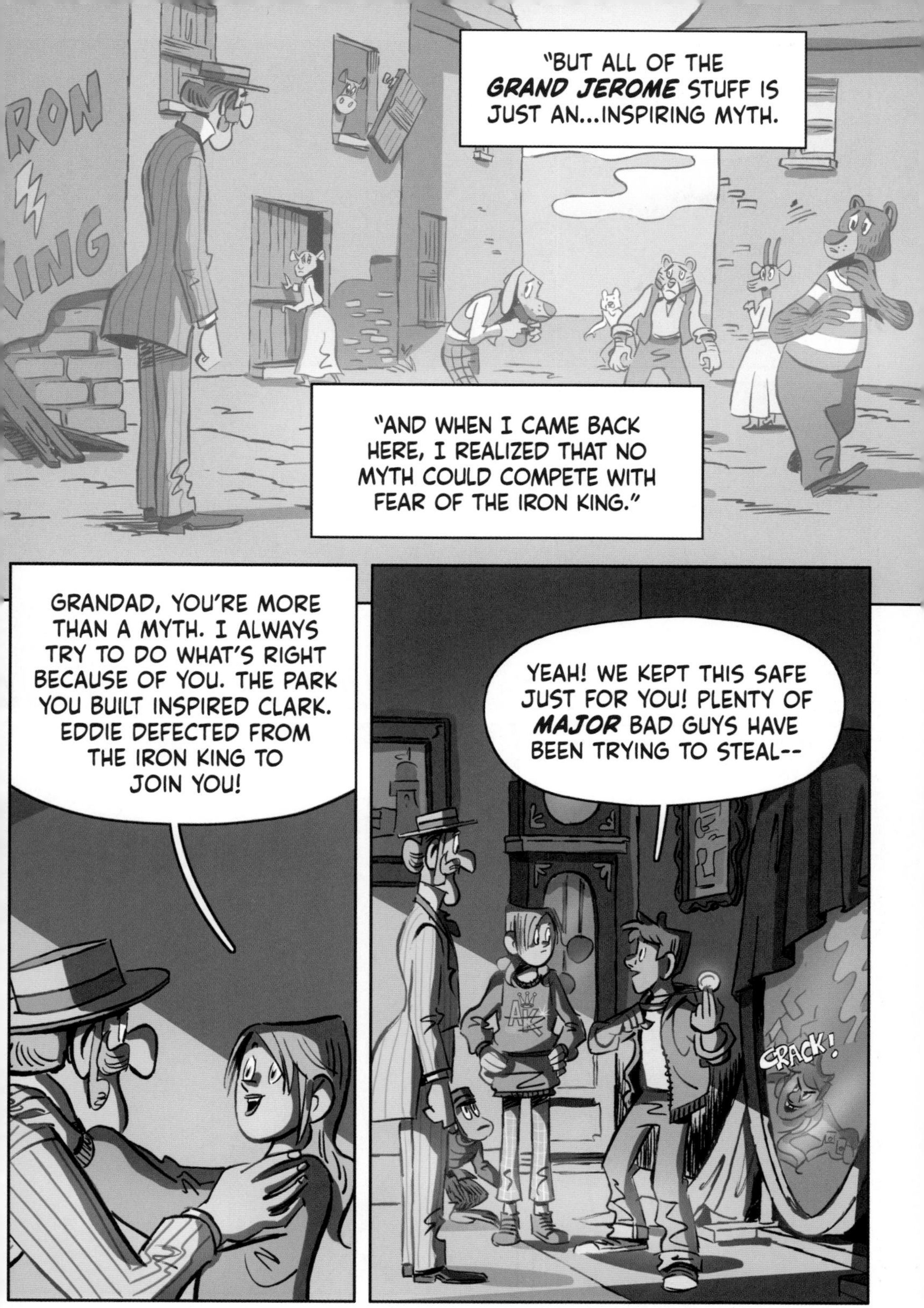
"BUT ALL OF THE GRAND JEROME STUFF IS JUST AN...INSPIRING MYTH.
"AND WHEN I CAME BACK HERE, I REALIZED THAT NO MYTH COULD COMPETE WITH FEAR OF THE IRON KING."
GRANDAD, YOU'RE MORE THAN A MYTH. I ALWAYS TRY TO DO WHAT'S RIGHT BECAUSE OF YOU. THE PARK YOU BUILT INSPIRED CLARK. EDDIE DEFECTED FROM THE IRON KING TO JOIN YOU!
YEAH! WE KEPT THIS SAFE JUST FOR YOU! PLENTY OF MAJOR BAD GUYS HAVE BEEN TRYING TO STEAL--
CRACK!

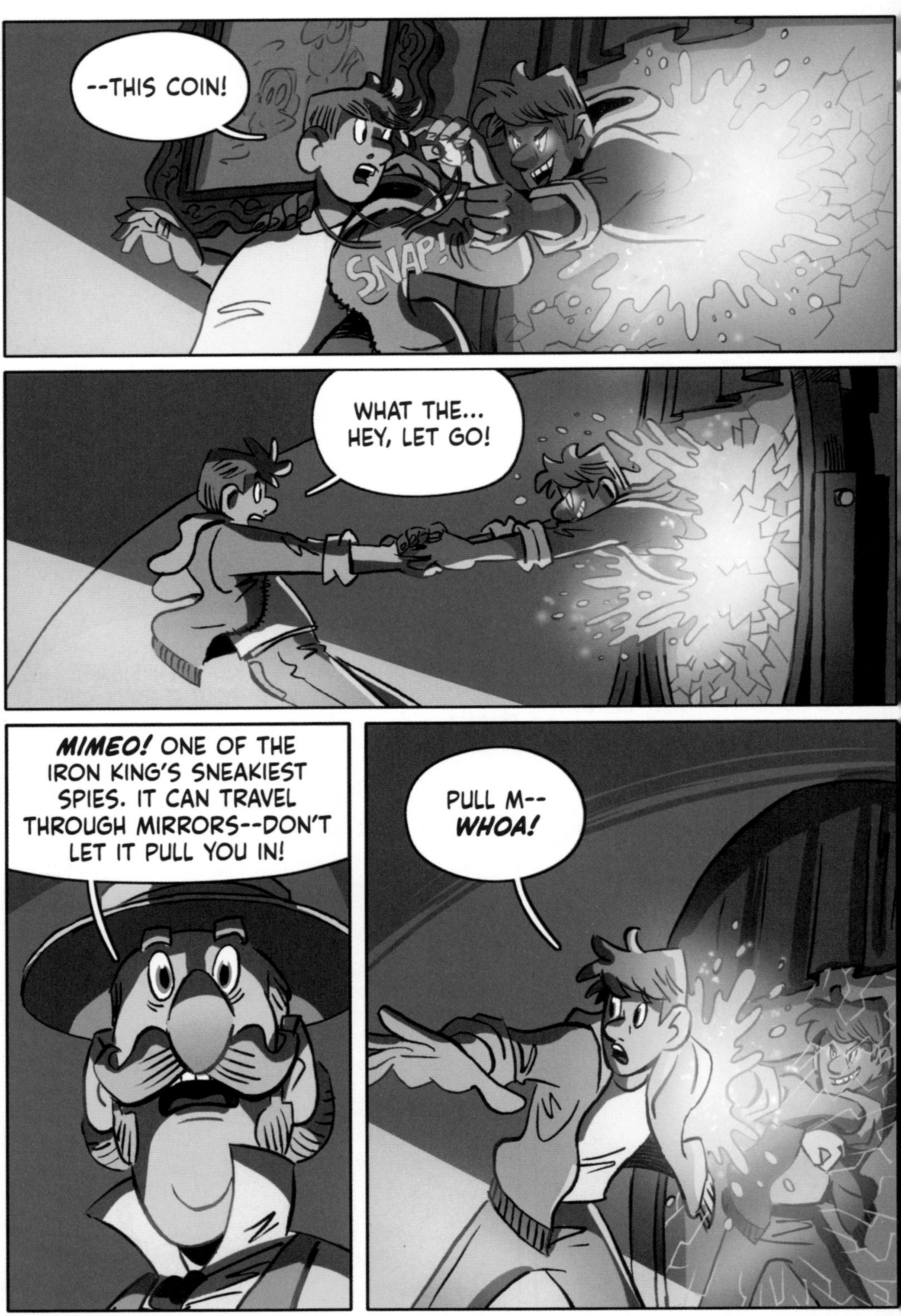
--THIS COIN!
SNAP!
WHAT THE... HEY, LET GO!
MIMEO! ONE OF THE IRON KING'S SNEAKIEST SPIES. IT CAN TRAVEL THROUGH MIRRORS--DON'T LET IT PULL YOU IN!
PULL M-- *WHOA!*

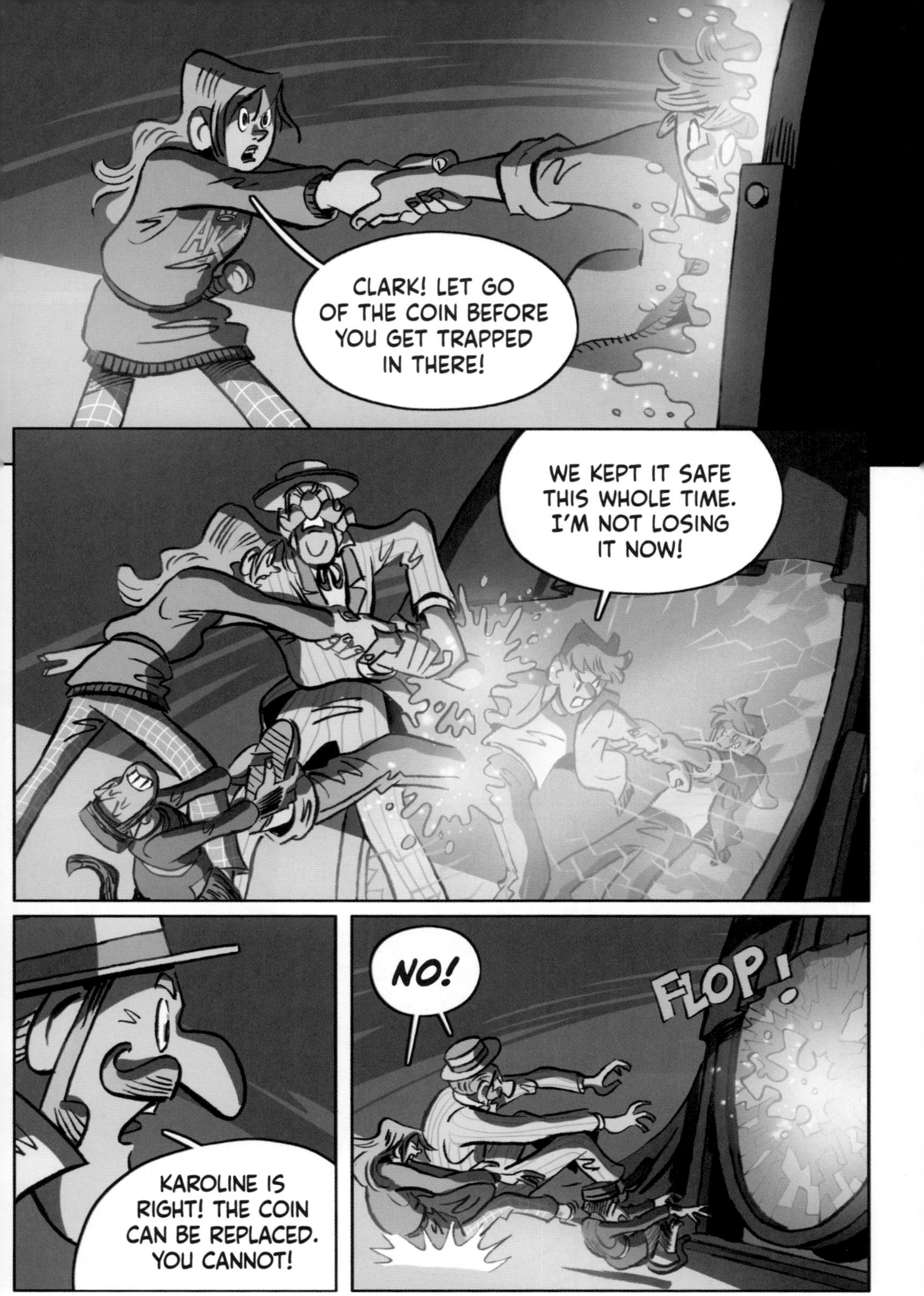
CLARK! LET GO OF THE COIN BEFORE YOU GET TRAPPED IN THERE!
WE KEPT IT SAFE THIS WHOLE TIME. I'M NOT LOSING IT NOW!
KAROLINE IS RIGHT! THE COIN CAN BE REPLACED. YOU CANNOT!
NO!
FLOP!

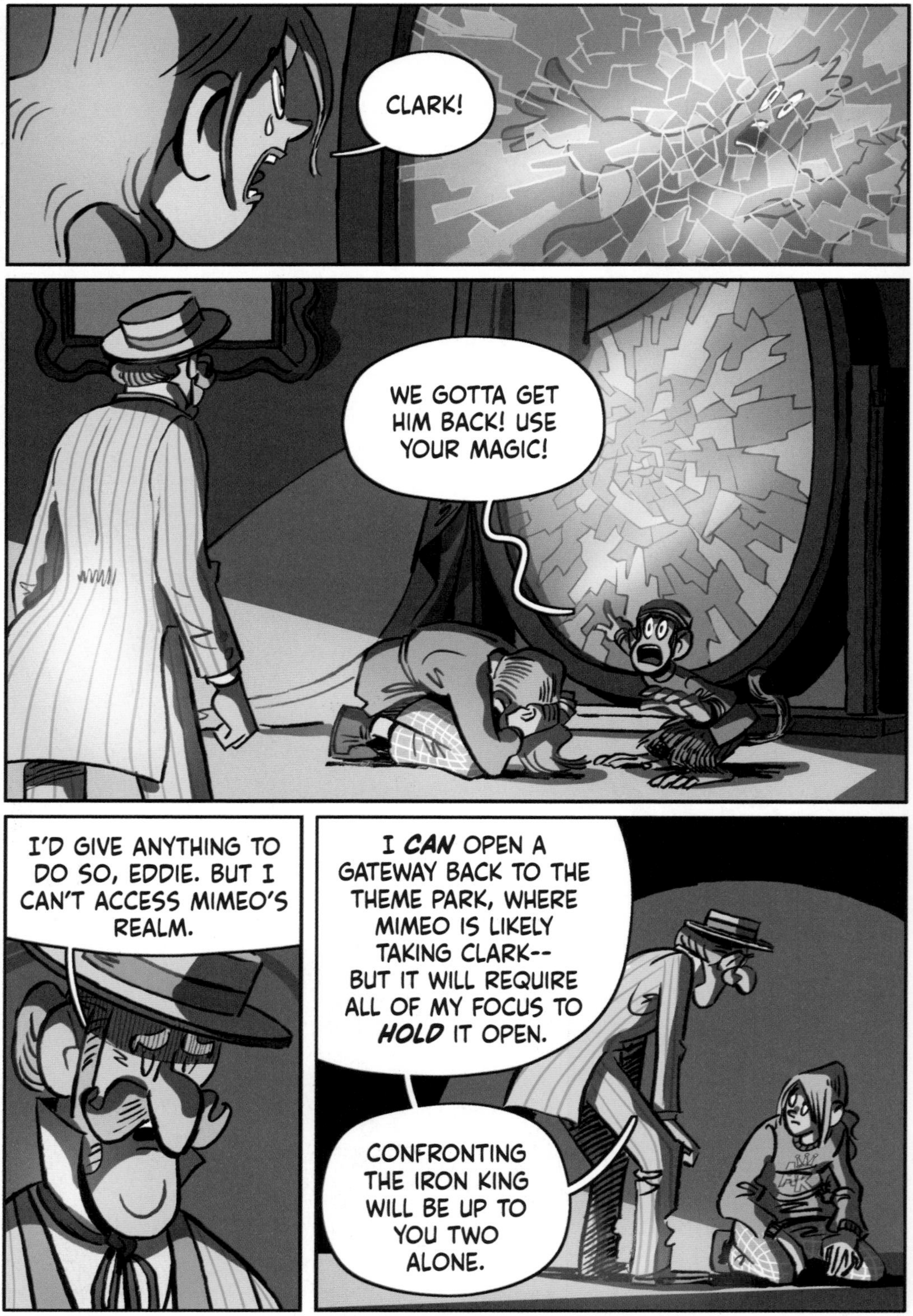
CLARK!
WE GOTTA GET HIM BACK! USE YOUR MAGIC!
I'D GIVE ANYTHING TO DO SO, EDDIE. BUT I CAN'T ACCESS MIMEO'S REALM.
I *CAN* OPEN A GATEWAY BACK TO THE THEME PARK, WHERE MIMEO IS LIKELY TAKING CLARK-- BUT IT WILL REQUIRE ALL OF MY FOCUS TO *HOLD* IT OPEN.
CONFRONTING THE IRON KING WILL BE UP TO YOU TWO ALONE.

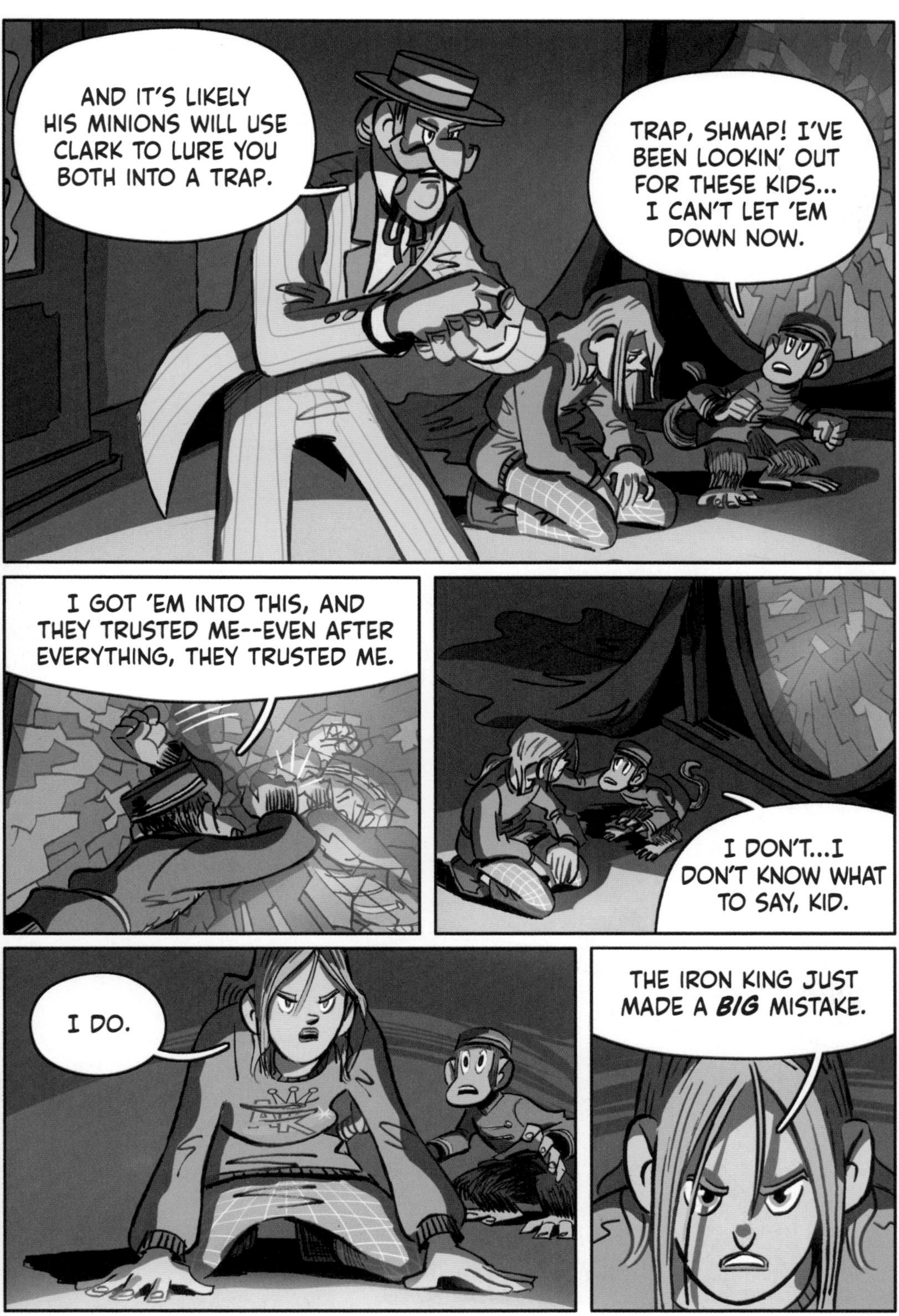
AND IT'S LIKELY HIS MINIONS WILL USE CLARK TO LURE YOU BOTH INTO A TRAP.
TRAP, SHMAP! I'VE BEEN LOOKIN' OUT FOR THESE KIDS... I CAN'T LET 'EM DOWN NOW.
I GOT 'EM INTO THIS, AND THEY TRUSTED ME--EVEN AFTER EVERYTHING, THEY TRUSTED ME.
I DON'T...I DON'T KNOW WHAT TO SAY, KID.
I DO.
THE IRON KING JUST MADE A *BIG* MISTAKE.

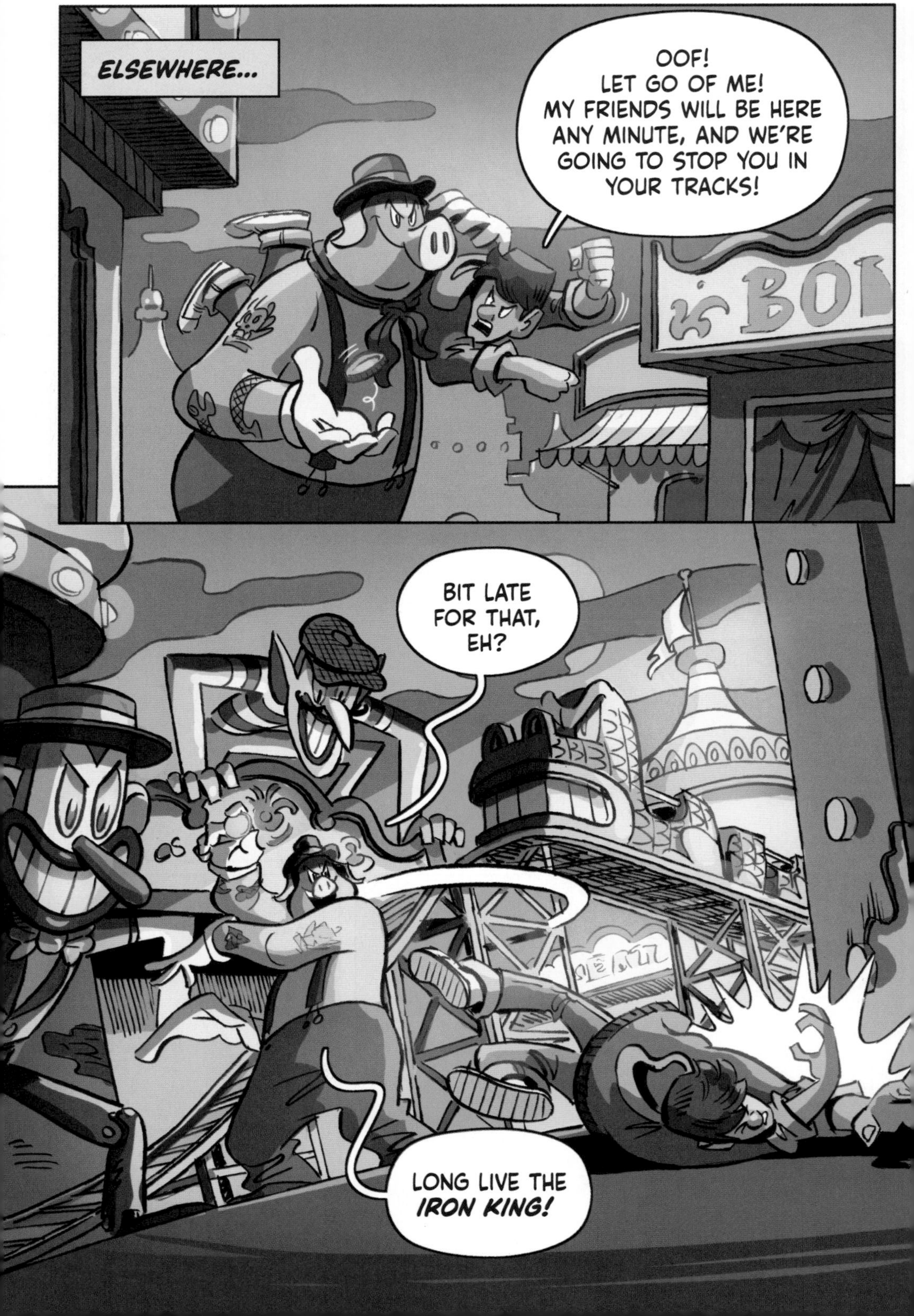
ELSEWHERE...
OOF! LET GO OF ME! MY FRIENDS WILL BE HERE ANY MINUTE, AND WE'RE GOING TO STOP YOU IN YOUR TRACKS!
BIT LATE FOR THAT, EH?
LONG LIVE THE *IRON KING!*

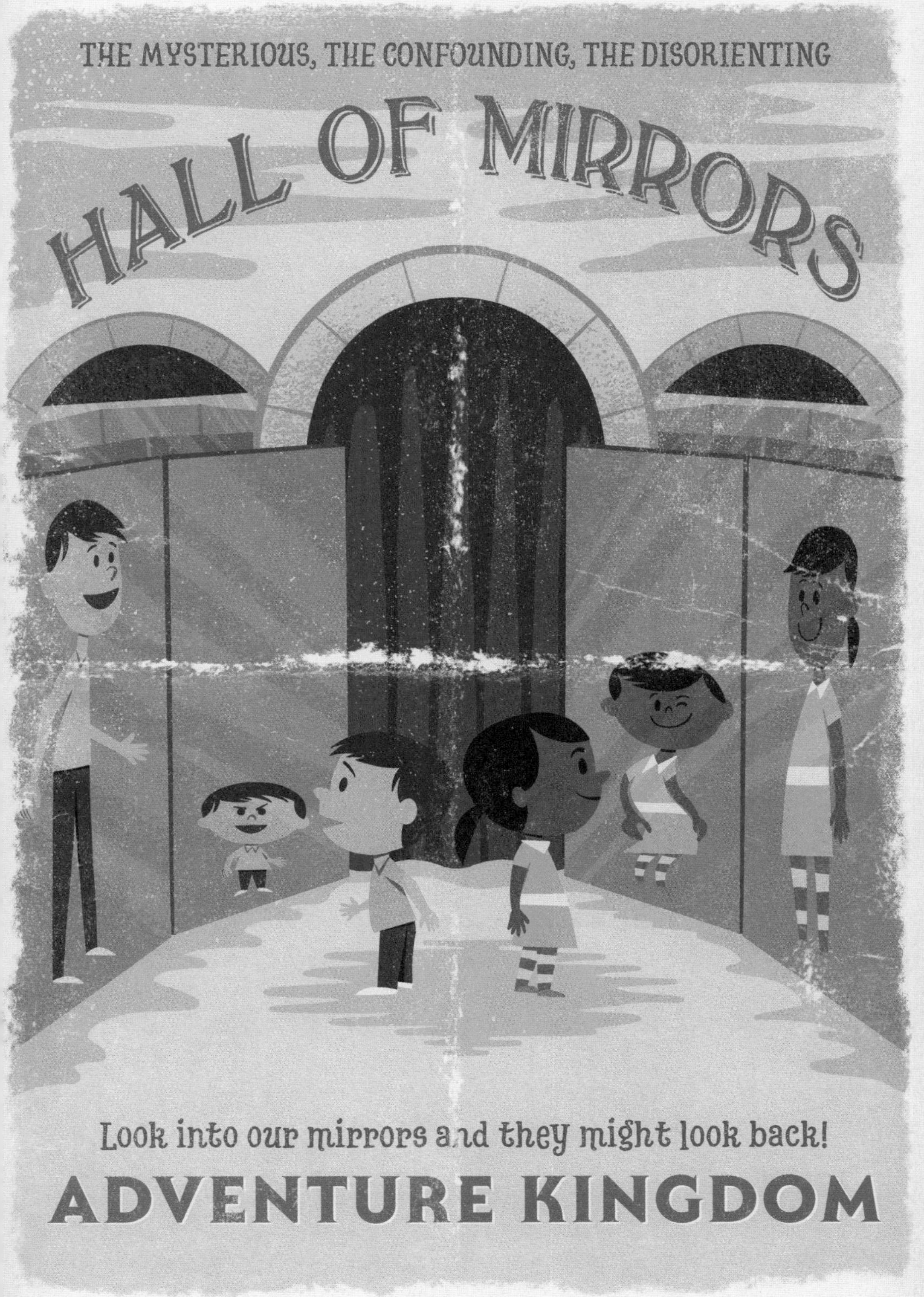
THE MYSTERIOUS, THE CONFOUNDING, THE DISORIENTING
HALL OF MIRRORS
Look into our mirrors and they might look back!
ADVENTURE KINGDOM

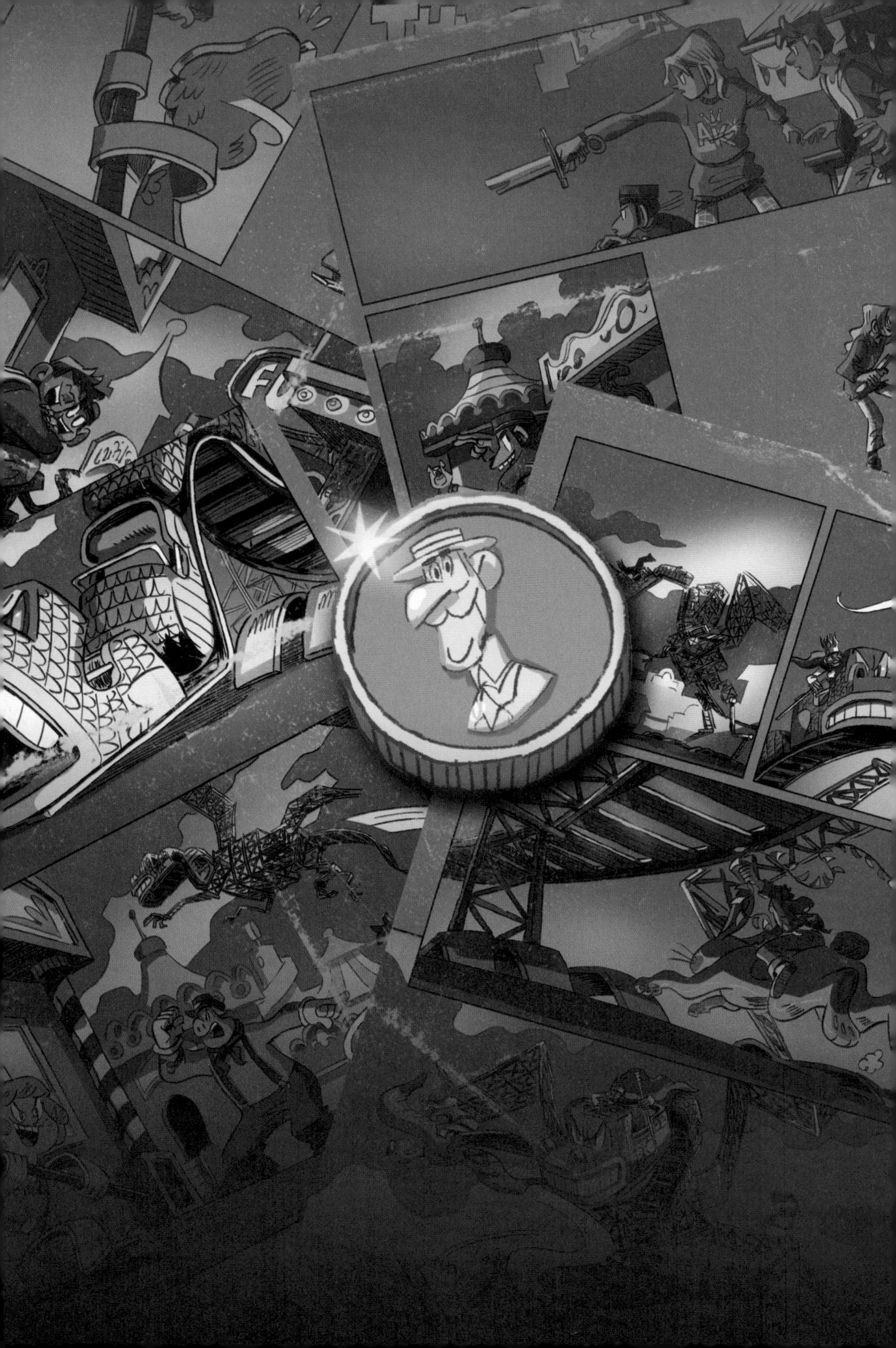

CHAPTER 5
THE GRAND FINALE

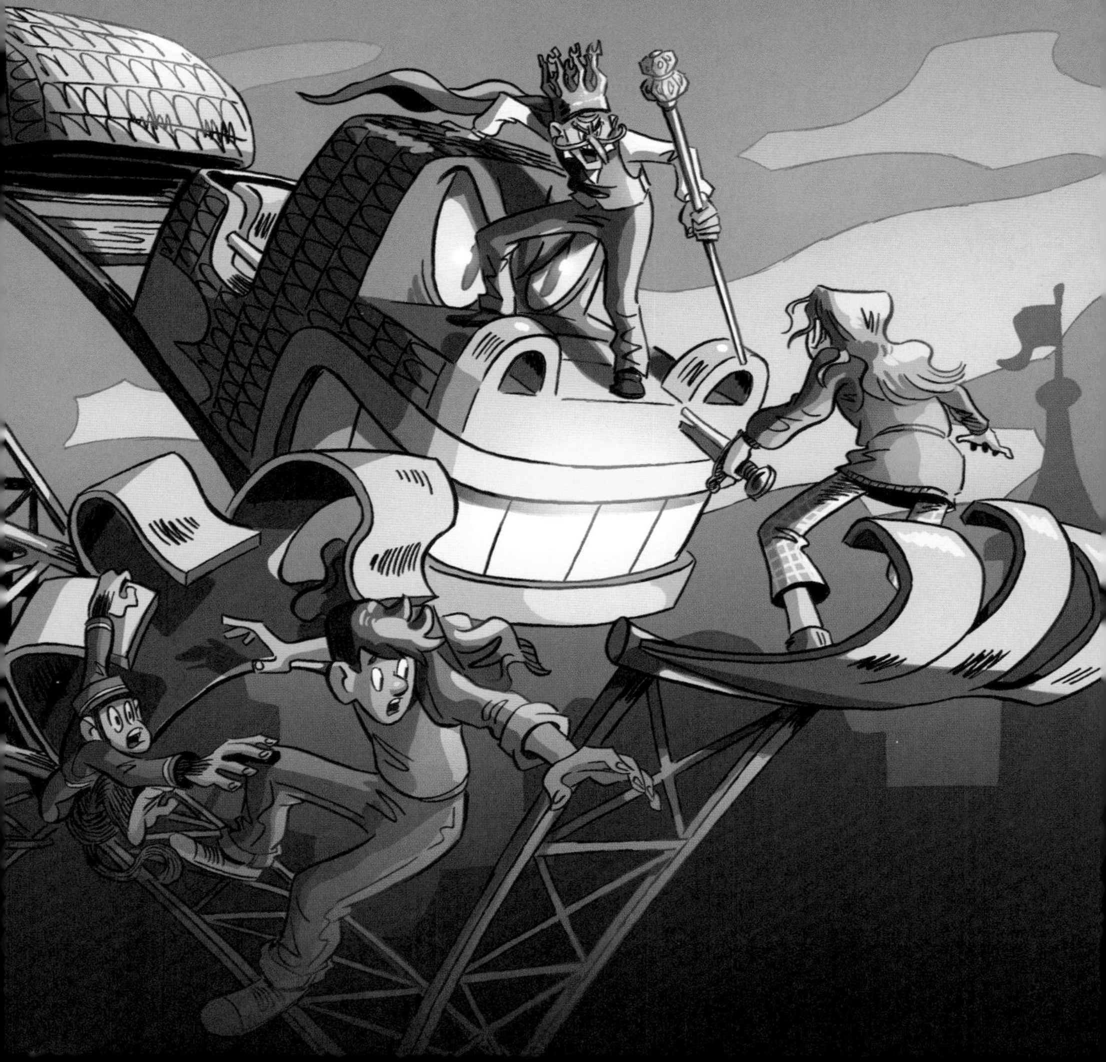

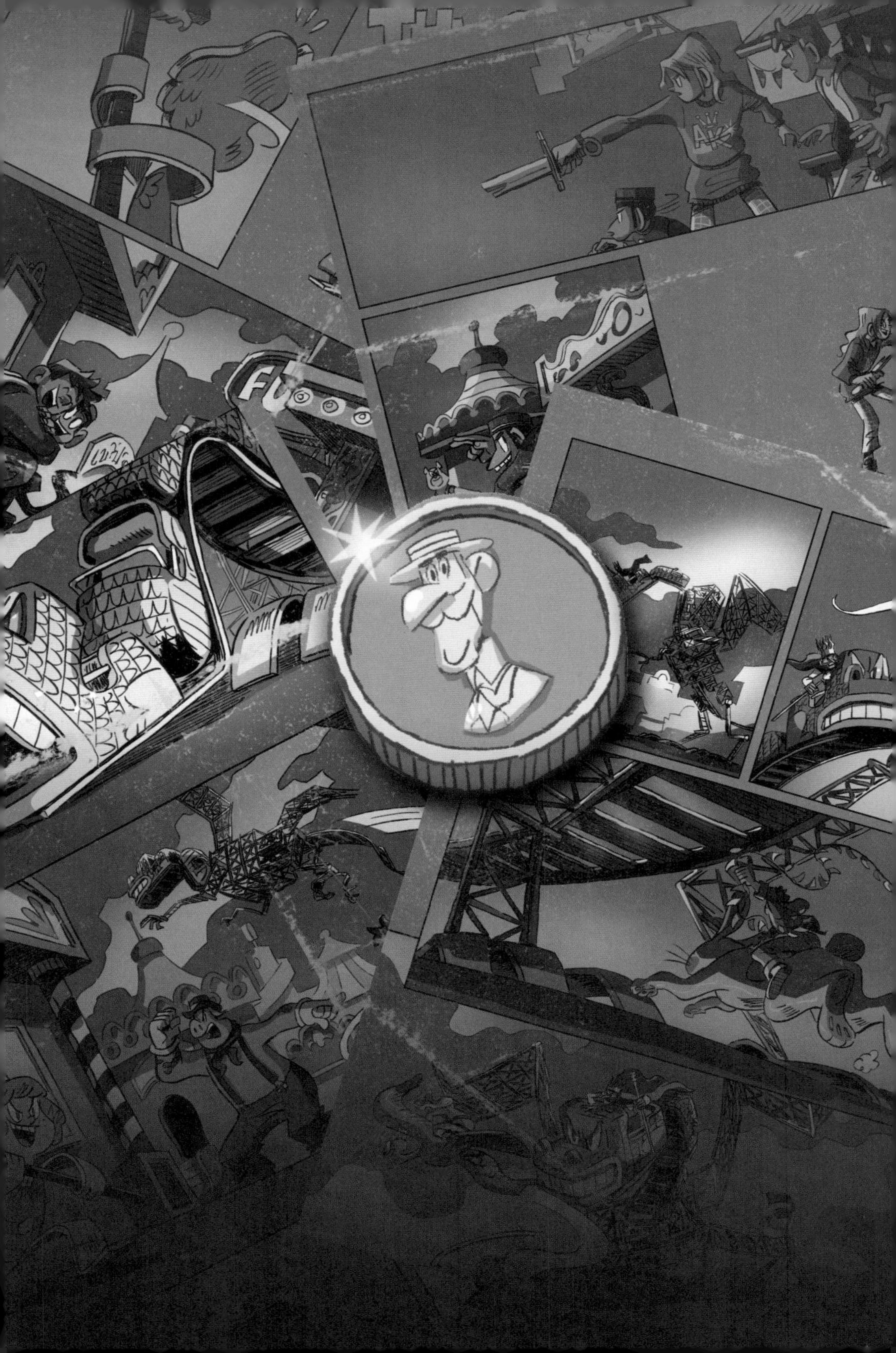

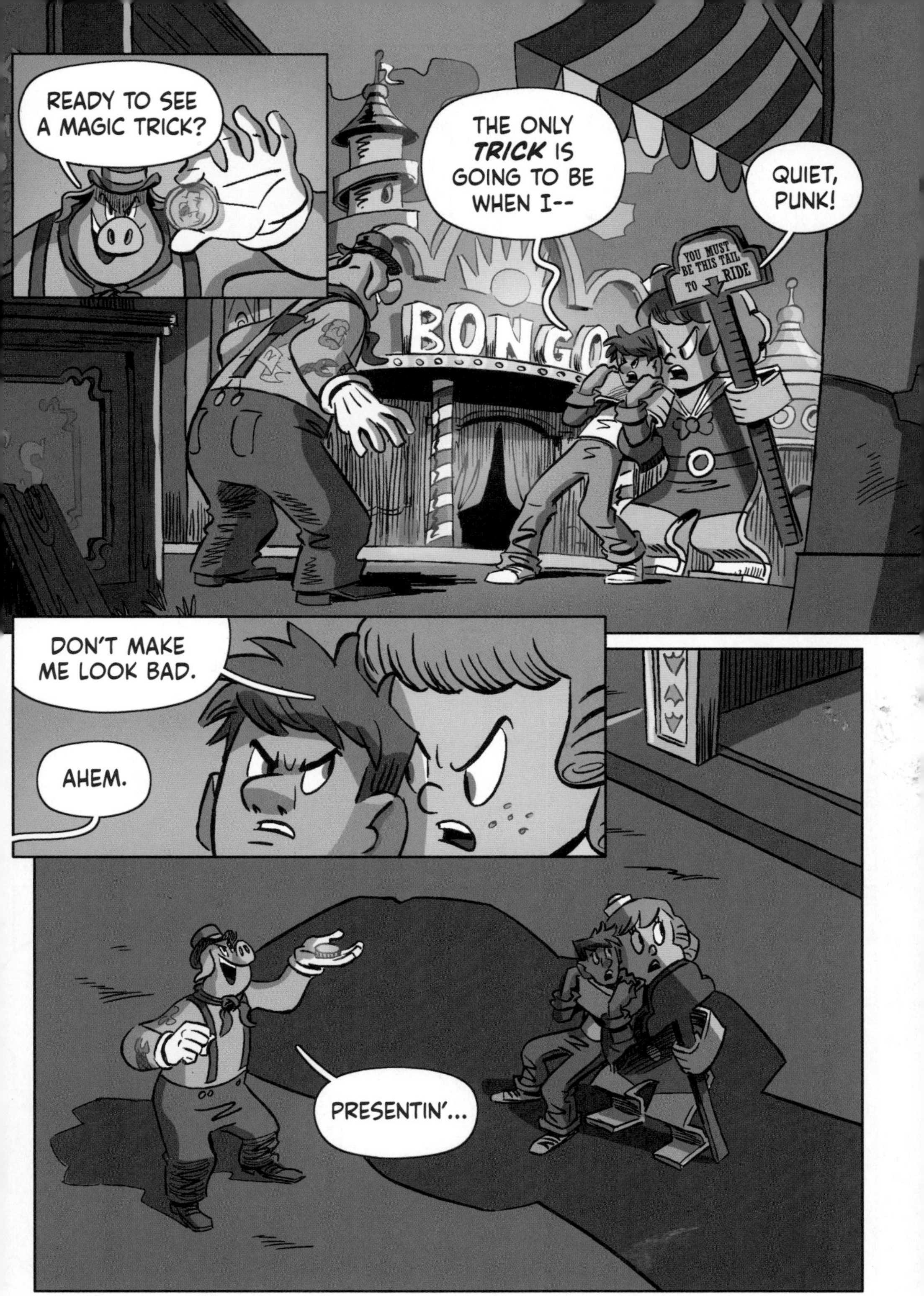
READY TO SEE A MAGIC TRICK?
THE ONLY TRICK IS GOING TO BE WHEN I--
QUIET, PUNK!
YOU MUST BE THIS TAIL TO RIDE
BONGO
DON'T MAKE ME LOOK BAD.
AHEM.
PRESENTIN'...

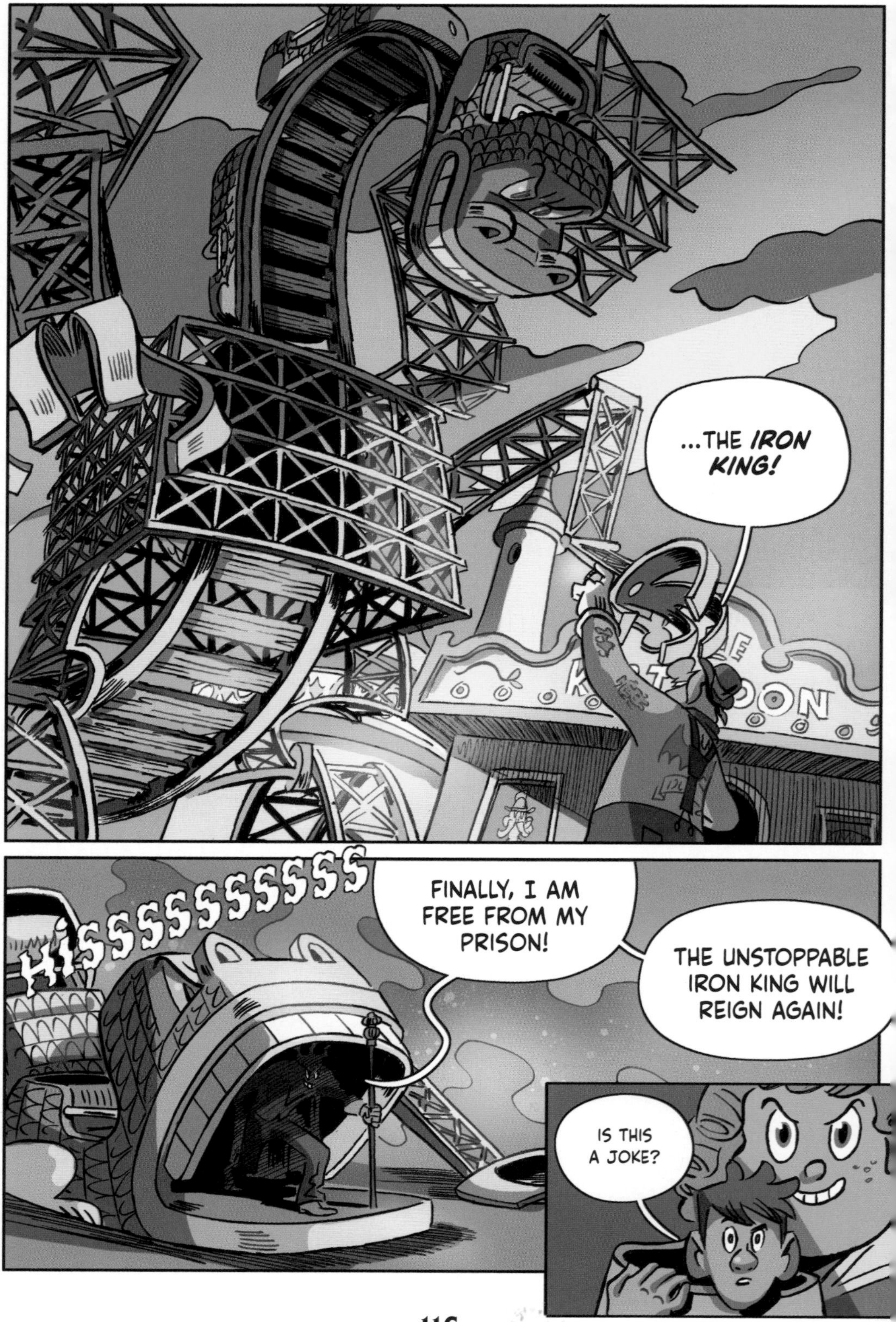
...THE IRON KING!
HISSSSSSSSSSS
FINALLY, I AM FREE FROM MY PRISON!
THE UNSTOPPABLE IRON KING WILL REIGN AGAIN!
IS THIS A JOKE?

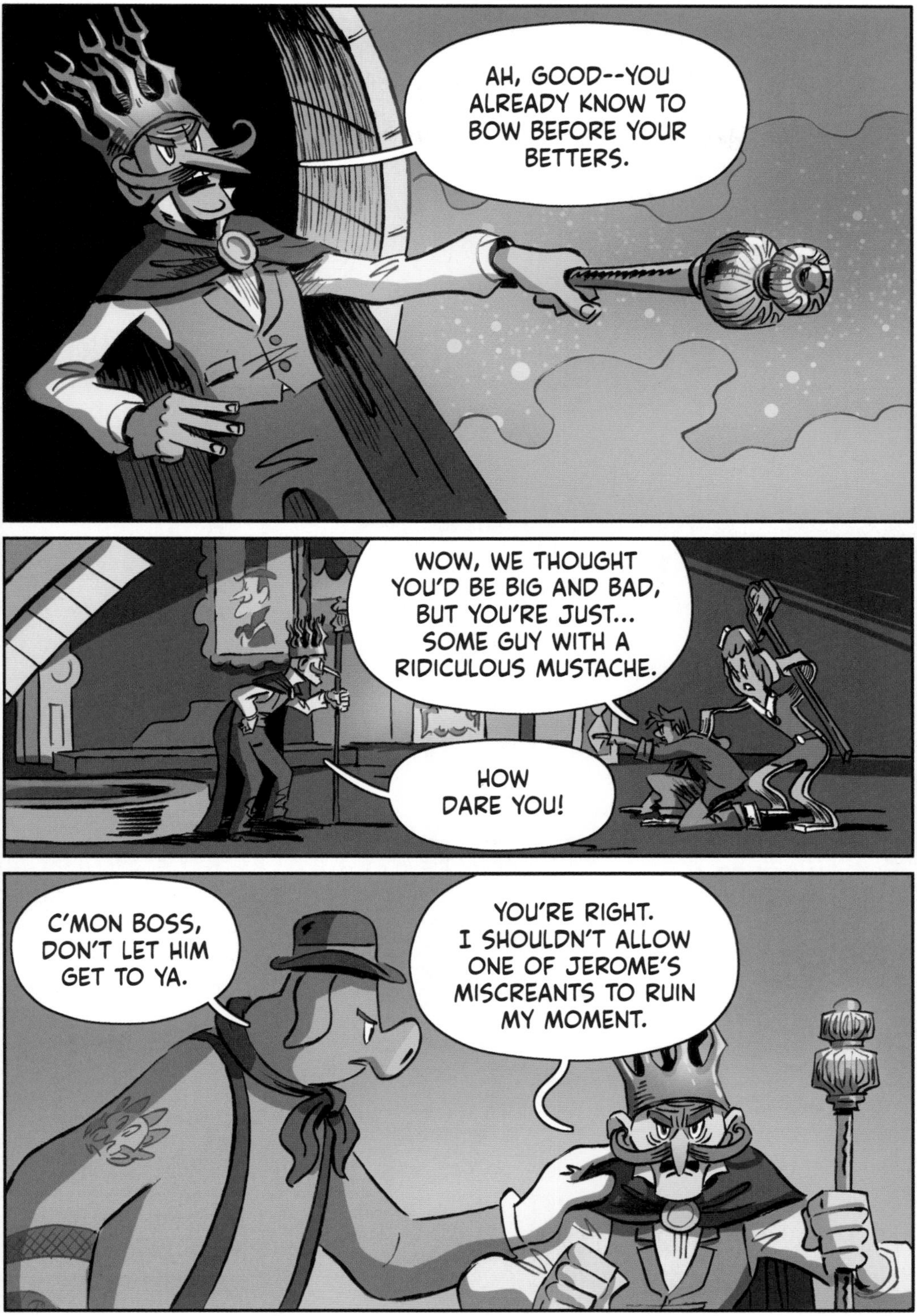
AH, GOOD--YOU ALREADY KNOW TO BOW BEFORE YOUR BETTERS.
WOW, WE THOUGHT YOU'D BE BIG AND BAD, BUT YOU'RE JUST... SOME GUY WITH A RIDICULOUS MUSTACHE.
HOW DARE YOU!
C'MON BOSS, DON'T LET HIM GET TO YA.
YOU'RE RIGHT. I SHOULDN'T ALLOW ONE OF JEROME'S MISCREANTS TO RUIN MY MOMENT.

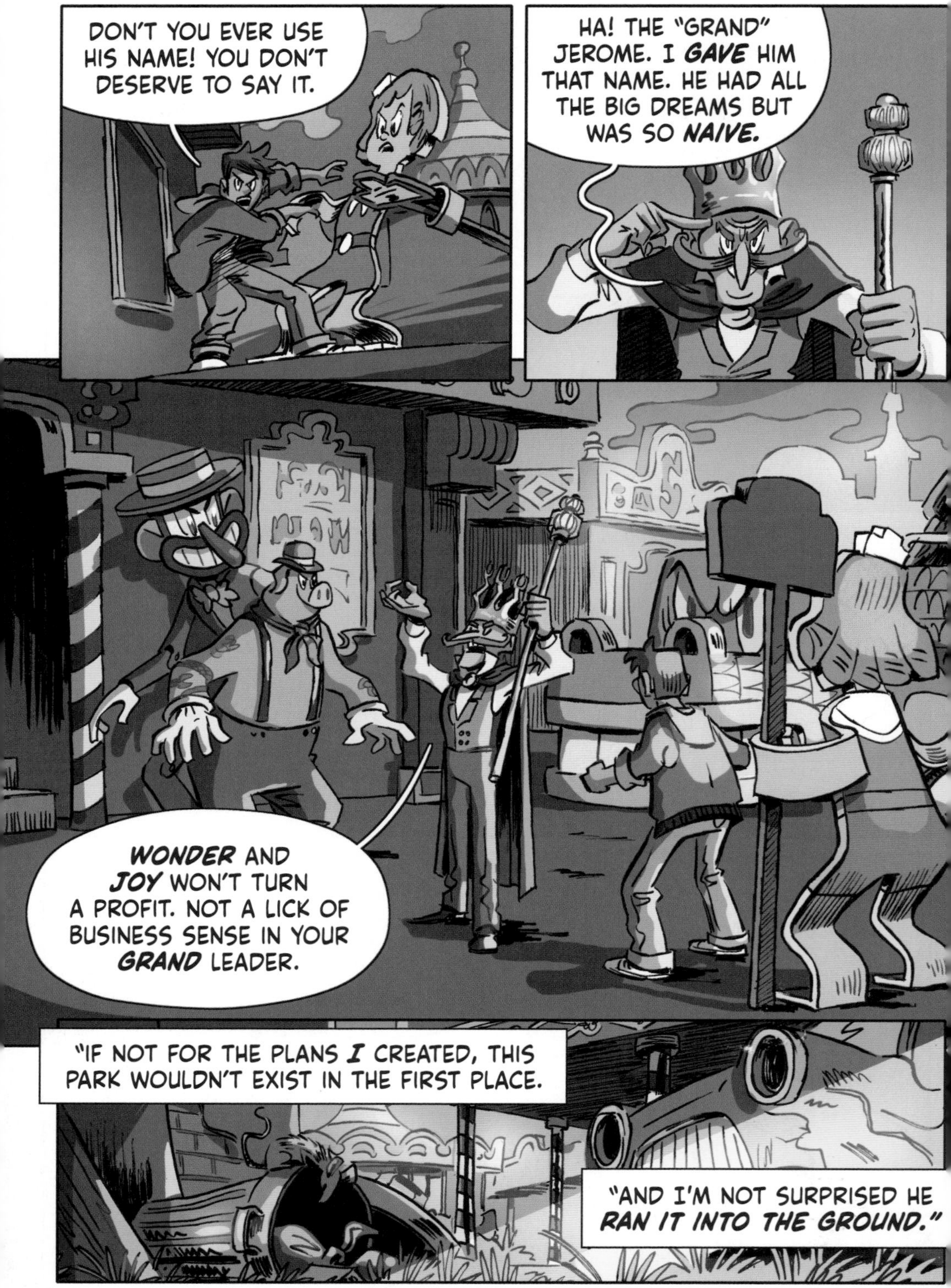
DON'T YOU EVER USE HIS NAME! YOU DON'T DESERVE TO SAY IT.
HA! THE "GRAND" JEROME. I GAVE HIM THAT NAME. HE HAD ALL THE BIG DREAMS BUT WAS SO NAIVE.
WONDER AND JOY WON'T TURN A PROFIT. NOT A LICK OF BUSINESS SENSE IN YOUR GRAND LEADER.
"IF NOT FOR THE PLANS I CREATED, THIS PARK WOULDN'T EXIST IN THE FIRST PLACE.
"AND I'M NOT SURPRISED HE RAN IT INTO THE GROUND."

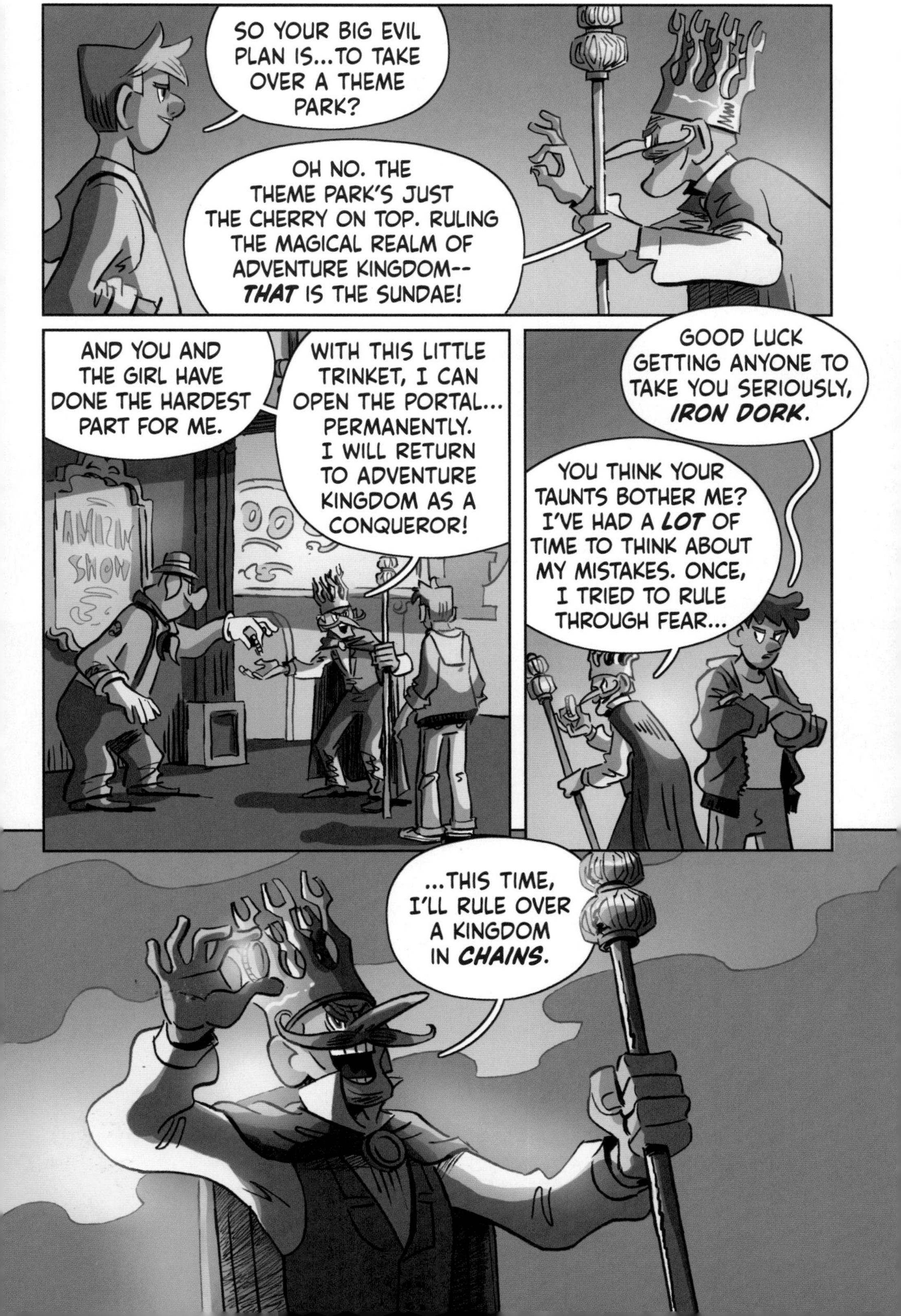
SO YOUR BIG EVIL PLAN IS...TO TAKE OVER A THEME PARK?
OH NO. THE THEME PARK'S JUST THE CHERRY ON TOP. RULING THE MAGICAL REALM OF ADVENTURE KINGDOM-- *THAT* IS THE SUNDAE!
AND YOU AND THE GIRL HAVE DONE THE HARDEST PART FOR ME.
WITH THIS LITTLE TRINKET, I CAN OPEN THE PORTAL... PERMANENTLY. I WILL RETURN TO ADVENTURE KINGDOM AS A CONQUEROR!
GOOD LUCK GETTING ANYONE TO TAKE YOU SERIOUSLY, *IRON DORK*.
YOU THINK YOUR TAUNTS BOTHER ME? I'VE HAD A *LOT* OF TIME TO THINK ABOUT MY MISTAKES. ONCE, I TRIED TO RULE THROUGH FEAR...
...THIS TIME, I'LL RULE OVER A KINGDOM IN *CHAINS*.

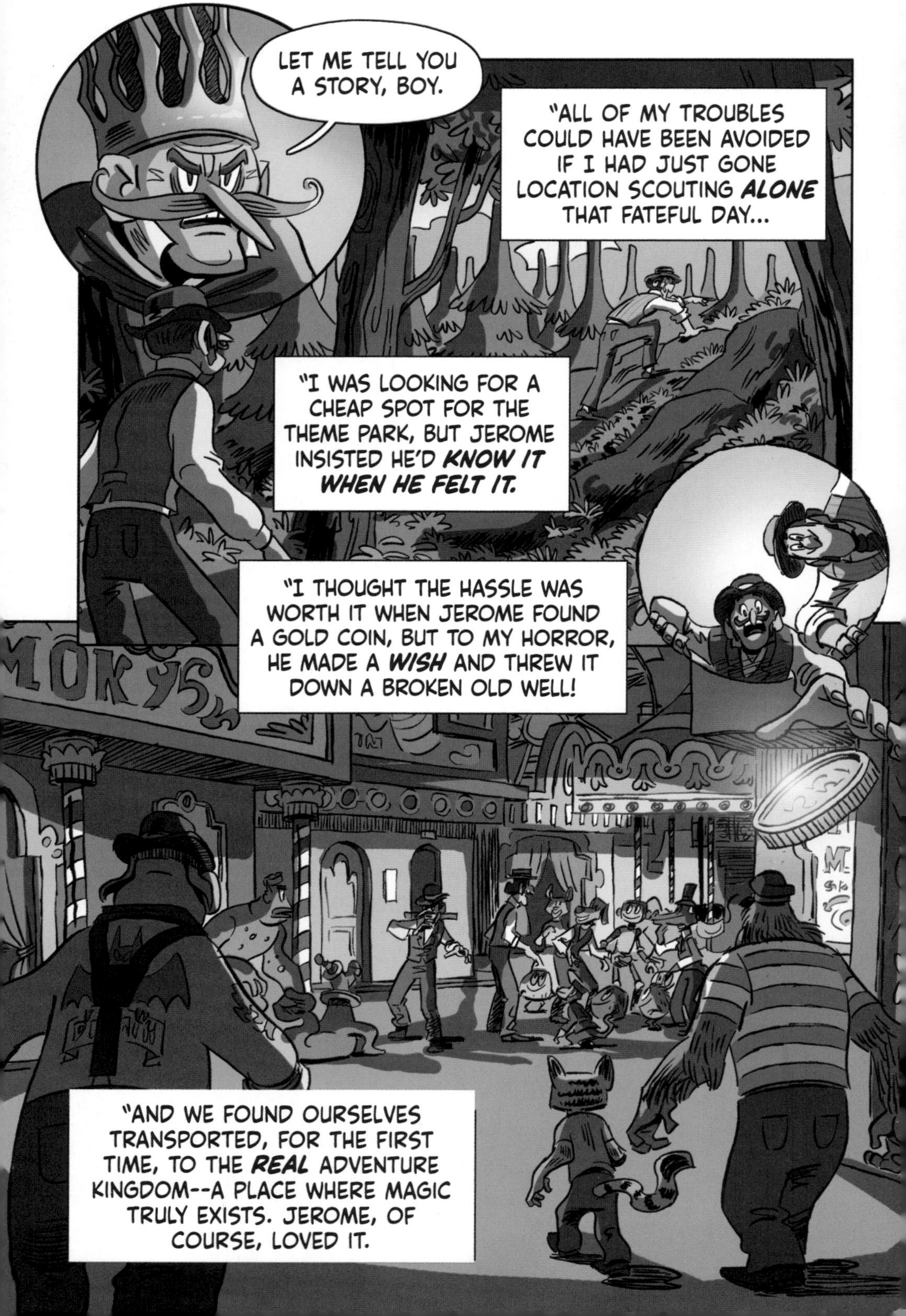
LET ME TELL YOU A STORY, BOY.
"ALL OF MY TROUBLES COULD HAVE BEEN AVOIDED IF I HAD JUST GONE LOCATION SCOUTING ALONE THAT FATEFUL DAY...
"I WAS LOOKING FOR A CHEAP SPOT FOR THE THEME PARK, BUT JEROME INSISTED HE'D KNOW IT WHEN HE FELT IT.
"I THOUGHT THE HASSLE WAS WORTH IT WHEN JEROME FOUND A GOLD COIN, BUT TO MY HORROR, HE MADE A WISH AND THREW IT DOWN A BROKEN OLD WELL!
"AND WE FOUND OURSELVES TRANSPORTED, FOR THE FIRST TIME, TO THE REAL ADVENTURE KINGDOM--A PLACE WHERE MAGIC TRULY EXISTS. JEROME, OF COURSE, LOVED IT.

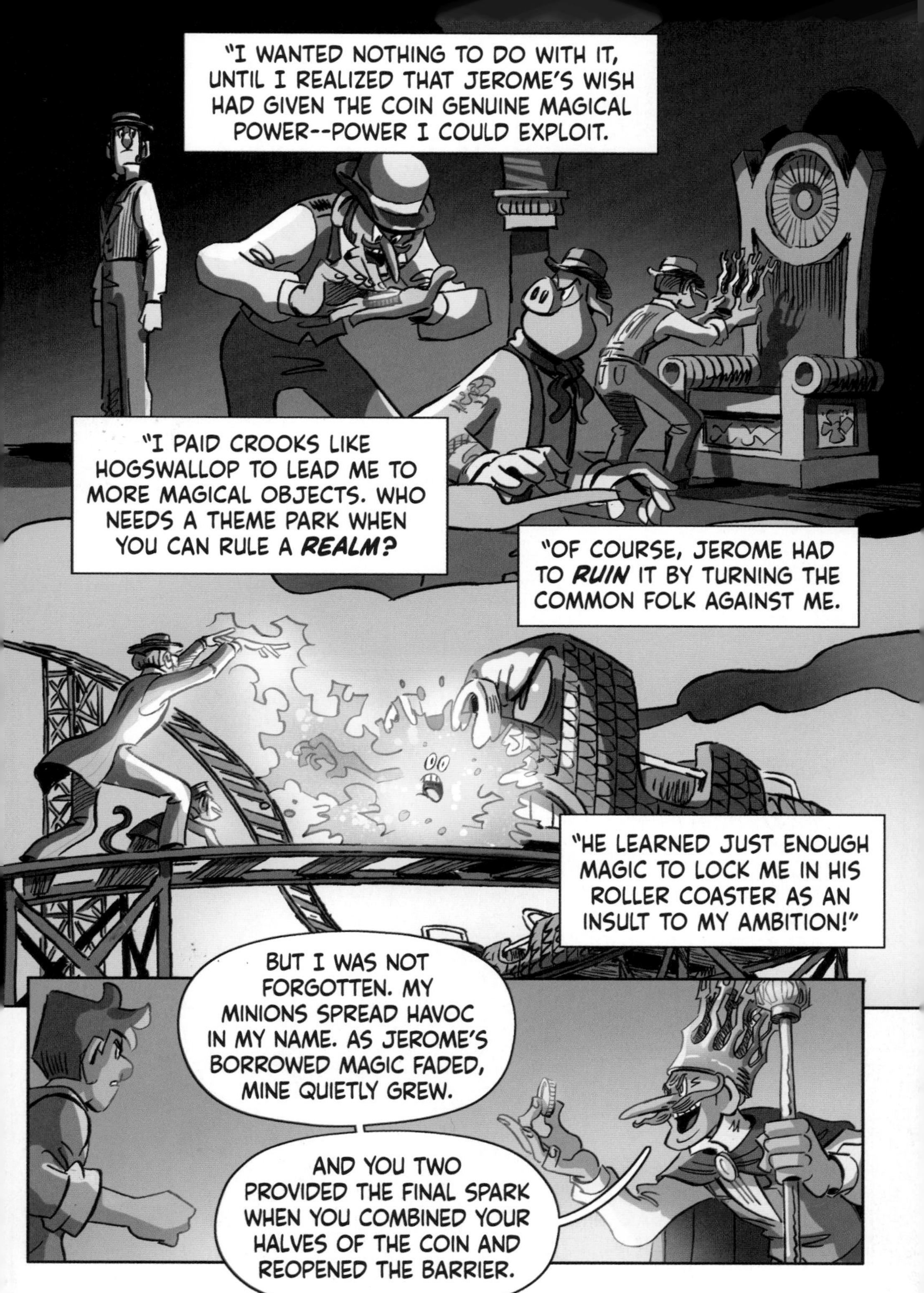
"I WANTED NOTHING TO DO WITH IT, UNTIL I REALIZED THAT JEROME'S WISH HAD GIVEN THE COIN GENUINE MAGICAL POWER--POWER I COULD EXPLOIT.
"I PAID CROOKS LIKE HOGSWALLOP TO LEAD ME TO MORE MAGICAL OBJECTS. WHO NEEDS A THEME PARK WHEN YOU CAN RULE A ***REALM?***
"OF COURSE, JEROME HAD TO ***RUIN*** IT BY TURNING THE COMMON FOLK AGAINST ME.
"HE LEARNED JUST ENOUGH MAGIC TO LOCK ME IN HIS ROLLER COASTER AS AN INSULT TO MY AMBITION!"
BUT I WAS NOT FORGOTTEN. MY MINIONS SPREAD HAVOC IN MY NAME. AS JEROME'S BORROWED MAGIC FADED, MINE QUIETLY GREW.
AND YOU TWO PROVIDED THE FINAL SPARK WHEN YOU COMBINED YOUR HALVES OF THE COIN AND REOPENED THE BARRIER.

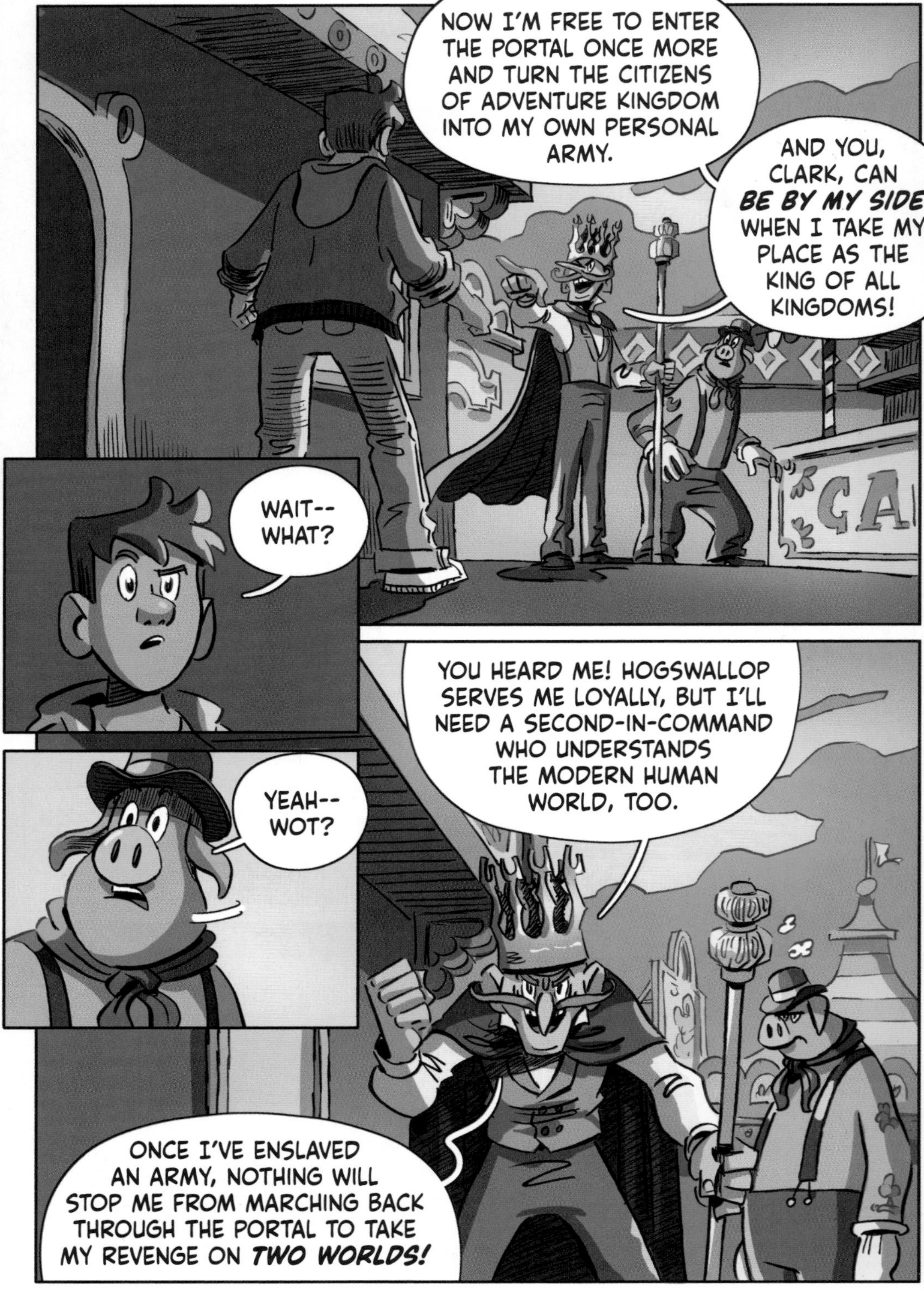
NOW I'M FREE TO ENTER THE PORTAL ONCE MORE AND TURN THE CITIZENS OF ADVENTURE KINGDOM INTO MY OWN PERSONAL ARMY.
AND YOU, CLARK, CAN ***BE BY MY SIDE*** WHEN I TAKE MY PLACE AS THE KING OF ALL KINGDOMS!
WAIT-- WHAT?
YEAH-- WOT?
YOU HEARD ME! HOGSWALLOP SERVES ME LOYALLY, BUT I'LL NEED A SECOND-IN-COMMAND WHO UNDERSTANDS THE MODERN HUMAN WORLD, TOO.
ONCE I'VE ENSLAVED AN ARMY, NOTHING WILL STOP ME FROM MARCHING BACK THROUGH THE PORTAL TO TAKE MY REVENGE ON ***TWO WORLDS!***

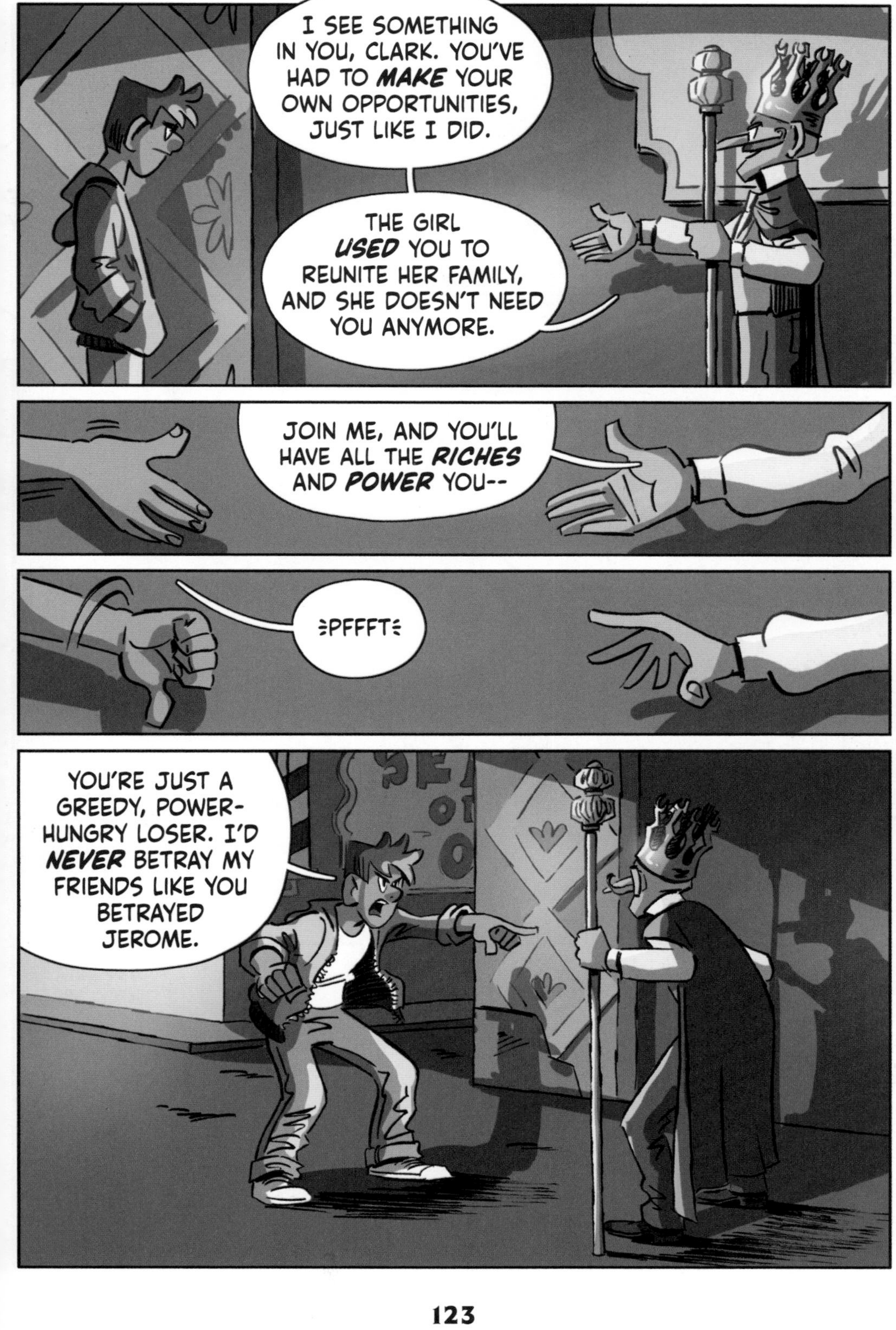
I SEE SOMETHING IN YOU, CLARK. YOU'VE HAD TO *MAKE* YOUR OWN OPPORTUNITIES, JUST LIKE I DID.
THE GIRL *USED* YOU TO REUNITE HER FAMILY, AND SHE DOESN'T NEED YOU ANYMORE.
JOIN ME, AND YOU'LL HAVE ALL THE *RICHES* AND *POWER* YOU--
PFFFT
YOU'RE JUST A GREEDY, POWER-HUNGRY LOSER. I'D *NEVER* BETRAY MY FRIENDS LIKE YOU BETRAYED JEROME.

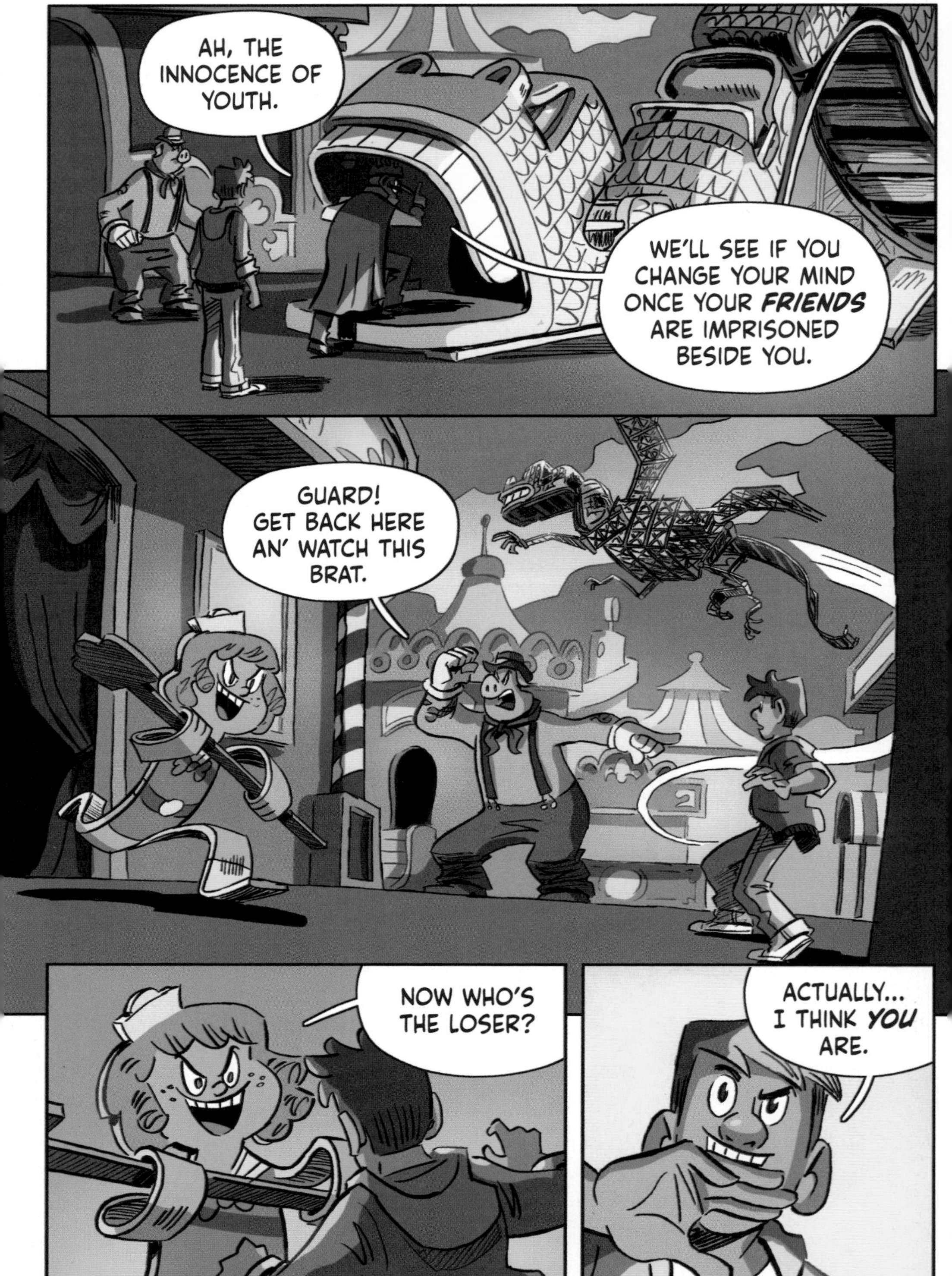
AH, THE INNOCENCE OF YOUTH.
WE'LL SEE IF YOU CHANGE YOUR MIND ONCE YOUR ***FRIENDS*** ARE IMPRISONED BESIDE YOU.
GUARD! GET BACK HERE AN' WATCH THIS BRAT.
NOW WHO'S THE LOSER?
ACTUALLY... I THINK ***YOU*** ARE.

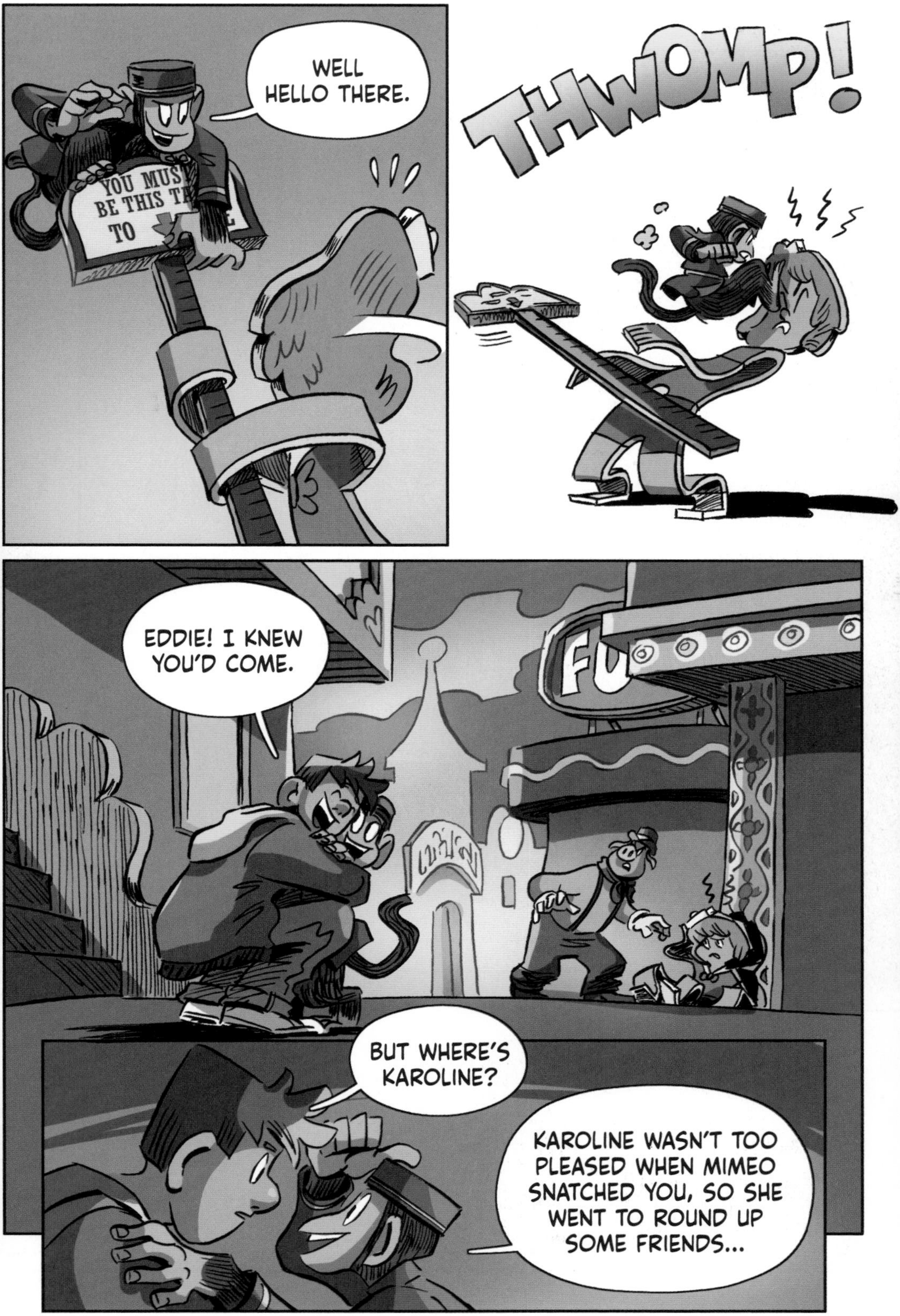
WELL HELLO THERE.
YOU MUS
BE THIS T
TO
THWOMP!
EDDIE! I KNEW YOU'D COME.
FU
BUT WHERE'S KAROLINE?
KAROLINE WASN'T TOO PLEASED WHEN MIMEO SNATCHED YOU, SO SHE WENT TO ROUND UP SOME FRIENDS...

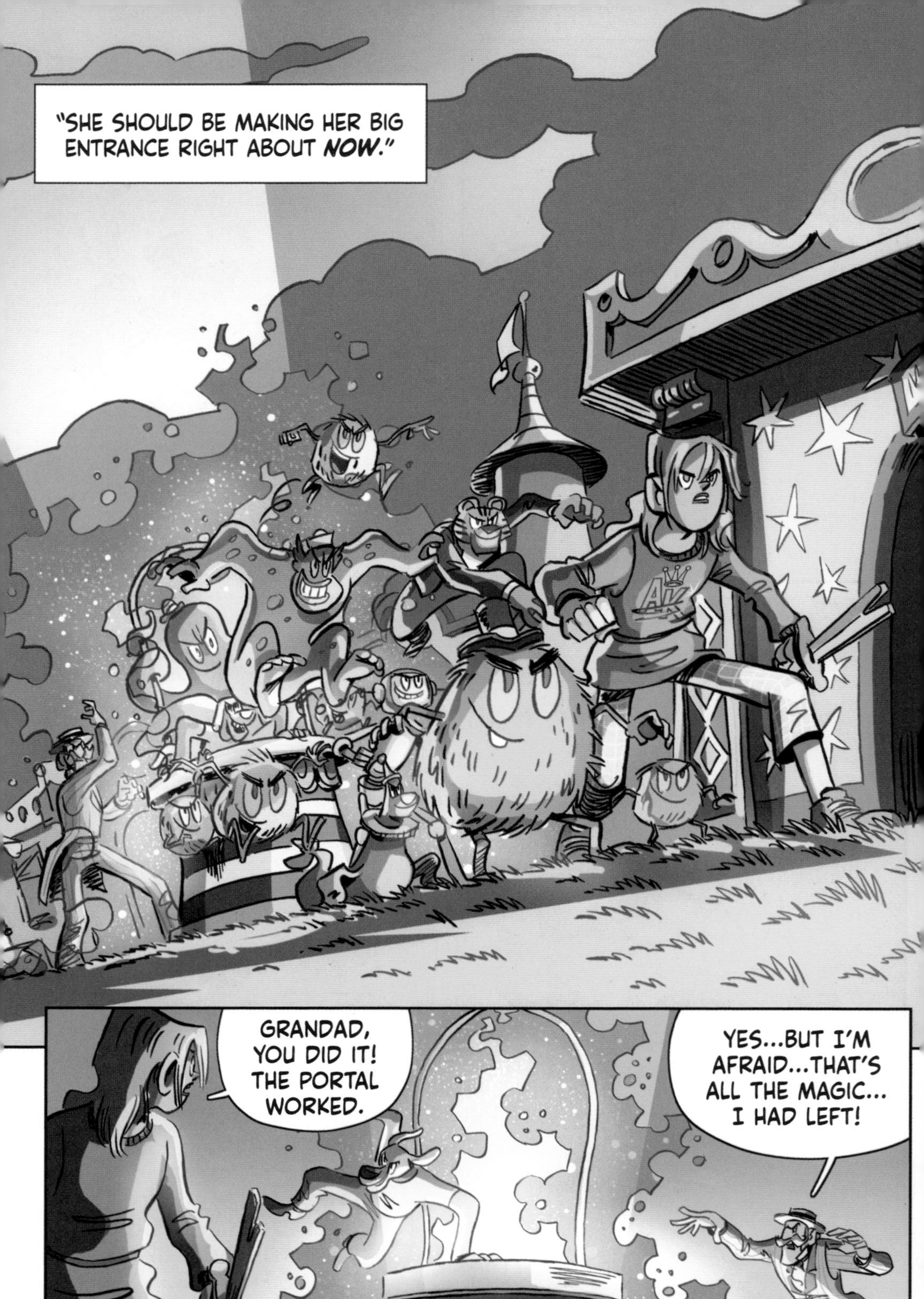
"SHE SHOULD BE MAKING HER BIG ENTRANCE RIGHT ABOUT *NOW*."
GRANDAD, YOU DID IT! THE PORTAL WORKED.
YES...BUT I'M AFRAID...THAT'S ALL THE MAGIC... I HAD LEFT!

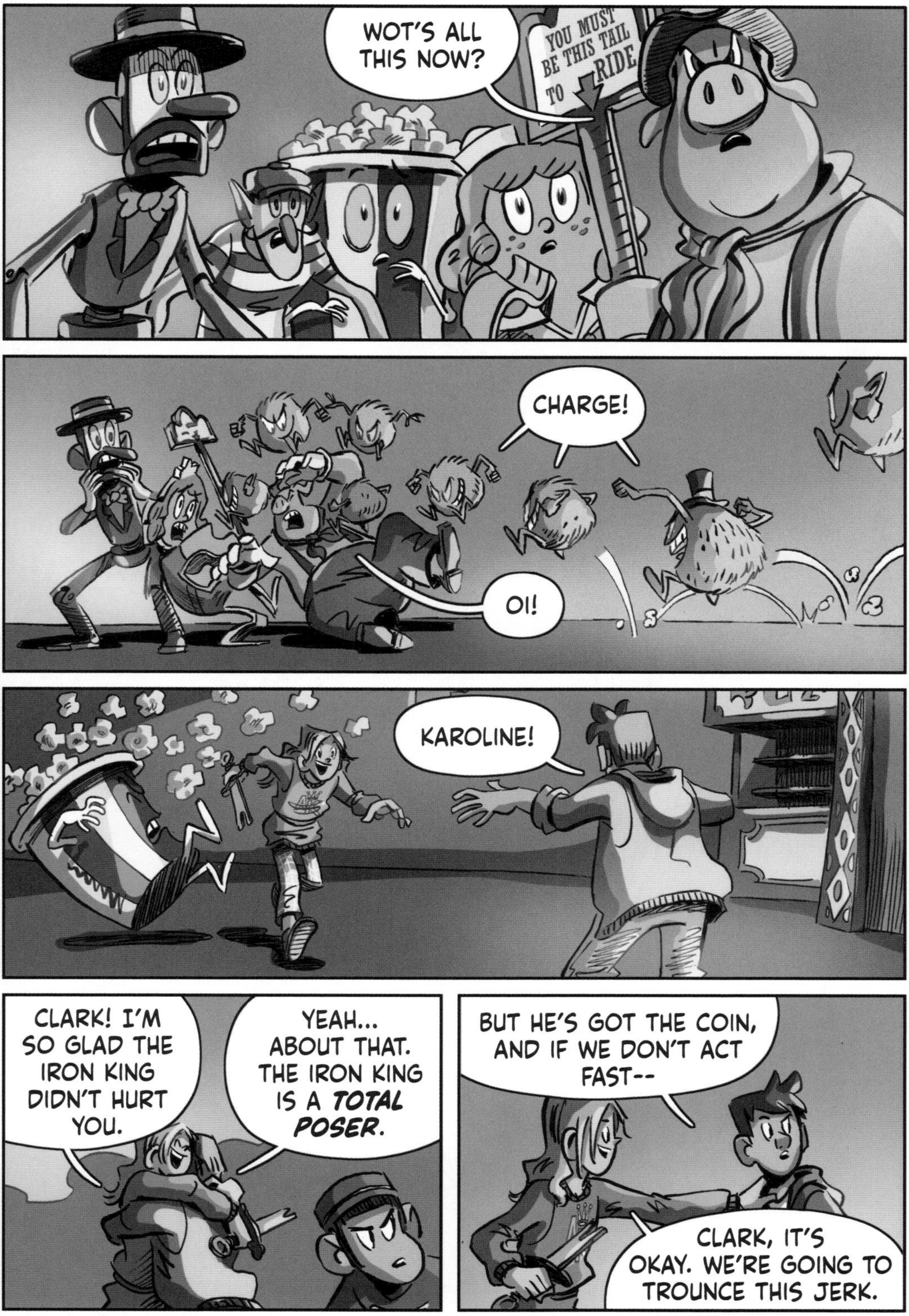

WOT'S ALL THIS NOW?
YOU MUST BE THIS TAIL TO RIDE
CHARGE!
OI!
KAROLINE!
CLARK! I'M SO GLAD THE IRON KING DIDN'T HURT YOU.
YEAH... ABOUT THAT. THE IRON KING IS A *TOTAL POSER*.
BUT HE'S GOT THE COIN, AND IF WE DON'T ACT FAST--
CLARK, IT'S OKAY. WE'RE GOING TO TROUNCE THIS JERK.

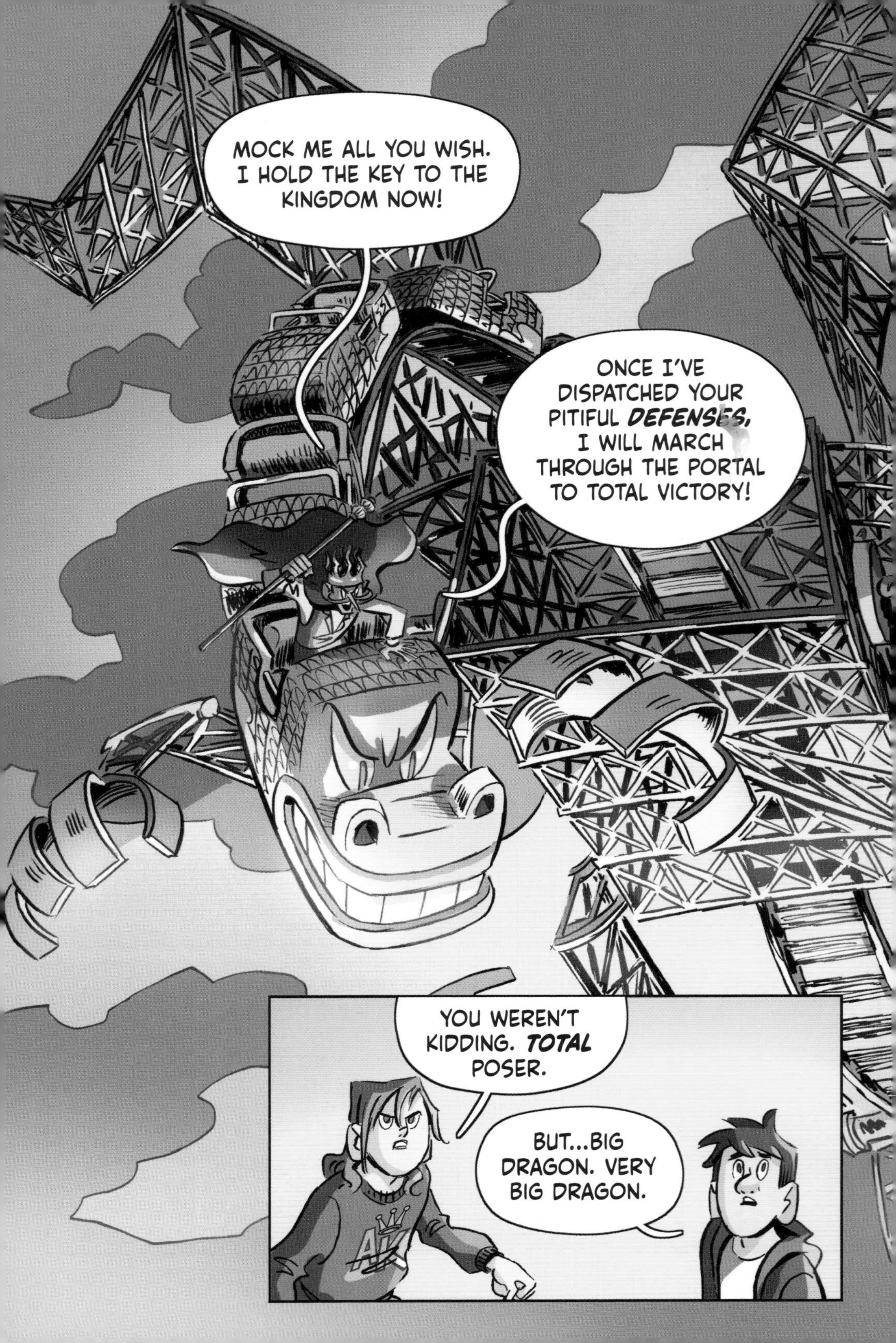
MOCK ME ALL YOU WISH. I HOLD THE KEY TO THE KINGDOM NOW!
ONCE I'VE DISPATCHED YOUR PITIFUL DEFENSES, I WILL MARCH THROUGH THE PORTAL TO TOTAL VICTORY!
YOU WEREN'T KIDDING. TOTAL POSER.
BUT...BIG DRAGON. VERY BIG DRAGON.

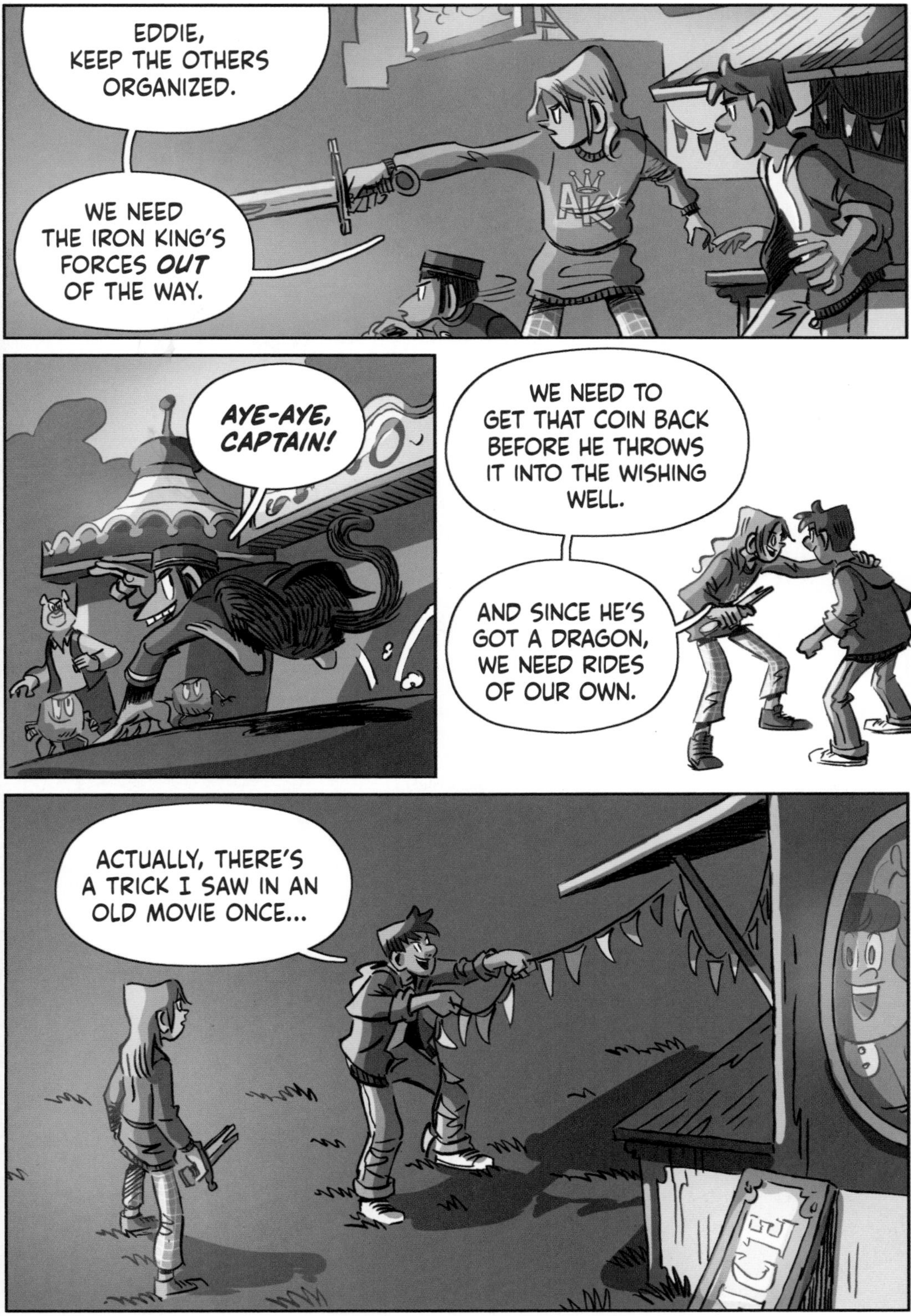
EDDIE, KEEP THE OTHERS ORGANIZED.
WE NEED THE IRON KING'S FORCES *OUT* OF THE WAY.
AYE-AYE, CAPTAIN!
WE NEED TO GET THAT COIN BACK BEFORE HE THROWS IT INTO THE WISHING WELL.
AND SINCE HE'S GOT A DRAGON, WE NEED RIDES OF OUR OWN.
ACTUALLY, THERE'S A TRICK I SAW IN AN OLD MOVIE ONCE...

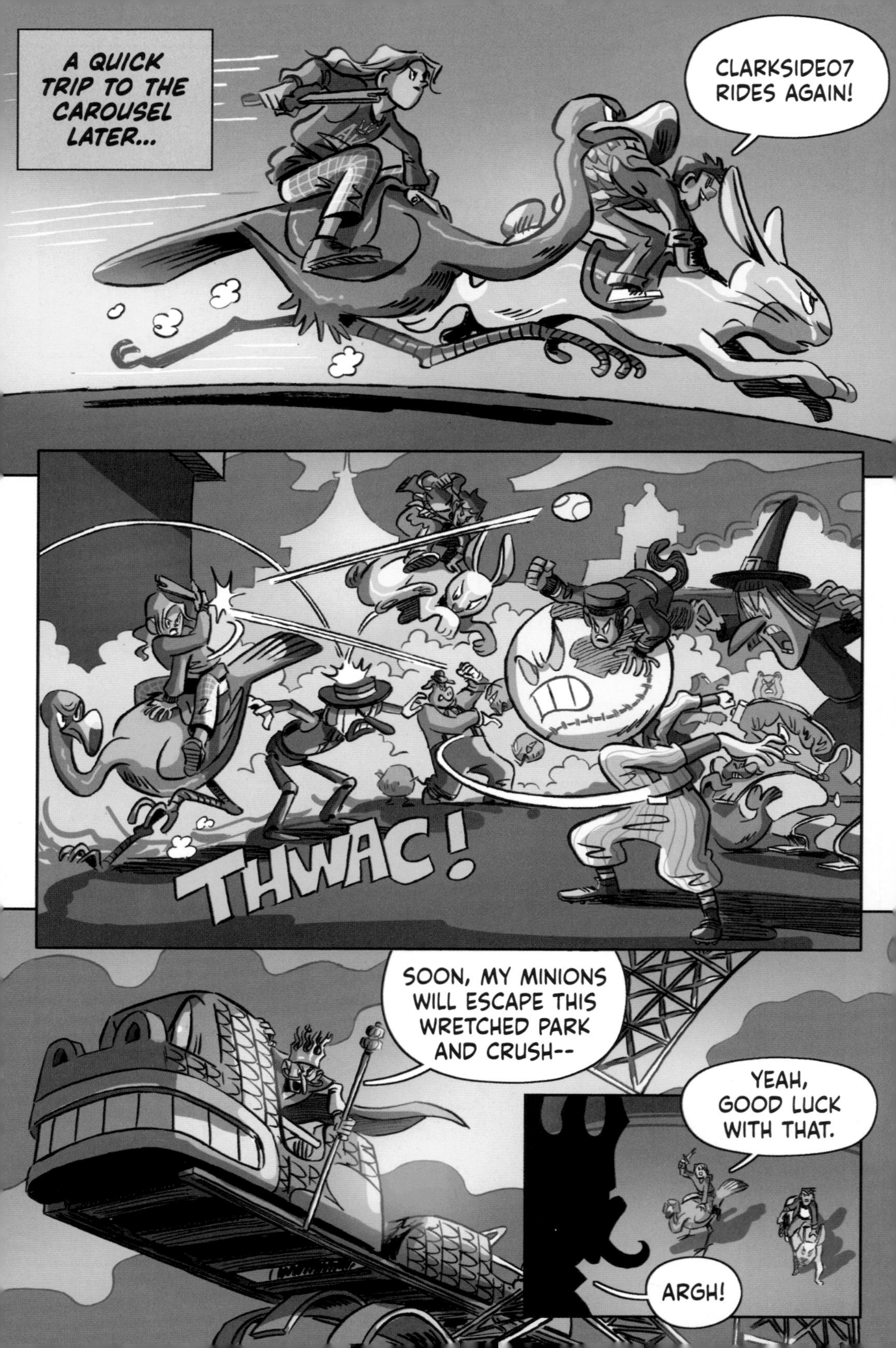
A QUICK TRIP TO THE CAROUSEL LATER...
CLARKSIDE07 RIDES AGAIN!
THWAC!
SOON, MY MINIONS WILL ESCAPE THIS WRETCHED PARK AND CRUSH--
YEAH, GOOD LUCK WITH THAT.
ARGH!

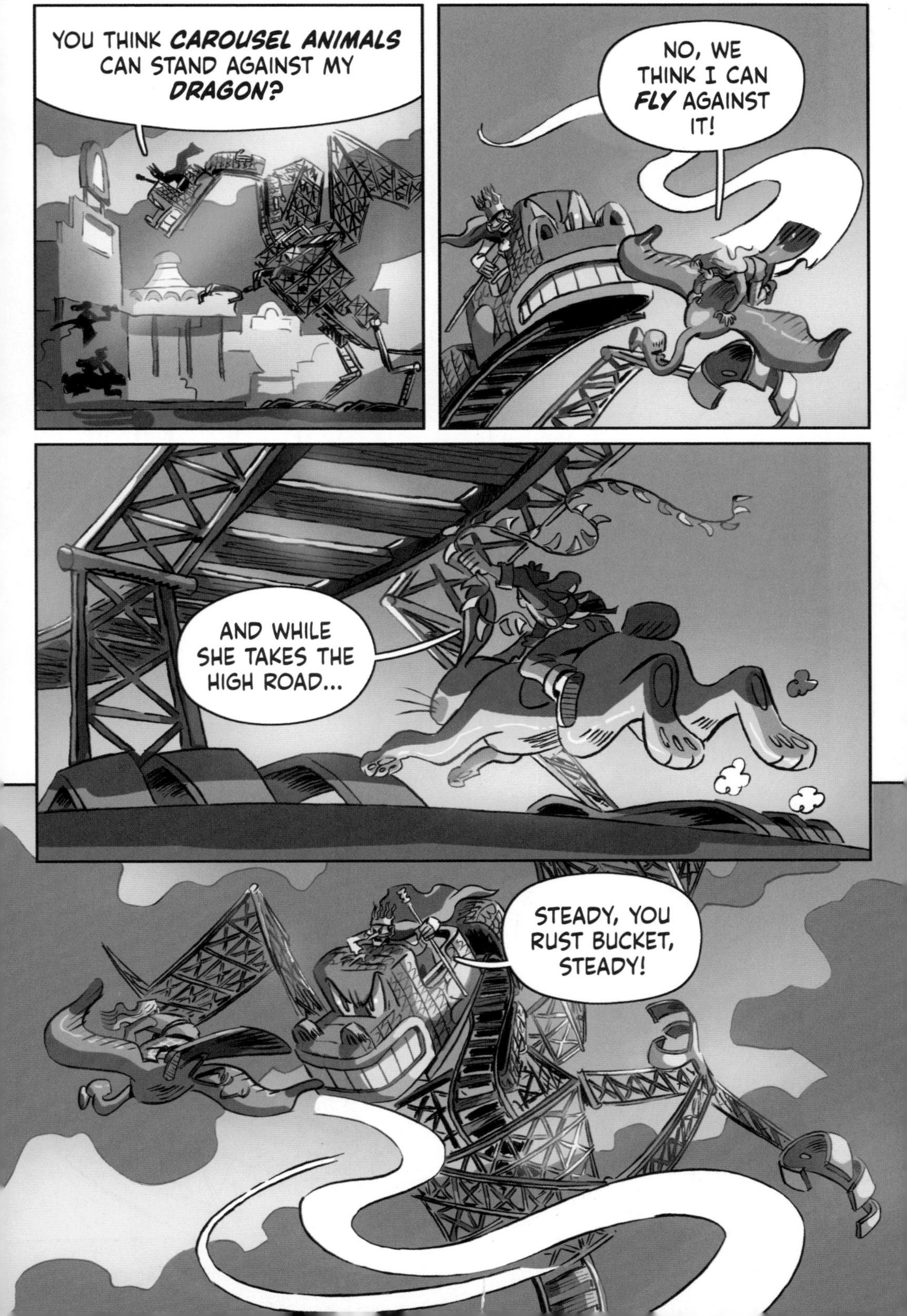
YOU THINK CAROUSEL ANIMALS CAN STAND AGAINST MY DRAGON?
NO, WE THINK I CAN FLY AGAINST IT!
AND WHILE SHE TAKES THE HIGH ROAD...
STEADY, YOU RUST BUCKET, STEADY!

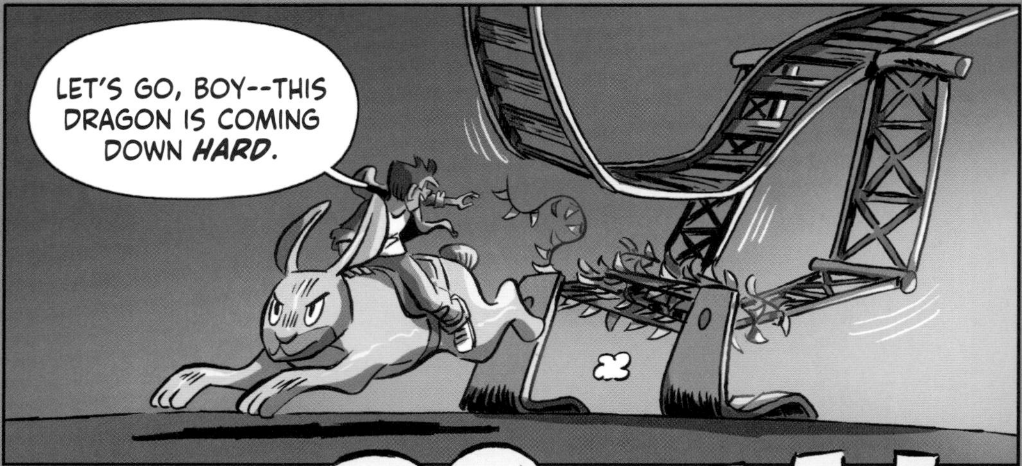
LET'S GO, BOY--THIS DRAGON IS COMING DOWN HARD.

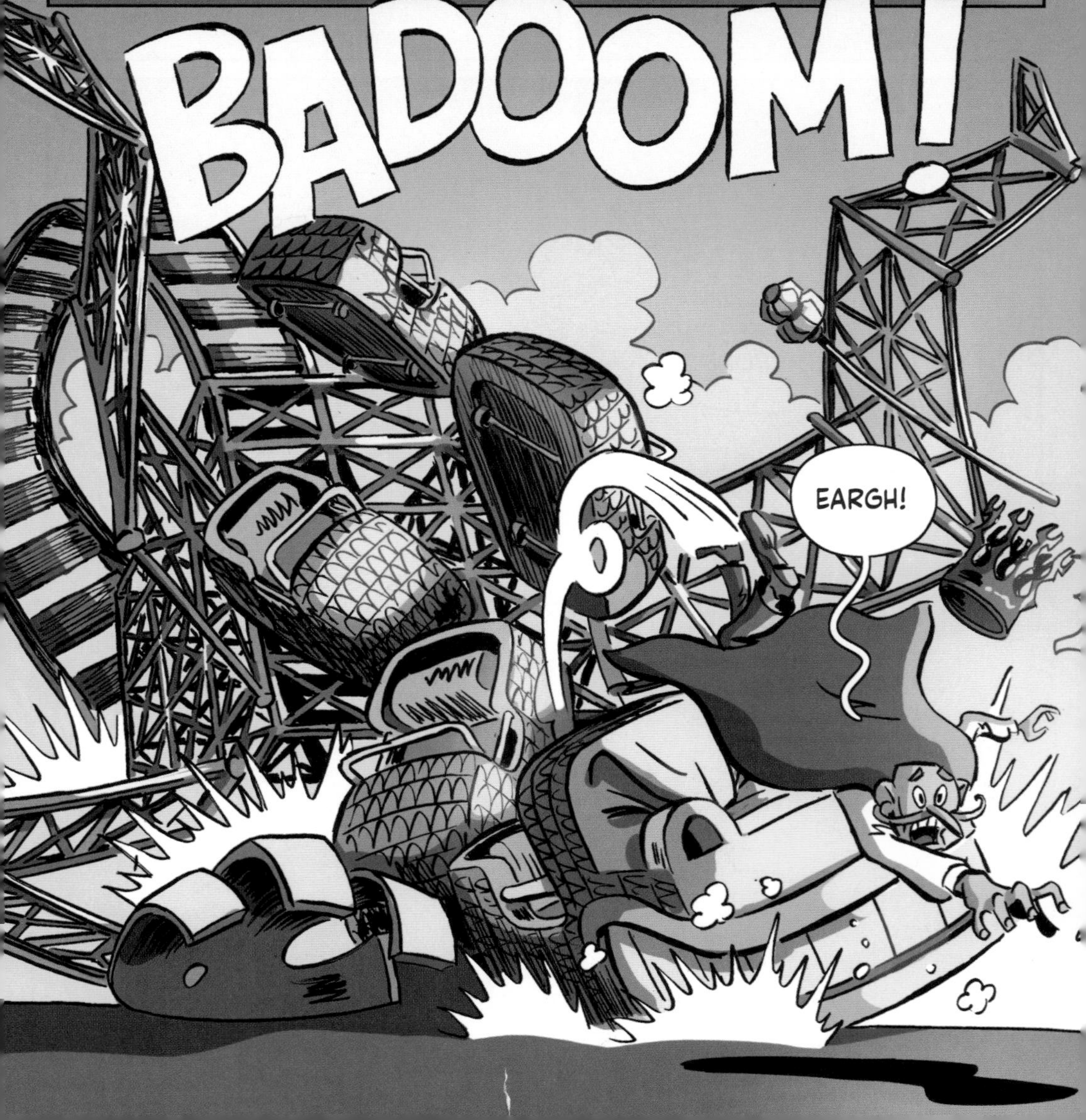
BADOOM!
EARGH!

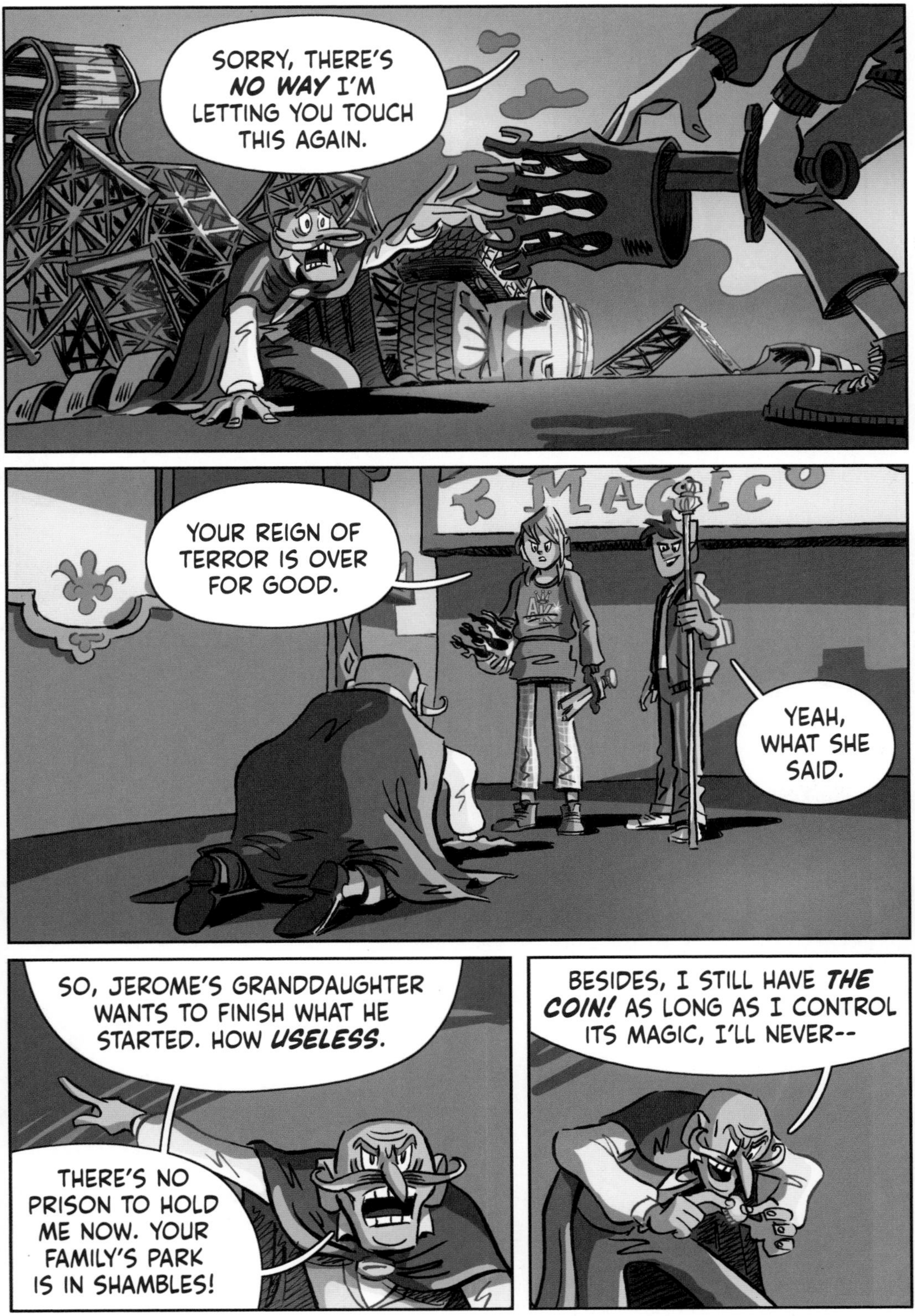
SORRY, THERE'S NO WAY I'M LETTING YOU TOUCH THIS AGAIN.
MAGIC
YOUR REIGN OF TERROR IS OVER FOR GOOD.
YEAH, WHAT SHE SAID.
SO, JEROME'S GRANDDAUGHTER WANTS TO FINISH WHAT HE STARTED. HOW USELESS.
THERE'S NO PRISON TO HOLD ME NOW. YOUR FAMILY'S PARK IS IN SHAMBLES!
BESIDES, I STILL HAVE THE COIN! AS LONG AS I CONTROL ITS MAGIC, I'LL NEVER--

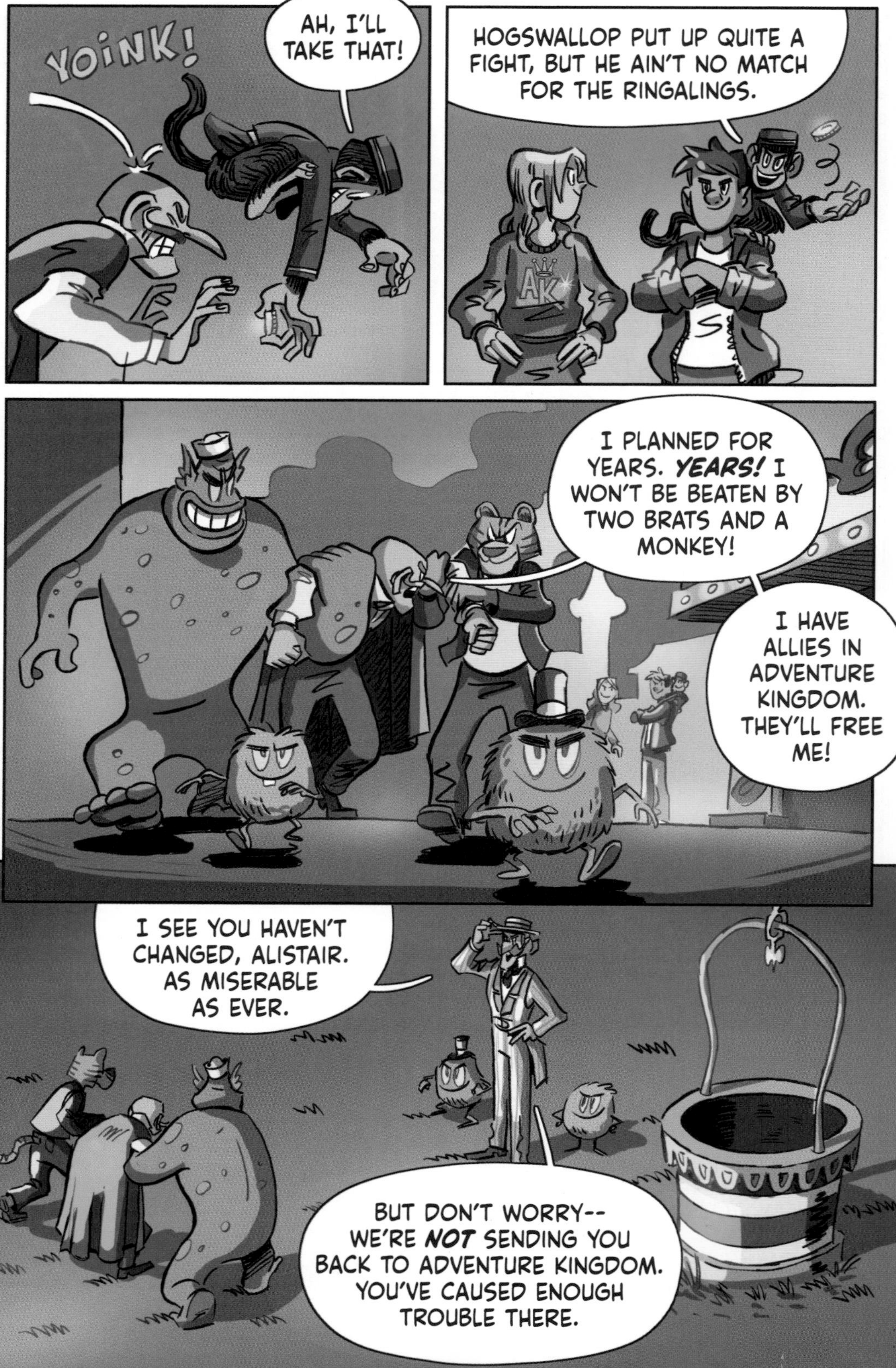
YOINK!
AH, I'LL TAKE THAT!
HOGSWALLOP PUT UP QUITE A FIGHT, BUT HE AIN'T NO MATCH FOR THE RINGALINGS.
AK
I PLANNED FOR YEARS. YEARS! I WON'T BE BEATEN BY TWO BRATS AND A MONKEY!
I HAVE ALLIES IN ADVENTURE KINGDOM. THEY'LL FREE ME!
I SEE YOU HAVEN'T CHANGED, ALISTAIR. AS MISERABLE AS EVER.
BUT DON'T WORRY-- WE'RE NOT SENDING YOU BACK TO ADVENTURE KINGDOM. YOU'VE CAUSED ENOUGH TROUBLE THERE.

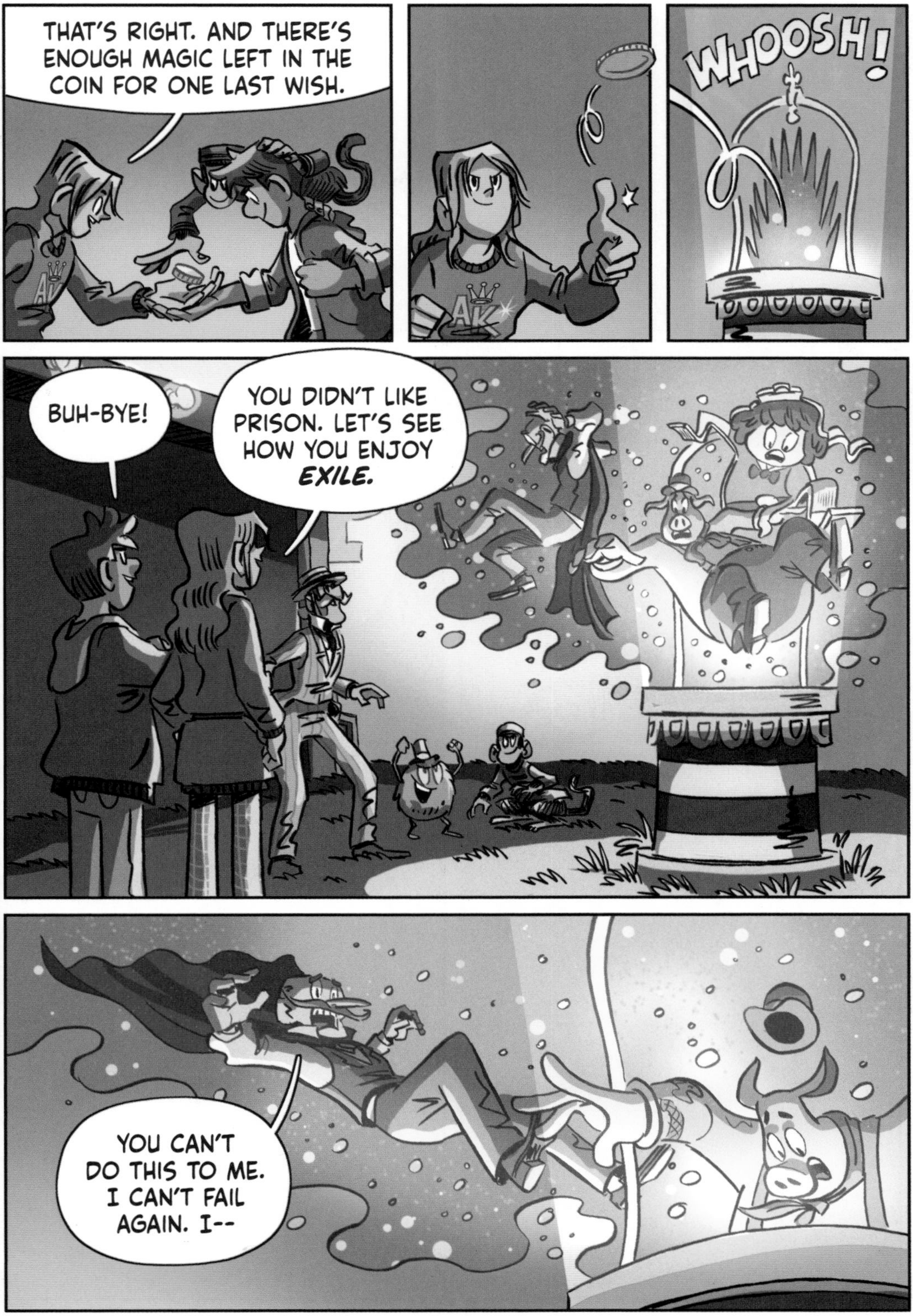
THAT'S RIGHT. AND THERE'S ENOUGH MAGIC LEFT IN THE COIN FOR ONE LAST WISH.
WHOOSH!
BUH-BYE!
YOU DIDN'T LIKE PRISON. LET'S SEE HOW YOU ENJOY *EXILE.*
YOU CAN'T DO THIS TO ME. I CAN'T FAIL AGAIN. I--

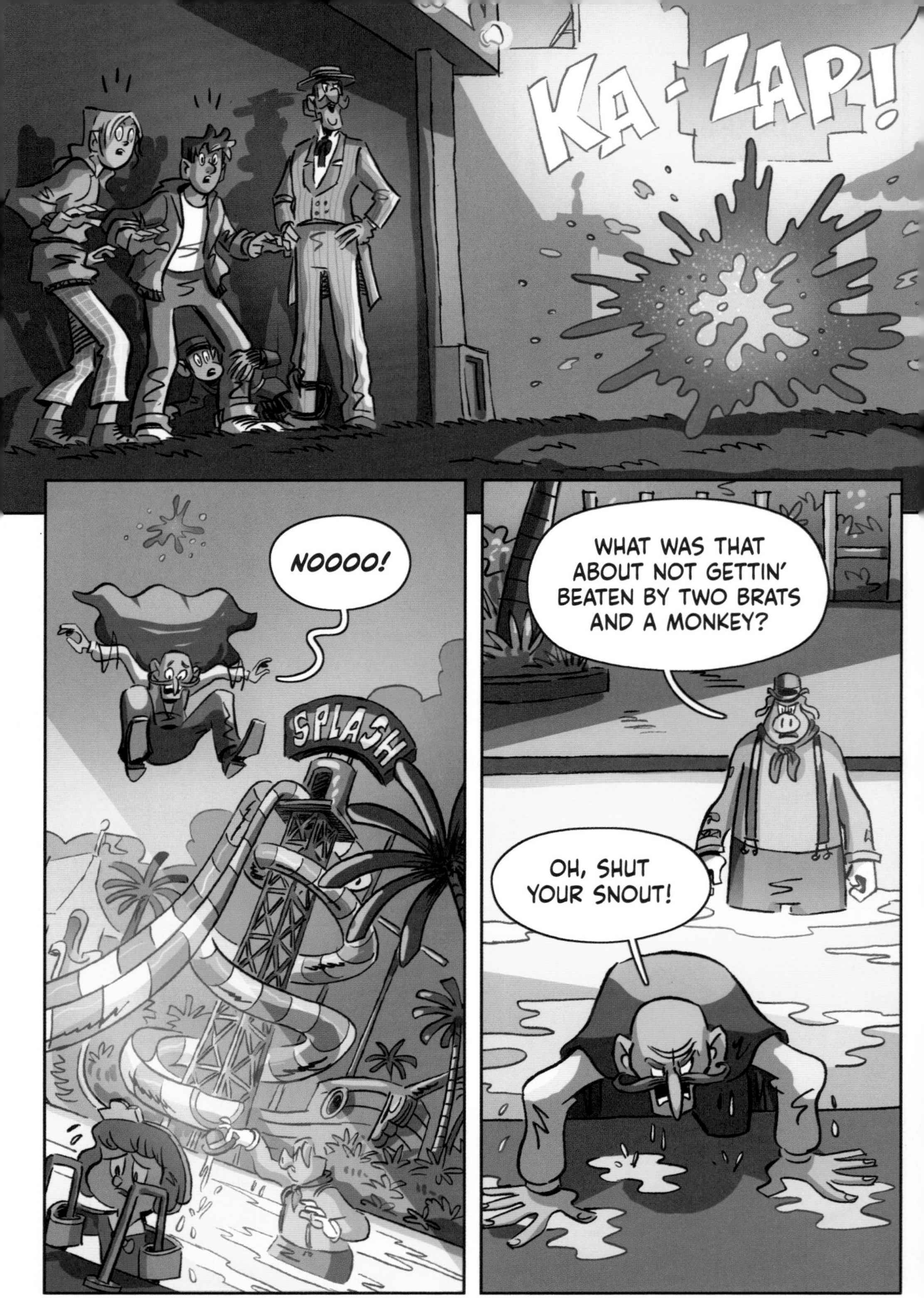
KA-ZAP!
NOOOO!
SPLASH
WHAT WAS THAT ABOUT NOT GETTIN' BEATEN BY TWO BRATS AND A MONKEY?
OH, SHUT YOUR SNOUT!

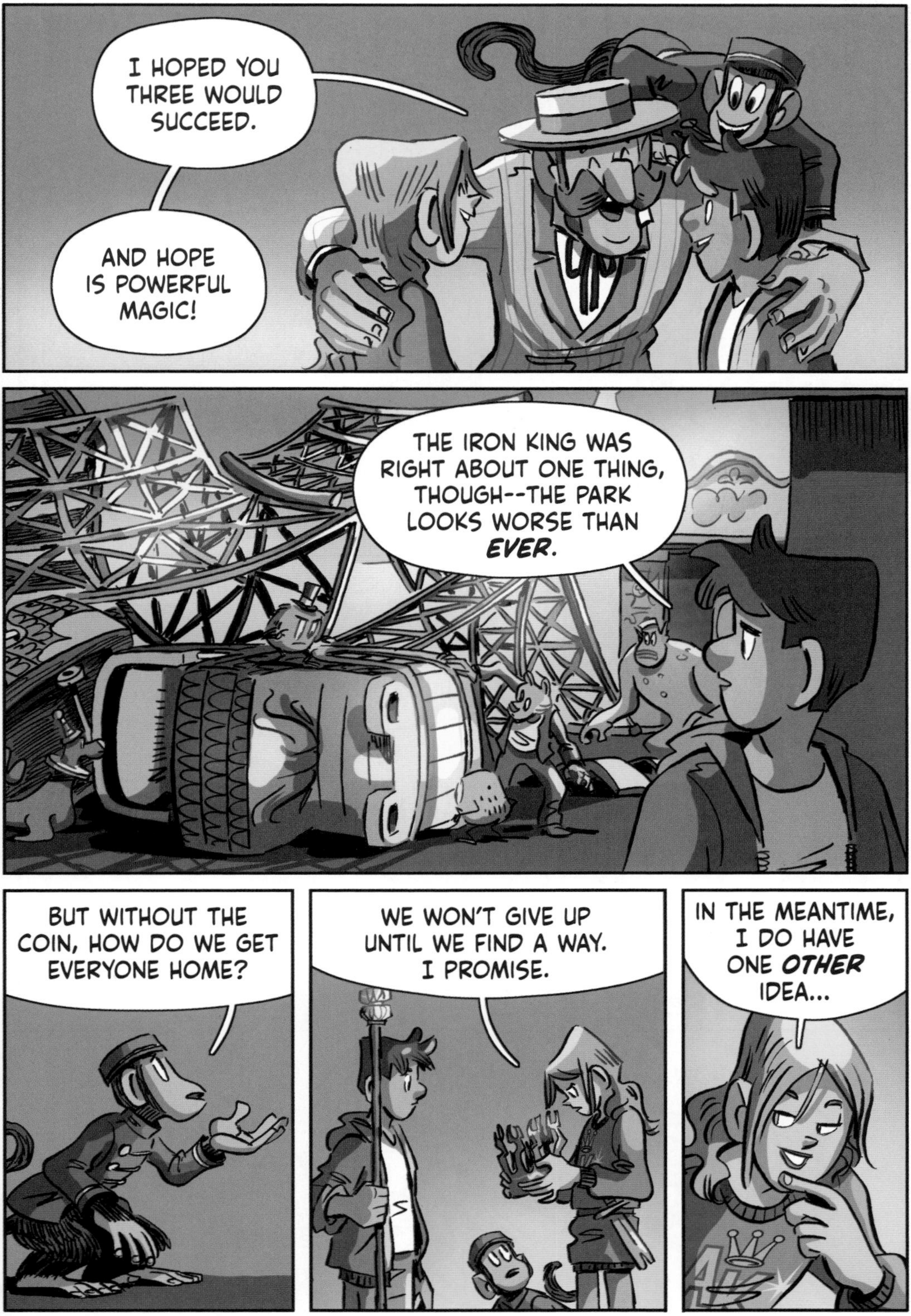
I HOPED YOU THREE WOULD SUCCEED.
AND HOPE IS POWERFUL MAGIC!
THE IRON KING WAS RIGHT ABOUT ONE THING, THOUGH--THE PARK LOOKS WORSE THAN ***EVER***.
BUT WITHOUT THE COIN, HOW DO WE GET EVERYONE HOME?
WE WON'T GIVE UP UNTIL WE FIND A WAY. I PROMISE.
IN THE MEANTIME, I DO HAVE ONE ***OTHER*** IDEA...

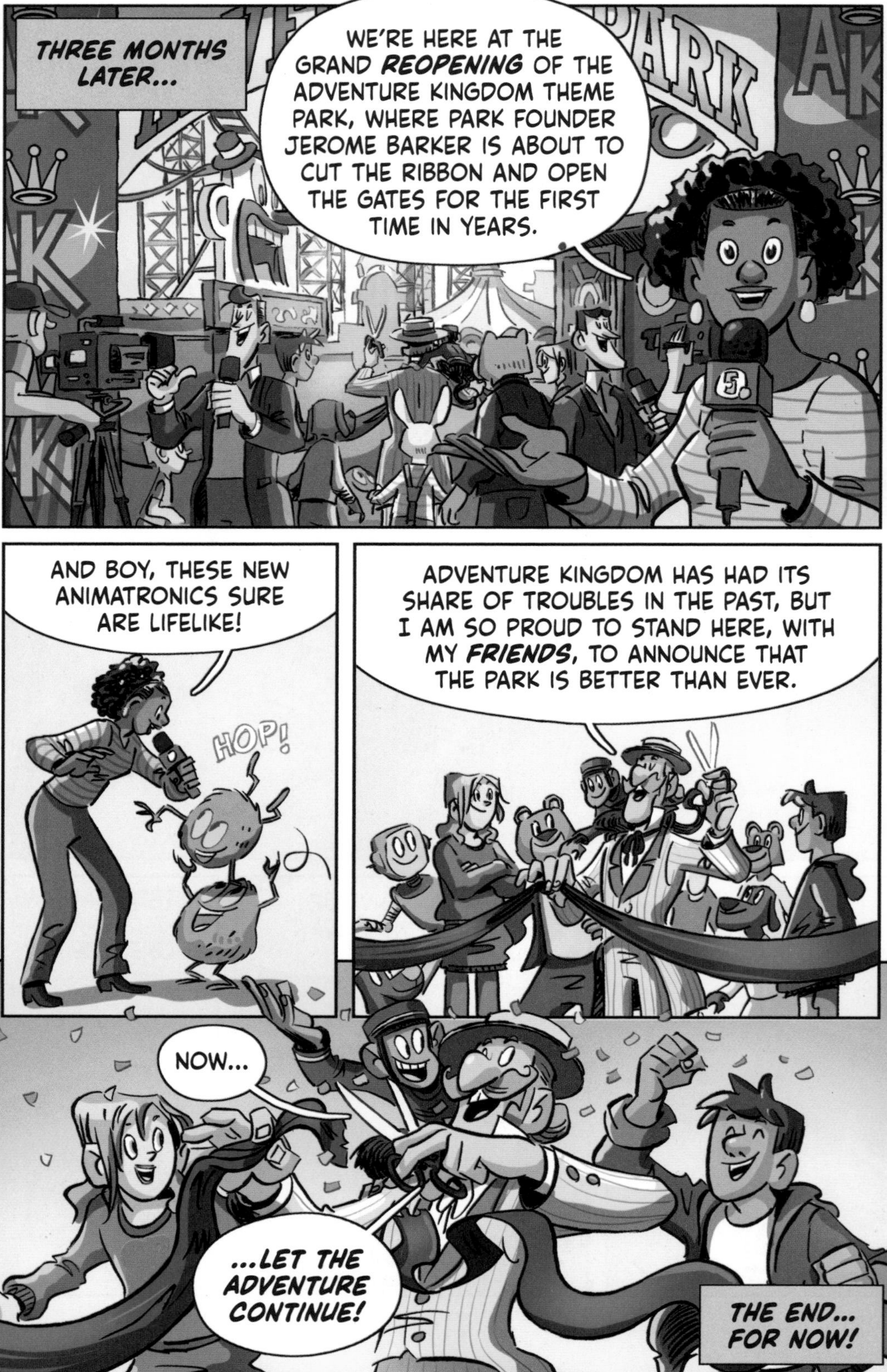
THREE MONTHS LATER...
WE'RE HERE AT THE GRAND REOPENING OF THE ADVENTURE KINGDOM THEME PARK, WHERE PARK FOUNDER JEROME BARKER IS ABOUT TO CUT THE RIBBON AND OPEN THE GATES FOR THE FIRST TIME IN YEARS.
AND BOY, THESE NEW ANIMATRONICS SURE ARE LIFELIKE!
HOP!
ADVENTURE KINGDOM HAS HAD ITS SHARE OF TROUBLES IN THE PAST, BUT I AM SO PROUD TO STAND HERE, WITH MY FRIENDS, TO ANNOUNCE THAT THE PARK IS BETTER THAN EVER.
NOW...
...LET THE ADVENTURE CONTINUE!
THE END... FOR NOW!

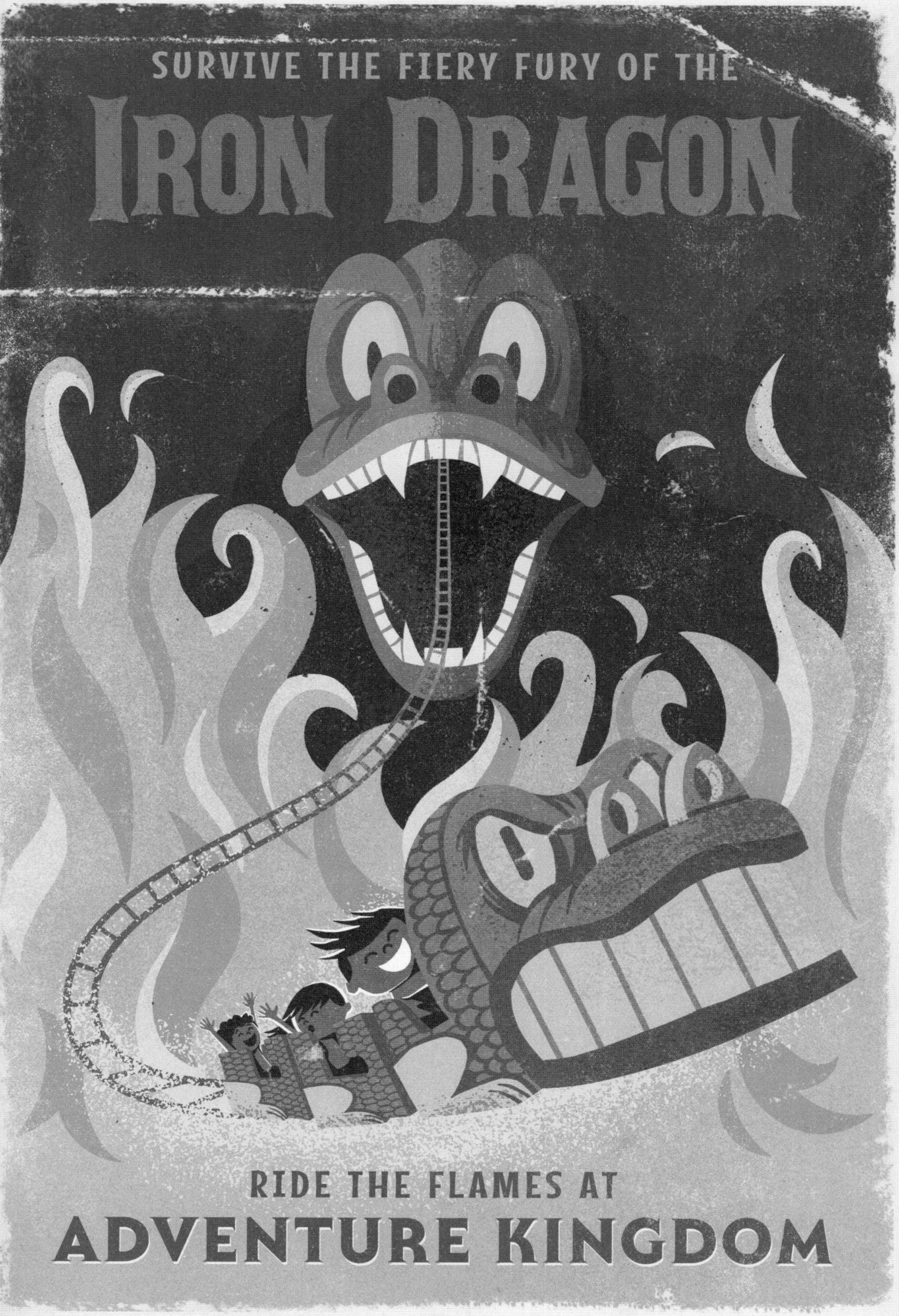
SURVIVE THE FIERY FURY OF THE
IRON DRAGON
RIDE THE FLAMES AT
ADVENTURE KINGDOM

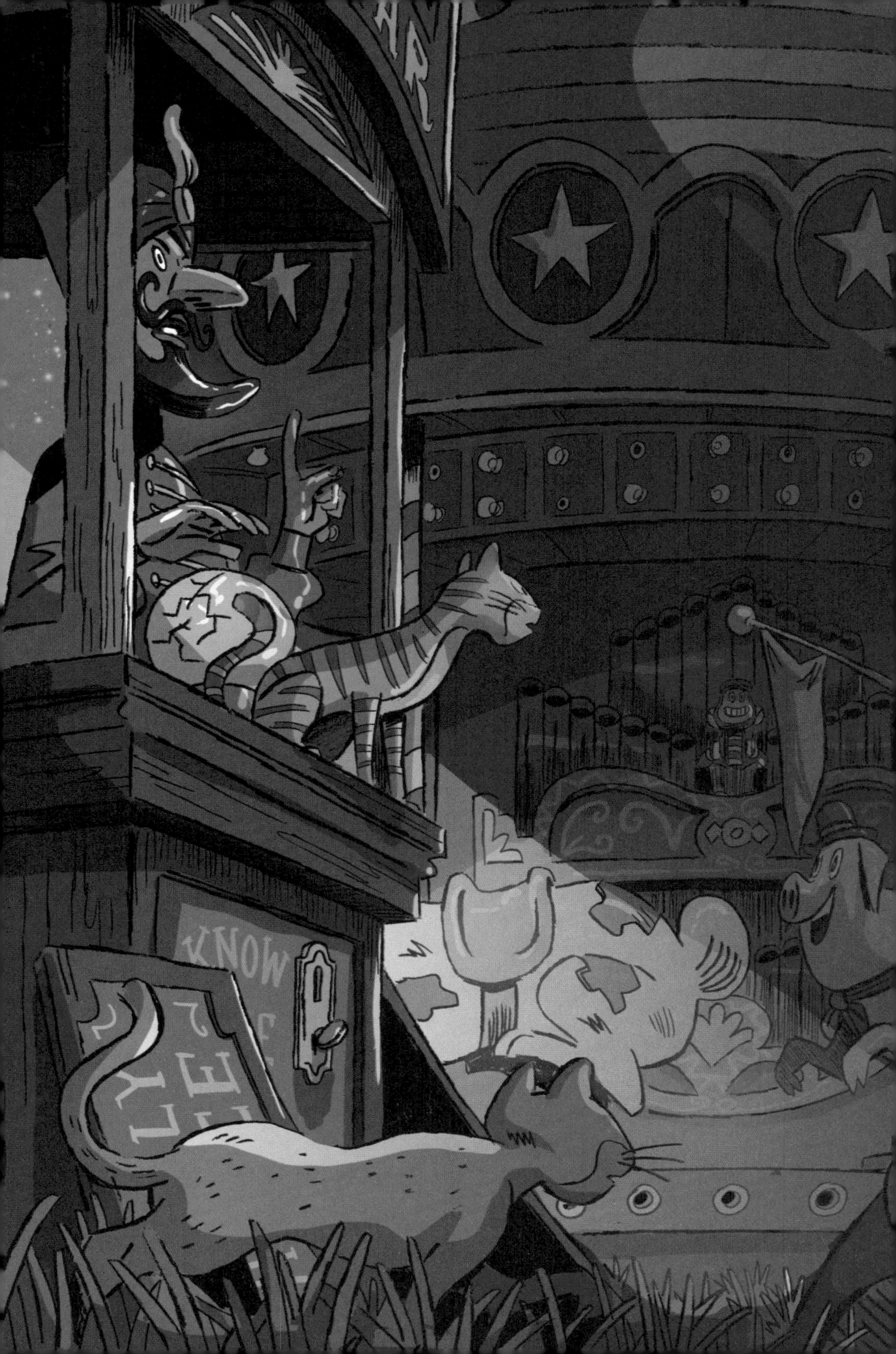
KNOW

ABOUT THE AUTHOR

STEVE FOXE is the author of more than fifty comics and children's books for properties including *Pokémon*, *Batman*, *Adventure Time*, *Steven Universe*, *Far Out Fables*, and *Spider-Ham*, as well as quite a few stories for adults. He lives in Queens with his partner and dog, but he visits theme parks every chance he gets.

ABOUT THE ILLUSTRATOR

PEDRO RODRIGUEZ studied illustration at the Fine Arts School La Llotja in Barcelona, Spain. He has worked on a variety of projects in design, marketing, advertising, publishing, animated films, and music videos. He has illustrated more than forty books and comic books. Pedro lives next to the beach, close to Barcelona, with his wife, Gemma, and their daughter, Maya.

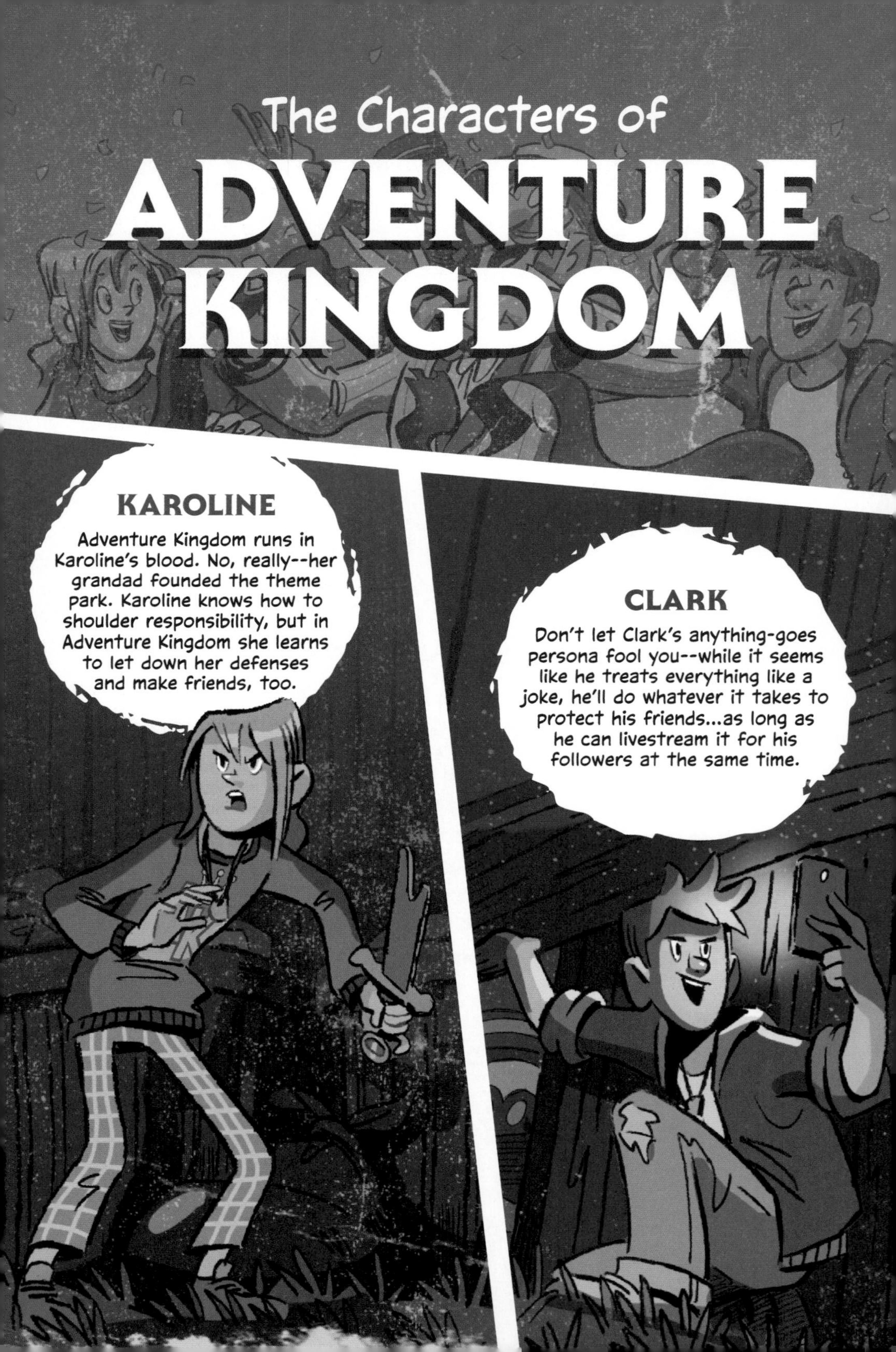
The Characters of
ADVENTURE KINGDOM
KAROLINE
Adventure Kingdom runs in Karoline's blood. No, really--her grandad founded the theme park. Karoline knows how to shoulder responsibility, but in Adventure Kingdom she learns to let down her defenses and make friends, too.
CLARK
Don't let Clark's anything-goes persona fool you--while it seems like he treats everything like a joke, he'll do whatever it takes to protect his friends...as long as he can livestream it for his followers at the same time.

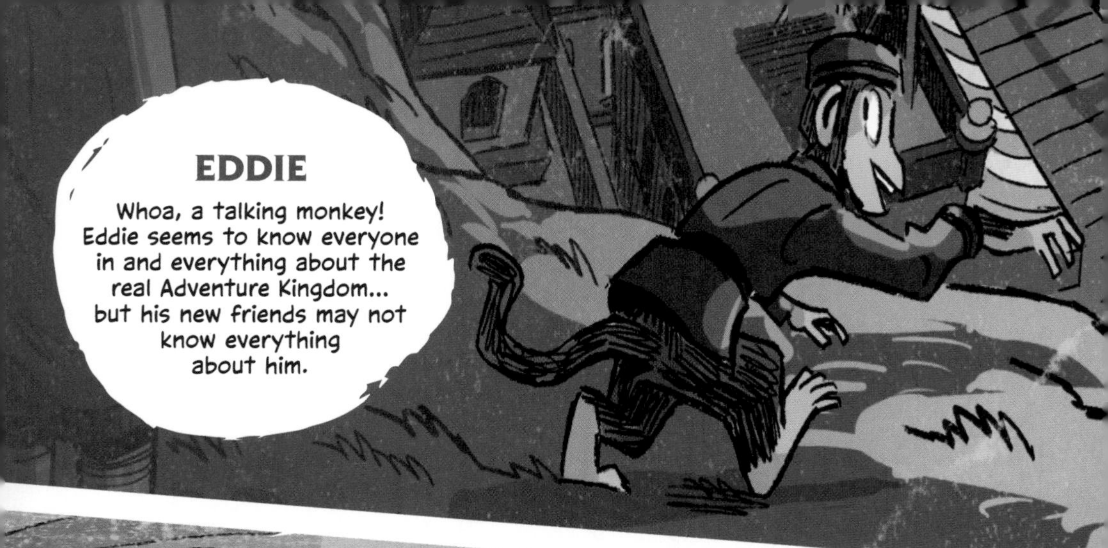
EDDIE
Whoa, a talking monkey! Eddie seems to know everyone in and everything about the real Adventure Kingdom... but his new friends may not know everything about him.

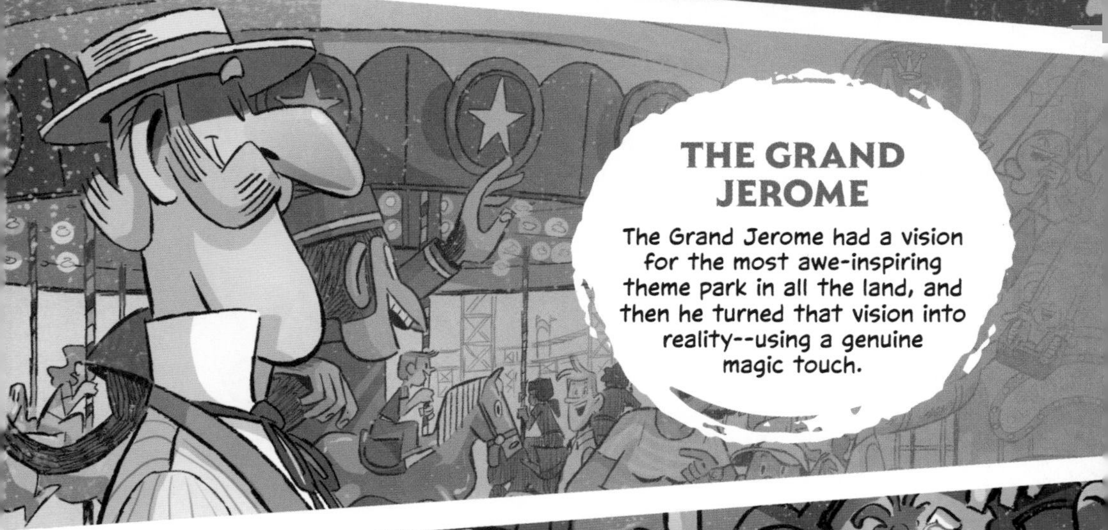
THE GRAND JEROME
The Grand Jerome had a vision for the most awe-inspiring theme park in all the land, and then he turned that vision into reality--using a genuine magic touch.

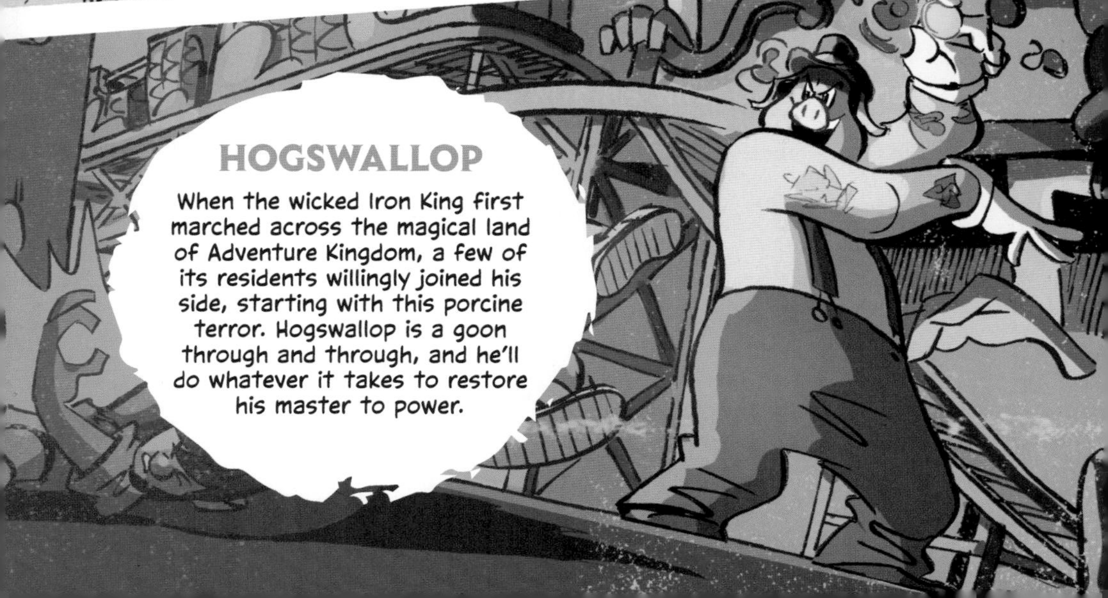
HOGSWALLOP
When the wicked Iron King first marched across the magical land of Adventure Kingdom, a few of its residents willingly joined his side, starting with this porcine terror. Hogswallop is a goon through and through, and he'll do whatever it takes to restore his master to power.

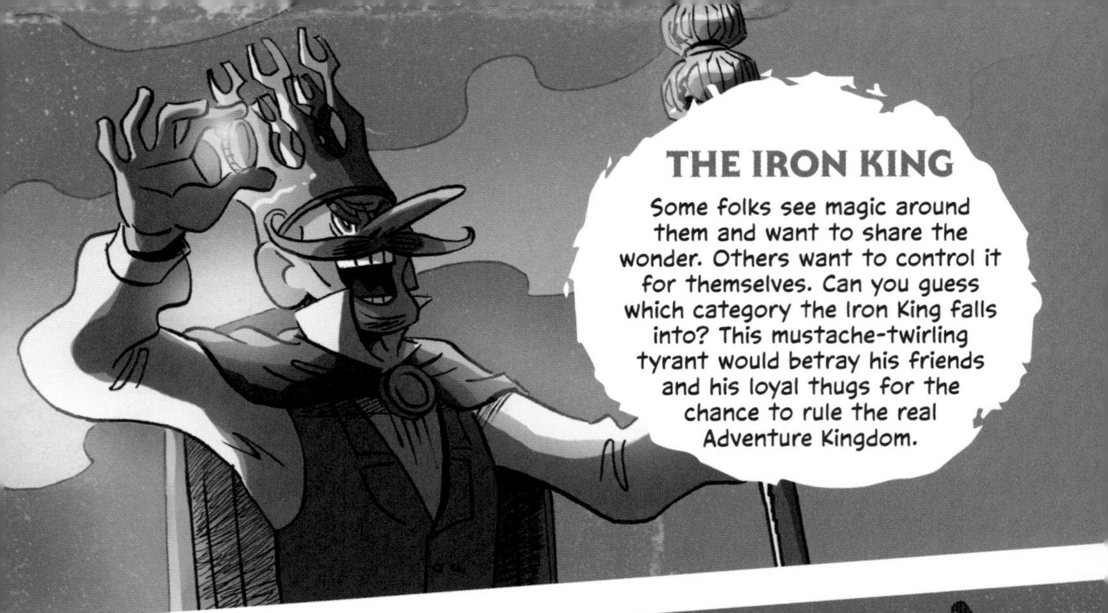
THE IRON KING
Some folks see magic around them and want to share the wonder. Others want to control it for themselves. Can you guess which category the Iron King falls into? This mustache-twirling tyrant would betray his friends and his loyal thugs for the chance to rule the real Adventure Kingdom.

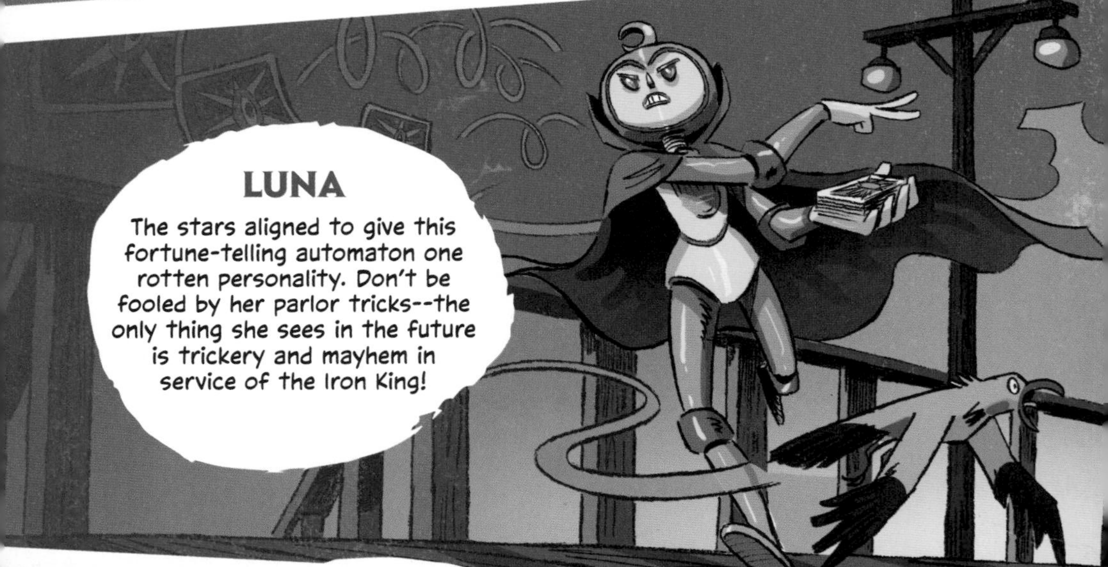
LUNA
The stars aligned to give this fortune-telling automaton one rotten personality. Don't be fooled by her parlor tricks--the only thing she sees in the future is trickery and mayhem in service of the Iron King!

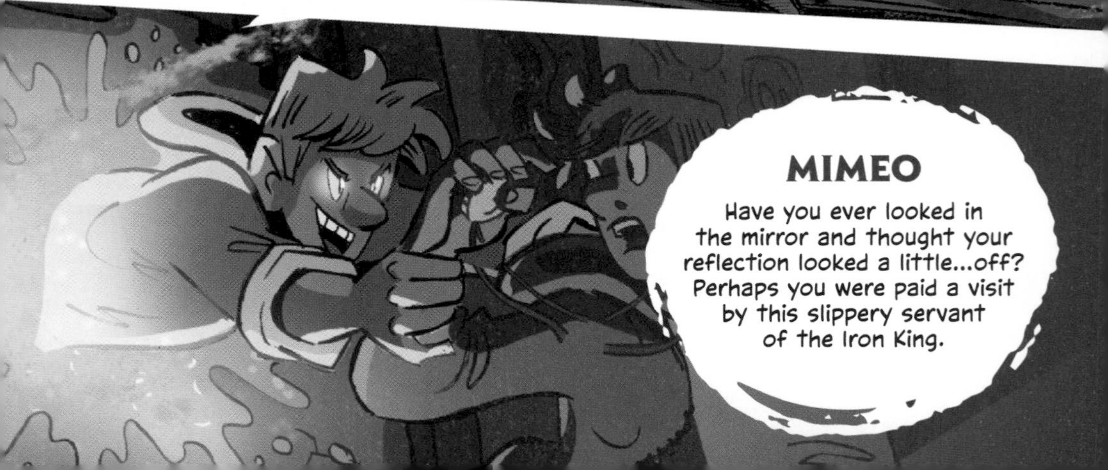
MIMEO
Have you ever looked in the mirror and thought your reflection looked a little...off? Perhaps you were paid a visit by this slippery servant of the Iron King.

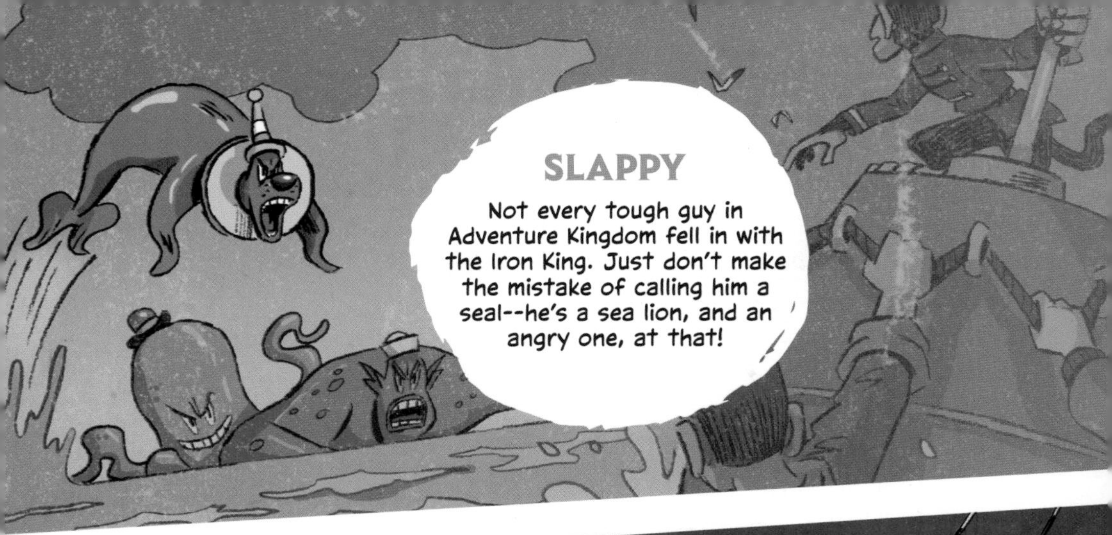
SLAPPY
Not every tough guy in Adventure Kingdom fell in with the Iron King. Just don't make the mistake of calling him a seal--he's a sea lion, and an angry one, at that!

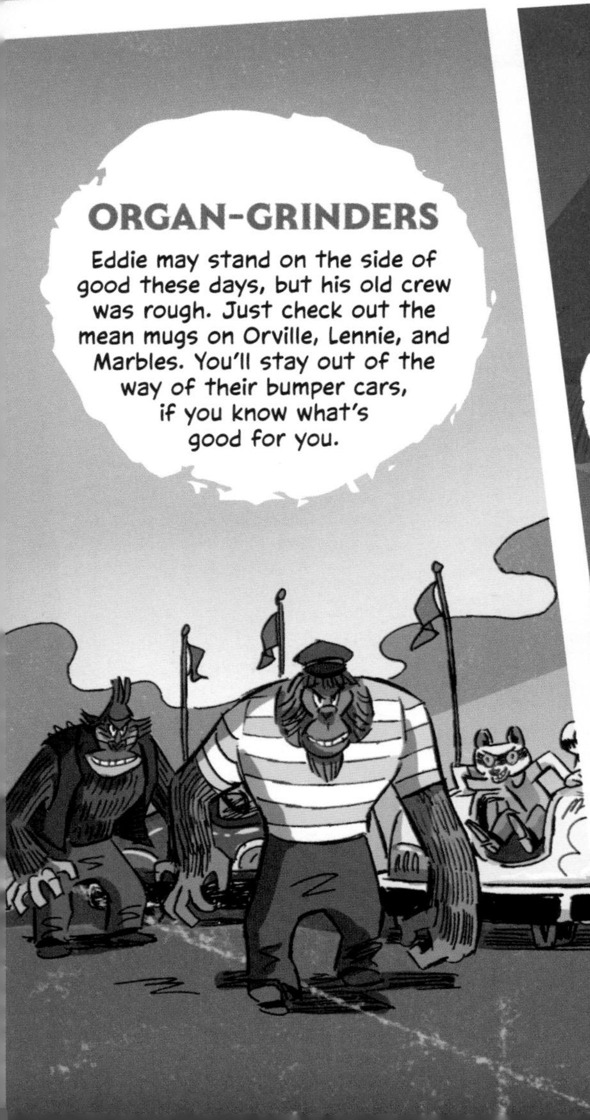
ORGAN-GRINDERS
Eddie may stand on the side of good these days, but his old crew was rough. Just check out the mean mugs on Orville, Lennie, and Marbles. You'll stay out of the way of their bumper cars, if you know what's good for you.

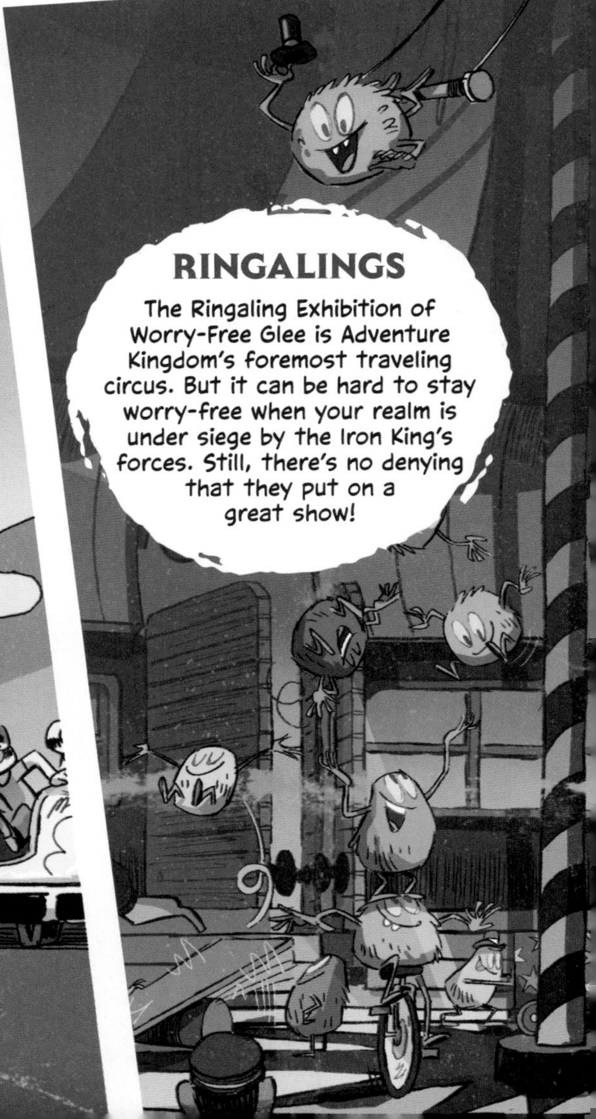
RINGALINGS
The Ringaling Exhibition of Worry-Free Glee is Adventure Kingdom's foremost traveling circus. But it can be hard to stay worry-free when your realm is under siege by the Iron King's forces. Still, there's no denying that they put on a great show!

BEHIND THE SCENES

Epic makes comics by bringing together the best writers and artists to collaborate on stories filled with action, humor, and heart. But that process takes time and work!

1. SCRIPT

The first step in creating any comic book is for the writer to come up with the plot and dialogue. Here's Steve Foxe talking about his process for *Adventure Kingdom*.

"One of the great things about a long-term creative relationship is learning more about your collaborator as you go along. For instance, I learned pretty early on that Pedro has a great sense of pacing, so I don't have to get too specific about how panels should be placed on the page. Pedro is also really skilled at depicting nuanced emotions, so I don't have to spell out how a character is feeling in the dialogue--he handles it right on their faces."

Page 3

Panel 1:
Soon after, Eddie crests up from a dip in the path and points into the near distance. Clark and Karoline both have concerned looks on their face.

1 EDDIE: Sorry kiddo, but your grandfather is kind of a legend in my world. The Iron King never could compete.

2 EDDIE: But why am I flapping my gums? We're here!

3 EDDIE: Bright-Sky Boardwalk! Our premiere seaside destination.

Panel 2:
Bigger panel as we see Bright-Sky Boardwalk, which is much gloomier than the name portends. Think classic early 20th-century boardwalks, now weathered and cast under never-ending grey skies. As for residents, let's at least stick to folks who look like they're in old-timey bathing suits or sailor suits, to stay on theme? In one corner of the shot, we should see SLAPPY the sea lion, dozing next to a half-deflated balancing ball. Slappy has smeared clown paint on, a hat, and maybe a neck ruffle too? The other thing we should definitely see, and potentially a few times around these scenes, is a balloon stand or cart with lots of balloons tied to it.

NO DIALOGUE

Panel 3:
Close on Karoline and Clark grimacing at each other.

4 CLARK: More like "Mostly Cloudy Boardwalk"...

5 KAROLINE: Yeah, is this the best this place has to offer, Eddie?

Panel 4:
Eddie, possessing of some wounded pride (and maybe a little guilt), stands up for the Boardwalk.

6 EDDIE: Ya don't have to be rude about it. I told you Adventure Kingdom has seen better days. But it'll all get fixed once we find the Grand Jerome.

7 EDDIE: Like I said, I know a gu--

8 SLAPPY [off-panel]: Eddie! Eddie, you rotten rat-monkey, is that you?

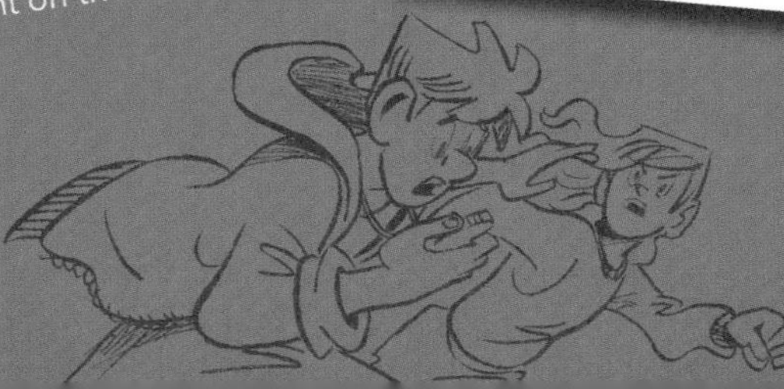

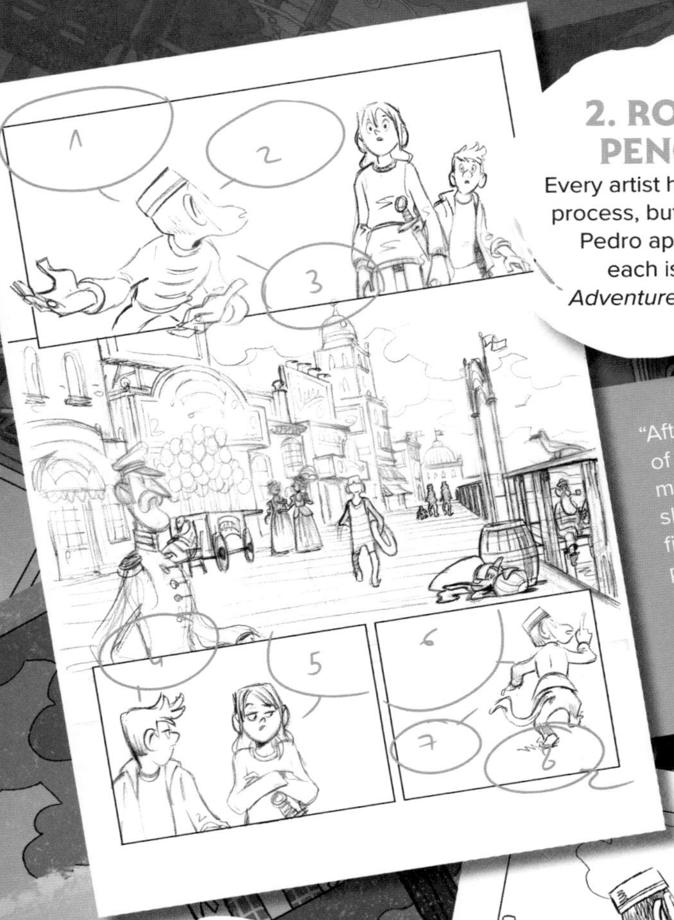

2. ROUGH PENCILS

Every artist has their own process, but here's how Pedro approaches each issue of *Adventure Kingdom*.

"After several readings of Steve's script, I make a first quick sketch in order to fit the scenes into panels. After that, I make another, more defined sketch according to what the script asks for."

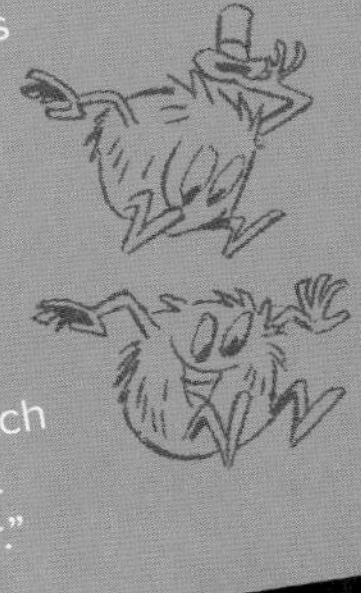

3. INKS

After the sketches are approved by the author and the editor, the artist turns them into final, inked drawings. Drawings will often change in response to feedback from Steve and Epic's team of editors and designers.

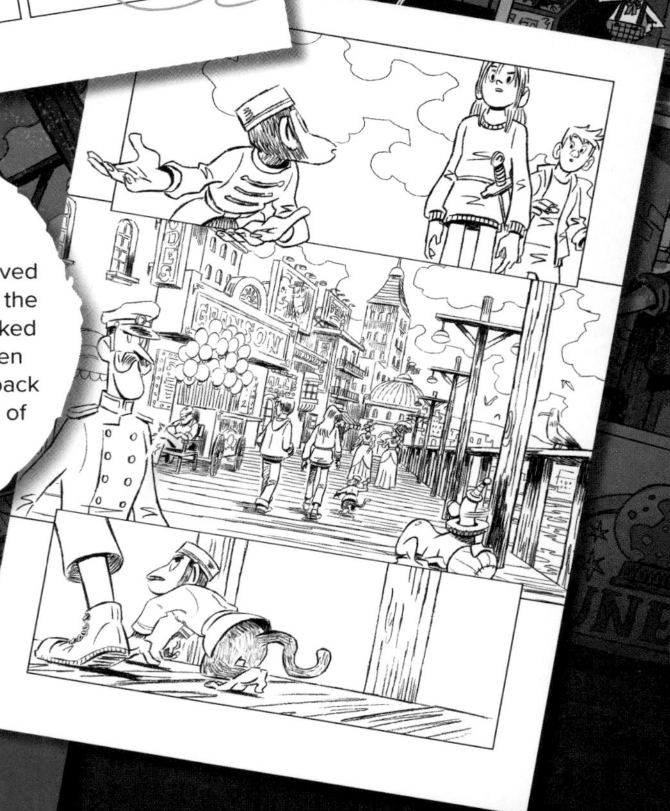

"When inking, I make small changes that would improve upon the sketch. I also work on additional details, as well as facial expressions."

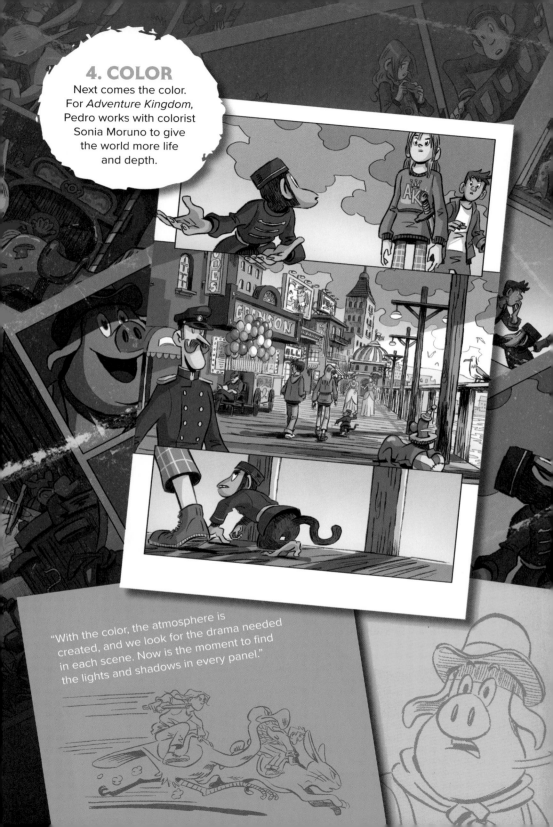

4. COLOR

Next comes the color. For *Adventure Kingdom*, Pedro works with colorist Sonia Moruno to give the world more life and depth.

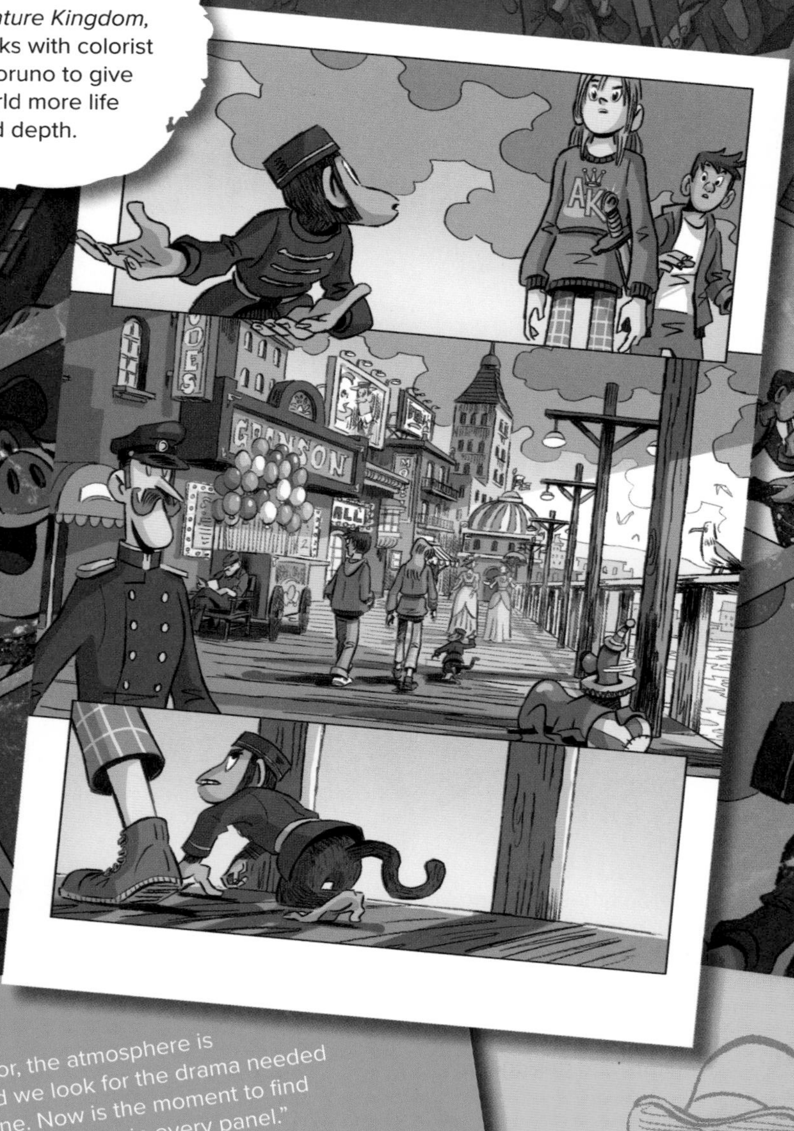

"With the color, the atmosphere is created, and we look for the drama needed in each scene. Now is the moment to find the lights and shadows in every panel."

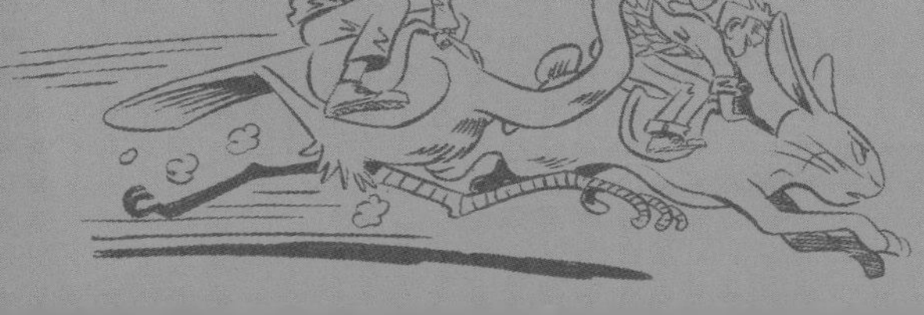

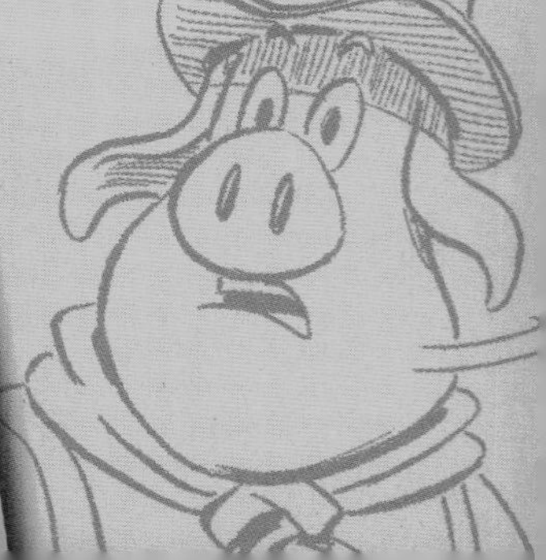

5. LETTERING

Finally, the lettering is inserted into speech bubbles and carefully placed. This is also the last chance Steve has to make any changes to the text.

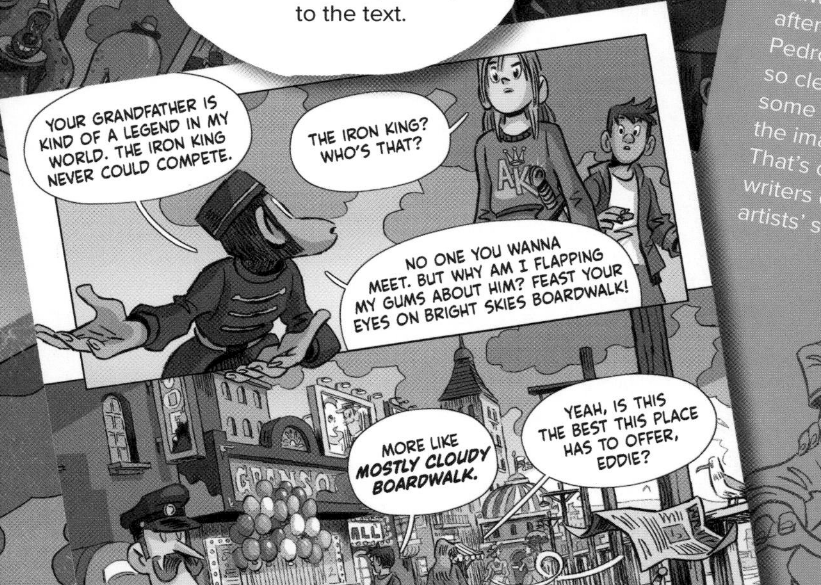
YOUR GRANDFATHER IS KIND OF A LEGEND IN MY WORLD. THE IRON KING NEVER COULD COMPETE.
THE IRON KING? WHO'S THAT?
NO ONE YOU WANNA MEET. BUT WHY AM I FLAPPING MY GUMS ABOUT HIM? FEAST YOUR EYES ON BRIGHT SKIES BOARDWALK!
MORE LIKE *MOSTLY CLOUDY BOARDWALK.*
YEAH, IS THIS THE BEST THIS PLACE HAS TO OFFER, EDDIE?
YA DON'T HAVE TO BE RUDE ABOUT IT.
EDDIE! EDDIE, YOU ROTTEN RAT-MONKEY, IS THAT YOU?

"I always revise dialogue after seeing the art. Often, Pedro has drawn things so clearly that I can cut some of my text to let the images tell the story. That's one big way that writers can adapt to their artists' strengths."

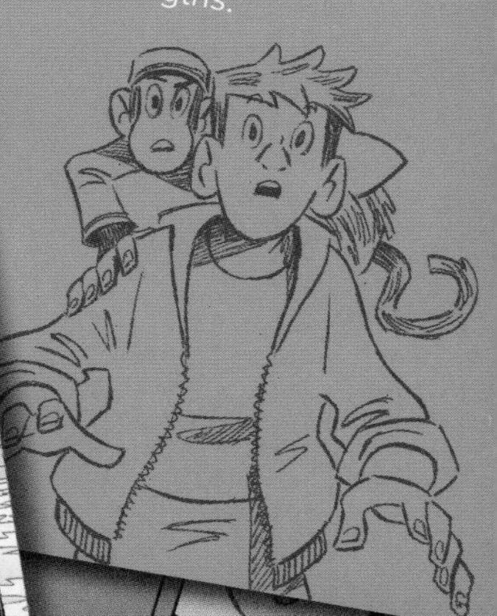

As you can see, it takes a lot to make a single comic page, and many things can change along the way. Can you spot the changes made from script to the final, colored page?

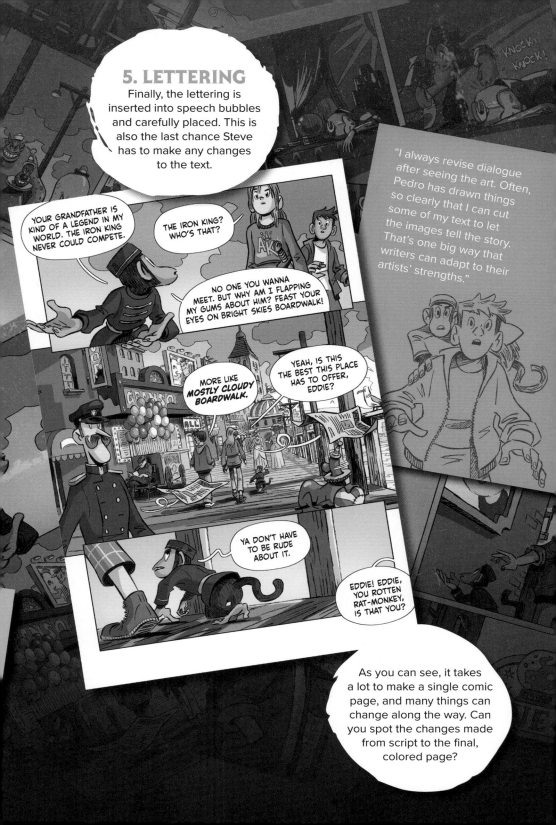

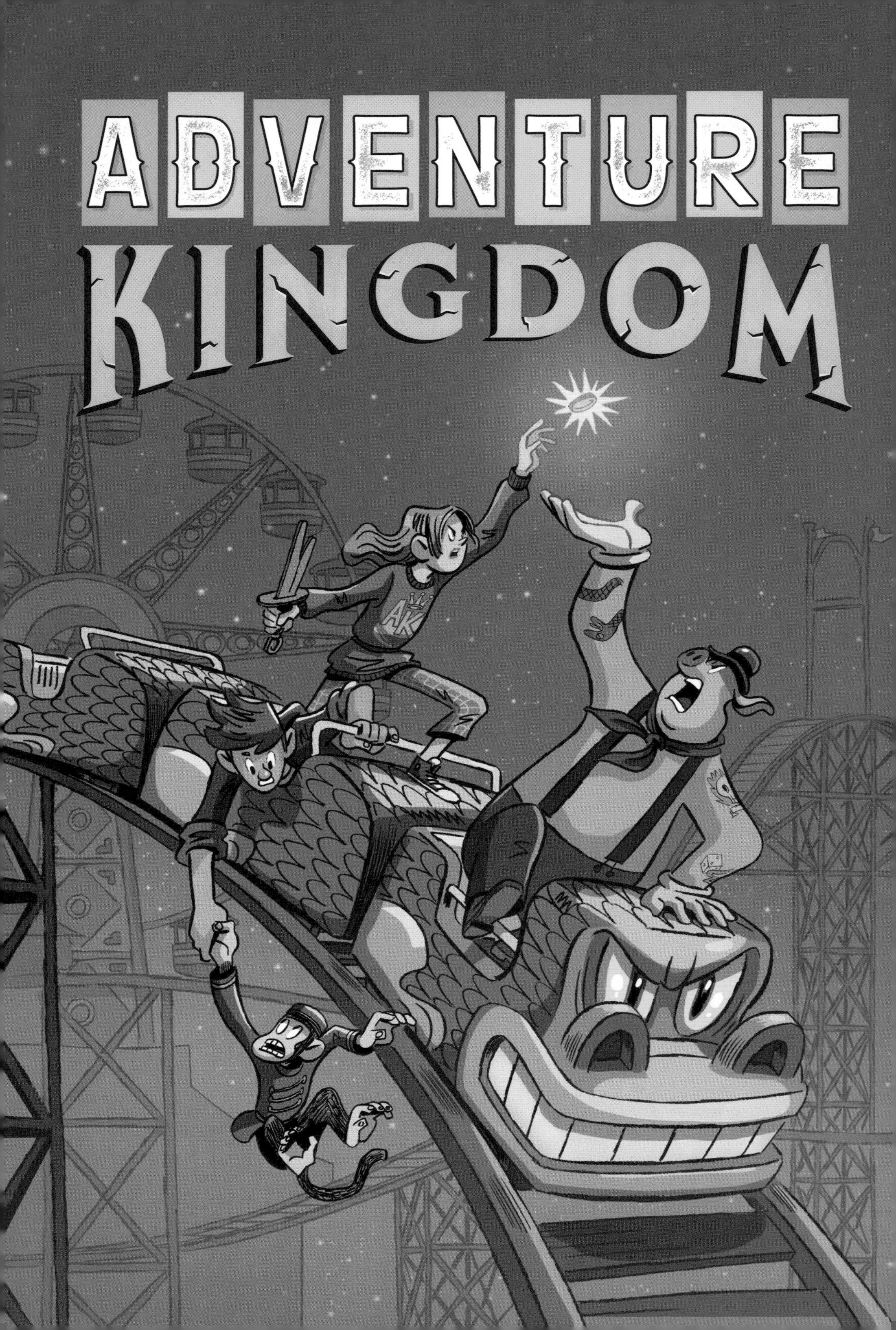
ADVENTURE
KINGDOM
AK

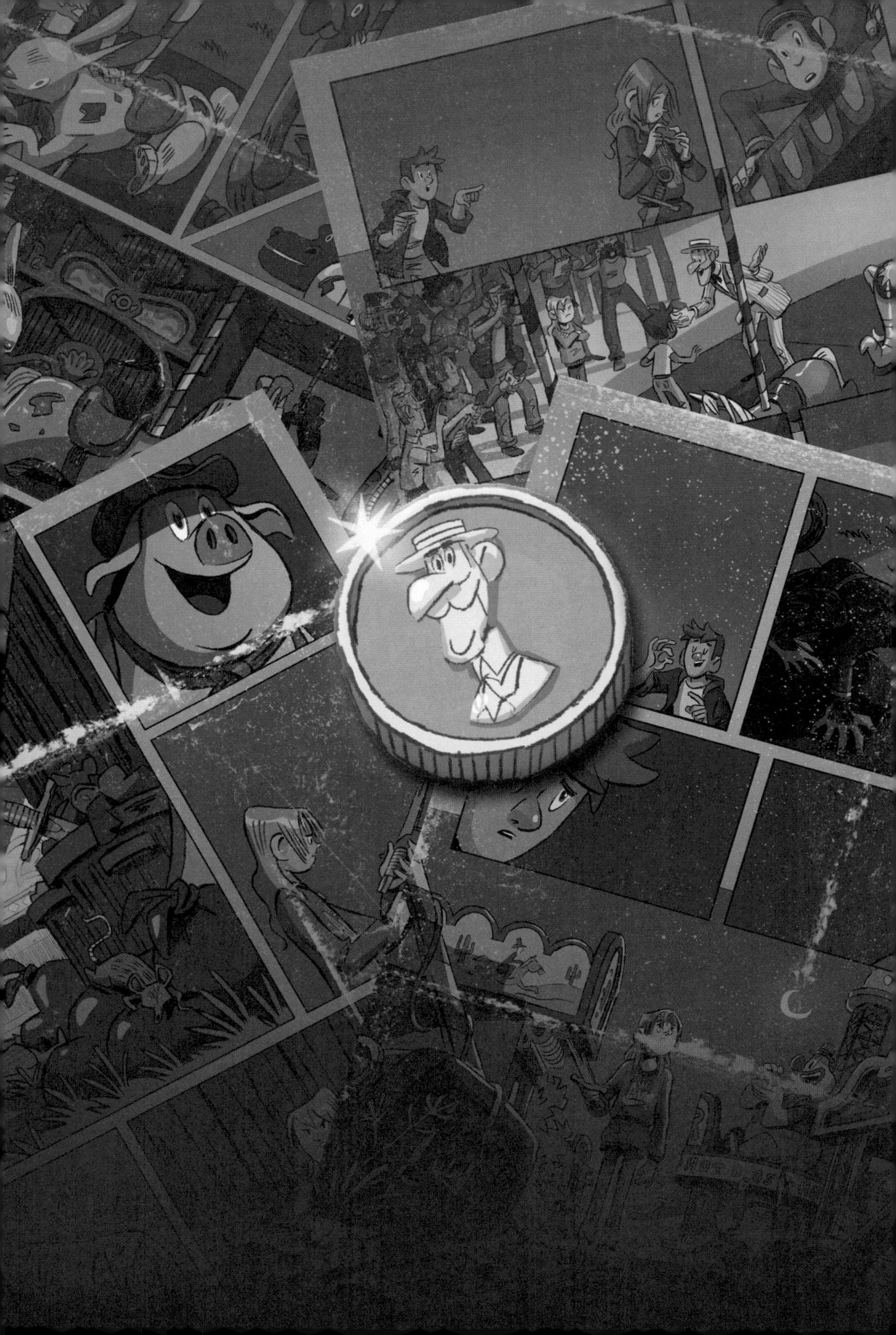

HAVE YOU HEARD ABOUT epic! YET?

We're the largest digital library for kids, used by millions in homes and schools around the world. We love stories so much that we're now creating our own!

With the help of some of the best writers and illustrators in the world, we create the wildest adventures we can think of. Like a mermaid and a narwhal who solve mysteries. Or a pet made out of slime.

We hope you have as much fun reading our books as we had making them!

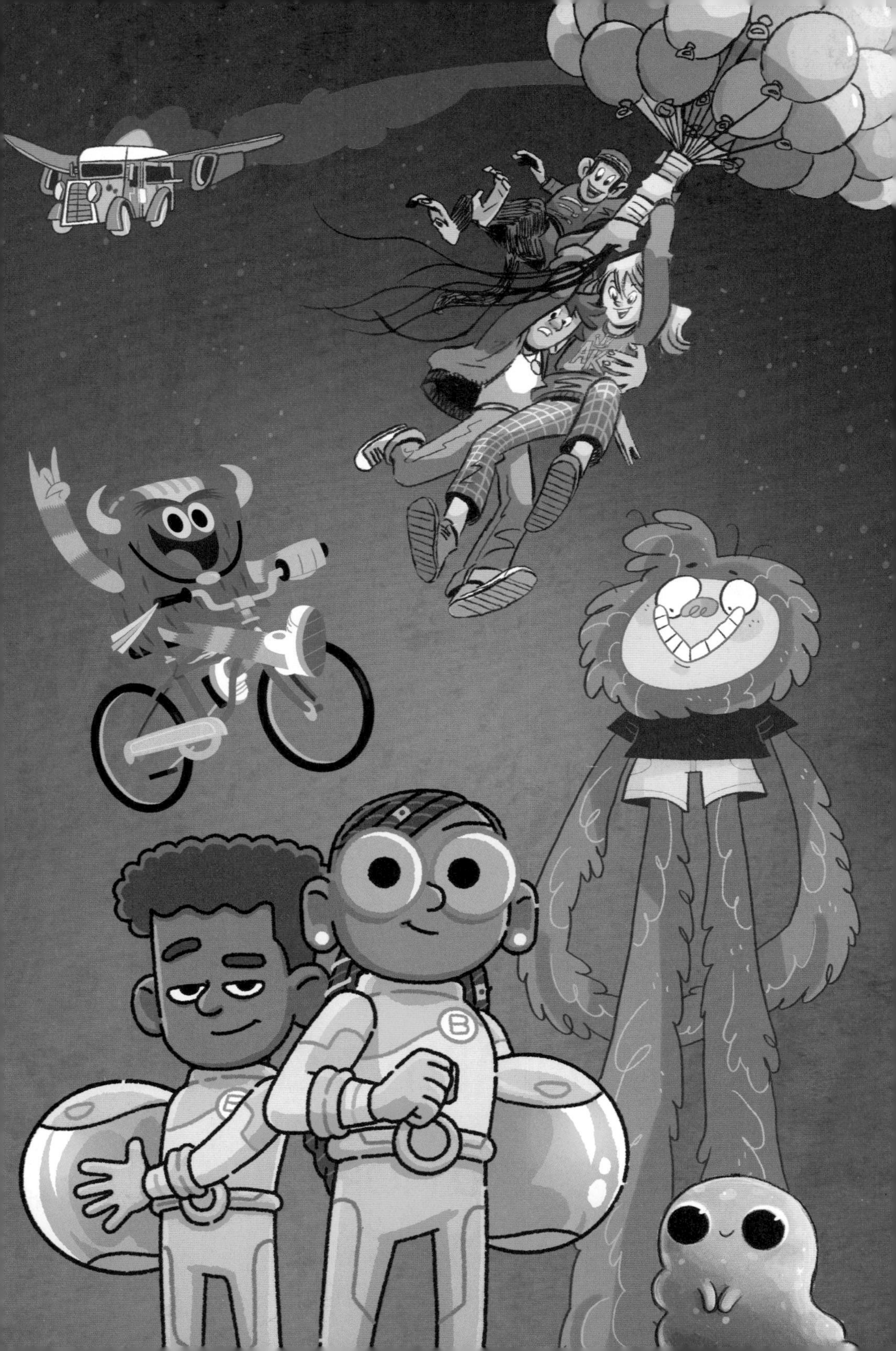

LOOK FOR THESE BOOKS FROM

epic!

AVAILABLE **NOW!**

TO READ MORE, VISIT
getepic.com